Bella Mason has been a bookworm from an early age. She has been regaling people with stories from the time she discovered she could hold the dinner table hostage with her reimagined fairy tales. After earning a degree in journalism she rekindled her love of writing and now writes full time. When she isn't imagining dashing heroes and strong heroines she can be found exploring Melbourne, with her nose in a book, or lusting after fast cars.

Carol Marinelli recently filled in a form asking for her job title. Thrilled to be able to put down her answer, she put 'writer'. Then it asked what Carol did for relaxation, and she put down the truth—'writing'. The third question asked for her hobbies. Well, not wanting to look obsessed, she crossed her fingers and answered 'swimming'—but, given that the chlorine in the pool does terrible things to her highlights, I'm sure you can guess the real answer!

AN ITALIAN TEMPTATION

BELLA MASON

CAROL MARINELLI

MILLS & BOON

First published in Great Britain 2025
by Mills & Boon, an imprint of HarperCollins*Publishers* Ltd,
1 London Bridge Street, London, SE1 9GF

www.harpercollins.co.uk

HarperCollins*Publishers*, Macken House, 39/40 Mayor Street Upper, Dublin 1, D01 C9W8, Ireland

An Italian Temptation © 2025 Harlequin Enterprises ULC

Strictly Forbidden Boss © 2025 Bella Mason

Italian's Pregnant Mistress © 2025 Carol Marinelli

ISBN: 978-0-263-34449-3

01/25

MIX
Paper | Supporting
responsible forestry
FSC™ C007454

STRICTLY
FORBIDDEN BOSS

BELLA MASON

MILLS & BOON

For Helena,
for all the calls, the sunshine by email
and helping me make Enzo and Charlotte shine.

PROLOGUE

Six months ago

ONE WOULD HOPE that on a day like this the sky would be dark and dreary. At least then it would reflect how Enzo De Luca felt. Instead, it was offensively bright.

The weight on his shoulders was heavier than he could ever have imagined. It wasn't just because of the polished mahogany coffin that rested there; it was the guilt of not having been present for his mother's last days. It was the grief of losing his only remaining parent. It was the knowledge that their family estate would hardly feel like home again. Not that it had for a while.

Enzo, the Conte del Perlano—a beautiful, lush region in Calabria with rolling hills of vineyards as far as the eye could see—tried to push away the thoughts and grief as he walked. One step at a time, in perfect sync with the other pallbearers. With his brother, Emilio. His mother's coffin rested between them. Enzo knew his brother would be grieving openly, but he couldn't. He wouldn't show any of the emotions he felt. He would keep his thoughts shielded as he always did. He could trust no one with them, and all of Perlano would be looking to him, the conte, for reassurance.

One foot in front of the other he walked with the three other men, away from the chapel and towards the meadow behind, where his family had been buried for generations. Enzo wished he could look around. See it all one last time because he knew he wouldn't return. Not to this place that he loved so much, that held so many painful memories of what he had lost. How painfully he had been betrayed.

Mechanically, Enzo and the others placed the coffin over the hole in the ground and stood back, watching as straps were looped through the handles. Everyone gathered around the gravesite with a stem of pink oleander. It was winter and the oleander shrubs had died for the season, but Enzo had them brought in so his mother could be around her favourite flowers just one more time. Not an easy task on short notice given the strict rules around its importation, but Enzo had made it happen.

He stepped forward as the mahogany box began to lower and tossed his flower in. Everyone else must have joined him because the wood was slowly disappearing beneath a carpet of pink. Heart breaking, he watched only as his mother was lowered and once she reached the bottom, he turned his back and began walking away.

'Leoncino…' He heard a voice call to him, but he would not look back. Let Emilio deal with everyone. Enzo was done. He could feel the burning gazes on his back as he walked away, but he ignored them all.

A black car waited for him outside the chapel. He opened the back door and slid in.

'To the airport,' he instructed. Enzo hadn't said a single goodbye. All he needed was to return to Sydney.

CHAPTER ONE

THE SILVER FOUNTAIN pen landed with a muffled thud as yet another email pinged on Charlotte Kim's computer. She swivelled in her chair to skim through the mail deciding it wasn't worth attending to immediately and flagged it for later. Picking her pen back up, she caught a whiff of a woodsy cologne. The same warning she received every morning before Enzo De Luca turned the corner and filled the very large and sleekly modern penthouse office with his presence. Somehow, he always made it seem smaller. Tall and broad with thick dark hair, cold green eyes and perfectly trimmed stubble, he was every bit as intimidating as his reputation suggested.

'Celeste,' he greeted in his deep voice still rich with an Italian accent, despite years of living in Australia, that made her heart beat a little faster every time she heard it.

'Good morning, Mr De Luca,' she replied despite the pang of discomfort she always felt at hearing that name. 'I will be through with your schedule shortly.'

He nodded once before disappearing through his office door.

She closed her eyes and imagined that he had said her real name in that voice. That he bathed her in his smile. It was so rare, but he would give it freely to her because he knew her. She opened her eyes and sighed at the ridiculousness of that dream. She shouldn't allow herself to think like that about her boss. He could fire her—or destroy her without even realising it. But as long as it remained a thought, never acted upon, she was safe.

Charlotte locked her computer, picked up her tablet and made for the private C-suite kitchen. There she prepared Enzo's espresso just as he liked it. While the machine buzzed and whirred as it filled the cup, she looked out the floor-to-ceiling window at Sydney spread out below.

It had been two years since she had moved here from Perth. Two years that she had been working for Enzo at De Luca and Co. and not once in that time had she ever felt herself relax. She couldn't. She was always so tense that she just learned to live with a constant ache in her shoulders. In her gut.

Charlotte had come to this city as Celeste. All the time she had been here, she had been extremely careful to maintain the image of the highly efficient PA with little personality other than being a workaholic.

She couldn't explore the city she now lived in because she was always scouting the area for threats. Anywhere she went had the hairs on the back of her neck standing on end. The only place she felt at all safe was in the office and in her home. But even then, she was ever vigilant.

A sharp twinge of pain in her stomach brought her attention back to the kitchen. She pulled the small cup out from under the portafilter and, reaching for a saucer, caught a glimpse of her reflection. Of the grey shift dress that was neither loose nor fitting, so unlike the bright, exquisitely tailored high-end clothes that she had once worn. Of her black hair hanging limply around her shoulders, not even slightly reminiscent of the perfectly styled tresses of her past. Of her plain black shoes with the smallest of heels that made her miss the closet full of designer shoes she'd left behind. And finally, the black glasses on the bridge of her nose that she didn't need, which diverted attention away from her nearly black, angular eyes.

Plain. She was utterly, heartbreakingly plain. But if she were to remain safe, that was exactly what she needed to be. It wasn't safe to stand out. Not to anyone. Definitely not to Enzo. The old Charlotte would have spoken to him. Flirted harmlessly with him. Maybe even befriended him. But now, she had to be invisible to him.

If beige was a person, Charlotte, it would be you.

She hadn't even been with a man intimately. Her virginity was beginning to be a point of frustration, but remaining hidden meant never being able to date. Being with a man was too risky if she was trying to hide. Who could she trust?

With a sigh, she ignored her thoughts and took the tablet and espresso to Enzo's office, only stopping at her desk briefly to swallow an antacid. As she placed the coffee beside his computer, she admired the view of Circular Quay as she did every morning, gazing longingly at the water.

'Ah, my coffee. *Grazie*,' he said. 'My usual blend?'

It wouldn't be a day if you didn't make me state the obvious, Enzo, she thought to herself.

'Brewed as you like it, sir.' It took a great deal of self-control not to emphasise the *sir*. Now was not the time for attitude.

'Seven grams?'

'Yes, sir.' Good Lord, did he make it hard to keep the attitude at bay, though!

'Eight bars of pressure?'

She was going to strangle him. If she didn't know him better, she would say he did it to mess with her. 'Of course, Mr

De Luca.' Could the man not let go for two minutes just to enjoy a cup of coffee, for heaven's sakes? He should just do it for himself. Damn control freak! Words she would never say aloud. Instead, she ran through Enzo's schedule with him.

'That leaves us with your eleven a.m. They insist on meeting with you so I pencilled them in. However, I believe you've mentioned before that they don't need to meet with you specifically.' Charlotte was well aware that Enzo had mentioned nothing of the sort. They were simply a company wanting to attract investors and, in her opinion, not bringing much to the table. But in a bid to remain as inconspicuous as possible, she often made her judgement calls seem like they had come from Enzo. That way if he thought back on it later, he could easily forget her part in it.

Enzo was a fiercely private and notoriously headstrong businessman, and with De Luca and Co. having recently celebrated its bicentennial, she could understand why he had to be. It was no small thing to own a multinational of its size with the legacy it held. The only reason he listened to her at all was also the only reason she had landed this job: because of her impressive education. It was the only thing she hadn't lied about in her application.

'You're right. I don't have time to deal with them. Get someone else on it.'

'Yes, Mr De Luca.'

'Close the door on your way out.'

She was almost out of his office when he called out to her.

'Oh, and Celeste?'

'Yes, sir?'

'The coffee is good,' he said with a barely there smile. And that was why she didn't strangle him. Today. Tomorrow? Who knew.

Charlotte smiled and closed the door wishing again that just once he would call her by her real name. However much his need for control might frustrate her, it was hard to be in his orbit and not get pulled in. By his brilliance and his intellect. That unflappable calm that he seemed to radiate to all in his presence as if it was his superpower. And those cold green eyes that she knew observed more than anyone really understood.

Still, the biggest part of her relished the distance she had with Enzo. He didn't know her real name; he didn't know much about her at all. In fact, if she was replaced by a robot, she doubted he would notice very much. That granted some safety. Not enough that the feeling of anxiety in the pit of her stomach ever went away, though.

She sat down at her desk and looked out the glass panes at the sprawling city. It was big, but nowhere was big enough if she wasn't careful.

She'd taken this job to hide. If anyone knew who she was, then she would have to disappear and start again in yet another place. She didn't want to have to do that. It was impossible to know who might have connections to her old life. She had come from a wealthy family. A family with far-reaching connections. She couldn't risk her freedom just for a *Good job, Charlotte*, no matter how much she craved validation from Enzo. She couldn't trust him with her real name. That would be beyond foolish. And he certainly wouldn't trust her if he ever found out she had been lying to him. Who knew how badly he would react?

She told herself didn't matter: it was still *her* work. *Her* intelligence that was appreciated, regardless of what anyone called her.

Pulling up her email programme, Charlotte got busy moving Enzo's meeting and dealing with everything she had flagged. She really did enjoy working at De Luca and Co. Here, she was as close to the top as she could ever allow herself to get without attracting attention. And then there was Enzo. Yes, he was arrogant, but she had to admit his integrity was admirable. He used his power to help others, even though he kept his altruism a secret. She only knew because she was his PA. He was good to his employees. She would know: she had seen how a lesser man treated his.

There was no way in hell she would do anything that risked making her face her father again.

The door clicked shut, and Enzo sipped from his cup, savouring the hot coffee while his emails streamed steadily into his inbox. Celeste had outdone herself—though, he probably had that exact thought most mornings. She was by far the most efficient PA he had ever had and so far had lasted longer than any other. She didn't just rise to meet his standards, she did so with calm professionalism. He was thankful for whatever circumstance brought her to him. He might even consider giving her a substantial performance bonus this year.

He took a deep breath. This was usually his only quiet moment of the day, one in which he took great pleasure. An impeccably made espresso and a gander at his emails, and he'd be ready to take on the hundred different things requiring his attention.

Enzo was proud of his routine, his discipline. As the head of one of the largest and oldest financial companies in the world, discipline was a trait he needed. Not to mention as the head of one of the oldest families in Calabria. He tried not to think of that—of what his family had become—but it was hard. Especially when one email in particular caught his eye.

It had come from the lawyers regarding his mother's will. Whatever they had to say, it couldn't be good. Dread settled in Enzo's belly. Just like that, he was thrown back to the day they buried her, six months ago. To the grief and anger. To her coffin sitting on his shoulders making him want to lash out. To the boulder on his chest whenever he thought about the fact that he hadn't been home in over two years before that, despite knowing how sick and frail she had become. He couldn't return. Not when all he could think about there was his fiancée, Gia, who had slept with his brother—a man he should have been able to trust above all others—in his family home. The pain of that betrayal had never dulled. It had broken him. Destroyed his ability to trust anyone again.

Enzo pulled at his tie which had begun to feel as tight as a noose around his neck. But as always, he had to hide his feelings. An issue had obviously come up, and feelings would help nothing. They would only cloud his judgement and make him react recklessly. But it wasn't easy to push them aside. Not when he was so angry. Angry at the world for his mother's death. Angry at himself for not being there. Angry at Emilio—with whom he had always had a fractious relationship—for tainting his home.

He swallowed what little was left in his cup and forced himself to calm down.

His mother's estate had been relatively easy to settle, especially when everything she had—save the vineyards—had been left to his brother. Valentina De Luca had come from a vastly wealthy family herself. Her fortune and properties, not to mention the charity she'd founded, had all become Emilio's for the simple reason that Enzo was the Conte del Perlano, a title he'd inherited from his father along with the vast De Luca estate. Everything that had been amassed over centuries belonged to Enzo, including the centuries-old financial and banking company, and the winery. So when he had found out that there was very little in Valentina's will that concerned him, he didn't much care. The vineyards were all he'd expected, and he already had enough on his plate. It all made little difference to the bond they'd shared. So to hear from the family lawyer now unsettled him.

Gritting his teeth, Enzo opened the email. His hands curled into fists as he read. Whatever grief he had momentarily felt was burned away by the anger that had fully taken hold of him. Cursing his brother's name, Enzo's shoulders tensed with every word.

...is in possession of a second will that bequeaths the De Luca vineyards to Emilio De Luca...

Enzo trembled with the force of his rage. No longer able to contain his ire, he threw back his chair and, grabbing fistfuls of his hair, marched to the window. He tried to take a breath, but it was no help. If anything, like a bellows, it fanned the flames of his fury.

Emilio wanted to take his vineyards. It shouldn't have surprised him. He often wanted what was Enzo's—and their mother had always swooped in and placated Emilio. Convinced Enzo with love and hugs to share what he had or give it up entirely to his little brother. And Enzo would, because he was the oldest, the firstborn. It was his job to look out for everyone.

But not any more. Not since Gia.

'A second will!' Enzo spat at no one. They all knew that his father had gifted the vineyards to his mother because she had loved them so much, but the condition had always been explicit. She had to leave them to Enzo, the next Conte del Perlano. That was exactly what the lawyers initially said she *had* done. So why would she make a second will leaving them to Emilio?

Those vineyards were Enzo's. He alone was the conte. He alone was responsible for hundreds of years of history. Legacy. And now he was responsible for every single person those vineyards provided with a livelihood.

'Why, Gia?'

'I wanted your brother. I've always wanted him. The only reason anyone would choose you over him is for what you have, Enzo. No one wants to come second or third or fourth to your duty.'

Gia's hurtful words came back to haunt him. As head of the De Luca family, it was his duty to take care of not just the vineyards but the entire estate. The family name and fortune. Just as his father had. Just as his father had taught him to do.

Enzo's heart constricted painfully as he thought of the memories he treasured. All the years he spent at his father's side. From an early age, he had been taken on business trips and sat in on meetings, learning about everything his father did. Everything Enzo would one day have to do.

Well, one day had come, and Hell would freeze over before he gave up that responsibility. He didn't want to, but he would go back to Perlano, do whatever it took to prove once and for all that it was all his. That the second will was some sort of lie.

His presence was a necessity because he trusted only himself to handle this situation correctly and permanently.

With far more irritation in his voice than he would have liked to show, he marched over to his desk and called his PA.

'Celeste, in here. Now.' He didn't sit. He was far too agitated. What he wanted to do was punch something. The very muscle in his arms vibrated with the need to act.

Within seconds Celeste was walking into his office with her trusty tablet in hand.

'What can I do for you, Mr De Luca?'

'We will be leaving for Italy.' His voice was barely more than a growl. 'Something has come up at the vineyards that I need to deal with urgently. We'll be taking the jet. Make the arrangements. Clear my calendar for the next week.'

'Will do. Shall I arrange for the usual accommodation?'

'No, just make sure that my car is waiting for me at La-mezia. I will deal with the accommodation.'

'Yes, sir. I can arrange for a driver to give you time t—'

'No. I told you only to ensure that my car is there. I will drive.' Enzo had only ever been driven in Perlano once, and that was when he left six months ago. He trusted no one but himself to tackle those winding roads. He didn't need time to prepare. He would get them to the estate faster than any driver and then sort this mess out himself.

'Understood.'

'See to it that everything is ready in an hour. I will have no delays.' His tone was brusque, and he saw a wince cross Celeste's face.

'Yes, sir.' Enzo watched her leave his office.

Dio mio! He had to calm down. While he was thankful that Celeste was so unquestioningly efficient, Enzo didn't talk to his employees like that. It hadn't even occurred to him until now that Celeste might need more than hour to get *herself* ready to fly. As his PA she should be ready to go with him at the drop of a hat when the need arose, but he was behaving like a brute. It was unacceptable and not the kind of behaviour that earned him the loyalty he had with his employees. He couldn't lash out at everyone when only Emilio deserved his ire.

He wasn't acting like himself, and it was because he knew how hard it would be to see his home again, even if his brother wasn't there. Perlano ripped open his scars. He didn't know how to prepare himself for that.

CHAPTER TWO

WHY, I HAVE nothing going on in my life and would love to drop everything to fly halfway across the world. Thanks for the consideration, Enzo.

Charlotte did, in fact, have no plans but it was his lack of consideration that irked her. He was lucky that she lived such a hermitic life. Knowing she could not say anything so revealing aloud, Charlotte simply pushed her glasses—that she did not need—up the bridge of her nose and ensured that the plane was fuelled and ready.

She glanced at her watch with annoyance. It would be incredibly tight to make all their arrangements plus get home in time to pack a bag for an unknown amount of time away and still be at the airport within the hour.

But not having much of a life and very few, mostly essential possessions meant that she was able to perform the miracles that Enzo needed. Just as he had ordered, an hour later, they were seated in the De Luca private jet and taxiing down the runway.

This wasn't the first time Charlotte had taken an international trip with Enzo, but it was always a source of great stress for her. The one place she couldn't lie about her name was in immigration. She constantly feared that it would be on one of these trips that her father finally found her. So far, her luck had held out. She clung to that knowledge now because there was nothing she could do while in the air. Nowhere she could go. No plans she could make. She would only know if she had to run again once she landed.

It hurt that she had to run from the man who should have wanted to love and protect her, but her father's only interest was in his business. That was why he had arranged her marriage to Grant Campbell, a crooked businessman in Perth who could get her property-developer father any land he wanted at any price. He was a slimy character who had been involved with her father for years. Had known her for years. Wanted her despite how young she was.

At twenty-five, Charlotte had already been in hiding for two years. Trying to remain safe from the two most unscrupulous and powerful men she knew.

'Please! I don't want to marry him!'

'I don't care. I won't let you cost me business.'

'Is Grant more important than me?'

'Yes.'

The memory that both angered and hurt her was never far from her mind. Always there ready to plunge a knife in her chest. It also motivated her to keep hiding.

Charlotte had done everything she could not to arouse suspicion. She had cleared her bank accounts when she left and split the money over several new accounts with several banks so none of them seemed conspicuous. Even her socials had been abandoned as they were when she left Perth. She had deleted the apps from her phone to never be tempted. She even avoided taking selfies because she knew how many millionaire heiresses had had their pictures stolen from the cloud.

Her life would have seemed extreme if anyone had seen how she lived, but Charlotte's goal was that no one ever would. Not when she couldn't trust anyone. Not when her tormentor had so many resources.

A breath-stealing ache in her stomach had her reaching for the antacid she always kept nearby.

It was always like this. Charlotte wished she could have just one day, one trip, when she didn't feel like she had to look over her shoulder.

The only bright side was that Enzo wasn't around to see her like this. While normally they would have spent most of the flight working closely, this time he had shut himself away. His corporate jet was huge, with a private office and a bedroom, as well as numerous public sections—a conference area, a lounge, guest bathrooms. But Charlotte had chosen to sit at a table by the window, always the quietest spot on the plane. Three luxurious cream leather seats sat empty around her, which was perfect. No one had to witness her falling apart just slightly. Not the cabin crew and certainly not Enzo. Not that he would notice.

It was the point of her disguise…but it made her miserable at times. Enzo was a smart man. How wonderful it would be to have an honest interaction with him! What would he think of her? Would he remain as calm and in control as he always did? He never allowed anything to get under his skin. Well, not until now. He had never snapped at her like he did in his office. Something was eating at him. There was another reason it was probably for the best that he wasn't around her, because she might have asked him what was wrong. And she couldn't do that. She shouldn't want to know more. Distance meant safety.

A soon as the plane levelled off, Charlotte pulled out her laptop. If her mind was going to race, she would at least try to give it something to focus on.

And it worked. She didn't notice the drink placed on

the table for her and certainly not when her meal arrived. She had worked so long and so hard that she only took a break once her eyelids began to droop. She saved her work and looked out the window seeing nothing but an illuminated wing.

The cabin was dimly lit when Charlotte blearily blinked awake. Having no idea how long she had been asleep, she lifted the window blind she had no memory of closing and instantly regretted it. The bright sun was an assault on her senses. She turned away for a second and rubbed her eyes before attempting to look out the window again.

They flew over green hills—*close* green hills. They were obviously going to land soon, and she had missed her opportunity to freshen up. She stood to get her bag and felt a blanket fall from her lap, something she didn't remember being draped over her. Enzo's crew was always attentive, but they'd gone above and beyond today. They'd never packed away her laptop before.

She retrieved her bag and pulled out a compact mirror to look at the frightful state she was in. Playing the role of the plain PA had its advantages: all she had to do was brush out her hair and pop a mint in her mouth.

A small part of Charlotte was excited. She hadn't been to Italy since she was much younger. It had been a different life back then, and all she had seen was Rome and Venice. This trip might not be the vacation she hoped to have—she didn't go on those any more: they were too risky—but at least she was still able to see new places in the world and admire the coastline she had dreamed of one day sailing along.

The plane touched down, and as soon as the doors opened, her passport was being stamped and, without another word, the immigration officials were gone. With a pounding heart, Charlotte gathered her things and made for the stairs. Taking a deep breath, she stepped out and found…a gleaming grey Maserati Quattroporte waiting on the tarmac, just as she'd arranged. No one but airport staff around, no one waiting to corral her into a waiting vehicle that would whisk her back to her father.

Only once her feet hit the tarmac and she knew she was safe did she feel like she could breathe again. Her shoulders relaxed a fraction, and she sprang into action.

She retrieved the key to the Maserati and dismissed the driver. With her tablet in one hand, she waited at the base of the staircase for Enzo.

Charlotte watched him jog down and cursed the unfairness of life. He looked every bit as fresh as he did when boarding, as if he could be stepping out of a glossy magazine cover, whereas she was in some sort of corporate ghillie suit that made her invisible. Not just to Enzo but to everyone. A part of her railed at being hidden. It wasn't fair that she lived half a life. It wasn't fair that she should be punished when all she wanted was freedom. But she had to swallow her irritation.

'Here are your keys, Mr De Luca,' she said.

'Thank you,' he replied, taking them from her, barely breaking his stride.

She had to almost run to keep up with his long strides, but after two years, she was used to it.

The lights on the car flashed as he unlocked it, and immediately their luggage was being loaded into the boot.

'You might as well put your tablet away. It's over an hour to Perlano,' Enzo said in his deep voice. While there was no emotion to his tone, it still felt like an instruction.

'Yes, sir.' She did as she was told and, when she walked

around the car, found that the passenger door had been opened for her. This was different. Normally she and Enzo shared the back seat and discussed his schedule, meetings and anything else that needed to be addressed for the trip. Now she was meant to sit beside him while he drove. Would she be expected to talk to him? They usually didn't discuss anything that wasn't work-related. What if she slipped up and mentioned something incriminating? Maybe it would be best if she found alternate transport. Except she didn't really know where they were going. All Enzo had said was that he would arrange their accommodation.

She was back in her spiral of overthinking, which was helping nothing. Buckling herself in, she pulled out her phone and decided to do some research on the area.

She typed *Perlano* into the search bar and pulled up an article on the history of the region. It was an old place, and she felt some relief knowing it would hold little value to her father. It was unlikely that he would think to look for her there. She flicked to the images tab, seeing hundreds and hundreds of beautiful pictures of hills and sea.

'It would be better if you looked out your window instead of looking at pictures that do it no justice.'

Charlotte started at the sound of Enzo's voice. They'd left the airport and were now driving along an undulating, curvy road with green hills on her left, dotted with stone ruins among tall trees. And on her right, the Tyrrhenian Sea stretched to the horizon in a rainbow of blues, the surface of the water shimmering in the afternoon sunlight. Charlotte noticed the number of yachts out on the water and wished she could be lying on the deck of one of them, having the sun kiss every inch of her skin.

And as they drove past one of the many little *borghi*,

Charlotte's breath caught. The little town cascading down the mountainside was something straight out of a fairy tale. It was as if she'd been transported back in time.

She had to admit, Enzo was right.

'Have you been to Italy before?' he asked.

'Once, when I was young, but we didn't see much of it. Though, I do wish that we had. Especially the coast.'

'Let me guess, you went to Roma?'

'And Venice.' Charlotte was a little shocked that Enzo was asking her about herself. While she revealed nothing of any real consequence, it would be far safer to steer the conversation away from herself.

'Those are beautiful places, but Perlano is different.' Charlotte hazarded a look at him and found his gaze firmly focussed on the road, his hands holding the steering wheel in the gentlest grip. For some reason she thought she'd never seen him so at ease, while still being so utterly tense. His body might be languid, holding all that effortless confidence that seemed so natural to him, but the lines around his eyes and mouth told a different story.

Not wanting to be caught staring, she shifted her gaze out the window.

'How so?'

'You will see when we get there. It's best to experience it. No explanation will be adequate.'

Charlotte caught the flicker of a smile in his reflection on her window. Well, there was information for her to store away. He might not return home very often, but he certainly did love it.

Within minutes the view changed, and gone was the sea. Instead, they were surrounded by hills, long green grasses dancing in the wind and, in the distance, what must have been farmland. It was beautiful. And the warmth of the afternoon sun on her skin was heaven. Sydney's winter chill was a distant memory here.

'I read that Perlano is quite old,' Charlotte offered when the silence in the car grew too thick and she could bear it no more. Her father had always wielded stilted silence like a weapon. Rather than endure it, Charlotte would escape with her friends, and then she didn't have to be quiet. She would be her natural self, talking and rambling without worrying about the consequences. Well, she had no friends now, but still she didn't have to bear any real silence. The office was filled with various sounds. At home, she kept the television on nearly constantly even if she wasn't watching.

This silence was different to the one she'd grown to hate. It felt overwhelming for a different reason, and she couldn't pinpoint exactly what it was apart from Enzo's presence. This was a big car, but it didn't seem like it with him in it. Charlotte was aware of every movement his body made, the way his hands splayed on the steering as he adjusted his grip. Perfect hands and long fingers…

'My family ruled over Perlano for hundreds of years from the very same estate. Each one changed it very little, but their marks are there. You may explore it when we are not working.'

Charlotte was pulled from the rabbit hole that she was mentally falling into and forced herself to pay attention to his words. 'I don't know if that's a good idea,' she responded automatically.

'I assure you, it's quite safe.'

She didn't reply. She wasn't about to argue with her boss when his idea of danger wasn't hers. While it was very unlikely her father would even know of Perlano—he never saw the value in things unless they were important to him—there was no place picturesque enough, no gelato sweet enough to risk being caught off guard and dragged back to Perth. Her heart raced at the very thought.

Charlotte discreetly wiped her sweaty palms on the skirt of her dress and remained uncomfortably quiet as they approached Perlano.

The wild grasses disappeared, replaced by rolling green hills. The closer they drew, the clearer she could see that each one was covered in neat, vibrant vineyards. Over on the right, the sea was once again visible, but so were houses, stacked close together down the hills and stretching to the water. Every single one had a dull red roof and aged, sand-toned plaster. It was like a postcard made real.

They turned off the highway and drove along narrow roads, climbing higher and higher, closer to the vineyards. Charlotte felt as if she could stick her arm out and touch the bright leaves that surrounded them. Nothing could have prepared her for the sight looming at the top of the hill. All she could make out was an obelisk of a tower, rectangular and tall with a portion of its ramparts visible. The stone, even this far away, looked aged. It could have been an intimidating sight, jarring, but it wasn't. Not with the great, silvery olive trees and lush oleander shrubs around it, pink blossoms bright against the monolithic backdrop.

Finally, they approached large wrought-iron gates that swung open, leading to a long driveway. Charlotte had always known that Enzo was the Conte del Perlano, but seeing and knowing were two different things. She had always thought of his title as nothing more than exactly that. A title. This was something else. She hadn't expected an estate as grand as this or a building that had seen so many centuries but still looked like a home. Inviting and warm.

'This is beautiful,' she remarked as the car came to a stop.

'You sound surprised.' She could hear the teasing in his voice and found the smallest of smirks on his face.

Well, that was new. Was Enzo a different man here? For some reason she found herself wanting to know. Wanting to uncover that side of him. An impulse she'd never once had before.

'I am, a little,' she admitted.

'Come,' he said, elegantly exiting the car.

She joined him as he made his way to a large door where an elderly woman with a kind face and salt-and-pepper hair tied back in a bun waited.

'What about our bags?'

'They will be placed in our rooms.' Gone was the playful Enzo from only a moment ago, and in his place stood a man even more tense than usual. '*Buonasera*, Isabella.'

'Enzo!' She took his face in her hands even though she had quite a height to reach. Her eyes sparkled, and there was clear affection in her voice as she said, 'You have been away too long, Leoncino.'

'I've been busy.' Placing his hand above Charlotte's elbow, Enzo urged her forward. At first, she felt the touch like a brand, the current startling. But then it changed. The gentleness of his grip and the warmth of his hand calmed that unsettled feeling into something even more unexpected. A feeling of being grounded. Charlotte wasn't used to being handled gently or, in the past two years, at all. But here was a powerful man who was tense and curt and clearly on edge, and yet he controlled all that, shielded her from whatever was raging within him. It made her feel safe. And curious. And confused.

'This is Celeste Park,' Enzo continued. 'Make sure she has a comfortable room. Celeste, this is my housekeeper, Isabella. She will help you with whatever you need.'

'*Benvenuta*, Celeste,' the old woman said, taking her hands. 'We will get you all settled, yes.'

'It's nice to meet you, Isabella.' She meant it. It had been a very long time since Charlotte had felt anything close to the warmth this old lady exuded.

Still grasping Charlotte's hands, Isabella turned to look at Enzo and added, 'Your room is ready. It's always waiting for you.'

'*Grazie*, Isabella.'

Charlotte watched him smile stiffly at the housekeeper and walk away.

Isabella sighed. 'Come, let me show you to your room.'

Charlotte was certain that it was sadness she now saw on Isabella's face and was filled with a burning curiosity to know exactly what had happened here, but she couldn't ask Enzo. They didn't have that relationship. The last thing she needed was to give him a reason either to fire her or remember her.

CHAPTER THREE

ENZO WANDERED THE GROUNDS. He had no idea how long he had been out there, but the sun had set, leaving golden streaks in the darkening sky. The long shadows cut by the trees were no longer distinguishable from the darkness around them. When he looked back, the house was bathed in light. Every lamp burned, casting a glow through every window. Hidden lights around the plant beds illuminated the walls, with only the faintest glimmer caressing the surrounding leaves. He could never forget how beautiful it was in Perlano, in his home, but it was also where he felt the rawest. Like every healed-over scab had been torn open.

He vividly recalled his brother approaching him in this very spot with a look of guilt, asking to speak to him privately. Enzo glanced up at the window to what had been his room. The place where Emilio admitted that he'd had sex with Gia. Enzo had wanted to get far away from the memories, but as he looked towards the chapel whose spire he could only just make out, he knew that move had taken him away from his mother too.

He had loved her. She had always told him how proud she was of him, how impressed she was by his readiness to accept his duty to the family. To protect all that was theirs, just as his father had. Enzo had spent so much of his life living up to that image. He'd always been included in his father's

work, and it pleased him to no end. And as he grew older
and better understood the business and would sometimes
offer his own take, the greatest validation his father could
give him was a nod of approval. He lived for those moments.

Enzo heaved a sigh. Emilio had taken the comfort of
home away from him, and now he was trying to take the
vineyards too. Would his brother not be satisfied until he'd
sullied every bit of Perlano for him? Enzo didn't want to
acknowledge it, but that thought hurt. He remembered
being so excited when he was three at his brother's arrival
in the world. It was his earliest memory. Being involved in
his father's business so much as he grew hadn't left much
time for him to bond with his brother, but he'd still tried.
Even when he noticed his mother coddling Emilio, with
her obvious favouritism, it didn't bother Enzo.

With another sigh, he turned around and walked back
to the house. He noticed how quiet it was. It seemed Isabella had retired for the night without turning out the
lights. That wasn't like her, but maybe she'd deliberately
wanted to remind him of the beauty here. Of everything
this home held. She was always trying to lure him back,
but the problem was that it was filled with ghosts. Of his
father preparing him to take over. Of his mother's affection. Of Emilio and Gia. The anger and pain.

He wasn't himself here. He wasn't controlled. His usual
discipline always seemed to escape him; his emotions got
the better of him. He hated it.

He really did not want to retire to his room yet. He was
glad that he no longer slept in the room in which he had
grown up, no matter how luxurious it was. No matter how
much of him it reflected. The master suite was now his,
but even to that he did not wish to go.

Hoping to delay what would obviously be a short and

troubled sleep, he went down to the cellar and picked out a bottle. A little quiet and some good red wine might at least allow him to relax a little. It was worth a try.

He ran his thumb across the label with pride and went to fetch a glass from the kitchen, but on his way, he noticed a figure out on the terrace. Celeste was out there. He couldn't blame her for enjoying the view. She was the first woman he had brought here since Gia, he realised, since that relationship had crashed and burned so spectacularly.

Celeste was different, though. Where Gia craved the limelight, Celeste shunned it. Where Gia was fashionable and glamorous, Celeste was muted.

There was something deliberate about it, as if she tried to erase all evidence of her existence from one interaction to the next. Enzo admired her professionalism, but he knew so little about her. Come to think of it, all he really knew about her was that she was well-educated and that she had once been to Italy. But on the plane, when he had found her sound asleep, frowning and curled in on herself, something about her struck him. He'd never realised how small she was, and it dawned on him that he had always thought that her presence simply…filled a space. He hadn't liked that look of discomfort on her face, so he'd reached over her to close the blind, catching a whiff of blackcurrant and vanilla. A pretty fragrance that he'd found he rather liked. He had put away her work and covered her in a blanket, watching as the frown dissolved away and was replaced by a small smile.

Why had he suddenly found her so intriguing?

Rather than try to figure it out then, he had gone into his private bedroom to sleep. It had been no use.

Now, though, instead of fetching one glass from the kitchen, Enzo took two, along with a corkscrew. What harm could come from sharing a drink? Besides, Celeste was in his home. Even if she was there to assist him, he could still be a gracious host.

He stepped out onto the terrace. The gardens before them were framed by the centuries-old stone arches. He placed the glasses on the wrought-iron patio table with a clink that clearly startled Celeste.

'Jesus!' she exclaimed, clutching her heart.

'Apologies, I didn't mean to scare you,' he said, pulling the cork from the bottle with a pop.

'Oh, it's fine. I just wasn't expecting anyone to be out here.'

'I have always enjoyed sitting out here.' He filled a glass with rich red wine that he placed at the vacant seat at the small table. 'Sit, have a glass of wine with me.'

'Thank you.' She turned the chair to face out towards the gardens and eased back, plucking her glass off the table and taking a small sip.

For some reason, the act gave him great satisfaction. He batted the thought away. It had nothing to do with Celeste herself. It was just the fact that she seemed pleased by the wine that he enjoyed. After all, he was proud of his heritage. The small smile curving her lips was not at all distracting. Just like it hadn't been distracting when he saw her smile in her sleep on the plane.

'It's good,' she said before taking another sip.

'Again, you sound surprised.' He filled his own glass and set the bottle down on the table, then stepped to the edge of the terrace and slid his hand into his pocket.

'I've never had it before.'

'I wonder, should I be insulted that my PA could not be bothered to sample our wines? Or is it that she didn't know about them, which would be no less worrying?' She wouldn't be able to see his smirk. Why was he teasing the woman? In two years, they had never had this kind of relationship. Nothing at all had changed apart from coming back to Perlano, to his home.

You know why. You've already compared her to Gia.

'Well, I *have* always known about them, Mr De Luca, but it's a little pricier than a PA can afford, you know.'

That was a lie. Enzo knew what he paid her. She could afford a few more luxuries than she seemed to allow herself.

'I can see why you enjoy sitting out here. It's so peaceful. We don't get to see the stars quite like this in Sydney,' she said.

She was trying to change the subject. His suspicion that she tried to remove traces of her presence came back to him. He asked her a question—an inconsequential one at that—and she moved on to a subject that required no revelations about either of them. But she was right, they didn't see the stars, not with the bright city lights, and he missed it. He missed his home; he missed his people; he missed all that was his. But he didn't miss the feelings this place made resurface.

'Perlano is a special place. There was a time when the people of Calabria moved north or emigrated to other countries. We took the opportunity to start another vineyard in Piemonte. But the people of Perlano stayed.'

'They were happy to be here.'

'And it is the conte's responsibility to make sure it stays that way.'

'It seems like you have all been successful.'

Was Enzo a successful conte? He did what he could, but he made sure to stay away. Could he do more if he spent his time in Perlano?

'I love the hedge maze,' Celeste said, breaking through his thoughts.

Was she offering up a little bit of information about herself? Ever since that moment on the plane, she was becoming a puzzle that he wanted to solve. He wasn't sure why, but if he could keep her talking, maybe he would collect a few more pieces.

'It was an addition made by my father's great-grandfather. His wife loved sitting in the gardens, but she particularly loved that fountain, so he created the maze around it so she could be surrounded by both things she loved. But they say he ensured the hedges were kept lower than the fountain so he could always see where she was, see over the walls.'

'That's a beautiful story. I imagine there are a lot of stories in this place.'

'There are. Every conte put their mark on it in some way. It was a favourite pastime of mine to find all of them.'

He was proud of his history. How could he not be? It was a privilege to be handed the legacy and ensure that it endured. A privilege and a weight, but not one he'd ever shied away from. He had taken it all on, and he hoped he had made his father proud too.

Enzo turned around to look at Celeste, at all the burning questions in her eyes. Her next question would likely be what everyone asked: *How does it feel to be the conte? Did you always want to be?* He would give his usual rehearsed answer. Feelings had nothing to do with it. It was always his destiny. But if he was honest with himself, he had always wanted to be. He wanted to honour his father, the man who'd spent so much time with him, preparing him for the duty, ensuring he was strong enough to lead. Their bond had been profound: Enzo had loved his father, but more than anything he had respected him.

Instead, Charlotte asked, 'What mark have you left?'

The question caught him off guard. He knew what he had changed, but he wasn't sure if that was how he made his mark. 'The kitchen.'

'I'm sorry?'

Enzo saw that she had drained her glass, so he refilled both his and hers. 'My mother loved this place, especially the vineyards, but she also loved to cook. So after my father passed, I had the kitchen remodelled to give her the scenery she loved plus the convenience of modern life. She was getting older, you see.'

'So you wanted to make it easier on her,' Celeste said as he resumed his place at the pillar. This time, instead of looking out at the garden, he only saw her and how, in the darkness, her black hair looked almost blue. How elegant she was, despite how much she seemed to try to hide.

'Yes,' Enzo answered.

'Did you ever learn to cook from her?'

'I'm Italian, *cara mia*.' He grinned. 'Of course she ensured both her sons were capable. And you?'

'And me what?' Charlotte asked, ignoring his mocking tone.

'You almost certainly asked me that question anticipating that the answer would be *no*. Probably so you could make some clever remark. I'm simply asking you the same.'

Enzo was being playful, something that both shocked and delighted Charlotte. He had certainly not shown her much of his personality in the office. Everything about him seemed so closely guarded. He always said just enough. Never once in all the time she'd known him had she seen him allow someone into his thoughts, but now he was offering her peeks into who he was underneath it all.

In some ways, he was just like her. Hiding. Maybe not

to the same extent as her, but there was an Enzo to uncover. And she wanted to see more. That cocked brow
made something curl in her belly. The way he looked at
her with those green eyes that were so startlingly bright,
even in the moonlight. They pierced through her and made
her mouth go dry. The reaction surprised her, but it felt
good to feel something exhilarating. It was as if she was
coming alive. She saw the man every day, but she'd never
felt pinned by his gaze, except now that was exactly what
was happening.

She shouldn't be thinking about him like this. But when
Enzo, the famed control freak, saw fit to be playful, maybe
it was safe to let go just a little bit. So she answered without thinking.

'Of course I can. In fact, I have learned under some of
the very best chefs in the world.'

'Oh, really?' Enzo challenged.

'Yes. It's called the internet. You should check it out
sometime.' She turned her nose up at him, taking a long
sip of her wine, and when she shifted her gaze over to him,
she saw that he was stifling a smile.

Enjoying herself more than she had in a while, she
curled her fingers around the frame of her glasses and
drew them off her face. It felt so much better to be without them. Without that constant weight, that reminder to
be someone else. She picked the bottle off the table and
walked over to Enzo, emptying what was left into their
glasses.

She could feel him watching her intently as she read
the label then placed the bottle back on the table. She
was always so careful not to splurge, not to buy anything
that could raise suspicions, but maybe when they returned
home, she could make an exception for this wine.

'Alla tua.' She clinked her glass against Enzo's and watched his eyes darken when she sipped.

'Usually the toast comes first,' he said, his voice pitched low. The gravel in his tone made her feel warm.

Maybe with the loss of her glasses some of her old boldness returned, because she found herself saying, 'Rules are meant to be broken.'

'Salute.'

She kept her gaze fixed on his, watching him watch her sip her wine. Seeing his green eyes dip to her throat as she swallowed.

'You are an intriguing creature, Celeste Park.'

'I'm glad you think so, Enzo.'

The hand holding his wineglass dropped to his side and hers followed, as if they were mirrors of each other. They seemed to move closer with every breath, breaths that seemed in perfect sync. Breaths that erased all thought and left nothing but the force of their locked gazes pulling them together. Charlotte's heart knocked against her rib cage. All she needed, all she craved was his lips on hers. Their softness and his warmth.

'I think it's time we retired for the night.'

Charlotte was dazed. As sense returned to her, she saw Enzo pull away. All that buzzing energy was replaced by the sheer horror of what had almost happened.

'Um…yes. Goodnight, Mr De Luca,' she said, avoiding looking at him. She placed her glass on the table and half ran to her room, which took more concentration than it should have, her head swirling with all the wine she had consumed.

She shut the door and locked it for good measure, engulfed in mortification.

'Rules are meant to be broken? What the hell were you thinking? Not our rules! Our rules keep us safe!' she

chastised herself in the mirror. 'What absolute madness overcame you?'

Great! Now she was talking to herself.

She should have known their little *tête-à-tête* was not a good idea when wine was buzzing in her veins. When she was so affected, and he seemed not to be.

She rushed into the en suite bathroom and stripped her clothes with vehemence, furious with herself. She had been on numerous trips with Enzo, but not once had they ever acted so inappropriately. Not once had they teased each other or chatted like that. She had called him *Enzo*, for crying out loud!

She yanked her pyjamas over her head viciously, further angered by a realisation: she found Enzo attractive. More attractive than she'd found anyone before. She wanted to kiss him more than she'd wanted any other. When she closed her eyes, she could still see the bright green of his.

'It's just the wine talking, Charlotte. Go to bed!'

But she couldn't blame the wine when she recollected the magnetised way their bodies had drawn closer. Maybe if she had had more experience, she wouldn't have been so lost to the current of their attraction. Maybe she would be more immune to Enzo's seductiveness.

She switched off the lights and climbed into bed, determined to erase the whole interaction from memory. A part of her resisted, though. It had been so long since she had spoken to anyone like that, so long since she had kissed anyone, and never once a man like Enzo. She wanted more.

It was just a craving, stupid and reckless and not something she would act on. Biting back a groan, she closed her eyes and resolved to be even more closed-off than before.

Loneliness was a small price to pay for freedom.

CHAPTER FOUR

CHARLOTTE WALKED DOWN a sunlit staircase, passing painting after painting that could rival those in any art gallery. She stopped to admire one but wasn't really seeing any of the details.

She was procrastinating.

Sleep hadn't dulled her mortification, and as much as she wanted to see Enzo to have a taste of that feeling again, she wanted to avoid him. She'd shut off her usual alarm and tried to doze, but it hadn't worked. So she had taken an extra-long shower and taken her time getting ready.

All to give her the best chance of missing Enzo.

Part of her wondered if her reaction was a bit extreme. After all, there was no guarantee that she would still feel the things she had last night. She had consumed a fair amount of wine—maybe it was just a fluke? Either way, she was committed to being even more closed-off. More efficient. She had taken a silly risk, but that was in the past. Now she had work to do.

'Good morning, Celeste,' came Isabella's highly accented greeting. 'Come, I have prepared you a breakfast.'

'Oh, you really shouldn't have worried. I have work to get to.'

'Nonsense. You will eat first.'

Isabella ushered Charlotte into the spacious kitchen

where a spread was laid out on a large island. A spread for one.

Charlotte laughed. 'There's enough to feed an army here, Isabella. Won't you join me?' She didn't know what it was about the older woman, but her presence was comforting. Since Charlotte was unlikely to return to Perlano, there was little risk in indulging in some company.

'Oh, I couldn't.'

'Please?'

With a motherly sigh and smile, Isabella said, 'Fine. Maybe just a coffee.'

Charlotte reached for a *cornetto* and was pleased to see Isabella sit down and do the same.

'I'm afraid Leoncino has already left. He said to inform you that he would return later.'

So Charlotte was in the clear for now. 'Was that all he said?'

'He also said you could work from the downstairs office. It used to be where his mother worked.'

Two offices. Maybe she could avoid her boss for a little while longer.

But avoiding Enzo didn't mean that Charlotte wasn't still curious. He had been different since they arrived: driving himself, teasing, talking—not to mention the wine. On the terrace she'd wanted to uncover more about Enzo, and to her surprise, despite her mortification about the almost-kiss, that desire hadn't gone away. It would be a mistake to act on it. A very bad idea. She had worked so hard all this time to keep him at a distance. To remain safe. So even though she was curious, and even though she was so starved for company, she needed to bury the curiosity. Bury it with all the other pieces of herself that she had to hide.

'Leoncino is—'

'Why do you call him Leoncino?' she blurted.

You complete idiot! What did we just decide, Charlotte?

Damn this sudden inability to control herself when it came to her boss!

Isabella chuckled, her face lighting up. 'Because he is my little lion. When he was young, he would walk around here like a little master. He was always so brave. From the youngest age, he was staring down an impossible path, but he always took it on. Nothing was too big for our Enzo. He thought he could protect everyone.'

Charlotte could see it. He still acted like the master of the universe. She ate thinking about the change in him in this place. Would he be back to normal once they were in Sydney again?

Thinking of the office had her looking at the time. She had wasted so much of it avoiding Enzo, she really needed to get a start on her day even if it meant leaving Isabella's company. It had been so long since she'd shared a meal with someone, chatted like this. Charlotte kept telling herself there was a reason why she lived the way she did—it was better than being dragged back to a place where she was just her father's pawn—but it was lonely.

She drained her cup and asked Isabella to show her to the office.

It was lovely. Books lined two walls, and beside the door on either side were large paintings of the estate and its grounds. Large glass doors opened onto the very same terrace Charlotte had shared with Enzo the night before, with a view straight to the fountain.

'Enzo's office is directly above you, but if you need anything, I am here,' Isabella said before leaving, closing the door behind her.

Charlotte's computer bag was already placed on the large desk. Beside it sat her glasses.

Her hands immediately went to her face. Sure enough, she wasn't wearing them. She cursed loudly and grabbed them, jamming them onto her face, her heart racing. Sweat beaded on her brow, and her palms became clammy as panic consumed her.

How could she have been so careless? What had Enzo noticed?

A voice at the back of her mind told her to calm down. People forgot or lost their glasses all the time.

'But I don't!' she yelled at herself, just as pain erupted in her stomach. She reached into her bag for one of her trusty antacids, chewing on it as she thought. What had she done after she took them off? Charlotte couldn't remember. Most importantly, she didn't remember doing anything to raise suspicions about who she was. It was impossible to forget the almost-kiss, but apart from that she could think of nothing that would have made Enzo distrust her. She had been flustered. He would chalk forgetting her glasses up to that, surely.

She threw the doors to the terrace open and took a deep breath. All was not lost. She just had to put the wall between her and Enzo back up, and there would be no more catastrophes.

It had taken all of Charlotte's willpower to concentrate on the work she had to do. She was grateful that Enzo wasn't around as a distraction because her mind already wanted to go constantly back to the night before. She had been working for hours, and her neck ached. Still, she concentrated until footsteps outside the office alerted her to Enzo's arrival. He marched towards her with a scowl on his face.

Instantly she was on her feet.

'Mr De Luca, what's—?'

'Get ready, we're going to the vineyards.'

'Yes, sir.'

Wondering what was going on, she gathered her bag and tablet while Enzo paced. His hair stuck up at odd angles as if he had been gripping it in frustration. He was agitated. That wasn't good. Charlotte had never seen him like this. He *was* the control in the room. He kept people calm. But this trip was already so different. There was a human under all that, breaking through as he came apart.

She had seen from his calendar that he had been at his lawyers. Whatever was happening, it couldn't be good. It was just like Enzo to keep his thoughts to himself, never to allow anyone into his plans until absolutely necessary. Charlotte knew she would only find out what was going on once he assigned her a task, so she rushed out behind him to a pathway that led away from the estate.

She was thankful that she had opted to wear sensible shoes because while it was always a mission to keep up with Enzo, it was even more so on the uneven ground and his impatient pace. She noticed his hands were fisted at his sides as he walked. He was an entirely different man from the one in Sydney.

They walked until they came upon a large building that seemed to defy time, looking like it had been standing an age while still new and modern in parts. It was obviously taken care of, refurbished numerous times over the centuries.

When they stepped in, the winery was cool and impressively clean. It screamed Enzo. The newer parts of the building didn't take away from the older. If anything, it celebrated the historical architecture. But she didn't have much time to appreciate it when Enzo was storming through the place.

Clearly, he was looking for someone in particular. Charlotte knew she was there to take notes, but it felt like it was going to be her job to calm Enzo down.

'Marco!' Enzo shouted as they walked between massive barrels.

A man at the end of the passage looked up from his clipboard with a frown and walked towards them.

'Did you give Emilio a walkthrough?' Enzo asked through gritted teeth. Charlotte looked at him in surprise. She'd never once heard him speak in that manner to anyone, let alone an employee.

Marco recoiled, obviously stunned. His mouth opened and closed soundlessly before he stammered a response. 'Um…y-yes, he was here about a month ago. He wanted a full tour. Is everything okay?' He looked to Charlotte for help, shock still plain on his face.

'Anything else?' There was a throbbing vein in Enzo's temple. This was wrong. Charlotte knew she had to do something. Her boss's respect and integrity were things she greatly admired. If he continued like this, he would only regret it later.

'Well, he asked how often Mrs De Luca would visit, which I thought was odd, but I just put it down to her death.'

'I don't pay you to make calls like that,' Enzo snapped. 'I pay you to—'

'Excuse me, Marco,' Charlotte said, having heard enough. 'Can you give us a moment? I need Mr De Luca to look at something urgent that has just come through.'

Marco looked between them and nodded before turning around and walking away, confusion clear on his face. She didn't blame him. She was confused too.

Enzo turned his furious glare on her, but Charlotte wasn't cowed by it. Instead, she placed her hand on his arm and pulled him between the casks.

'Enzo, is everything okay?' she asked, knowing she had to be the calm in this situation.

'What?'

'This isn't you. You don't treat employees like this. You have never spoken to anyone like you just did to Marco, and he didn't deserve it.'

Enzo cursed under his breath, rubbing his temples with his right hand, but Charlotte stepped closer into his eyeline, forcing him to look at her. A warmth flared within her, their proximity making her heart beat faster. His loss of control was somehow stirring. Even on the terrace he had summoned his self-restraint before they could kiss, but now there were no masks, his emotions on display. It made Charlotte wonder what it would be like if he lost control with her. What that kiss would have been like if he had been unleashed.

She pushed past the thought, past the curling in her belly. She needed to bring controlled Enzo back to the surface.

'Emilio is his boss too. Why would it matter if Emilio had a tour?'

A muscle ticked in Enzo's jaw as he looked into her eyes, but he was quiet, so she knew he was listening.

'Let's take a break and get a drink and then we can relook at what's going on. You can speak to Marco once you're calmer.' As soon as the words were out of her mouth, Charlotte realised she had broken one of her own rules. She always made everything seem like it was Enzo's idea, but now she had taken charge. She had essentially given her word that she would solve a problem with him, something she normally felt wasn't her place. It was a risk. She was stepping into the limelight, doing something that would make Enzo take notice of her. Not to mention Marco. Either of them could unwittingly let slip information about her to the wrong person and attract her father's attention. Her stomach throbbed painfully, but she had no antacids with her, and she couldn't focus on the pain when something serious was going on with Enzo. She couldn't leave him alone in it.

'You're right,' Enzo said at last. 'Let's go back to the house.'

Charlotte nodded and turned to lead the way out, but he didn't immediately follow.

'Wait for me out there. I have to apologise to Marco.'

She was glad to see that he was able to admit when he was wrong. *That* was the man she admired and chose to work for. And that was the man who was becoming increasingly more dangerous to her because her heart had not slowed. When he'd looked into her eyes, she hadn't wanted him to stop.

She couldn't allow this attraction to continue. It wouldn't end well for her.

Enzo walked beside Celeste in silence. He could feel her occasional glances at him, but he wouldn't acknowledge them. He'd behaved abominably, and she'd been right to pull him aside, getting him to see and think rationally. He couldn't remember anyone else having the power to reach him like that. Maybe one…but even Gia had only had that power because Enzo allowed her to have it. Celeste had simply barged through the red haze and pulled him out.

The path narrowed slightly, and he watched her step ahead of him. That was new, he realised. She always followed quietly behind, but in the winery she was bold. There was fire in her. Even now as they walked, she didn't look over her shoulder—she simply led. There was more to his PA than he had realised. Well, he had found that out the night before. He'd been so close to making a mistake on the terrace, so close to kissing her. He both thanked and cursed his sense for returning in time to make her run from him, so hurried that she'd forgotten her glasses. The same glasses that he'd left on her desk and that she now wore. Glasses that she obviously didn't need. He'd seen her read the label on the wine bottle. He'd watched her race away from the darkened terrace. Perhaps it was a style choice, but he greatly doubted that. It was yet another piece that didn't quite fit into the puzzle of her that, for some reason, he desperately wanted to solve.

That was exactly why he had left so early this morning: he needed space from Celeste. Going to the lawyers had successfully pushed her from his mind for a short while, but only because finding out that the second will—a will that had been sent only to Emilio as per Valentina's instruction—was valid had enraged him. If Enzo wanted to retain ownership of the vineyards, he had to find a way to invalidate the second will because his mother had indisputably left them to Emilio.

Enzo had no idea why his brother had kept the information secret for so long. Perhaps his visits to the vineyards had something to do with that. In any case, they had little contact, and he was certain if Emilio could have had the lawyers handle everything without ever letting Enzo know, he would have. Because he was a coward. It still didn't explain their mother's change of heart, however, and that betrayal weighed heavily on his mind. A constant hurt.

Enzo was angry that so much had been kept from him.

He was angry at the mother he still loved and still missed for doing this. He couldn't understand her motivations. He didn't understand why Emilio was so set on ruining Perlano for him.

The vineyards meant a lot to all of them. Enzo had wonderful memories of protecting his mother from the wasps and spiders while she tended to the plants. If he wasn't there with her, he visited with his father, who had taught him how to inspect the plants and winery.

Once when he was young, his father had placed Enzo on his shoulders and as far as he could see there were only grapevines. Every row laden with fruit.

'One day, Enzo, all of this will be yours, and you alone will be responsible for our people. For our family and our history.'

The memory made Enzo miss his father so much his chest ached.

He didn't realise where he was until they had walked into his office. How did Celeste know where it was? Had she been exploring? Searching through his home? Strangely, the thought wasn't upsetting. And it should have been. He hadn't shown her around for a reason. He didn't trust people, generally. But it had already been a trying day, and he'd been barely holding on to his temper for most of it, so perhaps he simply had no more capacity for anger.

He walked to the window, looking out at the vineyards that stretched in an undulating sea of green. They had existed even before the company did. Not a lot of people realised just how much the De Luca history was tied to these vineyards, but he did.

'Here you go,' Celeste said, handing him a glass of grappa. The spirit was made in their estate in Piemonte. Just like his father, Enzo used to drink it as a digestif after his meal, taking a moment just for himself in the privacy of his office. It had been a long time since he'd indulged in the ritual, but now Celeste had given that to him again.

Enzo took a small sip, relishing the spicy, floral hints. The vineyards were part of who he was as they were for every conte before him. It didn't matter what the second will said.

'He'll never have them,' he muttered under his breath.

'Who won't have what?'

'Emilio,' he responded, turning to face Celeste, unsure of why he was telling her this. Maybe it was because he was already trying to hold back so much anger and disappointment that he didn't have enough control left to stop the words spilling from his lips. 'Emilio wants the vineyards. All of them. He is in possession of a second will that states they should belong to him, and he wishes to take them.' Just like Emilio, always wanting to take what was Enzo's. He'd succeeded with Gia; Enzo wasn't about to let it happen again.

And what about his mother's betrayal? All three of them were aware that his father had gifted the vineyards to her, but that she was expected to bequeath them to Enzo. It had been so in the first will. Why did she create the second? Why didn't she warn him? Was he being punished for leaving? He couldn't stay. Not after the affair. She had always said she understood that.

Enzo looked down into the narrow long-stemmed glass, at the nearly colourless liquid, caught between hurt and anger, and said, 'I'll make sure that he will never have them.' After all, he was the conte. The vineyards were his.

The words made unease creep into Charlotte's belly. She had dealt with possessive men before. Had run from them.

If Enzo had a possessive streak, it was one more reason why what lay between them could only ever be an attraction that was never acted upon.

But she sensed that there was more to it than that. Enzo was so private, and so little of his personal life got out into the media that she didn't even know what his relationship with his brother was like. And Enzo wouldn't share more, she knew that. She was amazed he had shared so much with her already. Whatever was actually going on must be tearing him up, because she was certain it had been hurt that had flashed across his face before his expression hardened once more. It was possibly that brand-new vulnerability that had her speaking now, that had her wanting to offer comfort in some way.

'I have a half sister,' she said. 'We grew up together, mostly. I was four when she was born. I had hoped we would be close. I was so young when she came into the world, so excited, and I kept waiting for her to be old enough that we could do things together, but that never happened. She made my life as unpleasant as she could as often as she could. You see, she was always a little bit jealous that *she* wasn't the firstborn. That I was the one meant to take over…'

'Take over what?'

Charlotte looked up to see Enzo paying close attention, his glass ignored as he looked only at her, and she realised that she had almost slipped up and revealed too much. She couldn't tell him that she was meant to have taken over her father's business. There would be far too many questions—he might find out just how wealthy her family was. So she deflected.

'It doesn't matter. The point is the way siblings act out is usually just a symptom of another issue.'

* * *

Celeste had Enzo's complete attention. He wanted her to keep talking, so to keep the atmosphere as it was, he picked up his glass of grappa and took a small sip, pleased to see Celeste do the same. It really had been a long time since he had shared a drink with anyone without having to conduct business, and here he was, doing it twice with Celeste in as many days.

'Do you see much of your sister?' He almost regretted asking the question when he saw the sadness in her face that she quickly covered up.

'I don't really see my family anymore.'

Why? He wanted to find out more. He didn't understand this need. Why was he so intrigued? Why did he like the idea of knowing her?

What he did know was that he would much rather keep the focus on Celeste instead of saying any more about himself. He didn't confide in people. He didn't trust anyone enough to do so. His thoughts were safer if no one knew them.

But you did share your thoughts with her.

He couldn't lie to himself; he had done so, and he did it without thinking. What was it about her?

He moved closer to Celeste, catching the scent of blackcurrant and vanilla just like he did on the plane. For the first time, he noticed the sprinkling of freckles on her cheeks. She looked up at him, her gaze never wavering from his, and he realised that he was seeing a different side to her. She wasn't looking away. He had always known she was smart, but there was a confident, feisty woman that she kept hidden and now—just like the night before—she was trying to break free.

Closer. He kept drawing closer until his eyes dipped to

her slightly parted lips and all he could think about was kissing her. How sweet would she taste? What sounds would she make for him? How soft were her pink lips?

How was it possible that he was only just realising how beautiful she was? It was like waking from a dream. How could he have missed something so glaringly obvious when it was in front of him this whole time? She had been working for him for two years, for heaven's sake!

Exactly! She's been working for you for two years! What are you doing?

What was he doing? She was his PA. The realisation was like being doused in ice-cold water, and he pulled away, shocked that he had almost kissed her again.

CHAPTER FIVE

CHARLOTTE WAS STUNNED. Paralysed in the moment. Watching Enzo.

One heartbeat.

Two heartbeats.

And then she was moving. Rushing away. She wrenched the door open, not even hearing when it hit the wall. And then she was running. Down one passage and then another. Damn this house! Why couldn't she remember her way?

In her mind she saw Enzo yank himself away, a look of sudden realisation on his face. The same shock she was feeling now. They had almost kissed. Again. How could she have let this happen? She had been so adamant that she would keep her distance after what had happened on the terrace, but when he drew closer it was as if every thought had disappeared. Every reason that they shouldn't kiss dissolved away into nothing. His presence burned through it all, leaving all her resistance nothing more than smoke on a breeze.

Her heart was still beating fast. Maybe it was panic, maybe it was because she was fleeing, but mostly it was because he had been so close. The way he looked at her, as if he saw her—the real her. *Charlotte*, and not her invented persona. And she wanted him. She wanted him to pull her into his arms and kiss her.

Why now? Why was she so attracted to Enzo? It must

be this place. He had said she was safe here, but it was far more dangerous than anyone could have realised. It brought out his human side. It showed her his scars. No one was more surprised than her at how deeply it cut to see him hurt. But she couldn't be around him right now. She couldn't even blame the drink, because she had barely sipped at the grappa. This chemistry was all them, and it made her want to wail. How could life be so cruel? To have never been with a man, and then to have someone so close that she could never truly have. All because of her father and the groom he'd tried to force on her, a groom who couldn't be even a fraction of the man that Enzo was.

There was safety in Enzo's shadow, but Charlotte had to deny herself the man because the light shone far too brightly on him. That attention would be the end for her.

She paid no attention to where she went, hurriedly running down the stairs, looking over her shoulder as though she could see through the walls into Enzo's office. Her foot hit the landing, and her body slammed into another.

Soft arms came around her, steadying them both.

'*Dio!*' Isabella exclaimed. 'Celeste! Are you all right?'

'I'm sorry, I—I wasn't watching where I was going.' Charlotte had to fight to keep the panicked sob building in her throat from escaping. That would only draw questions from Isabella, and the less she said the better.

'I was just going to Leoncino to give him this, but since you are here, you can take it.'

Charlotte swallowed hard, trying to control every impulse to flee, to run from this house, from Perlano, from Enzo. But where would she go? Travelling privately with him was one thing, but the moment she set foot in an airport, it wouldn't be long before she was found.

'Sure.' She accepted the cream envelope. The stationery was very clearly expensive, and Enzo's name was printed on the front in a highly stylised script. 'Do you know who it's from?'

'A messenger brought it.'

Charlotte turned to go, but Isabella stopped her.

'Are you certain that you are okay?'

Charlotte forced a smile and hoped it didn't look as brittle as it felt. 'Yeah, I am.'

Envelope in hand, she glanced up the stairs. Instead of going back, she turned on her heel and walked outside. She needed a moment. Just to collect herself.

Fanning herself with the letter, she found herself walking to the fountain. Water had always soothed her soul, so she decided to sit on the edge and enjoy the cool mist that rose up around it. It was such a glorious day. The early afternoon sun was high in the startlingly blue sky, casting barely any shadow. Charlotte wanted to rail at all of it. It should be dull and oppressively grey to match how she felt.

The surroundings were so beautiful that it was hard to picture a world outside it. But there was one. A cruel world that forced Charlotte into hiding. That stole the possibility of passion or companionship.

This fountain, the maze…it was such a beautiful love letter. How she wished she could have that kind of love in her life, but fate had other plans. Instead, she had to hide from an arranged marriage to an atrocious man and face a growing attraction to her untouchable boss.

Charlotte pushed off the fountain, moving away from the flow of the water she so enjoyed, to walk through the maze. She never liked the idea of getting deliberately misled; if the maze were taller, she doubted she would have gone in at all. But right now she would have liked tall walls to hide behind. The privacy would have given her a chance to pull her own walls back up, to rebuild the barrier between her and Enzo. So unlike his great-great-grand-parents. With her low walls, no matter where the contessa wandered, her husband would have been able to see her. To reach her. Charlotte would never have that, with anyone.

From where she stood, she could see a small portion of the wrought-iron gates at the bottom of the long driveway and felt a part of her reach for them. Her instinct screamed at her to run. To escape this attraction before it became a bigger problem in her life. But when she looked at the en-velope, she knew she couldn't.

Regardless of what happened between them, she had a job to do. It was the only point in her life that gave her any fulfilment at all.

'You can do this, Charlotte,' she said to herself. After all, she had escaped without anyone's help. She had set up this new life for herself, and she had got the job at De Luca and Co. on her own. If she had to face an attraction to Enzo every day, she would do it. If she ran, there was no guarantee she would find an opportunity like this again. Through him, she could leave a mark.

So, inhaling deeply, she swallowed the ever-present urge to flee and walked back into the house. She would just need to be careful. All she had to do was try to stay away from Enzo as much as possible. With her own office and her own room, that shouldn't be too hard.

He's your boss. There's no Enzo. It's Mr De Luca to you.

The door was still open, and Enzo was standing at the window with his hands clasped behind his back. From his profile, she could see a frown on his face.

Charlotte regretted the almost-kiss even more now, be-cause it would have only added one more weight onto the shoulders of a man who already bore so much.

Act like nothing ever happened. An Oscar-winning performance. Understand?

'Mr De Luca,' she said clearly. She almost faltered when he turned at the sound of her voice and the frown slipped off his face to be replaced by something softer. She could have almost sworn that he was about to move closer to her but stopped when she ploughed on. 'This arrived for you.' She kept so much space between them that she had to fully extend her arm to hand the envelope to him.

He looked at her for a fraction of a second. Not moving. Assessing. And then he reached for the envelope, stepping back once he had it in hand. Granting the request for space that must be clearly legible in her body language.

'What is it?' She was relieved that his tone was back to business as usual. Relieved…and hurt.

'I don't know. Isabella said it arrived by messenger.'

Charlotte watched his hands work to open the envelope and had to look away. There was no way his *hands* were making her feel things.

'It's an invitation,' he announced.

That got her attention. She watched as his eyes skimmed over the card.

'To a ball in Milan. This is perfect.'

Yes, it was, because now Enzo would be away for a few days, and she would have the time to recalibrate. It was exactly what she needed. So why did she feel disappointed that he would be leaving?

'I'll go make the arrangements for your travel.' Before Enzo could say anything else, Charlotte was fleeing, her heart twisting as she put space between them.

Enzo watched her rush out of his office, but he wasn't going to let her hide from him again. So he followed her.

She must have run all the way because he found her seated behind her borrowed desk, trying to behave like the quiet, efficient PA when he knew it was a façade. He had seen the fire in her when he almost kissed her.

He was in a rage after seeing the lawyers, but Celeste had stepped in and pulled him out of his own head. She had reminded him who he was. He couldn't understand why a woman that strong was trying to hide or why, after he had seen under that mask, she was trying to pretend like he hadn't.

And it rankled that she was doing everything she could to avoid acknowledging their almost-kiss, avoid him. They needed to talk.

He sat opposite her, the table between them. 'You will arrange for *our* travel. We will first visit the vineyard in Piemonte, then attend the ball together. Book rooms for us, we'll leave in the morning.'

Celeste tensed.

'What's wrong?' He could hear his frustration leak into his tone.

'Nothing's wrong,' she replied, without taking her eyes off her screen.

Enzo reached over and pushed the lid of her computer down, keeping his hand on the device to prevent her from hiding behind it.

'Do you mind? I'm trying to work,' she snapped, then blinked as if the response caught her off guard.

Good.

He wanted to see more of that feistiness. He could see she tried to suppress it.

'I do mind. Is this about what happened in the office?' There had been two mistakes there. At least he had the sense to stop himself before he kissed Celeste. She was his employee, and he could have kicked himself for his behaviour. The second mistake was almost going to her when she had walked back into his office. She kept testing his control. Enzo would *not* pursue her, but it bothered him that she wasn't being her honest self with him now. He wanted her to talk about it. At least then he would know whether she was just as affected as he was. He would have her deliberate honesty, not just her body's reaction to him.

'I don't know what you are talking about, Mr De Luca.'

That got under his skin.

'So we're back to that? What happened to Enzo?' He realised then that he liked her using his name, the natural way it fell from her lips. 'In that case, Ms Park, I asked you a question.'

But she didn't answer. He watched her watch him. As if he could see her mind at work, he knew instinctively she was looking for an excuse.

'Well?'

'Yes. It's about that.'

Lie!

He had seen the way her eyes dipped to his mouth before she answered.

'I don't think it's a good idea for us to go together and blur the line of our professional relationship.'

Another lie.

They were stacking up now, and it grated on his nerves. He'd had enough of people lying to him, hiding things from him, deceiving him. The woman he had loved, his brother and now his mother.

It seemed like he was simply destined to keep learning that people weren't trustworthy. Maybe it was something about him that made the people around him behave that way.

His response to Celeste—however ill-advised—was honest. The woman on the terrace was honest. The woman in his office who wanted to be kissed as much as he wanted to kiss her was honest. There was very little in the world as honest as the natural attraction that seemed to be building between them.

And even though their attraction was a terrible idea and an impossibility to act on, at least Enzo could trust it and acknowledge it while remaining committed to keeping the boundaries of the work relationship in place. Now Celeste reminded him why he shouldn't trust her either. She was hiding things from him. Lying to him.

Enzo removed his hand from her laptop and sat back in his chair. 'Don't worry, Ms Park…' He saw her lips press into a thin line. Clearly, she didn't like it when he called her that. He was only returning the favour. 'You have nothing to be concerned about. I only wish for you to attend as my PA.' He noticed the frown on her face, but she said nothing, so he pushed on. 'This is an event to rub shoulders with some of the most powerful people in the world. There are relationships to be forged. De Luca and Co. needs to be represented. That's all you are there for. Nothing more.' Which was the truth. Whether she realised it or not, Celeste was popular amongst his clients. Nearly every one of them had remarked on her efficiency, her intelligence. More than a few had approached him with offers to poach her with something in return for him, and he had turned them down every time. Taking her to the ball could benefit him and the company greatly.

She looked out the French doors, and he wondered what she was thinking now. He had to fold his arms across his chest to stop himself from snatching those glasses off her face and forcing her to look at him.

Her throat bobbed before she could respond again.

'I have nothing to wear,' she objected.

Of all her excuses so far, this one was the most insulting. To think that he would drop her in a sea of sharks without any preparation annoyed him more than it should.

After all, it was a reasonable thing to fret about. Except, of course, he would ensure that his date was properly attired.

He always had when it was Gia on his arm, and she revelled in the attention—in the fine silks and jewellery and his giant diamond on her finger. But then it was the diamond she'd wanted, not him. She'd made that perfectly clear.

Celeste was different, but that didn't mean he wouldn't make the same effort for her. All these worthless excuses to get out of being in his company! Couldn't she see that going together would be for her benefit as much as his? She was the best PA he'd ever had, and he wanted to reward that. He had already decided she would earn a significant performance bonus, and attending the ball should have been a treat. Enzo was also certain that if she dressed up and immersed herself in some glamour for a night, maybe she could find her confidence. Be that woman he had seen on the terrace. He was trying to help her.

'I will take care of it. Any other concerns, Ms Park?'

Now he was taunting her, but he wanted a reaction. A peek behind the curtain. He wanted to crack through the wall she had erected. He wanted *his* Celeste back.

Yours?

When had he started thinking of her as his? He didn't hate the thought. She was *his* PA. But that wasn't a good enough explanation for how this felt. He felt possessive over the pieces she had shown him.

And now that he was looking, really looking, she was showing him another.

'I don't want to go!' she snapped.

'Then, tell the truth,' he nearly growled at her. 'Be honest with me, and I might consider it.'

'I don't want to end up in the socials,' she said, and this time he believed her. He believed the pleading in her eyes. The desperation in her voice that cut through him. 'You have to know who you are, Enzo…'

Finally, she was saying his name again, and the sound of it made him relax a fraction. But also, now he was listening because this wasn't just the mask speaking, it was the woman beneath.

'Your name is everywhere. On every social media app, on every news website, in every business and financial publication. There isn't a business in the world that hasn't heard of or had some connection to De Luca and Co. Your wines are in millions of homes. I know it's only your public persona that you allow out into the media, but people still know who you are. This trip has been one of the few where you haven't had to deal with press. So far, I've done a great job of keeping out of it, but if I attend with you, that will be the end of my privacy. Everywhere I go it will be violated. I don't want that. I don't want the attention.'

Enzo was dumbstruck. He had no idea she had felt this way. Of course he didn't—why would he? He and Celeste never really talked like they had on this trip. And he got it. This life wasn't for everyone. He had been born into it. Raised in it. The people in his circle accepted it. Gia… well, Gia had relished the attention. For an ordinary person it would be daunting. Was that why Celeste tried to hide?

But she was so strong beneath her mask, so beautiful— she could thrive in the limelight. Why was she so desperate to avoid it? What had happened to her? She had mentioned a jealous sister… Could that be the reason for her shyness?

He *had* to help her out of her shell.

'Please, Enzo. I like my quiet life.'

He uncrossed his arms and leaned towards her, gentling his voice to reassure her. 'Celeste, I will ensure that you don't end up splashed across the media. This event is very exclusive. There are no pictures allowed in the ballroom, and I personally know the host. I will make sure you remain anonymous to the world. You have my word.'

He would keep his promise, but he would also make sure that a woman as beautiful as Celeste who deserved to shine in the spotlight could find her true self. Her honest self.

'So, is there a problem?' he asked, but now it was a dare. Challenging her to step into herself.

He saw defiance in those coal eyes. Fire. Satisfaction curled through him at the sight.

Holding his gaze, Celeste replied, 'Not at all, sir.'

CHAPTER SIX

CHARLOTTE SLUGGISHLY OPENED her hotel room door. She was exhausted, and it had nothing to do with how she physically felt. She was mentally drained.

She'd spent the day with Enzo, and while that was nothing out of the ordinary, the atmosphere was. They had said little to each other since their conversation the day before in the office, beyond a couple of necessary instructions from him. They'd flown to Milan in the morning, then he had driven them to the vineyards in Piemonte, then back to their hotel. The whole time, the air had been thick with questions neither would voice.

Now Charlotte closed the hotel room door and leaned against it. Normally she would ensure her room was close to Enzo's suite, or book a shared suite with multiple rooms. This time she had made sure she was as far from him as possible to prevent her from doing anything reckless.

Her stomach protested loudly. Anxiety over the ball had made it impossible for her to eat. Her mind just kept going over and over all the possible ways everything could go wrong. Of course, she'd looked at pictures of Enzo at similar events, seen him all dressed up and felt envious that she couldn't share the experience. She'd always wished that one day she could attend with him. The old her loved social events, loved going out and getting glammed up. But that outgoing Charlotte could never be indulged. Just one picture of her floating around the internet would make all the running and hiding she'd done utterly pointless. She'd done so well to avoid the cameras. Was tonight really any different? If she went to the ball, surely it would get out that she had been at De Luca and Co. the entire time? Then it would be only too easy for her father to find her.

Charlotte's heart raced at the thought. It made her want to curl into a ball and hide.

Enzo's voice rang in her ears. *'I will ensure that you don't end up splashed across the media. You have my word.'*

While it eased her mind a little, she was still nervous. How could one man control an entire room of people?

Of course, she knew her father would not be looking through social media himself nor trawling the tabloids, but she knew, given how much her disappearance might cost him, he would have people looking for her. And who knew how ruthless those people were? Maybe Enzo could protect her, but he was a man of integrity. He didn't think like the lowlifes her father would happily employ to get his way.

This was a mess.

Then, run. Run like you always do.

She loved her job too much to do that. Her quiet life.

It's not a quiet life, Charlotte, it's a silent life. There's a difference, and you're being a coward.

Her stomach ached, and she reached into her pocket for her antacids. Just as she had done on the plane. Enzo had seen it, but he hadn't commented.

She just couldn't get their interaction the day before out of her mind. When Enzo had asked if she objected to the invitation because of their almost-kiss, it had seemed like the perfect excuse, but she hated that she'd lied. Really, even though she ran and even though she promised to be better at keeping her distance, she wanted more than anything to see where that kiss could have led. She realised now just how heady his presence had been since their first night. From the moment they had shared that bottle of wine, he had been in her thoughts constantly. He was consuming her in a way he never had before. The more of himself he showed her, the more she wanted to see.

The way he looked at her before they'd almost kissed made her shudder. It was so different to the coldness in her office afterwards, when she knew he could tell that she was lying. Until she had told as much of the truth as she could without giving herself away.

She'd felt his gaze on her when they walked through the winery that morning, as she jotted down everything that was discussed and making a mental note of the way Enzo tensed up when they reported that Emilio had been there too. On the drive back, she'd wanted to ask Enzo if he was okay. Comfort him somehow, because she could tell he was hurting and didn't understand how no one else saw it. She'd almost placed her hand on his thigh to do just that but thankfully caught herself just in time and ran her fingers through her hair instead. Had Enzo noticed? She'd seen him grip the steering wheel tighter afterwards.

Charlotte knew she couldn't remain against this door hiding from Enzo for ever.

Screwing up her courage, she walked into the room. The very first thing that caught her eye was laid out on the bed. A gorgeous long sequined black dress. She ran her fingers over the shoulder, dragging them down the diagonal neckline. It was exquisite. When she turned the tag around, she saw a haute couture label that she hadn't even had access to in her old life. Beside the dress waited a pair of black stiletto sandals and a velvet box that she opened to reveal a pair of earrings and bracelets.

When she had remarked that she had nothing to wear, Enzo had said he would take care of it—but she didn't expect this! She picked the dress up, holding it to her body as she stepped in front of the full-length mirror. It was perfection. Her concern might have been a convenient excuse, but it had been honest: she really didn't have anything to wear to a ball. She did have the money to buy something and they *were* right on the Via Monte Napoleone, surrounded by high-end stores. But the moment she swiped her card, she would have been paranoid that the transaction would alert people to her location. Now Enzo had taken that worry away.

As she placed the dress back on the bed, she noticed a cosmetics counter's worth of luxury makeup on the table. Her heart swelled at the sight. Enzo had thought of everything. It all showed her how much attention he really paid—especially when there should be no reason that her dress and shoe size should be correct. Then it struck her. On one of their previous business trips, her heel had broken, and Enzo had arranged for a new pair to be brought to her. At the time he had said he'd done it so that they didn't lose any productivity, but maybe, just maybe, he had been taking care of her.

Warning bells sounded in Charlotte's head. She was growing attached. Enzo had just proved that he had remembered something about her, when her aim was to be unmemorable. She had to hide, not get noticed. And in all this, she would *definitely* be noticed.

But she wanted it.

She wanted to wear this dress. She wanted to wear heels that made her feel tall and invincible. She wanted to do her makeup and style her hair. She wanted to let herself out of the cage. Toss away dull, quiet Celeste and let Charlotte shine. She wanted to stand in front of Enzo as the person she truly was and see if he would want her then. If he would sweep her up and let her bathe in that presence that made all else fade into nothing. She wanted to know if he would see her and know all of her, know that the intelligence she showed at the office came through a carefully controlled filter. That she was so much more than she seemed.

She was already showing him parts of her that she kept hidden, and every time she did, he came a little closer. And God, was it intoxicating!

Charlotte needed Celeste, but as scared as she was, she was liking who she was around Enzo. This trip had turned everything on its head, but she couldn't regret it because since coming to Italy, he had revealed so much more of himself. She wasn't deluding herself into thinking she knew him yet. He was so guarded, played everything so close to his chest, but some things were obvious to her now. He was witty and occasionally sarcastic. He liked taking care of people. He loved his home. There was an entire ocean of emotion within him, not to mention pain.

'What happened to you, Enzo?' she wondered, picking up a tube of lipstick and twisting it open. It was a stunning shade of red. Bold.

She looked around the room and laughed softly to herself.

'No one has ever treated you like this, Charlotte.'

Even before she had left her life of wealth behind, no one had made her feel special. And in this one gesture, Enzo had.

She thought back to seeing Enzo disembark the plane looking fresh and glamorous, remembered how badly she wished it could be her. She so badly wanted a chance to live again, just briefly, before she went back into hiding. And Enzo had promised to keep her safe. Maybe she could have just one night to make her soul happy.

She turned to face herself in the mirror. 'Maybe we could let Charlotte out, just this once?'

Enzo stepped out of the elevator on Celeste's floor. He adjusted the cuffs of his shirt peeking out of his black tuxedo sleeves and then stood with his hands clasped behind his back. There were two reasons he was waiting for her. The first—and the one he acknowledged most willingly—was that, given how reluctant Celeste was to attend at all, he wanted to make sure she actually turned up. One day she would thank him for it, if not for the fact that he would have helped her find her fire, then maybe for the considerable bonus she would earn from helping him attract more business. Besides, they were meant to be attending *together*.

The fact that he'd happily attended events alone ever since his relationship with Gia had crashed and burned was something he ignored now.

The second reason was that when Celeste had told him that she didn't want her privacy invaded, she had looked so vulnerable that he absolutely had to ensure that she was protected. He had given her his word, and he stood by that.

But even he had to admit that there was one more motivation behind this. And when he saw Celeste walking towards him, that third reason revealed its name. Desire.

His breath caught. His PA was gone, erased entirely. Walking towards him, like some fairy queen wearing the night sky as if *she* controlled the stars in the galaxy, eclipsing the beautiful marble pillars and dissolving the sculpted walls into nothing, was the woman he had almost kissed twice. Images flashed in his head. Celeste pouring wine. Celeste pulling off her glasses. Celeste dragging him out of his fury. Celeste in his office, waiting to be kissed. With every step she took, he felt the weight of each moment in his whole being. Those were just peeks into the woman he saw now. Uncovered. Exposed. Utterly breathtaking.

Desire and arousal unlike anything he had ever felt coursed through him now. He wanted her. He wanted her so badly that part of him wanted to take her up to his suite and forget about the ball. Forget about everything apart from her.

He would kiss that bare shoulder while slipping that single strap off the other. He would worship at the leg that was revealed to her thigh with every step. His hands would settle on her tiny waist, stroke at the teasingly small part that two sheer stripes exposed. The rest of her was hidden away in swathes of black sequined fabric.

He had to get his thoughts under control because he could feel the pressure in his trousers from her effect on him, and he was not some adolescent boy. But when he saw the white gold earrings with the rare blue garnet that he had bought her dangling down her elegant neck, he wanted to kiss her there. Leave a mark for all to see.

Desperation gnawed at him. He wanted her in his arms because for all their attraction and near misses on this trip, he still hadn't experienced that, and he felt bereft of something he had never known. It was pure insanity, wasn't it?

He couldn't stop himself when Celeste came to stand before him. Leaning down, he kissed her cheek and saw her eyes follow him.

'You look beautiful.' That wasn't enough of a compliment. Enzo was struggling to keep his hands to himself and not brush them through her long dark hair that she had styled in a way he had never seen on her.

Different. Celeste was changed in every way, and yet he had never seen her more herself.

There had been a look of apprehension on her face, but it had morphed into satisfaction when she saw him, telling Enzo that she'd known all along who she was beneath her camouflage. Satisfaction then morphed into triumph when her gaze roved over his body displaying his overwhelming desire for her.

'You look pretty good too, Enzo.' She smirked. 'I imagine you're going to get all kinds of attention tonight.'

He chuckled at her joke, self-satisfaction rolling through him. His plan was already working. He'd had no doubt, of course, but to see Celeste already being herself, being bold, made him happy in a way he hadn't felt in a long time. He offered her his arm.

There was only one person's attention he wanted.

He walked with Celeste, arms linked, through the marble foyer of the hotel with its grand, sweeping staircases and sparkling chandeliers with an eye for none of that beauty, nothing but the woman by his side. He led her through a private exit where an Italian sports car with dark tinted windows waited. Dressed as they were, on one of the most expensive streets in the world, he couldn't risk taking Celeste out the front doors where paparazzi might lurk. He'd given her his word that he would protect her, and he would.

More and more, it was becoming something he wanted to do. Something that gave him great pleasure.

He opened the door for her, closing it once she was all settled, and rounded to the driver's side. Ensuring that they were alone, he stepped into the car. It came to life with a loud growl before settling into an aggressive purr.

He took one more look at Celeste before easing the car onto the road, secure in the knowledge that no one would see them. But as they began driving towards the Palazzo Felce, Enzo quickly realised that it was not just being photographed that he had to worry about. He could feel Celeste's gaze on him, burning through to the heart of him, heating his blood. He wanted to reach out and place his hand on her exposed thigh. Claim her. And it didn't help that she seemed to be just as aware of him. Even when she turned away, it seemed like she couldn't help looking back towards him, finally shifting in her seat, angling her body towards his. He had to fight for concentration.

'You seem tense,' Celeste said.

He was tense. He was trying to wrestle his want for her into something manageable. He gritted his teeth to stop himself from telling her precisely what she was doing to him without doing anything at all. He couldn't even come up with a witty comeback.

Out the corner of his eye, he could see her fingers toying with a sequin on the edge of the slit that was going to put him in cardiac arrest.

'Stop that,' he said, his voice low.

'Stop what?'

'You know what. It's distracting.'

He heard her chuckle to herself, sounding almost surprised, and turned to look at her as she crossed her arms over her chest and looked out the window. It did nothing to help his out-of-control libido.

Dio! She was going to be the death of him.

'I have a question,' Celeste said, breaking the silence.

'What is it?'

'I don't understand the issue with the vineyards. Why can't you share ownership? I mean you and Emilio are both De Lucas. Surely you have enough power to see that they remain as you wish them to.'

Enzo would have thought that a bit of conversation would be a good thing to distract him from his thoughts, but this was the last topic he wanted to discuss. 'It's simple. Those vineyards, the company, the estate, are mine. They belong to the conte, and I take care of what's mine. My brother…he will want it, take it and then do nothing with it. He'll let it fall into ruin. That's what he does. But this time he will know that I don't let go of what's mine.' He looked at Celeste, at her frown, then back at the road, hoping she wouldn't push further. It seemed like he always wanted to tell her more than he should. Thankfully, the gods offered him a little reprieve because just then, the grand Palazzo Felce came into view. Enzo knew what the front would be like. A red carpet extending all the way to where the cars would stop. Cameras clicking as the elite made their way inside. That wasn't an option. He turned down a side road and parked at the back of the palazzo, where there was no one waiting but a single man in a sharp suit, just as Enzo had arranged.

He brought the car to a stop and helped Celeste out before handing the keys to the young man. He said nothing as he offered Celeste his arm. When she took it, it was as if fire licked up it. Together they walked up the stairs, and Enzo couldn't help but feel a sense of rightness. Attending these events was something he simply had to do. Frankly, he felt more excitement going to the office each day than making these appearances. But with Celeste—as she was now—he felt powerful in a different way than he did as conte. He *wanted* people to see her with him. He wanted to see more of her himself, because now that this woman was uncovered, he didn't know how she'd managed to dull her shine so much that she had slipped under the radar for two years.

While it was a joy to discover the woman she really was, the fact that there was anything to uncover at all had Enzo conflicted. It was a reminder that he didn't know Celeste. That he couldn't truly trust her. But did that matter? He didn't trust anyone with his thoughts, and he certainly didn't trust anyone with his emotions anymore. He didn't need to trust her with either tonight. He just needed her to be his PA, the woman that seemed to have the golden touch with his clients and business partners alike without realising it, despite her reserved façade.

He couldn't allow himself to grow any attachment to her, but that didn't mean he couldn't enjoy watching her shine. And she'd shine even more brightly if she could find the real Celeste. Be her.

And with how she'd looked and acted since leaving her room in that dress, that was already happening. Just as he knew it would.

A security guard in a dark suit with an earpiece opened the door for them, and in they stepped to a gilded world filled with so much history. But as Enzo navigated them through the maze of passages until they entered the grand ballroom, he wasn't looking around at the splendour. He was looking only at Celeste, at the look of awe on her face. At the smile that made him weak.

Enzo had never seen a look like that on Gia's face. She'd expected to be treated like this, to attend events like this. The expression of hers that Enzo most remembered was one of almost bored expectation.

Without realising it, Celeste had satisfied a craving he didn't know existed until now.

'Welcome to the Ballo del Sforza,' he said quietly.

'I've been to one ball in my life, but it was nothing like this,' she said, looking around at the neoclassical architecture, the white walls with gold accents, the hanging chandeliers and marble floors, the waitstaff in black suits with gold masks, carrying trays of golden drinks and morsels of food that were more like bite-size works of art.

'Come, we need to mingle.' As much as Enzo wanted to keep watching Celeste, he always attended these events for one reason: business. He was a De Luca, and his presence was expected; there were deals to be made and hands to be shaken. Though, he wasn't quite sure how *he* would accomplish that tonight when Celeste commanded his attention.

They waded into the crowd together and started their rounds, but after the second conversation where Enzo barely took in what was said, he knew he needed a break from Celeste's presence. He could feel the current between them crackling over his skin. He needed to get himself under control.

'I suggest we split up,' he said, leaning down to speak into her ear, inhaling that intoxicating perfume she always wore.

'We'll cover more ground that way,' she agreed. 'Only...'

'Don't worry, Celeste, there are no phones in here. As long as you don't leave this room, you will be fine.'

He watched her nod and sashay away, hips swaying in that dress. It didn't matter if she was beside him or walking away, Celeste had a stranglehold on him.

Charlotte looked around, mentally noting all the businessmen and women she had only heard or read about. A few she had met thanks to being Enzo's PA, and it was to one of them that she walked now.

'Celeste Park! How good to see you.' The tall brunette woman greeted her with kisses on her cheeks.

'Lucia, it's good to see you too,' Charlotte replied, surprised that Lucia Bianchi remembered her at all. She had last seen her over a year ago, and Charlotte had only sat in on two meetings with her and Enzo. The thought made anxiety creep into her belly. She strove to be unmemorable, but she couldn't panic here where there were witnesses. She looked away, trying to control her thoughts before they spiralled, and caught Enzo watching her. She saw his lips move as he continued his conversation, but his gaze stayed locked on her, his attention never wavering. The look in his bright green eyes settled her.

'You look incredible!' Lucia was saying. Charlotte tore her eyes from Enzo. 'I've always thought you were wasted as Enzo's PA—any chance I could steal you away?'

Charlotte forced herself to laugh. She didn't want to be anywhere else. 'I'm flattered, but probably not.'

'Loyalty,' Lucia remarked. 'A rare commodity these days. Your boss is a lucky man.'

Charlotte didn't have a moment to respond because Lucia was calling someone else over.

'Charles, come here. I'd like you to meet someone.'

Charlotte watched as a young blond man with a lean build and hazel eyes joined them.

'Charles Moreau, I'd like you to meet Celeste Park. Enzo De Luca's PA,' Lucia said in introduction, with a hand on Charlotte's shoulder.

'Pleasure to meet you,' he said, and Charlotte noted his French accent.

'And you,' she replied amiably, feeling a little more anxious. She had to remind herself that in Europe, no one would know her. Celeste wasn't her real name. No one would connect her to this event once she left.

'Charles here is taking the finance world by storm,' Lucia said, just as the music morphed into another melody.

'Would you care to dance?' Charles asked.

Charlotte felt a burn at the back of her neck and turned to find Enzo still watching her.

When she had seen him waiting at the elevators, something took flight in her belly. Enzo was utterly devastating in a tuxedo. The bow-tie and cummerbund had her fingers itching to touch him. And every time they *had* touched, she felt scalded. Especially when he did nothing to hide the hunger in his gaze. The same hunger she saw now.

'So, would you?' Charles asked.

'I'm sorry?'

'Dance.'

'Oh.'

It's a bad idea, Charlotte.

'I'd love to.'

Idiot.

Dancing with Charles would stop her looking at Enzo and distract her from the need growing in her core from his gaze. She took Charles's hand as he led her to the dance floor and swayed with him. It had been a long time since she had danced with anyone, and it felt wrong now. Uncomfortable. As if she was forcing a square peg through a round hole.

'This seems like a very nice perk of your job,' Charles commented.

'What's that?'

'Getting to travel the world with your boss. Attending balls. My own PA has the night off.'

'What's your point, Mr Moreau?' Charlotte wasn't sure if she liked the man just yet but was interested to see where the conversation would lead. She hadn't been able to interact with people like Charles outside of Enzo's office for years. And since she was letting the real Charlotte out to play just a little, she was determined to enjoy it. The real her liked this, liked being able to dance and chat and socialise. All of the things that had disappeared from her life once she became Celeste. She just needed to remember to be careful about what she exposed of herself and to whom.

'Just that it's interesting,' Charles said, with a smile she didn't quite trust. 'I've been wanting a meeting with Enzo. Think you could schedule me in? He's so rarely in Europe these days.'

And until she could figure out Charles Moreau's intentions, wanting a meeting was as far as he would get. 'I'll see what I can do.'

'That's all I can ask,' he said, swaying with her. 'You know, you are a beautiful woman, Ms Park.'

'Thank you, Mr Moreau, but that's not why you're dancing with me. You're just trying to get an in with Enzo.'

'Why can't it be both?' He gave her a flirtatious smile which she returned, trying not to roll her eyes. She couldn't let her attitude show. Charles Moreau could forget dancing with someone's PA at yet another event on his calendar, but he might remember the woman that challenged him. Sass wasn't her friend. Especially when Moreau already made her anxious.

Suddenly she wanted to get away. They had been dancing too long. The song was nearly over. Perhaps she had pushed her luck far enough. She'd already broken several of her rules because Enzo had promised to take care of her and she had trusted him, but now her anxieties were quickly working their way back, the sheer number of people around making her want to escape.

'You seem uncomfortable,' Charles observed.

'What makes you say that?'

He leaned down, lips brushing her ear. 'I have pretty good eyesight. And I can feel it in your body.'

'I'm sorry,' she apologised, forcing a smile to return to her features. 'It's a lot more people than I'm used to.' She hated having to lie. Hated to have to use Celeste as a barrier. Hated having to dull herself to feel safe. Before she could say more, she heard someone clearing their throat beside her.

'Mind if I cut in?' Enzo wasn't giving Charles much of a choice as he smoothly took her palm in his and placed his hand on her waist, slipping her out of Charles's arms and into his embrace.

The moment they touched, Charlotte felt a zap, as if they were lightning itself. She felt herself take a breath, as though she had been holding it the whole time she was with Charles. Tension finally melted away from her shoulders. If she'd felt uncomfortable with Charles, it was the opposite with Enzo. Like puzzle pieces effortlessly falling into place.

Enzo hadn't even fully waited for Charles's response before they were spinning away from the man into a quieter corner. The look he gave Charlotte made warmth spread through her core. The longer they danced, the easier it was to forget her worries of just a moment before, until she was so swept up in Enzo that she stopped hearing the music altogether and the din of voices faded away.

'So here is what I propose…' Enzo said.

'I'm listening.'

'We take the night off. No business. I'm not your boss. We simply enjoy the evening.'

'I think I could find that acceptable.' Especially when his hand was on the small of her back and dragging upwards, allowing his thumb to caress her bare skin. When his gaze was intense and his attention so focussed on her.

'Have I mentioned how beautiful you look tonight?'

'Nowhere near enough times,' she joked. It was so easy to talk to Enzo. Banter with him. Be herself. Could they have always had this if she had been braver before?

'A crime.'

Her breath grew shorter. 'I believe some punishment should be in order.' The words slipped from her lips, surprising her and making a smile curve Enzo's full lips. That was almost unacceptably bold, something the old Charlotte would have said, but Enzo destroyed her filter, allowing the real her to flow out, washing away Celeste—the barrier that just moments ago Charlotte had drawn on to distance herself from Charles.

'Believe me, I'm being punished enough right now.'

She felt it in the way his fingertips pressed into her back. In the tension in his shoulders. Saw it in the flame in his eyes. She couldn't believe she had once thought of his eyes as cold. They were anything but. Enzo's eyes were a green flame, like burning copper. Scorching.

He was restraining himself, but only just, and that knowledge made the air thick, hard to breathe. And yet all she wanted then was to pull him closer and breathe him in.

'Come with me, *cara.*'

Enzo led her through the throng of people, and Charlotte plucked two golden drinks off a passing waiter's tray, handing one to Enzo as they moved towards a Juliet balcony. The air was less stifling here, but no less thick when Enzo was so close.

'*Salute,*' she said, clinking her glass against his, and she could tell that—just as she was—he was thinking about their last toast.

Charlotte took a sip of the Franciacorta. It should have been delicious, but with Enzo's eyes dipping to her lips and back again, she could taste nothing. Her being was consumed by him. By his presence.

'Like it?'

'I can't taste it,' she replied breathlessly.

'Why?' He was moving closer to her now, crowding her.

'You,' was all she managed.

'And what about you?' Enzo asked. Charlotte swore that in this moment, he was the embodiment of flame, and like a moth, she was drawn in regardless of the danger. He was uncovering a side to her she hadn't even known existed. She wasn't dull Celeste. She wasn't even bright, talkative Charlotte. She was just a woman who craved the man before her.

'What about me?'

'The way you affect me. I am not blind, *cara*, but I have seen nothing tonight. Nothing but you.' He took another step forward, and Charlotte had to crane her neck to look up at him. 'I have spoken to people, but all I hear is your voice. I don't want this drink in my hand or anything they could serve because I have no taste for it.'

'What do you have a taste for?' Charlotte asked.

'Do you really not know?' Enzo challenged. His lips were so close to hers that they shared breath, and it only made Charlotte more light-headed. As if she was floating.

'I want you to say it,' she replied boldly, closing the distance between them a little bit more.

'You.'

'Then, kiss me, Enzo.'

The words had barely been set free when his lips met hers, and all that crackling current built by those burning touches was finally freed in the most explosive feeling Charlotte had ever experienced. His warm hand found her jaw just as she wrapped her arm around his neck. Her fingers sank into his thick hair, grabbing hold in a fist that had him growling low in his throat. The sound made butterflies take flight in her stomach. And then he bit her lip and, as she gasped, plunged his tongue into her mouth, and Charlotte felt it in the most intimate part of her. She was lost to the taste of him. To the sensations in her body. It was as if she was awakening from the hibernation her life had become. Brought back to life by Enzo, by this kiss.

'Gioia,' he whispered against her lips, never breaking the connection. *Joy.*

And when his tongue danced with hers again, Charlotte moaned into his mouth and felt his arm wrap around her, pressing her into his body. Felt the hardness pushing against her stomach. She wanted all of him. She was too lost to care where she was. She didn't even feel the glass of Franciacorta in her grip. Didn't feel it slip through her fingers.

Crash!

Glass hit the stone floor, shattering into a million pieces. The sound was dull and distant, only just reaching Enzo, making him pull away from Celeste's intoxicating lips. The first things he noticed were her still-closed eyes, but then, almost in slow motion, he saw heads snap in their direction. The silence was suddenly deafening. The music had stopped. Every eye was on them, and just like that, sense returned to him. There was too much attention on them. Attention Celeste didn't want.

That set him in motion.

'Cara,' he said softly, 'look only at me.' When she opened her arresting eyes and he was confident she was with him, he said, 'We're leaving. Don't give anyone your attention. Don't even look at them.'

He couldn't take her back the way they had entered: they'd have to walk through the entire ballroom. Then he remembered that there was a second way out. Gripping Celeste's hand tightly, he used himself as a barrier between the guests and her. Barely breaking stride to place his glass on a passing tray, he kept walking until they were back in the passage they had used before.

'Have my car ready to go,' he said into his phone without greeting or farewell. As they reached the back doors, he put his arm around Celeste's shoulders, forcing her close to his body to ensure no one could directly see her face.

The valet had his car ready, the engine idling throatily, but Enzo paid no attention to the man until he'd ushered Celeste inside the car, still shielding her with his broad frame. Once he was in with both doors closed, he turned to face her. Her face was flushed, red slashes on her cheeks and neck.

'What about the ball?' she asked in a small voice.

'I don't care about it. What I care about is you and whether you are okay.'

'I'm fine, Enzo. I—I didn't mean for you to have to leave.'

'Look at me,' he instructed. It took a moment but she obeyed, and he cupped her cheek. 'I don't care about any of that. All I want is you, if you will have me.' He'd had to get Celeste out of there so quickly that he hadn't had a moment to process that kiss until now. It had rocked him to his soul, and he'd had nowhere near enough of her. The fact that he was still hard was testament to how badly he wanted her.

'Yes.'

Music to his ears. Enzo kissed her hard and fast, then tore through the streets of Milan.

CHAPTER SEVEN

THE ELEVATOR DINGED on the topmost floor of the hotel, opening into a penthouse suite that would have certainly been big enough for Charlotte to have shared with Enzo. But she had fled from him, from all that he saw. From their attraction. After that kiss, she didn't know why she had. That kiss was everything she had hoped for and more. That kiss was a factor in why she had run from an arranged marriage. Because how could she be married to a man she couldn't tolerate when the world held so much passion?

The man beside her held so much passion.

He burned with it, and she wanted to dance in the flame.

Never had Charlotte craved a man so badly. Yes, she'd had her share of boyfriends when she was a teenager and in her early years of studying, but those relationships—while sweet and innocent—couldn't compare to how she felt now.

How she felt when Enzo let go of her hand and pinned her against the wall with his body. When his lips swooped down on hers and lightning crackled in her veins once more.

His tongue moved with hers, and his body pressed against hers, but it wasn't enough. There were still too many barriers between them. She wanted him. She wanted to feel his skin on hers. This was what it was like to be overcome with need. To crave someone. It was a new feeling and a dangerous one, because Charlotte didn't know how she could go back to living as she had before experiencing this. These heaving breaths. Goose bumps running down the length of her body. Her heart thrumming like a hummingbird's wings. She never wanted to leave this place where pleasure was such a drug.

And she desperately, *desperately* wanted Enzo to take her. To be her first. To brand her soul in that way.

Acting on instinct, she reached between their bodies and undid his coat, but the need to touch him, feel him, was too urgent to bother pushing it away. Instead, she pulled at his shirt until she could slip her hands beneath, tracing the cut planes of his torso, moaning at the body he kept hidden in those designer suits.

His lips trailed to her ear where he whispered, *'Tesoro, mi fai impazzire...'*

His voice had grown even lower. Strained. She needed to see him.

Charlotte pushed against him, and he stepped back. His jacket was open, shirt creased and hanging out, bow-tie askew. It was the most unravelled she had seen him, and it only made her burn hotter at the fact that it was she that did this to him. Despite her inexperience and despite the fact that she hid, Enzo reached in and pulled her to the surface. And in front of him, she was every part of her true self even if she couldn't tell him. So she grabbed his hand and led him to the couch, where he sat back with a smirk.

'What now, *tesoro*?'

'This.'

Through the long slit in her dress, she placed one knee on the cushions, leaned over him and kissed him lightly. Teasingly. And when he tried to follow her lips, she pulled away, making him growl.

'Would you like me to beg, *tesoro*?'

'I want you to make me yours. I want you to take me, Enzo.'

Bold. That's what he made her. Because when he was looking at her like that, as if she was the very sun, how could she not be?

Enzo slid his hand down her leg and, with his fingertips just grazing her skin, collected her dress up to her hips, making her shiver. Making those butterflies take flight once more. She straddled his lap and yanked on his bow-tie, tugging it free and tossing it over her shoulder, not caring where it landed. She smiled when Enzo laughed, a deep rich sound she wanted to hear again and again. But now? Now she needed his clothes gone, but it was hard to concentrate on his shirt buttons when his thumbs were rubbing circles on her hips under the fabric of her dress. Feeling a sense of great accomplishment when she undid the final button, she pushed the fabric aside to reveal his golden skin. A sculpted body that surely had to have been bestowed upon him by a Roman god. Except she knew of his discipline, knew how hard he worked to become this singularly spectacular man.

Charlotte ran her fingers over the light dusting of hair on his chest that disappeared, only to reappear in a single line below his belly button trailing downwards until it was hidden by his pants.

Just as her finger was about to follow the line and plunge beneath his belt, Enzo caught her wrist and brought her hand up to his mouth, kissing her palm. Making her melt.

'I will endure your punishment, *tesoro*, but know that this is truly torment.'

And she knew then how patient he had been with her. And how little of that patience he had left.

'Then, do something about it.'

Enzo hooked a hand around her neck and pulled her down, kissing her hard, urgently, biting on her lip and entwining his tongue with hers. And Charlotte couldn't help it: her hips ground against the bulge in Enzo's pants, looking for relief from the powerful sensations overcoming her.

Enzo groaned, bucking his hips to meet with hers. 'Take what you want, *tesoro*. Take it from me.'

There was only one thing she wanted. The one thing she had never had. And it occurred to her that she could simply let Enzo take her to bed and never tell him that she was a virgin. Her inexperience would be her secret, just like she kept her identity a secret. But a much bigger part of her wanted to reveal this to him, wanted to show him that she trusted him. That she trusted he would take care of her. The thought made her already frantic heart beat so much faster.

'Enzo, I have to tell you something first,' she said, with their foreheads touching and their breaths coming in pants.

He pushed her back and looked her in the eye, all pleasure replaced by his utter attention. 'You can tell me anything.'

Charlotte swallowed hard. 'I... I haven't done this before.' She was sure she was beet red. 'This will be my—'

'*Tesoro*, are you a virgin?' he asked, more serious than she had ever seen him. She nodded, and he replied, '*Dio!*'

'Are you angry? Or disappointed?'

She saw his eyes soften, and he tenderly grasped her chin. 'Never. I'm just surprised. But thank you for telling me, and now I know this isn't enough.'

'What isn't?' she asked, afraid of the answer. Was *she* not enough? Of course she couldn't be. He was experienced, and while she had kissed others before, it was nothing like being with Enzo. She needed to run. She tried to get off his lap. To pull her dress down around her, cover herself up. But he grabbed her hands in a gentle grip.

'Don't hide from me. I don't like it when you hide,' he said with an intensity that made it impossible to look away. 'This,' he said as he glanced at the couch, 'isn't good enough. You deserve better. And I can fix it.'

Her heart gave a lurch as he scooped her up and stood. Carrying her as if she weighed nothing at all, Enzo took her into his bedroom. With the utmost care that made Charlotte's heart sing, he placed her in the centre of the very large bed. If she wanted to, she could look out of the window at the beauty that was Milan at night, but when Enzo rounded the foot of the bed, the view behind him faded into insignificance. Especially when he was shedding his coat and shirt. He draped them over the armrest of the couch to the side, never taking his green eyes off Charlotte. When he slipped off his pants, Charlotte was certain that she had forgotten how to breathe.

Enzo was undoubtedly the most devastatingly beautiful man she had ever seen. Would ever see again. It made her sad that she would never be able to call him hers. Not when he lived his life in the light and she was forced to the shadows.

She pushed the thought aside, refusing to mourn when there was pleasure on offer. She would savour it and lock it away. Store it somewhere safe to return to in the future and remember what happiness felt like.

'*Tesoro*, I have been craving this.' He kneeled at the foot of the bed and bunched her sparkling dress up to her hips, then slowly, surely knowing precisely how crazed this was making her, pulled down the scrap of lace she called panties and dropped it behind him.

Charlotte couldn't describe how glad she was that he called her *tesoro* because she wouldn't be able to handle being called Celeste now. She hated it, she realised. She hated the name. She hated who Celeste was. Celeste wouldn't be this open. Celeste wouldn't have the honest reaction Charlotte had now, moaning at the kiss Enzo placed on the inside of her thigh.

Higher.

She must have said her thought out loud because Enzo replied with a chuckle. 'Patience.'

She didn't have any of that.

'Please, Enzo.'

Enzo lifted his gaze to meet hers. 'Don't beg. You never have to beg with me.' The words went right to Charlotte's heart. She had begged her father to reconsider her arranged marriage, but it had got her nowhere. She had begged her sister to tell her how to make their relationship better, and that too had fallen on deaf ears. Now here was Enzo telling her she never had to beg.

'Kiss me.' The words were out of her mouth before she had a moment to consider them, and Enzo obeyed. Closing his mouth over her mound, he kissed her deeply. His sinful tongue delved into her core making Charlotte's back arch off the bed. His arm snapped over her hips, keeping her still as he feasted on her. Her hands sunk into his hair, gripping the long strands as she fell apart under his kiss, feeling utter euphoria. The blood in her veins was replaced by heat. A tightening built in her core, so much more powerful than anything she could make herself feel.

'Enzo,' she breathed, and the vibration from his moan pushed her over the edge. She shattered against his mouth, her body writhing, and then he was kissing her, her taste on his lips. On his tongue. It was the single most erotic

BELLA MASON 91

thing she had ever experienced. He kissed her and kept kissing her until her body settled against his and her eyes finally opened.

Magnificent. That was what Celeste was. She was a drug entirely consuming him. How she had remained a virgin all this time was beyond Enzo. A primitive part of him, which he hadn't known existed until a few minutes ago, was glad of it. He didn't like the idea of any other man touching her. It had taken everything in him to remain cordial when he had seen Celeste dancing with Charles Moreau. He'd wanted her in his arms. Now he had exactly that.

'How do you feel?' Her kisses drove him crazy, but he couldn't forget how inexperienced she was.

'Good. Better than good. I want more.' Her shining skin flushed, and with her broad smile, he had never seen her look more mesmerising. Had never seen a woman more beautiful.

'You will get everything you want, *tesoro*.'

He unzipped the side of her dress and eased it off her. Given the cut of her dress, it wasn't exactly a surprise to find that she hadn't been wearing a bra, but actually seeing the evidence still felt like taking a punch.

Celeste would be the death of him. Of this, he was sure.

Dropping her dress off the side of the bed without looking, he took her nipple into his mouth, feeling satisfaction burn through him at her mewl. His fingers trailed down her body, over her belly button, down, down, down, until they teased the bundle of nerves at the junction of her thighs, making her pant his name. Enzo would never tire of hearing that.

'I need you,' she breathed.

He kissed her lightly on the lips, then retreated to the couch, fished his wallet out of his pants and pulled out a foil package. He held it in his teeth as he removed his underwear and heard Celeste's audible gasp.

Smirking at her, he rolled the latex onto his impressive length and crawled over Celeste, kissing up her body as he did. He wanted her. He wanted her in every way, on every surface, in every position. But what he *needed* was to see her.

He positioned himself at her entrance, feeling a primal urge to plunge into her and claim her as his. Instead, he asked, 'Are you sure, *tesoro*?'

'Yes,' she whispered.

He covered her with his body, holding his weight on one elbow as he slowly pushed into her.

'Open,' he instructed, with his thumb at her mouth. She obeyed, drawing it in and sucking on it, making him curse out loud. With difficulty, he pulled it free and slipped his hand between their bodies, teasing her with that same thumb, making her relax and moan and writhe.

He pulled out a little and slowly thrust back in.

'Heaven,' he panted and saw her response to his praise in her nearly black eyes. Felt it as she began to meet him thrust for thrust.

His name became unintelligible on her lips. His heart was throwing itself against his rib cage. He felt it everywhere—felt *her* everywhere. As if with every moment, with every slide against each other, she burrowed a little further under his skin.

Mine. Mine. Mine.

His mind shouted it. After this, she would be his. Celeste was in his blood. He was marked. He lowered his head to the crook of her neck, kissing her there. Sucking on the skin. Now she was marked too.

A coiling began at the base of his spine. He would not last much longer. It was beyond any comprehension that she should feel this good, that she would affect him so. But he felt her arch under him, felt her tightening hold around his hardness, and knew she was equally affected.

He held her to his body, his pace becoming rapid. They were soaring together, and they would fall together. It was never something he'd needed before, but this time was different.

'With me, *tesoro*.' He could hear the strain in his own voice. Barely a breath or pant or a growl and yet, somehow, all three.

And then she was right there with him.

His rhythm faltered as she squeezed around him, calling his name as—just like a firework exploding brilliantly and loudly in the night sky—they burst in rapture so intense it had Enzo seeing stars.

In the aftermath, the room was silent save for their breaths. Enzo had lost touch with time, not knowing how long it was before he could gather himself enough to slide out of Celeste and look down at her. She was beaming at him, and he kissed her temple in a tender touch that he didn't think came naturally to him.

'We should do that again,' she said before he could ask how she felt. The real Celeste, never failing to surprise him.

He laughed, eyes crinkling, feeling lighter than he had in an age. 'I concur.'

'Smart of you to agree with me,' she teased.

He kissed her passionately, tugging on her lip with his teeth. As he got out of bed, he knew he wasn't anywhere close to done. He wanted to keep Celeste in his bed all day, and that was exactly what he was going to do.

Charlotte watched Enzo disappear into the bathroom. She lay back on the pillows, taking in the room for the first time. The giant vase of flowers in the corner, another on the coffee table. Framed artwork hanging on the various walls. It felt wrong that the world around her should seem so unchanged when her own had been changed irrevocably.

Enzo had been so thoughtful with her and yet so powerful. A perfect summation of the man she knew. He had more power than most people could even dream of, was ruthlessly efficient in business. And yet, hadn't he shown his thoughtfulness in small ways over the years? With his mother and her kitchen, with Charlotte.

'What are you thinking so hard about?'

Charlotte gave a small start and turned to look at the man himself, leaning casually against the doorframe.

'We need to put a bell around your neck,' she said.

He pushed off the wall and stalked to the bed, sliding between the sheets and pulling her close. He took one of her hands in his and placed it on his neck.

'This space is reserved.' His light kiss made Charlotte melt into him. 'But I believe I asked you a question.'

Charlotte thought about lying but found herself wanting to tell him the truth. 'I was just thinking about you. This… What we did.'

'Do you regret it?' Despite the way Enzo held her, caressing her skin, his light touches, she could see caution in his gaze.

'No.' She shook her head. 'Is it always like this?' She hated that she had to ask at all. That her life hadn't really been hers to live. That even before Grant, she'd had to maintain a certain amount of caution. It had been a necessary part of being who she was. There was always someone who would want her for her family's money, so making them wait for her to be ready to share such a physical connection kept her safe. It weeded out those who weren't worthy. Who she couldn't trust. Of course, the list of people she could trust had shortened drastically over the years.

But it was different with Enzo. She didn't mind asking him. She only hoped the answer wouldn't be something to make her run.

Enzo brushed her hair back away from her face. 'No, *tesoro*, it's never like that.'

It wasn't just the answer—it was the fact that he answered honestly that settled her.

'You are incredible,' he said.

'Why do I feel like there's a *but* coming?' she joked.

'I don't understand why I was your first.'

That was a fair question. She was a twenty-five-year-old woman who was a PA to one of the most powerful men in the world. Academically, she had achieved so much, and in working at De Luca and Co. her business acumen had only grown, but she had stagnated in this one area of her life.

'Because I was running from it. At first sex was a test to see if someone would stay with me on my terms. Respect *me* enough to respect my wishes.'

'I take it there were those who chose to leave,' Enzo guessed.

'Yes, but I was happy for them to go. With the type of family I came from, it was important to me that I could trust them.' Of course, as it turned out, her family—especially her father—were the ones she couldn't trust. In that moment, Charlotte wanted so badly to tell Enzo everything, tell him what she was running from. But after what she and Enzo had shared, she found another reason why she was afraid to do so. Uncovering this attraction, their physical connection, had made her the happiest she had felt in a long time. The brightest point in her life so far. She didn't want to see that desire turn to hate. She couldn't bear it.

'Unfortunately, it was my family I couldn't trust.'

'What happened?' The low growl in Enzo's voice comforted her. Protective anger tinted the air, and it made her want to hold him more tightly. Instead, she rolled onto her back and looked up at the ceiling but saw only the face of Gordon Kim. Her father. Her tormentor.

'Please! I don't want to marry him!'

'I don't care.'

She shook the memory away and answered Enzo's question. 'I was being forced to marry someone I didn't want to. Someone I detested. So I left.'

She could see Enzo had a great many things he wanted to say. She could see the anger that had fully taken hold in his eyes, and he felt like a protector, but he couldn't be the protector she needed. Nothing had changed. Enzo was still a businessman with near-celebrity status. People all over the world were fascinated by him and his family's wealth. Charlotte could only really enjoy this temporary connection behind closed doors.

'You're safe with me, Celeste.' How she'd craved hearing those words. But that damn name! It was tearing her up inside.

The safest thing would be to turn the focus onto Enzo and away from her.

'Can I ask you something?'

'Anything, *tesoro.*'

'Why don't you ever have anyone in your life? I've been

with you for two years, and never once in that time did I see you with anyone or make any reservations.'

Enzo huffed a humourless laugh. 'You noticed that.'

'Of course.'

This time it was Enzo's turn to look away. As he rolled onto his back, Charlotte moved closer, propping her head on her arm so she could look at him while he spoke. Silence stretched between them. Just when she thought he wouldn't say anything at all, he spoke.

'I was once in a relationship. Her name was Gia. I met her before I had become conte but was already heading up De Luca. My father had been forced to take a step back for health reasons.'

Enzo spoke so emotionlessly that Charlotte thought this story could only end badly. Part of her regretted asking, but a different part of her was thrilled that Enzo, a man who famously kept his thoughts to himself, was opening up to her. She placed her hand on his sternum. Her heart rejoiced when he covered it with his own.

'Over that time we grew close, and I asked her to marry me…'

Charlotte was shocked. She had seen multiple old pictures of him with the same woman, but she knew nothing of the engagement. Of course, he would have managed to keep all of it out of the media.

'Shortly after that, my father died, and I became conte. Gia seemed supportive. She understood what the role meant for me and my family. What it meant *to* me, and I loved her.'

Jealousy. That was what pounded in Charlotte's veins now, but it should be ridiculous to feel jealous over the thought of someone from the past meaning something to a man she would never truly have. She tried to force past the feeling, irrational and grating as it was.

'At least I thought I did.'

'What happened?'

'She betrayed me. Emilio came to me and confessed that he and Gia had slept together.'

'Oh, Enzo!' Charlotte was horrified. She couldn't imagine being hurt like that by two people he should have been able to trust. To count on.

'When I confronted Gia about it, she didn't deny it. You see, while I trusted her, confided in her, she was lusting after my brother. She wanted the fame, the money, the jewels I showered upon her but not me. Things I had confided in her, she had spread to Emilio.'

No wonder that Enzo was always so guarded. That he so smoothly deflected questions he didn't want to answer. That it was usually impossible to know what he was thinking. In his place Charlotte would have likely clammed up too. It was so much safer not to trust people.

Except Enzo had trusted her, hadn't he? Even though it was only a little. He had let her in a small amount, but there was no way Charlotte was going to lie to herself and assume that Enzo would be an open book to her from this point. After all, she wasn't letting him in completely either. They had been so intimate, were lying in bed together after having the most explosive sex, speaking of things they kept well hidden—and Enzo was still calling her Celeste. The barrier was still up between them. Her whole life was fractured. She was two people, and she hated it more than anything now, but she didn't know how else to remain safe.

Enzo kept safe in a whole other way, but just like her, he kept people away too.

'What did you do?' Charlotte asked, needing to know

exactly how Enzo would deal with someone utterly destroying his trust.

Like you will, Charlotte?

'I made her leave the house. She put up a fight. How else would she get the fame and fortune she wanted? Emilio is a wealthy man, but he didn't inherit centuries' worth of legacy. She wanted to keep the ring, so I let her and paid her handsomely to leave.'

'You said the house. You don't mean the estate? Right?'

'The very same.'

It made so much sense now that he hardly ever travelled back to Perlano. In all the time she had been with him, he had gone back once—six months ago, in fact—and had only been there a few days. She remembered because she'd arranged for his flight back on the day of the funeral. At the time she had thought him cold for leaving so soon. What kind of arrogant, cold-hearted man would want to go straight back to work after his mother died? What kind of man would put his business first? One who was hurting more than anyone realised, it turned out.

Charlotte was happy that she had never met Gia. The woman sounded horrible, more horrible than anyone she'd known. Well, almost. Her father came pretty close. Grant Campbell definitely came close. She still remembered Grant telling her that once they were married, she wouldn't be allowed to work again. She was meant to submit to him.

Stifling the shiver that ran down her spine, Charlotte cuddled in close, placing her head on Enzo's chest, listening to his heartbeat.

'It must be really hard for you to go back there,' she said. Enzo didn't respond, but Charlotte remembered the pitying look on Isabella's face when they had arrived in Perlano. How many people knew what had transpired? Did the people of Perlano know? A few pictures of the funeral had emerged in the press. Charlotte remembered seeing not even the slightest hint of emotion on his face. He had just looked strong. Impassive. Immovable. The resilience that performance would have required took her breath away.

It also explained why he had been so different on this trip. Why he was so angry that day in the winery.

'You said Emilio has a second will. Is it real?' Enzo seemed to be in a sharing mood, with at least *some* of his walls down, and Charlotte wanted to make the most of it.

'My father had gifted the vineyards to my mother many years ago. His condition was that upon her death, she was to bequeath them to me, and she did. However, it turns out she made another will in which she left them to Emilio.'

'Why did your father give them to her?'

'Because she loved them. We all knew it. She spent most of her time in Perlano because of it.'

'But if she already left them to you, why did she change her mind?' She saw Enzo close his eyes, heaving a small sigh. Clearly, he had asked himself the same question.

'Can you invalidate the second will?' she tried instead.

'I'm trying, but so far it doesn't seem like it.'

'So what are you going to do?'

'What I *have* to do is prove that the vineyards belong to me. As far as I am concerned, they do. Emilio is *not* getting his hands on them,' he said through gritted teeth.

Charlotte was taken aback by his possessiveness. She understood why he would feel that way after everything his brother had put him through, but still…

'I can't wait until you're mine, Charlie.'

Charlotte pushed away Grant's voice. Enzo was different. He was good and hurt and protective.

But he still held on to things even if the best course of

action was to share. To find a way forward with his brother that would have benefited the vineyards and the company.

Charlotte understood what it was to be unable to trust your own sibling, even if her sister hadn't betrayed her in the same way. To have a sibling steal one's happiness left a deep wound. Enzo was more than entitled to his anger. However, that didn't make her uneasiness abate.

'But that's not anything for you to worry about, *tesoro*. I will deal with my brother,' Enzo said, tilting her face up to his. 'I have much more pleasurable things in mind for us.'

He kissed her hard. It was a dominant show of his passion, and she knew he was distracting her. Putting up a barrier between them. More than ever she understood why he did it, but she didn't like it. She wanted to be there for him, to show him that she would always be on his side.

But she could say nothing because she still had her own barrier in place. She wasn't being honest with him, so she could expect nothing.

CHAPTER EIGHT

DESPITE THE EARLY HOUR, the sky was already bright as Enzo stood at the hotel suite's window, gazing out at the slowly rising sun and the street below. Via Monte Napoleone was always busy, but it was far too early for any sort of traffic into the shops renowned the world over.

This was the first morning in a long time that he hadn't woken to go for a jog and then a punishing gym session. Another break in his absolute discipline. This entire trip had been a challenge to him in every way.

Celeste had been a challenge.

He thought about the beautiful woman asleep in his bed. How long had it been since he had woken next to a warm body? Since Gia and Emilio's betrayal, Enzo had tried to keep everyone at arm's length. On the rare occasion that he had found the need for someone's company overwhelming, he was always able to find a willing partner. And always just for the night. Always in secret, because he wanted to be seen with no one. It was a release for him, not a moment to share with the world.

With Celeste, it was all different.

Since the flight to Perlano it had been different. He had tried so hard to convince himself it was a bad idea to indulge in this maddening chemistry, but when he had seen her before the ball, he was lost. Lost to Celeste. Even creating some space at the ball had been a waste of time, because he felt pulled by her. Orbiting around her like she had become his sun. And seeing Charles Moreau's hands on her, his whispers in her ear, seeing her smile at him had unleased a beast in his chest.

Enzo didn't trust the man. If it was business he was after, he could go through the company. If it was Enzo's knowledge of banking from his family's long history of ownership, he could think again.

But it had been seeing Moreau with Celeste that had forced him to act, to claim her. To end the ridiculous charade of wanting to network when Enzo couldn't give a damn about any person at that ball apart from her.

That kiss…he couldn't stop thinking about it. And when she had confessed that she was a virgin… He was surprised by how much he liked the idea of her being *his* alone. Of never having to share her with anyone. It was irritatingly primitive, but he knew exactly what prompted it. Gia's betrayal had changed a great many things.

Celeste was so different. There was nothing false about her reactions to him.

He wanted more of her. He would never love her. That was an absolute truth. If he'd had the capability once, then that was another thing Gia had destroyed. But he desired Celeste fiercely. A desire she reciprocated. So there was no harm in continuing what they'd started. It might not last for ever, but love didn't last either. Love was fickle. Calling Celeste *his* was a truth. Their chemistry was honest. Enzo saw no reason why they couldn't enjoy the wonder of their physical connection.

Last night had been a wonder. After years of not really seeing Celeste, finally seeing her walls down had been a joy, and he wouldn't let her hide again, not from him. Not when he needed to see who people really were. Not when he vowed he would never be fooled by anyone again.

Enzo had cut Gia out of his life entirely, and if Emilio wasn't his brother and an irreplaceable part of the family business, he would have faced the same fate. He didn't care what face Celeste wanted to show the world, but with him—now that he had seen the real her—that was all he would accept.

Sighing, Enzo sipped at the espresso he had ordered from room service. Rich, aromatic coffee burst on his tongue. It was arguably one of the best he had tasted but still didn't feel as right as the cup he had every morning in his office. That cup Celeste made him. She was in his blood. Was she already too close? Recently he seemed to say more than he meant to around her. He didn't trust her yet, so he didn't understand why he had told her about Emilio and Gia. When she asked him that question—*Why don't you ever have anyone in your life?*—his mind had automatically begun sorting the pieces of the story in a way that made sense. Before he knew it, he was telling her everything.

Why had he wanted to? Why did it make the weight of that betrayal easier to bear?

He hadn't seen pity in her eyes. He had been so angry at himself for not having realised what had been going on under his nose, but she didn't think less of him.

Draining his coffee, Enzo walked back to the window, depositing the cup on the nearest flat surface without a thought.

He should be in that bed. Not out here trying to sift through his thoughts. His body ached for Celeste, despite the fact that he had kept her awake long into the night, showing her pleasure until her voice had grown hoarse and her eyes heavy.

This attraction, this chemistry was so different from anything he had known before. The intensity of his release with Celeste was mind-blowing. He'd marked her as his. And he held on to what was his.

Raking his fingers through his hair, Enzo stepped in the direction of the bedroom when he heard his phone ring.

Rushing back to the bedroom where he had left it, he hurried to answer before it could wake Celeste. He grabbed the phone and hurried out into the lounge, then looked at the number. It wasn't one he recognised, but the Australian code caught his attention. For a second he considered ignoring it and letting it go to voicemail, but an instinct he had always listened to told him to answer.

'De Luca.' His voice was still slightly rough given the early hour.

'Enzo De Luca,' said a sneering voice he did not recognise. A voice that knew his private number. Several alarm bells went off at once in his head.

'You have three seconds to tell me who this is or I'm hanging up,' Enzo demanded.

'Gordon Kim.'

Enzo had heard the name before. Now the number that flashed across the screen made sense. But what on earth did the property developer want with him?

'We haven't met,' Kim said, 'but you have something of mine.'

The man was out of his mind. They'd never even met. But Enzo had been in business a long time. He knew when to give an inch and when to stand his ground. Right now, he would not give any indication that he had no idea what Kim was talking about.

'If I have it, then it's not really yours anymore, is it?'

'Hand over my daughter, De Luca.'

Enzo was not prepared for that response. He looked towards the bedroom as if he could see through the wall at the sleeping form of Celeste. Celeste who wore drab clothes to work. Celeste who couldn't afford their signature wine. Celeste who had cut off her family for forcing her into an arranged marriage.

There was no way in hell Kim was talking about her. Was there?

'What makes you think I *have* her?' Enzo needed to know where he stood. He needed to figure out what was going on here. Men like Gordon Kim didn't just call people up randomly. If he thought Enzo had his daughter, it meant she had left without telling her father. And whether or not the man had confused Celeste with his own flesh and blood, Enzo wouldn't give up a woman to a situation she was trying to escape.

'Don't take me for a fool, De Luca. I saw you with her in Milan. I believe the event is called the Ballo del Sforza?'

Enzo cursed forcefully in his head.

Some small part of him was still hoping this was a case of a simple misunderstanding. He'd had spoken to numerous people last night. It was possible Kim could mean one of them and not the only woman who had held Enzo's attention.

'It's a big event. You'll need to refresh my memory.'

'This isn't a game, De Luca. I saw her with you on the balcony.'

Blood rushed in Enzo's ears. His grip tightened on the phone as he tried to control his anger—anger, initially, at the fact that despite the strict rules of conduct at the ball, someone had still snapped a picture of them, and secondly, and perhaps more painfully, at the fact that Celeste Park was not who she claimed. He had been played for years! A red haze coloured Enzo's vision. His hand curled into a fist that he very nearly drew back to throw into the wall. But he couldn't because that would give up the game to Kim. So he fought to summon all the control he possessed.

'Your daughter is an adult, Kim. If she wants to enjoy Milan with me, there's nothing you can really do about it, is there?'

'I'm telling you now, De Luca, return Charlotte to me or you won't like what happens. I'm not a man to cross.'

'Is that a threat?' Enzo asked, voice smooth as silk, the smile on his face clear in his slow, deliberate speech. White-hot heat was coursing through him. He had been underestimated by his brother, by Gia and now by Celeste, but he would not be underestimated by a man like Gordon Kim.

'And what if it is?'

Then, Kim would see what Enzo was truly like when he was unleashed.

'I don't take well to threats, Kim, so for your own sake, I suggest you stop now, or you will regret it. And unlike you, I don't make threats. I make promises and I keep them.'

'Am I supposed to be afraid of you?'

'I don't care what you fear,' Enzo said calmly. 'And I especially won't care when I stand on your ruins. So heed my suggestion. Your daughter will decide if and when she returns to you. I don't want to hear from you again. If you decide to be stupid and not obey my very polite request, know that I have the power to ensure that no bank backs any of your developments in the future.'

'You're lying.'

'Try me.' Enzo hung up. Gently he placed his phone

on the table. Heat radiated from every pore. His hands were trembling. Running them roughly through his hair, he cursed and tried to take a breath.

It was no use.

He swore loudly, giving into the rage that he couldn't control.

Celeste. Charlotte.

She had lied about everything!

For two years she had had access to all. Two years she had dealt with his business. His *family's* business. Two years of late nights and overseas meetings, all the while pretending to be someone else.

Enzo felt ill. He was pacing now, too agitated to remain still. Too far gone into his rage to even attempt control.

He had confided in her. Had wanted to hold on to her, and all this time he'd had no idea who she was. What did she want?

What about De Luca and Co? Had she been planted in his company?

Betrayed. Again!

Enzo was beyond reason. People kept proving over and over that they couldn't be trusted. But this—this hurt even more than Gia and Emilio's betrayal. Maybe it was because he should have known. He had hardened himself so much to the world, worked so hard to keep anyone from getting behind his barriers, but he'd *wanted* for Celeste—Charlotte—to be different.

Thinking back to the terrace, it felt like the knife in his chest was twisting. Wringing out every last drop of agony. He thought he had become smarter, but maybe this was the final lesson he needed to learn.

The pieces were finally falling into place. How she seemed like two different people. The glasses she wore but didn't need. Her clothes, her manner that made her so inconspicuous in the office. It wasn't that she was shy or lacking confidence. She had been hiding. But for what reason?

Enzo stopped pacing and turned to face the closed bedroom door. Celeste or Charlotte, whoever she was, was about to find out why Enzo wasn't a man to cross. He needed answers and, want to or not, she was about to give them to him.

Charlotte burrowed deeper in the duvet. She tried to move closer to the warm body beside her, but cold met her bare skin. Slowly opening her eyes, she realised that Enzo wasn't there and the sheets were cool to the touch. Goose bumps prickled her arms.

Rolling over, she plucked her phone off the bedside table. It was barely six thirty. How long had Enzo slept? He must have been awake a good long while. Charlotte didn't understand how anyone could subsist on so little sleep.

She pushed herself up to rest against the pillows, feeling a pleasurable ache in her body that brought a smile to her lips. Images from the night before replayed behind her eyes.

Enzo's mouth worshipping at her. Torturing her. It seemed to bring him as much pleasure as it did her. He had drawn her a bath afterwards. Gently and teasingly taking care of her. Caressing her skin with soap on his hands.

They had ordered room service but hadn't eaten much when their hands were all over each other again.

It was as if that kiss at the ball had unleashed all their desire upon the world, and there was no hope of containing it now.

Not that Charlotte wanted to.

Their night hadn't only been about passion. Enzo had opened up to her a little. But then he'd kept her busy, almost as though he wanted to prevent her thinking on his revelations. Or asking much more. She understood that need for privacy, so she'd let him sweep her away to a place where there existed only him, her and this unquenchable thirst for each other.

Charlotte would have liked nothing more than to get a few more hours of sleep, but there was no hope of that now. So she tossed the covers and padded, naked, to the bathroom where in the mirror she saw a red mark on her neck.

Enzo had left another on her breast and one far lower on the inside of her thigh. He was possessive, normally a thought that unsettled her, but the anger she'd felt radiating from him when she told him of the arranged marriage she'd escaped had eased that flare of unease. He wasn't like Grant or her father. He would give her the choice of being his. He had proved as much in the way he made certain that she wanted him.

How could she not?

The more of him she saw, the more she craved him. His warmth. His safe embrace.

Temporary.

She reminded herself it had to be temporary. They couldn't have a relationship in the light. Even though he had seen the real her, he still thought she was Celeste. She had to acknowledge that she was already playing with fire. She just prayed that she could prevent anyone from getting burned.

Charlotte freshened up and brushed through her dark hair. She would go in search of Enzo. Perhaps she could persuade him that breakfast in bed was a far more appealing proposition than work.

The thought made her stomach unfurl in that way it did only when Enzo was around.

She picked up the fluffy white robe that had been discarded on the bench at the foot of the bed. She was tying the belt around her waist when Enzo entered. He always sucked the air out of the room with nothing more than his presence, but with his hair tousled, his chest bare and those dark blue pants sitting on his hips in the most delicious way, bare feet carrying him towards her, there was not a force on earth that could get air back into Charlotte's lungs.

She wanted to go to him. To run her hands over the planes of his torso. Trace her fingers over the corded muscle that held so much strength, but when she looked at him, desire faded away. A plummeting sensation replaced it in the pit of her stomach.

His eyes were burning. There was a look in them she had never seen directed at her. Fury.

He was a tempest of rage as he walked towards her. Tense. Lips in a thin line. A muscle feathering in his jaw. She felt every step like a cataclysmic earthquake and took a step back. Shrinking away.

Something was very wrong, but a small voice told her that he could have heard bad news about the vineyards. There was no need to panic just yet.

'Are you a spy?'

'What?' Charlotte asked. Her heart beat frantically.

'I *said*—' Enzo shouted, then grit his teeth, speaking calmly, icily, terrifyingly '—are you a spy? Have you been planted in my company to steal information?'

Charlotte's mouth had gone dry. 'Enzo! No!'

'Then, to steal information from me?'

She knew then that he had found out who she was. Knew of her lie. She'd known this day would come. It was inevitable, but it was so much worse than she could have imagined. Why did it have to happen now, when she just wanted to pretend she could enjoy a little bit of happiness? A little bit of the joy that been missing in her life for so long.

She didn't know exactly how much Enzo had uncovered, so she tried to hold on to the charade for a little while longer. Maybe she could calm him and convince him that she was the same Celeste he had known these past two years.

'What are you talking about?' Breathless. The lump in her throat made it hard to talk. To swallow. To breathe.

'Do you take me for a fool?' His voice was hard, trembling slightly at the obvious difficulty he had in controlling his ire. The tone sent shivers down her spine. She had never seen him this angry, and now it was hard to breathe for a different reason from only moments before.

Her eyes welled with tears that she couldn't control. Scared for herself. Upset that Enzo would feel that she too was a liar. Someone who'd betrayed him just like the others. She wasn't that person, and she needed him to believe her. She needed him to listen because being in his shadow made her feel a little safer.

'Enzo, please,' she begged.

'Please what?' He stalked towards her, and she took another step back. Her stomach gave a painful lurch that had her clutching at it. Hands searched the pockets in her robe, but she was in Enzo's suite. There were no antacids here. Bile rose in her throat as her tears fell. She wanted to dash them away, but she couldn't. She wanted to run, but there was no way around him.

'You think I haven't noticed?' he spat. 'You think I haven't seen that you could be sitting in my chair, doing my job instead of outside my office as only a PA? You think I don't know that you're smart?' He laughed, and it was terrifying. 'Clearly smarter than I gave you credit for, because I fell for your trick, didn't I? I saw your mask. I saw the plain woman you wanted me to see and didn't question my instincts. The woman happy in her job. But I was the fool, wasn't I?'

'No!'

'No? I have seen how different you are from your act! We came here, and your mask slipped. The clothes, your name, the glasses—it's all a lie. I saw you forget them. I saw you read that wine label. Tell me, was seduction part of the plan too?'

Charlotte tried to say his name, but nothing would come out.

'Thank you. Thank you for showing me exactly why I don't trust anyone,' Enzo said, enraged.

'Please, Enzo, you have it all wrong.'

She saw it then. Her words had only thrown fuel on an already raging inferno. He was nearly wild with fury, and she retreated. The hard, immovable wall pressed against her back, and she had nowhere else to go. And then Enzo was against her, his hands slamming on the wall on either side of her head. His breath ragged.

'I want answers, Celeste.' He huffed out a breath. 'I should stop calling you that. Since you haven't given me your actual name, shall we go with *Liar*?'

Charlotte couldn't stop her tears from flowing now.

'I want the truth before I throw you out and never think of you again.'

His words were like knives plunging deep into her chest. She had wanted to be unmemorable, but the thought of Enzo forgetting her hurt. The thought of him hating her was nearly unbearable. And the thought of her father finding her was suffocating.

She opened her mouth to respond, but again nothing came out. Once Enzo threw her out, she would have nowhere to hide. She would have to fly back to Sydney, and it would be only too easy for her father to find her. To take her back to Perth and force her to marry Grant Campbell. His leering face in her mind had her nearly hyperventilating.

'I—I can't,' she sobbed.

'Why?'

Fear. Pure undiluted fear was coursing through Charlotte. Her body felt as if it wasn't hers. As if she was levitating. Adrenaline pumping. Making it hard to think. To speak.

It must have shown on her face, because she saw Enzo pause. His face that had been all hard angles a second before softened a touch.

'Are you afraid to tell me?' His voice was still a growl but had lost the edge of absolute hate.

All Charlotte could do was nod.

Enzo pushed off the wall and took a deep breath. His gaze still held cold heat, but she could see the control he had mastered over himself.

His hands settled on her robe-covered shoulders, and she let him steer her to the couch.

'Sit,' he ordered.

She obeyed at once. A few short hours before, they had been entangled on that bed before her. Now she sat stiffly, an ache forming in her back. Awaiting Enzo's sentencing of her.

'Speak,' he said, in what Charlotte imagined was as calm a tone as he could manage. The fact that the growl hadn't left his voice nor had the tremble in his muscle abated showed he really wasn't that calm at all.

Charlotte had to force air into her lungs. Force herself—against every instinct she had—to tell him the truth.

'My name,' she started in a small voice, 'is not Celeste Park but Charlotte Jane Kim. My father is Gordon Kim, the property developer.'

She saw Enzo nod, his face impassive, encouraging her to keep speaking. She had to. For her safety. For what she and Enzo had shared.

'What I told you before is true. My father was trying to force me into an arranged marriage with a businessman in Perth, where I'm from. His name is Grant Campbell, and he is well-connected but not in the way you are. Grant has local councillors in his pocket so he could get any property he wanted. Any land in a whole host of different councils.'

'Your father would do the development, and they would split the profits,' Enzo said, sitting on the coffee table in front of Charlotte.

'Yes.'

'Why were you being forced to marry Grant, and what does this have to do with me?'

Charlotte felt nauseated by what she had to say next. 'Grant had been in the picture for a while—I mean years, Enzo,' she said, trying to get him to understand her horror. 'He had his eye on me, and then when it suited him revealed to my father the extent of his influence. Grant's condition for the deal was that my father hand me over. He coveted me as a possession. I was twenty when this happened, and by twenty-one I was forced to become engaged to him. It was insurance that I would be his. He would tell me that once we were married, I would remain at home. I wouldn't need to work. It would be my job to see to his needs alone.' She fought the shudder that passed through her body and could see the simmering anger in Enzo's eyes reignite.

'If you were removed from play, would the deal fall through?'

'Yes. It would be proof that my father couldn't follow through on his word. Couldn't do whatever was necessary.' The tears that Charlotte had managed to control fell once more. 'I pleaded with my father, Enzo. I begged him for years to get me out of this situation. He refused. When they set the wedding date, it was the final straw. I couldn't… I asked my father then if Grant was more important than me and he said *yes*.' Her voice broke just as her heart had then and as it had every time she replayed the words in her head. 'I had to leave. I knew he would never pick me over Grant. Money would always come first to him. I would be alone in a loveless marriage, treated as nothing more than an object. I couldn't do it. I worked hard in my studies. I had my own ambitions, and it all meant nothing.' Charlotte dashed the tears away with the back of her hand and noticed Enzo's twitch towards her, but he held back.

'So you left.'

Charlotte nodded. 'I pretended that I was coming around to the idea of marrying Grant. My father bought the act and was pleased. When I told them that I was going to check out a place for the very specific décor I had in mind, it just looked like I was getting caught up in the excitement of the wedding. The ceremony was a means to an end, so no one else really cared about the details. I packed one bag and fled. I left my engagement ring behind in a drawer. It was a shackle. I wasn't asked. I hadn't said *yes*.'

'Where did you go?' Enzo asked in a voice that was

no more than a growl. She could tell he was still angry, but there was a shift in it, and she didn't know what that meant. Was he still angry at her? Where would she be at the end of this conversation?

'Straight to the airport. I had planned my escape. I knew how much time I would have to empty my accounts. I dumped my car and bought a cash ticket to Sydney and started over. I invented Celeste as a secret identity so my father wouldn't find me. I had to split the money I brought with me into so many different accounts so that no one account had an amount worth noticing.' Charlotte stood and dashed to the lounge where she retrieved her purse from the night before. She pulled out her wallet, opened it and held it out to Enzo, showing him all the bank cards. It was like showing him all the fractured pieces of her she had to hide. Had to be constantly aware of. Showing him what her life had become.

Enzo flipped through the various bank cards. Each with a different name.

'How did you manage to fake your identity with the banks?' He had been so angry at Celeste—Charlotte— after the call, but now he felt only sympathy. Anger still swirled within him, but it was only for what she had to endure. She was brave beyond measure, despite how scared she looked right now. That fear only made him angrier. Her tear-stained cheeks. Wide eyes. The nervous way she fidgeted with her robe. Nervous, he realised, not just because of what she was running from and what she was revealing, but unnerved by him. He had scared her. The way she'd backed away from him until she met the wall, the look on her face—it was like a deer being hunted. Enzo had done that to her, and he had never felt such disgust at himself. But he could make it right. He had to. He would make Charlotte understand that she was in no danger from him. That he wanted to help her. He had always wanted to help her; that was why he'd pushed for her to attend the ball. The very reason they were in this predicament now.

But he preferred this. No matter how hard it was, the truth was always preferable to any lie.

'Let's just say a very substantial chunk of money disappeared on the way,' Charlotte said. Enzo slipped the cards back into her wallet as he listened to her talk. 'I don't go out. I don't have friends. I can't risk anyone taking a picture of me or recognising me, but a quiet, lonely life is better than the alternative.'

Was it?

The life she lived wasn't a life at all. Marriage or not, Charlotte had lost the ability to live the moment her father had traded her for business.

Enzo could understand her reasoning. He had chosen a lonely path too. One without anyone he could trust. Relying on himself was always the smartest play, but it was hard. But at least he didn't have to hide.

Charlotte's reluctance to go to the ball made so much more sense now. Her concern was warranted because her father *had* seen her, despite the measures Enzo had taken to protect her. But Enzo knew he *could* protect her; he just hadn't known what he was facing—what she was facing—but now that he did, he could make sure she remained safe. Help her untangle her life so she didn't need to hide pieces of it.

Pushing to his feet, Enzo swore under his breath.

He knew of Grant Campbell. The name had come up once when De Luca and Co. had been looking for land to erect a satellite office, but Enzo hadn't trusted the man and opted to do business with someone else. Grant was nearly forty. The thought made his skin crawl.

Enzo heard Charlotte speak behind him as he went to the dresser, retrieving a pack of antacids.

'I can't go back, Enzo. Even if I'm costing my father money. I just can't.'

He crossed back to her, handing over the box. A momentary look of confusion flashed on her face before she pushed out a tablet from the blister pack and popped it into her mouth.

'When you told me you were meant to take over, you were talking about inheriting your father's empire, weren't you?'

'Yes,' Charlotte said, toying with the box in her hands. 'With my half sister.'

'And whichever way this works out for you now, she gets the company, I take it.'

Charlotte nodded.

'Which is why she never bothered to help you.'

'Yes.'

The flash of anger in his veins at that small affirmation was so intense that his vision blurred with it.

'I wasn't aiming to involve you, Enzo. I just saw a job I wanted. A place I could use my education. Somewhere that would make me fulfilled. Plus you're known for keeping your private life private, so I jumped at the chance. I didn't mean for any of this to happen.' Charlotte fiddled with the box in her hands. 'I was convinced that it wasn't really a lie to be someone else. I thought I would only ever be Celeste to you. To everyone. I was trying to *become* her, because being Charlotte wasn't safe. Celeste would have allowed me to have a life on my own terms. Safety. I could lie to everyone else, but it was hard to lie to you,

Enzo. I wanted to tell you every day. I wanted you to call me Charlotte. I wanted it so much that you're the only person I slipped up with. Only you.'

Seeing Charlotte like this cut through him like a sword. She was bright, sexy, intelligent, breathtakingly beautiful—but the woman before him now was worn down. Scared. It was unacceptable.

Kneeling before her, Enzo took her hand in his and held her chin, forcing her to look him in the eyes. 'Your father called me. He wants you back, but I won't let that happen. I wish you had told me sooner, but it doesn't matter now. I will protect you, Charlotte. All I ask is that you are always honest with me.'

'I can do that.'

He scooped her up as he stood and moved to sit against the headboard with Charlotte on his lap. Cradling her head against his bare chest, he could feel her quiet tears. The hand against her head travelled down to her neck where he felt her pulse thrum rapidly.

'Relax, *tesoro*. I won't let anything happen to you.'

CHAPTER NINE

CHARLOTTE FOUND HERSELF in Enzo's plane once again. Except this time, she was in the one area she had seen the least. The bedroom.

After she had confessed everything to him, Enzo had held her until she was able to breathe and then for a while longer, his tight grip becoming a soft embrace.

It wasn't long after that that he announced they would be leaving. All he said was that they were going somewhere safe.

'Will you still not tell me?'

'No.' He smirked, pulling her closer so their bodies pressed together in the most delicious way under the covers. 'You said you wanted to see more of Italy. Well, now you will.'

'My father knows where I am, Enzo. I can't go anywhere.' Ever since Enzo had told her that Gordon knew where to find her, Charlotte had an uneasiness in the pit of her stomach. Her neck constantly prickled as if she was being watched. And while she did feel safe around Enzo, it wasn't enough to overcome years of anxiety.

'No one will find you where we are going. I promised to protect you. I am not a man to go back on my word.'

She knew that. Integrity was important to her, and she had always admired his.

He kissed her forehead, fingers combing through her inky hair. 'You're safe with me, Charlotte.' How she had craved to hear him speak her name. She loved the way it sounded when he spoke it. Freeing, that's how it felt. A weight had fallen off her shoulders in being honest with Enzo. It made her hopeful that maybe she could live as herself again, but that was a terrifying prospect.

'You're thinking too much, *tesoro*. You have kept yourself safe alone for all this time. Sharing this burden with me will make it easier.'

He was right. She forced herself to remain calm and closed her eyes.

When Charlotte awoke, she was in the passenger seat of a car, with Enzo driving, his dark sunglasses perched on his nose. His powerful legs were clad in dark blue denim, a black V-neck T-shirt hugging his incredible physique. The sight made everything below Charlotte's waist tighten.

'Good, you're awake,' Enzo said. She felt her cheeks redden at having been caught staring, but it was an impossibility not to. 'We're almost there.'

'And where is that?'

'I am glad that you don't give up. I admire your tenacity.'

'But you're still not going to tell me.'

'You would be correct.'

'You know, you can be very aggravating, Mr De Luca.' Charlotte folded her arms across her chest, but Enzo reached over and threaded his fingers with hers, bringing them to his lips, kissing her sweetly on the back of her hand. The touch sent sparks shooting all the way down her arm.

'It will be worth it.'

Charlotte fell silent, choosing to look out the window for clues as to where she was, but nothing was familiar to her. When a town finally appeared in the near distance, Enzo spoke.

'Welcome to Ravello.'

Charlotte turned to him with a beaming smile. She had heard of Ravello's beauty, had always wanted to sail along the Amalfi Coast, but after she ran, she had said goodbye to those dreams. The very last trip she had taken for herself had been a girls' getaway with her friends to Santorini. In her heart, it had been her way of saying goodbye without having to say anything to them.

Now Enzo was giving her the things she wanted and needed. The ability to be herself. Safety from her father. The opportunity to see the parts of Italy she had really wanted to experience.

Now that her father knew that she was with Enzo, he would likely suspect that she would hide in Perlano. That would be until they booked in somewhere.

'Where are we staying?'

'My home.'

'Your...' Charlotte trailed off. As his PA, she knew of every single one of Enzo's private properties. But she had no idea that he had so much as a bench in Ravello.

'It's my private residence. No one knows about it. No one has been there.'

'Then, how do you maintain it?'

'I bought the property and manage it through a fund. I don't deal with anyone personally, and everyone who has access to the property has had to sign a strict non-disclosure agreement. Believe me, you are safe here.'

If Enzo had gone to such lengths to keep the place private, it was obviously important to him. Living life in the public eye must get tedious, so she could understand him needing somewhere to retreat. What struck her the most was that he was opening up this secret location to her.

'When you say no one knows about it—'

'I mean no one. I have brought not a soul here, Charlotte. Not even my mother.'

Charlotte was lost for words. She watched as they navigated the narrow, winding road to the top of a cliff, then turned onto a private lane with high walls on either side. At the end was a large gate, laced with lush creeping leaves that formed a solid-looking barrier. Not even sunlight seemed to poke through the green lattice.

Slowly the gate swung inwards, and when they drove through, Charlotte saw nothing but a plot of grassy land. They followed the drive as it swept to the right, turning in a hairpin until they came to a large garage door surrounded by a stone structure. She realised that part of the grassy plot was directly overhead as they drove into a cavernous garage.

Enzo parked the car and led her to a biometric sensor. He pressed his thumb to it, and the large wooden doors opened, admitting them.

Soft light flicked on as they walked through the house. Charlotte followed Enzo in silence, and when they reached the large open-plan living area, her breath caught. The villa was huge, made up of cascading levels cut into the cliff. Lush grass and hanging gardens flowed from one level to the next. The outside of the house had looked old, historic. The inside, however, was a marvel of modern design, technology embedded into every aspect of the villa.

This place reflected Enzo perfectly. His love and respect for history. His passion for modernity and efficiency. Yes, the estate at Perlano was beautiful—glorious in its long history, its legacy—but this was spectacular for a whole other reason.

'This place is amazing.' Charlotte walked to the large window affording unparalleled views of the coast.

Enzo wrapped his arms around her waist, his lips brushing against her neck. 'No one will find you here. The glass is one-way. No one can see in.'

Charlotte could scarcely breathe. 'Thank you, Enzo.'

'I keep what's mine safe,' he said, fingers working to untie the belt that kept her wrap dress closed. He split apart the fabric, hands trailing down her stomach until they slipped beneath the band of her panties, making her gasp and throw her head back against his shoulder.

His words and his fingers sent shivers down her spine. She did feel safe in this place. She was utterly vulnerable at this window, but she felt nothing apart from intense pleasure. She was at the mercy of his wicked fingers.

'Let me hear you,' he demanded, and with a keening cry she called his name. She turned in his arms, seeing the satisfied smirk on his face. Feeling against her stomach the effect she had on him.

She was about to kiss him, about to turn the tables on him, when a hard vibration from his pocket caught both their attention.

Enzo took a look at his phone, his smirk falling from his face.

'I have something to take care of,' he said, slipping his phone back into his pocket. 'Why don't you go for a swim?'

Charlotte looked over her shoulder at the pool outside. She was safe inside. While the crystal blue water looked more than inviting with the sun brightly baking down, there were no barriers outside. No biometric doors or smart-glass walls.

'Charlotte,' he said, cupping her cheek, 'do you trust me?'

Of course she did. She'd told him things she'd hoped no one would ever know. 'Yes.' She hoped he heard her fervour.

'It doesn't matter where you go on this property, no one will see you. I wouldn't have brought you here otherwise.' She saw him drop his head and sigh before he touched his forehead to hers. 'You're not living, *tesoro*. You've run so you could have freedom, but you don't have it. You won't let yourself. You can't deprive yourself of everything that could give you joy and still call that living.'

Charlotte had no answer. He was right. She kept telling herself that she'd fled to have freedom. That everything she sacrificed was worth it. That being alone, being lonely, was worth every minute of freedom she had. Yet she couldn't remember the last time she'd been to the beach or eaten out or laughed with friends. She didn't even have any friendly acquaintances at work because she was too afraid it would lead to her being dragged back and forced into a marriage with a vile man. She used to love going down to Leighton Beach, her favourite place, with her friends. But she had given it all up.

Charlotte was away from her father and Grant, but mentally she was no more free now than she had been back then.

'You're free to do as you wish here. Just know that whatever that is, you are protected.' Enzo kissed her forehead and left her standing near the kitchen.

Charlotte watched him leave, knowing what choice she should make to live again, but she couldn't make it right now. Glancing over her shoulder to take one last look outside, she followed Enzo. She was certain that whatever message he had just received had something to do with the vineyards.

She walked into his study and saw him behind his glass desk with his laptop set up, clicking through something, a look of intense concentration on his face.

'What's going on?'

'Before my mother's death, I contacted a company that specialised in the restoration, preservation and archiving of historical documents.'

'I remember that.' Charlotte had been the one to re-search the different companies and hand a shortlist to Enzo. Every single piece of historical paper, no matter how old, had been entrusted to them. It had surprised Charlotte that no one had thought to preserve the docu-ments before—she would have—but it hadn't surprised her that Enzo had been the one with the foresight to se-cure the De Luca legacy. The process was long and ardu-ous. Each page had to be carefully handled and scanned, turning it into an accessible digital copy, then storing the delicate document safely away from air or light.

'Even copies of my father's documents were handed over.'

'From the office in Perlano?'

'And elsewhere. The recording process is finally done.'

With the ownership of the vineyards hanging in the bal-ance, Charlotte could see the value in it coming through now. She was glad she'd chosen Enzo over a swim, because whatever he found now could either lose him the vineyards or ensure his claim. Either way, she would show him he could trust that she would be there for him.

Enzo scanned through each document, quickly opening and closing various files, looking for the agreement his father would have had his mother sign when he transferred the vineyards to her. It would undoubtedly have contained the terms of her ownership, giving Enzo definitive proof they were meant to be his. His father was far too scrupulous a businessman and dedicated to his duty to their family legacy not to have put something in place. It was only a matter of finding it.

He felt Charlotte's presence close by him. He was grateful for it, but he didn't take his eyes off the screen skimming through each file but not finding what he was looking for. In fact, there was no record of his mother ever having owned the vineyards at all.

'Something is missing,' he said out loud.

'What is?' Charlotte asked beside him.

'My father gifted the vineyards to my mother, but there is no record.' Having the exact date of the transfer would make his search easier. Hoping to find it, he pulled up the land registry in a new tab and searched through the database. He only knew the year—twenty-five years prior, when he'd been seven years old. Old enough to remember the conversation when his father had informed his mother of the gift. Old enough to remember her happiness.

What he found in the registry brought him to a halt. 'This makes no sense.'

Enzo saw his own name staring back at him. For eight years the vineyards had belonged to him. He'd inherited them when he had inherited everything else from his father's estate.

'What doesn't?'

He didn't answer Charlotte and instead searched through the site and then the files he had digitised.

'Enzo, talk to me.' Charlotte moved to stand in front of him.

'My father told her that he had already done it. That she

would have to leave them to me in her will, but they were hers for life. He lied.'

An uncomfortable prickling covered Enzo's skin. His father, the man he had looked up to, had wanted to emulate, had lied.

He pressed his fingers to his eyes.

'I don't understand,' Charlotte said.

'Emilio has no claim on the vineyards because my father never transferred them to my mother,' he replied gruffly, showing Charlotte the evidence on the screen. 'He lied to her. I never bothered to look into it because I trusted him. Ownership went straight from him to me. They have been mine since his death.'

How could his father have lied? Of everything in the world, trust was the most important to Enzo, and he trusted his father. Wanted to be half the man that his father had been. The man who had protected hundreds of years of legacy and made it thrive. Enzo couldn't believe that that man would have done anything without a very good reason. So maybe there was one to explain his actions. After all, he had never lied to Enzo, only his mother. The mother who had given Enzo his birthright and then tried to take it away to give to Emilio, the son she had always favoured.

There was a burning lump in his throat. Holding on to Charlotte's hips, he pulled her down onto his lap.

'Oh, Enzo.' He felt her arms wrap around his neck, holding him to her.

'He didn't trust my mother. Maybe she never trusted him either. After all, that second will exists.' Enzo's hands clutched at Charlotte's dress in a tight fist. His teeth were clamped together so hard it felt as if his jaw might shatter.

'Do you think he was justified in lying to her?' Charlotte's words were gentle, but there was an undercurrent to them.

'She defied the one condition he placed on the gift, Charlotte. Maybe he knew her better than I did.'

'He still lied, Enzo,' Charlotte said, patiently.

Yes, his father had lied. And his mother had lied to him. And Emilio had lied to everyone.

Would the betrayals never end? His family were incapable of being trustworthy. His father's lie felt like a splinter in Enzo's skin. But he couldn't deny that it *had* protected the vineyards.

'My father isn't the problem here. My mother did betray him.' Enzo laughed without mirth. 'They betrayed each other. There was no trust.' The realisation was like acid in his throat. He had always thought of his parents as having the perfect marriage, one that compared to his great-great-grandparents'. To him the vineyards were exactly the same as the fountain at Perlano: a symbol of the love they shared. But he was blind. Blind to so much. Looking back, he could have—no, *should* have—learned his lesson on trust from watching them. It would have saved him from learning it the hard way.

His mother was never included in decision-making, not at De Luca and Co. nor at Perlano, despite being the contessa, and she never included their father in her business dealings either. Emilio had inherited all that belonged to her. His father had left nothing to her, only to Enzo. There was such a clear divide between them that Enzo couldn't believe he hadn't seen it for what it was it before now.

'Enzo,' Charlotte whispered, cradling his head against her chest, 'I'm sorry. I'm sorry that you're having to question things when you can't get answers, but maybe they both did what they thought was best in their own misguided way.'

'Misguided? From where I'm standing, my father is the reason those vineyards are safe. He must have known that my mother might give them to Emilio.'

Charlotte looked at him. 'But Emilio was his son too. Even if they did fall to him, it wouldn't be the end of the world. You would have had everything else. The company which owns the winery. All Emilio would have had would have been the grapes. The wealth would have remained in the family, so why would the idea of Emilio getting the vineyards be so upsetting that your father would betray your mother's trust?'

The question had Enzo reconsidering his childhood. Every memory he had of his father was of just the two of them. Alone. He'd been trained to take over alone. Had Emilio been deliberately excluded?

Except what Emilio had been *excluded* from was never meant for him. Emilio had always had their mother's affection. All that time that Enzo had spent with his father, Emilio had spent with their mother.

Really, Enzo should have expected her to betray him for Emilio.

'I was the one qualified to take over, not Emilio. Since I was a young boy, my father took me to the company, to the wineries, on his business trips. When his health failed, he was happy to have me take the reins because I had been trained since I could walk. I was the one he could rely on.'

'Did he do any of that with Emilio?' Charlotte asked.

'No, Emilio was tutored privately in Perlano. My mother looked after him.'

'Do you have any memories of your father that don't relate to work?'

Enzo was forced to think hard, and he came up with nothing. 'Only that he would have dinner with us. That was our mother's rule.'

'Enzo, don't you see? Maybe Emilio was jealous of the affection you received, and maybe that's why your mother defied your father's instructions, but you need to see that *you* didn't receive any affection either. You were groomed to be the *Conte del Perlano*. That's not how a father should be with their child. You were more than a project, meant for more than duty. But you didn't have a chance to think of anything else, have any dream other than the one your father set out for you.'

'How can you know that?' Enzo sniped, trying to push her off his lap, but she stubbornly refused to move. She took his face in her hands, and he was forced to give her his attention.

'Because *I* was raised to take over my father's empire, and when I was more useful as something to be traded, he did that for his company to prosper. We are more than just pawns for our fathers' legacies.'

Enzo shook his head, refusing to believe Charlotte's words. 'That daunting path, the legacy, was my own, laid out before birth. I never shied away from it, Charlotte. I took it all on. Emilio has nothing to complain about. Nothing to be jealous of. He wasn't deprived of affection, and I wasn't a pawn.'

'Isabella told me she calls you Leoncino because even when you were little you wanted to protect others. You updated the kitchen because you wanted to take care of your mother. Did you ever consider you wanted others to feel what you didn't?'

That drew him up short. No. He hadn't ever thought about it. Given Charlotte's history he could understand why she saw things that way, but they weren't the same. Enzo's father hadn't failed him.

'Being groomed to take on the family legacy isn't the same as care and protection,' Charlotte continued. 'It isn't love. I have chosen something different for myself, and you can do the same, Enzo.'

Charlotte had chosen a path for herself, but Enzo didn't need to. There was no reason to hide from who he was. Yes, his path had been set by his father, and even if it was disappointing that his father had lied at all, Enzo still respected his utter devotion to the family legacy. And what was more, his father's actions had confirmed to Enzo that he was right not to trust anyone. His distrust of his wife meant that the vineyards were safe, that Enzo could be done with this whole second-will situation.

Enzo would hold that lesson close. Especially now that he had someone else in his home. His parents had been married for nearly thirty years without trust. He would bear that in mind with Charlotte too.

'None of this matters,' he finally said. 'This—' he pointed at his laptop '—settles the issue of ownership. That was the only goal.'

Charlotte sighed. 'Send the email,' she said almost tiredly, 'but Enzo, it matters a great deal. How you and Emilio were treated caused this conflict in the first place. Coming to terms with who your father really was will be hard. You wish he was the person in your head, but the reality of it hurts.'

He read longing in her eyes. Hurt in her downturned lips. That was her reality, not his.

'I don't have any words that can make this better,' she said. 'You need to allow yourself to grieve the loss of who you thought your father was, but, Enzo, maybe this could be a chance to get some of your family back.'

'There's nothing to grieve, and there's too much history there. What my father did to Emilio might have been mis-guided, but to have sex with my fiancée in my home was Emilio's own choice. *He* broke that trust.'

Emilio was the reason Enzo was so unforgiving. Why he didn't love or trust or give second chances. Too much had happened. An entire lifetime. All Enzo truly wanted now was peace so that he could go back to his company, and Charlotte. Because when he sank into her, he could pretend the world was exactly as he wanted it to be. He could ignore the unease in his gut.

'It's up to you. Just know you control your path,' she said, getting off his lap. And as if she was showing him how to make a different choice, she tugged him along as she made her way outside, shedding her clothes. When they reached the pool, she let go of his hand and dived in.

CHAPTER TEN

CHARLOTTE SAT CROSS-LEGGED on an armchair, wrapped in a sheet, gazing out the window at one of the most breath-taking views she had ever seen.

It had been days since their arrival. Days since Enzo had made some painful discoveries. Since he had sent what he had uncovered to the lawyers, his sole focus had been on her. They hadn't left the house at all. The only times they ventured outside was for a swim in the pool, and even then it would end with them tangled in each other with frantic kisses and an urgency that never seemed to abate.

Enzo had cooked every single day while she watched. And when she had commented that she had never seen anything sexier, he had taken her right there on the counter. After that he'd taught her to cook, but his methods of teaching were incredibly distracting. With his body against her back and his arms around her, guiding her hands through every process, all Charlotte remembered was the near-painful need for him he had aroused in her.

This felt like paradise. Happiness. Just the two of them trapped in their own little bubble with the world shut away. Here there weren't any money-hungry fathers, or jealous siblings or people they couldn't trust. All that lay beyond the doors, but Charlotte was happy pretending they didn't exist for just a little while. She just wished with all her heart that this life with Enzo could be hers permanently.

Ridiculous, of course.

Nothing had changed. Enzo was keeping her safe, but she had no idea what that could mean once they were back in Sydney.

'You're thinking too hard again.' Enzo's voice made her jump, and she cursed softly, which he still heard.

'Really, a bell,' she said.

He placed an espresso cup beside Charlotte and kneeled before her, placing her hands on his bare neck. 'I told you, this space is reserved.'

He kissed her sweetly but was already retreating when she wanted more. His darkening eyes told her that he knew. He was already shirtless—a state she was happy to note that he was frequently in these days. It would be so easy to slip her hand under the band of his pants and...

'Stop.'

'What?' she asked, confused.

'The way you're looking at me, *tesoro*. You're making me want to take you back to bed and keep you there when I have planned a surprise.'

'What kind of surprise?' Charlotte reached for the coffee, taking a small sip. She had never been much of a coffee drinker, preferring the same ginseng tea her mother had favoured before she had passed. Charlotte didn't have many memories of her, but that one had stuck. But maybe Enzo was some sort of magician, because the espresso he made was one of the most delicious things she had ever tasted. Charlotte had even told him that *he* should be the one making the coffees at work instead of her. All he had done was laugh in response, but it had fed her unease about returning to Sydney.

'The good kind,' he replied cryptically.

'Any surprise you think of would seem good to you because it was your idea. It's *my* unbiased opinion that determines whether it is in fact a good surprise. So you should just tell me now and find out.' She lifted the cup to her mouth, hiding her smug smile.

'Were you on the debate team?'

'Maybe. Also, if you know about it, it's not even a surprise to you, so you definitely don't get to judge if it's good.'

He shook his head at her. After spending so many years tense and scared, it was wonderful to experience this lightness between them.

'You wanted to see Italy, so I am going to show it to you.'

'How?' Charlotte's heart fluttered. She didn't want to be too hopeful just in case there was an element of her safety that Enzo might have overlooked, but even she had to admit that was a ridiculous thought. As it had been her habit, she was looking for reasons to deprive herself.

'You'll see. Get dressed,' Enzo instructed.

A short drive later, they were at the marina in Amalfi. Boats and yachts gleamed in their berths.

'What are we doing here?'

'We are going sailing,' Enzo replied, pointing at one of the boats. 'In that.'

Charlotte looked in the direction he was pointing where a sixty-five-foot sailing yacht waited, the gentle waves lapping at its large sides. Despite Charlotte's privileged upbringing and how much she enjoyed the water, she had never been on a yacht of any type.

'Is it yours?'

'Si, tesoro.'

He led her towards it, and for once, Charlotte could think of nothing clever to say.

'Are you going to sail it?'

'No. I have a two-man crew that I trust to be discreet.'

Enzo helped her aboard, then instructed one of the crew to fetch their luggage while he took Charlotte below deck. The living and kitchen areas were modern and furnished in creams and light wood with soft cove lighting. But they didn't stop there. They moved through the cabins, and in the farthest one, she found the master suite.

The bed was huge. The wood-panelled walls enclosed them like a hug and the en suite was like something straight out of the world's best hotels.

'What do you think of your surprise?'

Charlotte was blown away. How did Enzo continuously surprise her like this? How was he able to give her exactly what she wanted without compromising her safety?

And in that moment, she realised that her heart was softening to Enzo far more quickly than she would ever have thought. All the things she had noticed about him in the last two years were only a small part of the man he truly was, and her admiration for that man just kept growing.

Enzo was fire and passion and consideration and intelligence and kindness in one being, and she kissed him then. She kissed him hard and with abandon. He responded instantly, and before she knew it, he had her on the bed, and she was calling out his name.

She was so consumed with him, she didn't even really notice when the yacht left Amalfi.

'Where are we going?' she asked against his lips in the shower that followed.

'Everywhere,' he replied.

And he meant it.

They sailed first to Ischia and took the dinghy to the island to enjoy the hot springs, and from there they went to Sorrento, Capri, Positano. They spent days out on the water as they sailed along the Amalfi Coast, slowly making their way towards Perlano.

Enzo had made it possible for Charlotte to have something she thought she never could again. He showed her a life worth living. A life with safety and travel. He took her to numerous small towns where she enjoyed being anonymous. Never once did she feel the need to look over her shoulder.

Moored out on the water somewhere off the coast of Calabria, Charlotte stood at the rail on the aft deck looking at the twinkling lights of the distant towns with Enzo's arms around her and his lips on her neck. The sky was inky black, stars bright overhead in a spray of silver.

They were utterly alone. Enzo had instructed the crew to return to land for the night. Charlotte hadn't seen all that much of them anyway with Enzo keeping her so occupied, but she was grateful. They both knew that their time in Italy was coming to an end. They had lives in Sydney. Enzo had a company to return to, and Charlotte—well, she didn't know what awaited her.

So before real life could barge its way back in, she would enjoy what freedom she had left.

'It's funny. I was so scared to go to the ball, but now I'm glad I did. Without it, we wouldn't be here.'

She knew Enzo was listening, even though he said nothing and his kisses hadn't even stuttered a moment. But she wanted a reaction from the man. Unable to resist poking the bear just a little, she said, 'I guess I have Charles Moreau to thank.'

Enzo's low growl had her laughing.

She turned in his embrace and hooked her arms around his neck. 'Why, Enzo, I think you might be jealous,' she teased.

'I don't get jealous. If I need to be jealous over something, it means it was never really mine, and you, *tesoro*, are mine.'

She didn't want to point out that she was her own. After all, Enzo had given her freedom. Right now, being his didn't seem like a bad thing, even if the whole debacle with the vineyards had shown her just how possessive he was. She was also certain that he was denying the truth. Of course he had been jealous. She had seen it then. Seen it in the way he guarded what belonged to him.

But that wasn't a path she wanted to travel down now. In this moment, she wanted another memory to cherish.

'Kiss me,' she demanded. Her lips parted, ready. Enzo's green eyes glowed in the pale moonlight. His hands cupping her face steadied her and made her heart race at the same time. A moment passed between them, and then his lips were on hers in a ferocious kiss. Breathing her in. Charlotte plunged her tongue into his mouth, and he pressed his body to hers, backing her against the rail. The slide of his lips, the taste of him, was making her frantic with need, but she wasn't alone. She could feel his hardness pressed against her. His breath as harsh as her own. The kiss morphing into a punishing, bruising force that couldn't contain what they felt for each other. She knew they were only this explosive because he reflected the same intoxicating attraction, the same passion that he ignited in her. The same insatiable need she felt for him. Mirroring their desire to infinity.

And just as her hands had gone to his shirt, tugging it apart and pushing it off his shoulders, he was pulling her dress over her head and tossing it onto the deck. She ripped her lips from his, kissing and nipping at his throat, down to his chest. Tasting the skin there.

Overwhelmed and on fire, she needed him now. Needed an outlet for these feelings, emotions that were so big it felt like her heart was bursting with them.

And then Enzo surprised her again. Stepping away from her, he shed his linen trousers and stood before her bare.

She drank in every inch of moon-kissed skin, even more golden from their days at sea.

'Show me what you want,' he said. His voice was like gravel.

He was giving up control to her. Knowing exactly what she needed. Knowing she hadn't ever truly had it in her life. Enzo, the man who controlled so much, could control the world if he had half a mind to, with all the power he was born to and had amassed on his own, was handing it to Charlotte. In that moment, when he had given her everything, Charlotte knew. Without any doubt at all, she knew in her soul that she loved Enzo. That there had never been another, never would be another person who she could love as much as she loved him.

Power coursed through her veins, Enzo's pleasure the ultimate drug. Charlotte stepped up to him and with her finger on his chest, pushed him down onto the large, plush cushions that had been converted to a deck bed. He sat, watching her. She noticed his hand curling and uncurling into a fist to stop himself reaching for her. And holding his green flame gaze, she removed her bikini top and then bottoms—part of the sailing wardrobe that he had procured for her—slowly, letting them fall from her fingers.

A string of curses fell from his lips, and Charlotte smiled knowing that the moment his hands touched her, all this control would be lost. She would be drowning in him. She wanted to stretch this moment out, the anticipation building exponentially. The hunger in Enzo's eyes growing. She craved the moment he lost control, pushed to the edge of sanity. Deliberately, with sure, slow steps, she walked to him. Knees sinking into the plush cushion, she straddled him.

'You will be the death of me,' he said in a strained whisper.

'You are the life of me,' she replied and kissed him hard and full. His arms snapped around her. His fingers travelling over her skin. Raising goose bumps and sucking the air from her lungs. And just as she knew would happen, all thought left her mind. Especially when Enzo's hardness pressed against her core, and she ground her hips against him, making him swear loudly.

'I need you. I can't wait.'

She hovered above him, but just as he teased her entrance, he pulled away.

'We don't have protection. We need to go to the bedroom.'

'No, I need you. I've only been with you,' she said and felt his fingers press into her skin at the words. 'And I'm on birth control.' For once, Charlotte was thankful for the bane of hormone headaches. But even though she wanted him so badly she could weep with it, this choice was just as much Enzo's as it was hers.

'I'm clean too,' he said. Charlotte already knew that since she dealt with his physicals, but being his PA was the last thing on her mind now.

Enzo had never wanted to be with someone like this so badly before. The trust Charlotte placed in him was beyond

heady. As the head of one of the largest and oldest companies in the world, he was trusted by thousands of people,
but that paled in comparison to the utter trust Charlotte
put in him now. And when he slipped into her warm, wet
core, he stopped breathing.

He wanted to pull her down on him, to slide into her
over and over again. But she was in control. She needed it,
and if she faltered, he would be there to make sure she only
felt pleasure. So he threw his head back, muscles in his
neck straining, as she slowly sunk onto the length of him.

'Please look at me.'

His eyes snapped open before the command had even
taken hold, so strong was the effect she had on him. When
he was fully inside her, they moved together.

'Heaven,' he breathed against her shoulder, his teeth
marking her. Just when he thought he would lose his mind,
he felt her shudder. She needed him to take the reins so he
moved her hands around his neck and held her tightly as
he thrust into her, forcefully pulling cry after cry of pleasure from her until he could no longer tell his name from
a moan, and a tingling took hold in the base of his spine.
His body became a guitar string pulled too taut, the feeling of Charlotte pushing, shoving, rushing him to the edge,
but he would not fall alone. Sliding his hand between their
bodies, he teased her where she needed it most, and then
she was right there with him.

'Enzo, I'm going t—' She couldn't finish her sentence,
but he understood because he was just as far gone.

'Now, *tesoro*,' he commanded, and they both plum-
meted over the edge in the most intense climax he had
ever felt.

He couldn't let go of Charlotte. He couldn't pull out
of her either. He wanted to stay in this moment for ever.

A moment that had changed his world even though the world beyond them remained stubbornly the same. Nothing would ever be the same for him.

Charlotte placed her sweaty brow on his. He breathed her air. Held on to her slick skin. 'Enzo, I—'

He didn't let her finish that sentence, silencing her with a kiss into which he poured everything he felt. The gratitude for having her in his life. For seeing him, the man he was in private.

He pressed her back into the cushions. Lying over her, kissing her under a sky that was a tapestry of stars, floating alone at sea, he filled the embrace with all his lust and admiration and need to protect, knowing he wasn't even close to the same man who had left Sydney.

CHAPTER ELEVEN

ENZO HELD ON to Charlotte until the first streaks of gold appeared on the horizon. The start of a new day. Another day that he wasn't in Sydney.

This had turned into the most extraordinary trip. The best return to Italy he could remember, and Charlotte was the reason for that. Unfortunately, life beyond this yacht wouldn't pause for ever. Their time away wrapped up in only each other was coming to an end.

He scooped Charlotte up as gently as he could and carried her to the master bedroom where he tucked her into the plush bedding and then stepped into the shower.

Powerful jets of water rained down on him, washing the salt and sweat off his skin. It wouldn't be long until his crew returned, and when they did, he would have to instruct them to sail to Perlano. He had taken enough time to indulge in this maddening chemistry with Charlotte. Once he was assured all was settled with the lawyers, they would leave. He had responsibilities and a whole list of things to deal with once they were back in Australia.

He would move Charlotte to a more secure property, then get her to close all the bank accounts in various names and move the funds into ones in her own name. Changing her details at the office would be simple. It was time she stopped hiding and started living, and under Enzo's protection she would be able to do just that. Perhaps he would move her someplace close to his own apartment. It would be a lot more convenient when they wanted to have sex.

Is that all it is?

Of course it was. It had to be. Enzo had no interest in starting another relationship. He had no interest in love. Once burned, twice shy, after all. No, there was nothing more to this thing with Charlotte than a powerful attraction and the need to protect her from men that he would love nothing more than to destroy.

Enzo shut off the water and dried himself off. Charlotte was still soundly asleep, so he went back up to the deck in time to see his crew arrive.

'Take us to Perlano,' he instructed.

By the time they had reached the marina, the sky was pale blue, the sun only just risen.

'*Tesoro*, it is time to go,' he said, waking Charlotte.

She stretched, bathing him in a smile that felt like a punch. 'Where are we going?'

'Home.'

She frowned, sitting up. The sheet fell to her lap, and Enzo had to fight the urge to take her again.

'Home? Home to Perlano or home to Sydney?'

'Both. We have been away long enough.'

He didn't miss the look of disappointment on her face, but she must have known that things would go back to normal.

'Let me get dressed, and I'll meet you up top.'

He waited on the side deck for her. When she emerged in a summer dress, he briefly questioned why he would want to return to Sydney at all. But this wasn't his life. His company was.

It was time to return to reality. This time, Charlotte

could assert herself in the office without trying to make her ideas seem like his own.

Looking back, he was almost disappointed in himself that he hadn't figured things out sooner. So many things he'd dismissed, when they had been glaring clues as to who his PA really was.

'What's on your mind?' Charlotte asked, when they'd disembarked and climbed into his waiting car.

'Nothing for you to worry about, *tesoro*. We have a lot to do when we return.'

'Why do I feel like you're not just talking about work?'

Enzo glanced over at her. Once, she would have broken the connection of their gaze; now she refused to back down, willing him to tell her the truth. 'Because we're not. We will have to make some changes if you're to remain safe. And you will have to do away with Celeste Park.'

She fell quiet after that, but Enzo couldn't have her pretending to be someone else when she worked at one of the most respected financial institutions in the world.

As soon as they reached the estate, his phone chimed with an email.

'Perfect.'

'What is?'

'Emilio has been informed that he has no claim.' Enzo was happy that everything was in hand. He had accomplished exactly what he had set out to. No one would ever question what was his again. But he couldn't shake the unease his father's actions had inspired in him. He pushed the feeling away, not wanting to acknowledge it at all. This was still the man who had taught him everything.

He spotted Isabella entering the large entrance hall. 'Isabella, we are leaving for Sydney.'

'Will you not stay the night?' It crushed Enzo to see

the sadness his choice caused Isabella, a woman who had shown him nothing but love. But he couldn't stay here.

'Tell me, Isabella. Would you have told me that Emilio had been here if I had not returned?' The answer was more important to him than anything in that moment.

'No,' she admitted.

He couldn't trust anyone.

'We're leaving for Sydney. I will not be returning home.'

'For how long?'

Enzo didn't give her an answer. He didn't have one. It would be impossible to stay away for ever, but he had no plans to return anytime soon.

'Leoncino, you call this home even now. Sydney isn't home.'

Sydney wasn't filled with memories of lies and betrayals. Enzo turned his back on Isabella and walked away.

'Enzo!' Charlotte called, but he climbed the stairs, slipping from view.

'Let him go. I wish to tell you something, *piccola*.' Isabella took Charlotte's hands in hers, a gesture that was so earnest Charlotte would have done anything she asked. 'Be patient with him. I have seen him grow up. I have seen him before he closed his heart.'

Charlotte nodded. 'Goodbye, Isabella.'

All the way to the airport and even after boarding, she couldn't stop thinking about what Isabella had said.

'...before he closed his heart.'

She sat across the table from Enzo. His eyes were firmly fixed on his laptop. Charlotte knew Italy was a moment in time. A moment she wished could have lasted for ever, a moment where she knew happiness and freedom and what it was to love someone. But now that it was over and they were heading back to Australia, she no longer knew where she stood.

A closed heart didn't bode well for her. Yes, he was caring and protective. He had promised to protect her, but he hadn't said a word about anything more than that. What would happen once they reached Sydney? What would happen at the office? To her career? People would question why the CEO's PA had gone from Celeste to Charlotte. She didn't work in a vacuum.

Protection didn't mean love. No words of a future had been exchanged, so where did she stand? What would happen if Enzo decided he'd had enough of her? This relationship, whatever it was, was a risk, and Charlotte had lived avoiding risks.

She cursed herself for not thinking this far ahead when they were in Milan. A spell had been woven around them, but this flight was carrying them away from the magic and back to real life.

'Enzo?'

'Hm?' He still didn't take his eyes off the screen. She reached over and pushed the screen down, just as he had once done to her.

'What's going to happen once we're back in Sydney?' Her heart beat erratically as she waited for the answer.

'I told you—'

'I'm not talking about my protection and undoing all of my precautions. You know exactly what I mean. Do we have a future?'

Surprise flashed in his eyes, but he quickly covered it with a mask of neutrality. Whatever his answer was, Charlotte would hear it. He wanted trust, and she wanted the truth.

'Charlotte, I don't have it in me to love again. To trust that much.'

She was ready for his answer, but it didn't stop the words from shattering her heart. A heart that she had foolishly given to him. A good man. But a hurt man.

He moved his laptop aside and reached over, his hand sliding over her neck, thumb caressing her cheek. She wanted so badly to lean into the feeling. She could let him kiss her, then she wouldn't have to think at all. Passion would be the only thing coursing through her, and none of this would matter.

But that would be running. And this one time, she wanted to face her problem.

'Would it not suffice to enjoy this chemistry we have? To enjoy the protection I offer?'

Charlotte didn't respond. What could she say?

Think. You need time to think.

She agreed with the voice in her head, and being around Enzo was too distracting. Green eyes bored into her soul. Watching her. Waiting for a response that wouldn't come. At least not now.

'I'm going to rest,' he announced, leaving her at the table, and made for the bedroom. She was sure he did it because he knew what she needed. He wouldn't force her to do anything she didn't want to, not even give him an answer. Except she did need one. For herself.

Would it be enough? Would it be worth it? To have run from the prospect of an unwanted, loveless marriage into a loveless relationship with only protection and sex on offer? Offered out of a duty to her, not love. Enzo wasn't Grant. Enzo didn't want to cage and control her. He offered her pleasure and excitement. Even now her cheek still tingled from the spark of his gentle touch. He offered her a life.

But not a life with him. His hurt was deep, his inability to trust warranted, and perhaps in his place she would not want to love again either. But what they shared in Italy had felt so much like love. Giving her the gift of travel when she had given up on it as a possibility. His anger at her treatment. The way he had pleasured her, especially that last night under the stars. Control. He had given her control.

But none of it made any difference if he didn't believe he could love. He would never give that to her. She would never break into his heart.

Charlotte groaned and placed her head on the table in front of her. A headache was forming behind her eyes. Maybe aspirin and sleep would help clear her thoughts. She was about to reach for her bag but froze. The thought of aspirin conjured visions of Enzo handing her an antacid box, back in their hotel. The fact that he had one for her had touched her beyond measure, but that wasn't what had a hold on her now. It was the fact that she had been so calm with him since they had gone to Ravello, had felt so safe and relaxed, the stress of her father's constant threat so far from her mind, that she hadn't needed them at all.

When had anyone's affection been so healing to her?

'I don't have it in me to love again.'

Charlotte curled up on the seat, soft leather hugging her. Lulling her into a state of semisleep where she could escape the swirling thoughts that plagued her.

When the plane touched down, she was no closer to an answer. A car waited for them, and without thinking, she approached the front door but realised the driver had the rear door open for them both.

They were back to reality. Enzo allowed her to enter first, then slipped in after her.

'We're going straight to the office. Something has come up. I have to go into a meeting.'

'Will I be taking the minutes?'

Enzo's features had settled into the usual professional mask he wore for the world, but now they softened a touch. Charlotte noticed his hand twitch towards her, but he kept it firmly, stubbornly, on his thigh. The driver's eyes flicked to hers in the rearview mirror. Charlotte didn't know if she was grateful that Enzo was keeping their relationship private or if she was irritated to be shown affection in secret. Especially when she was meant to come out of hiding, stop living her life in the shadows. But she was still the PA. That's where she would have to be.

'No. You have other more urgent matters to address.'

There was no *tesoro*, no *Charlotte* here. Enzo wanted her to start unravelling her web of lies. She had his protection—she didn't need to hide. But he was hiding his feelings for her. And even though she understood how having a relationship with the boss could look, she was certain the man who could provide her protection could also deal with that aftermath.

She nodded, saying nothing because there was nothing she could say. A part of her wondered if Enzo wasn't punishing her a little for the trust she had broken with her charade.

As soon as they arrived at the office, Charlotte—tired from the long trip, heart aching from going from soaring happiness and freedom only a day before to feeling like she was standing on quicksand now—went straight to her desk and fired up her laptop. Enzo didn't spare her a glance as he walked toward the boardroom.

She opened up a blank document, fingers poised over the keyboard, thinking. Why had she run in the first place? She didn't want Grant. She was scared of him. She didn't want to be controlled. She didn't want to be a pawn. She felt betrayed that she was promised one life and was being forced into another while having to watch her sister get the life, the career she wanted.

But beneath all those valid reasons, Charlotte also wanted to choose her partner and wanted to be chosen back. She wanted to be loved. To feel loved. The closest she'd ever got was in Italy when she had foolishly fallen for Enzo knowing how closed-off he had become, knowing about Gia and Emilio.

She wanted love, and Enzo wouldn't love her. Every day would be torment. Every day that she gave to him would be another when she might have found someone to love her back.

So Charlotte began typing. Ignoring the sting in her eyes, she didn't stop until she was satisfied with what she had written down. Hitting Print, she raced to the larger of the printers on that floor to pick up her document before anyone else could see it, and as if the fates were watching her every move, she saw Enzo emerge from his meeting. One look from him had her heart racing. Her stomach coiling. Dampness pooling at the apex of her thighs. She wondered how she could have such a primal response to him when her heart was breaking from knowing he would never be hers.

'Come with me,' he said, lacing his fingers with hers and pulling her into his office, giving her flashbacks of a woman in grey admiring the view of Circular Quay. Of placing an espresso cup on the table. Of a man being difficult when he received it. They were like spectres living in the same place but in an alternate dimension.

But she was yanked from the vision when the door closed and Enzo had her pressed up against it, his lips coming to hers in an urgent, fiery kiss. She kissed him back, lips roving over his. His tongue danced with hers, unleashing sparks everywhere in her body. She wanted this. Wanted to drown in him. Wanted him to crave her in the very same way, as if he needed no nourishment in the world other than her touch. She wanted him to love her. And as much as this kiss made her feel and made her forget, it didn't make her forget that.

So she placed her hands on his chest and, as much as it hurt to do so, pushed him away.

'Enzo, we can't do this.'

She watched the lust clear from his green eyes as he took in the look on her face. She wasn't sure what he was seeing there because she could don no masks. There was no strength in her for that. Nor did she want to, because she wanted him to know that even now she would be honest with him.

'Tell me what you are thinking.' It was an order.

Charlotte handed him her letter and moved away, creating some space between their bodies. She watched him read it, wondering exactly what he was thinking. When he looked at her, she saw confusion on his face.

'You're resigning.'

'I'm leaving, Enzo.' The words she had hoped for so long that she wouldn't have to say. Hope was a dangerous thing. She had stayed at De Luca and Co. hoping she could make her mark through Enzo. She loved working here, but now, in the end, she couldn't say that it had been the people she loved or the work particularly, it had been getting to work with Enzo. He had been such a big part of her life even when they hadn't been involved. Ideas and decisions she had made only came to life through him. She didn't agonise over anyone else calling her Celeste; it had only bothered her on Enzo's lips. But she couldn't stay and hurt. Somewhere else, alone, she would give herself the possibility of forgetting him. Dulling the effect he had on her with time.

'Why?' He took a step towards her, and she took one back. Just like she had in the hotel in Milan when he had learned the truth and she had wanted to run. 'Does this have something to do with your father?'

'No.' She shook her head, swallowing to dislodge the lump in her throat. 'I've just had time to think. To realise that we can't be together.' She threw her hands up in the air and walked away from him, looking out at all of Sydney. Silently saying goodbye to a city she had only really got to know from afar. Where would she go from here? How much would it hurt to walk away? Right now, she was sure peeling the flesh from her bones would be less painful.

'God! Enzo... I want you, but not a relationship at arm's length.'

'Charlotte...'

That one word had her scraped raw. The strain in his voice. The longing in her for a life that was different was so consuming. If she could have been born anyone else, maybe they would have had a chance. If she didn't crave what he couldn't give. But that wasn't who they were, and it made no difference to wish for it now.

'You're not someone who will truly let anyone in. You're not someone who will love another, and I want that, Enzo.' A sob she had tried so hard to stifle escaped her and had him trying to close the distance, but she couldn't let him.

Accepting his comfort would only make this harder. 'Look at what we're doing here. Hiding in your office. This is what we will have. Kisses in secret. Touches that no one sees. Whispers that mean nothing. I don't want a secret affair. I want affection in the open. I want to be loved in the light.'

'Charlotte, you know I can't love you,' Enzo said with a calm that made her want to rage. But his eyes betrayed him. They were anything but calm.

'I know, and I won't ask you to. You've been too hurt. Your heart is scarred and beaten and bruised, and I have to accept that. I don't want to change you when I...'

'When you what?'

He walked towards her, but this time she didn't retreat. She simply stared up at him unable to say the words on her lips.

When I love you.

'When you what, Charlotte?'

'It doesn't matter. What matters is that I fled one life without love—I can't trade it for another. For whatever this relationship is. It would be too hard to be around you, Enzo. I *can't.*' And that was when she lost control of the emotions she was trying so hard to keep a lid on. She wrapped her arms around herself, tears slipping down her cheeks.

Enzo could see Charlotte breaking apart in front of him.

And it made him panic.

He wanted nothing more than to pull her into his arms, to comfort and soothe her. To tell her the words she wanted to hear to make her stay. But he couldn't do that. Not any of it. He had never lied to her, and he wasn't about to start now. But he couldn't let her go either. His body called to hers and hers to his in a way he had never experienced before.

Attraction. Chemistry. Whatever he had called this thing between them hadn't been adequate. It was more than that. It was primal. It was a force of nature.

He couldn't lose her. His body pulsed with…fear? Was he afraid of her leaving?

His breathing grew ragged as he realised that was exactly how he felt. He had feared nothing in his life, but he feared this. Everyone who had lied to him or betrayed him had been cast from his life, but Enzo didn't want that with Charlotte.

He *could not* lose her.

'You can't leave,' he said, his voice low, full of authority. 'You're *mine*.' He felt the truth of it in his bones.

But it wasn't heat or affection he saw in her fathomless eyes in response, it was pure sparkling anger.

'I am *not*!' Charlotte snapped, the strength of her tone surprising him even when he knew of the fire within her. 'I am *not* a possession, Enzo. I am not my father's to bargain with. I am not a trinket for Grant's whims and schemes. And I am not yours. I am my own person. You don't get to tell me that I *belong* to you just to make me stay. To control me.'

Control her…

That was the last thing he wanted to do. How could she get it so wrong? He wanted to hold on to her. Keep her by his side.

She was glorious in her rage, coming to stand toe-to-toe with him, but she didn't reach out, and when he tried to, she shrugged off his touch, taking him back to a different time. A different woman.

'I never wanted you.'

'I deserve to be happy,' Charlotte said, eyes shining with tears. 'I deserve to be free.'

'Free? What freedom will you have out there without me? Hm, Charlotte?' Enzo challenged. Surely, she had to see the best life she would have was with him, with the protection he could provide? 'Will you crawl back into the dark? Make yourself sick?' He threw the slim card of antacids he had taken to keeping in his pocket in case she needed them onto his desk. 'Live an empty life?' The words were unkind, a wound he inflicted on them both, but they were nonetheless true. He hated the idea. He hated that she wanted to put an end to them. Hated that he would be the one left missing her when she could so easily walk away.

'I've looked after myself before. I can do it again.'

'Fine!' he yelled, losing the tether to his self-control entirely. 'You're welcome to protect yourself!' Teeth gritted, he curled his hands so tightly his arms trembled. And Charlotte? All she did was place her hand on his heart and, with a sigh, walk towards his door.

He wanted to grab hold of her wrist and yank her back into his arms, to kiss her until she saw sense, but he did none of those things because if she didn't want to be his, she could leave.

Almost as if it happened in slow motion, he watched her open the door and walk away. She stopped only briefly at her desk just outside his door, to pick up her bag. One bag. After two years with him, working for him, all Charlotte had to show for it was the handbag that she carried anyway. Proof that he was a temporary stop. A place to hide until it no longer suited her. He'd been used. Not just him this time, but De Luca and Co. too.

And just like that, a blistering, consuming anger poured

through his veins, erasing the panic, the desperation to hold on to her that he had felt just moments before. Fine. Enzo didn't need her. She needed him. Charlotte may have squirrelled a fair chunk of money away in different accounts, but that didn't compare to his resources. His power and influence. She would never know true safety on her own. Not from her father.

Enzo marched to the door and slammed it shut. How dare she compare him to that man? He raked his fingers through his hair roughly. He was trembling with anger and had no way to rid himself of it.

It wasn't bad enough that she had likened him to Gordon Kim, she thought he wanted to control her, just like Grant Campbell. Knowing exactly the kind of filth Campbell was made Enzo want to break something.

It just went to show that one could never know what someone really thought, what was in their heart. Once again he had let someone into his life only for them to prove that he couldn't trust anyone. As if he hadn't learned the lesson enough. This time it had been his own fault. What the hell had he been thinking? Charlotte had been lying to him from the day they met. When he uncovered her deception, he should have rid himself of her right then in Milan. Not have wanted to protect her. Take care of her. Gift her the freedom she longed for.

And that thought had him replaying their time together on the yacht. In Ravello. If he'd thought he had reached the limit of his fury, he was wrong. Now he grew angry not just at Charlotte but at himself, for all that he had said to her. Had shown her.

Did she think he allowed everyone into his life the way he did her? She had been the first person he had taken to Ravello. That place was his sanctuary. The yacht was for him alone. But he had let her into these pieces of him no one knew about. Had told her about his family.

If she thought that was worth nothing, then he was better off without her.

'A possession,' he spat.

That showed Enzo precisely how little she thought of him.

He took a deep breath. It did nothing to calm him, but it did get him moving, walking stiffly to his chair. Every muscle in his body was bunched as he sat down, staring daggers at the door. At the empty table beyond.

She lied to me, he thought to himself. *What use do I have for a PA I can't trust?*

CHAPTER TWELVE

CHARLOTTE'S HEART BROKE as she turned the door handle. She was leaving everything she loved behind. Just as she had done before. She had loved her friends in Perth, loved so much of the life she'd built there, and she'd walked away from them. But as much as it had hurt to do that, it wasn't even a fraction of the pain she felt now.

The burn on the back of her neck told her that Enzo was still staring at her. It took every bit of willpower to pick up her handbag and keep walking. Away from the job she loved. The man she loved.

Love didn't overshadow anger, though. And she was mad. Angry that Enzo, too, had seen her as a possession.

'You will be mine and you will cater to my every whim. That is your place, Charlie.'

She tried to shake Grant's voice from her head. Enzo had called her his before. In Milan, it had felt like a promise. On the boat, it had seemed like passion, even though it niggled. This time, it felt like control. Enzo had called her his to stop her from leaving. He had given her choice after choice, except now when she needed it. So she used that anger as armour and walked away, forcing herself not to glance back so she wouldn't see the look on his face. She didn't want that to be her last memory. Not of him. Not of the only man in her heart.

Her eyes burned, but she refused to let herself cry, and as she walked down the corridor for the last time, she heard the almighty thud of a slamming door.

It felt like the door had slammed on this life. It was done, and she needed to leave.

'Breathe, Charlotte. Just breathe,' she told herself softly.

Yes, Enzo was angry. She understood why he would be. She even understood why he so jealously protected everything. But she was not a *thing*.

Jabbing the Down button, Charlotte willed the elevator to come up to her faster. As soon as it dinged, she was stepping in, not even waiting the second for the doors to fully slide open.

Breathe... That became her mantra as she half walked, half ran home. When she'd moved to Sydney, she'd forgone the luxury of a car. It was one more thing tied to her fake identity, and she didn't need the stress. Now she wished she had purchased one because to keep her composure in public was proving an almighty challenge. She couldn't even put her head down and shut everything out: now that her father knew where she was, she had to be aware of her surroundings again.

Relief pulsed through her when she finally entered her apartment. The stinging in her eyes grew unbearable, and a sob broke free but she covered her lips with a hand, trying desperately not to fall apart. Not to think of Enzo.

The studio apartment was small.

'*...an empty life...*'

It really was empty. Looking around her home, the only companions she had were plants that she couldn't take. Her possessions were limited. She never bought more than she could pack in a suitcase in a hurry.

Are you going to run again?

What choice did she have? She no longer had Enzo's protection. More than that, there would never be a time when Sydney didn't make her think of him. When she wouldn't be looking around every corner not just for danger but also for the man who had her heart but couldn't give his in return.

'Think, Charlotte,' she told herself. 'Now's not the time for tears. You can do this.'

She couldn't fall apart. Now was the time to think clearly. A new life waited on the other side of this ordeal. She just had to get there.

Throat burning from unshed tears, she swallowed hard and fetched a suitcase from her closet. She grabbed the clothes hanging up, not bothering to fold them before she dumped them in her bag. She hated the look of them now. Greys and beiges. She longed for the clothes she had worn in Italy, the closet full of holiday wear Enzo had given her. All of that lay forgotten in a bag at the office, and Charlotte wondered how long it would be before someone noticed them or Enzo threw them out. It was just as well. They were far too flashy. When she was trying to get by unnoticed, they would not help in the least.

Where would she go?

Melbourne? Adelaide? Some small town where no one would think of looking for her?

She was wasting time trying to think of it now. She would decide when she got to the airport. Anywhere would do, as long as it was away from here.

She called a cab and took one last look around the place she had called home for two years. A place that she had rented on a month-to-month basis just in case she had to run again.

'Will you crawl back into the dark?'

The words had sliced through her when Enzo had said them, but he was right. That was exactly what she was going to do. The moment she left Sydney, Celeste Park would be behind her, and she would find a new identity.

The cab was waiting for her by the time she had made it to the ground floor. She didn't even bother placing her suitcase in the boot. It was small enough to fit on the back seat with her.

Her heart was desiccating in her chest. She wanted to run back to Enzo and tell him to forget everything she'd said, that she would be happy to have a purely physical relationship with him, that she would love him even if he couldn't love her back. But she couldn't do it. She'd meant it when she'd said she deserved more. She wanted more from life than having powerful men try to control and possess her.

Charlotte put on her dark sunglasses, ensuring the driver knew she had no interest in conversation, and looked out of the window at the M1. All the people going about their lives. What would it be like to be one of them, to never have to look over her shoulder? To fall in love with someone she chose and be with them? What had she done to deserve this life?

'Ma'am, we've arrived,' the driver said.

'Oh. Thank you.' She climbed out of the car as quickly as she could, trying not to lose her balance as her suitcase caught in the tactile paving in her hurry to get inside. Unfortunately, she hadn't made it two steps before her phone rang. Without thinking, she answered just as she always did. The only person to regularly call her was the same person who had her shattered heart.

'E—'

'Hello, daughter.'

Every muscle in Charlotte's body seized. Every joint locked. Her stomach fell. She couldn't breathe. She couldn't move. Adrenaline flooded her system and her tongue turned to lead.

'It's been a while.'

Still she was silent. Tears welled in her eyes for a different reason now.

'Come, now. The least you can do is greet your father.'

Charlotte swallowed hard. 'You've got the wrong number.' Her voice was barely a breath.

'Nice try, Charlotte. I must say, you did a rather good job of hiding these last two years.'

Screwing up all her courage, Charlotte tried desperately to keep her fear from her voice. 'What do you want?'

'You know exactly what I want.'

'No.' Charlotte was choosing herself. No matter what it took. She had left Perth, and now would leave Sydney no matter how much it hurt to do so.

She was just about to end the call when her father said, 'You *will* be coming home, Charlotte. Don't be difficult.'

Charlotte hung up on him, on the man that scared her beyond all others purely because he knew exactly what Grant Campbell was like, knew exactly what kind of life awaited his daughter as Campbell's wife, and still traded her for a business deal.

She was so close to leaving it all behind.

Shoving the phone in her handbag, Charlotte grabbed the suitcase and stepped towards the door, but a large hand grabbed her arm tightly, yanking her back. She turned to see who had seized her, and it took her a moment to compute.

A man held the back door to a dark sedan open. Another clutched her arm in a bruising grip. She paled. Gordon Kim was looking down on her with a sneering smile.

'It's rude to hang up on your father. I taught you better than that.'

No. This couldn't be happening.

Charlotte tried with all her might to pull free, but she was no match for his brute strength. Especially not when she hadn't been to a gym in two years. In hiding, she had let herself become weaker. A mistake she was now regretting.

'Let me go,' she demanded. The strength in her tone shocked her when she was so aware of her fear. Her racing heart. Her sweaty palms.

'I already told you, Charlotte. You're coming back with me.'

'I don't want to! I don't want to marry Grant! You know what he's like.'

And my heart belongs to another.

'I really don't care. He is making this family a great deal of money. I raised you to know your duty to the company. Play your part.'

'My part?' Charlotte had thought she was consumed by fear. Now she was learning of the depth of anger she possessed too. 'My part was supposed to be making a mark within the company. My ambition, my education is just as valid as everyone else's. My part wasn't to be traded like a possession. I am not a trinket, Gordon.' Charlotte had respected her father even when she didn't agree with him, always addressing him formally. He was her flesh and blood. Now she realised she didn't have to. There was nothing worth respecting about the man, and she saw just how angry calling him by his first name made him.

'You are my daughter and will do whatever I tell you to. If you don't, I will hurt Enzo De Luca. I will hurt De Luca and Co. What do you think will happen when the press finds out that his PA is a fraud? A little girl that out-smarted the CEO.'

'You wouldn't.' Horror. She knew Gordon could see it on her face. It wouldn't matter that Charlotte only lied about her name; people wouldn't see it that way. Gordon could say whatever he wanted, and then it would be up to Enzo to prove them wrong. People lost faith in companies for lesser reasons, and the company was everything to Enzo. What if he was forced to step down?

It wasn't just the company Charlotte had to worry about. It was Enzo too. How would Gordon hurt him?

'Please, I'm begging you, leave Enzo out of this.'

'You don't understand, Charlotte. You have cost me so much money already. This is all the mercy I'm willing to show. Come quietly or De Luca becomes collateral damage.'

Charlotte couldn't stand the thought of anything happening to Enzo. He had been through enough. She couldn't be the reason he suffered any more. But Enzo was also powerful and vastly wealthy. Surely he could handle her father? Except she knew the only reason Gordon was even threatening Enzo was because of her. After Enzo had refused to hand her over and she'd essentially disappeared from Milan, Gordon would have understood that it was Enzo that was protecting her.

Maybe she could make a scene. There was security all around the airport. That way her father would have other problems to deal with, and she could slip away. But what would happen afterwards? He could make good on his promise. Charlotte couldn't let that happen to Enzo. And she realised even though Enzo couldn't love her, she loved him more than she valued her safety. This time, *she* would protect *him*.

So she stopped fighting.

'I'll go with you, but I need your word that you will leave Enzo out of this. He's done nothing to us.'

'I don't care about De Luca, Charlotte. As soon as you are married to Grant, I will forget the name De Luca even exists.'

She had to believe him. No other options existed for her. She had to face this nightmare, face her sentence, even though she'd done nothing wrong except be born to the wrong family. But if she had been born to any other, she would never have met Enzo, and she couldn't regret that.

So for the first time in a very long time, Charlotte didn't run.

She let go of her suitcase. The man who had been holding the door open wheeled it into the airport.

'Good choice, daughter.'

Pure, unfiltered hatred filled her at the word. She didn't want to be Gordon's daughter. She wanted to run back to Enzo. All the strength, all the adrenaline ebbed from her body and left nothing in its place. She was hollow.

Gordon placed his arm across her shoulders. To onlookers it may have seemed like a caring gesture. Charlotte knew the truth. He was simply making sure she didn't run. Steering her to her demise.

Charlotte paid no attention when they were checked in, not even when they boarded and settled in first class. Nothing was worth paying attention to. Not when she was fracturing. She would never see Enzo again. Yes, that had already been her plan, but now she realised that a small part of her had hoped that maybe she would have seen him. Maybe he would have tried to find her. The possibility had been limited, but it had existed. Now that possibility was gone.

She clamped her teeth together and put on her sunglasses. She would show no emotion, none of the grief ripping her apart.

Closing her eyes, she replayed her last night with Enzo in her head. Being with him under the stars. She would never know a feeling like that again. And she knew, every memory they'd made in Italy would have to sustain her for the rest of her life.

The plane barrelled down the runway and took flight, Sydney falling away below her and taking her heart with it.

Maybe it wasn't the smartest move for you to hide in Enzo De Luca's company.

It certainly hadn't been the best way to remain hidden, but when she thought of Enzo's touch, his affection, she couldn't bring herself to regret it.

CHAPTER THIRTEEN

ENZO SAT AT his desk staring unseeingly at the screen in front of him. It had been a week since Charlotte had stridden out of his office and out of his life, leaving him a shell of the man he once was.

It had been seven days of constant *what-if*s. Of anger that she'd rejected all he had to offer, which was everything he could give. Of anger at himself for letting her leave at all. Shame at his parting words, knowing they'd found their mark and hurt her as much as he was hurting.

Seven days of being merely a shadow of the leader his company needed. Getting barely any sleep because Charlotte's warm body wasn't moulded to his. Rolling over onto cool sheets and jerking awake in panic at her absence, before reliving the hell of watching her leave.

He couldn't bring himself to work out. Something that should have got his blood pumping, given him the energy to tackle the day, seemed like a waste of time. His discipline had faded, his routine smashed to pieces.

He had heard back from the lawyers. The issue with Emilio had been settled. Apparently, his brother wasn't happy, but there was nothing Emilio could do. Even that brought Enzo no joy.

What a difference seven days made.

After hearing from the lawyers, he could think only of

the things Charlotte had said in Ravello. They didn't stop replaying over and over in his head.

'I have chosen something different for myself, and you can do the same... You control your path.'

His obsession with the vineyards had deafened him to her then, but now that he had what he'd thought he wanted, Enzo had found himself finally understanding what she had been telling him. And it made the itch he felt about his father's lie turn into a wound he couldn't ignore.

The truth of his childhood was unveiling itself. All his life he'd wanted to make his father proud. Without complaint, he had picked up every challenge his father had laid down. It had turned him into the leader De Luca and Co. needed, into the conte Perlano deserved, but at no point had his father shown an interest in who Enzo was. In what he might have wanted. He was only ever given a goal to aim for and was encouraged to make that his whole life. Well, now he'd accomplished everything his father wanted of him, and instead of basking in his pride, Enzo was alone in his lofty office with no brother to talk to and a tainted memory of his mother.

'He lied, Enzo.'

His father *had* lied to his mother for years, and instead of dealing with that, with the truth of who his father was, Enzo had defended his actions. God! He was a hypocrite. How could he hate lies so much and yet still accept it just because it came from his father? Just because it won him the vineyards? His mother had been betrayed. But Enzo had been so angry at her for trying to give the vineyards to Emilio. His brother who had spent so much time with their mother.

He'd thought Emilio was jealous, but now he saw it was so much more than that. His brother hadn't received the slightest bit of attention from his father or any affection at all. No wonder their mother doted on Emilio. Favoured him. It didn't excuse what she'd done, but maybe in her place Enzo would have tried to even the scales for Emilio too.

'You didn't receive any affection either.'

Enzo hadn't received a *Well done!* He hadn't received praise. Just acknowledgement that he had done what was expected.

He thought his father hadn't failed him, when in truth his father had been so singularly focussed on his duty he'd failed his whole family. Enzo had wanted to secure the vineyards to honour his memory, the love his parents had shared. Now that he had his victory and no one to share it with, he realised how hollow it all was. His parents hadn't shared anything at all.

He knew what it was to share a life now. He'd had a taste of it with Charlotte.

Her affection had been a wondrous thing. Her boldness. Her sass. He'd lost himself in it for a little while. She didn't just dull the hurts he tried to bury deep within, she made them disappear. Pulling him from his anger. Saving him from his angst. Trying to show him the truth of his childhood. She'd wanted him to choose a better life for himself. Charlotte was in his corner. Until she wasn't.

And that was his own fault.

Enzo looked beyond the door at her empty desk. A taunting reminder of what he'd lost.

HR had sent him options for a temporary replacement. As much as he needed someone, he didn't *want* anyone. He didn't want to see another person in that chair. He didn't want to spend his days with a stranger who would pale in comparison to Charlotte. And he *would* compare them to her.

Without him realising it, Charlotte had become the benchmark against which all others in his life would be measured, and he knew he was ruined. For as long as he lived, he would crave one person for ever.

He missed her.

He missed her bright smile every morning. When he'd thought she was Celeste, he had considered her plain. When he thought back now, she was anything but. He couldn't recall the drab clothes she wore. He remembered how her greeting formed such an integral part of his morning routine. Put him in the right headspace to lead. They had been a team. And he'd loved working with her. How her opinions lined up with his. How, whenever they didn't, she challenged him in her own unobtrusive way. How she would try to pass off her own ideas as his. He had let her get away with that. He'd always been thinking along similar lines anyway.

A white empty espresso cup sat on his table. Enzo glanced at it. He had made his own coffee this week. Exactly as he had taught her. There was not the slightest difference in process, and yet he preferred it when she made it. He preferred everything she did. Charlotte had made his world better by just being in it. And he'd been blind to it.

Enzo cursed. How could a cup make him want to rip his heart out of his chest?

He pushed away from the desk and stood at the window. Pressing his palm to the glass, he looked at the city below. It didn't take his mind off Charlotte because he'd noticed how she used to look out at the view every day and try to hide her smile. She'd loved it, even though she'd never allowed herself to be a real part of this city.

There was a lot he'd pretended not to notice.

Then it struck him. He'd trusted her so much more than he realised.

Whenever he picked up on anything that made him doubt people, question who they were, he called them out—but he hadn't done that with Charlotte. As if he had known instinctively that she could be trusted regardless of her disguise. His throat clogged and his eyes misted when he—the man who trusted no one—realised the extent to which he had trusted Charlotte. Finding out about her true identity hadn't really shaken his trust. If it had, he would not have taken her to Ravello or on his yacht. He had been clutching at straws when he told himself he couldn't trust her. He had trusted Charlotte with his company. The life-blood of his family. His family's legacy.

He had trusted her so much that he had let her work in his mother's study in Perlano. Had trusted her enough to open up to her about his heartbreak, the reason he couldn't love. Enough to confide in her and let her comfort him.

Why had he been so blind to it before? His trust in Charlotte went so far beyond anything he should have felt towards a PA because she had never been just a PA to him. She had been a dependable constant in a life where he could depend on so few people.

He hadn't been that for her.

Charlotte hadn't been able to depend on him. She'd had to keep her identity a secret so long He had seen how the stress of it was wrecking her, but he'd done nothing about it until Milan. Bile rose in his throat when he thought of what he had said to her.

'You're welcome to protect yourself!'

'Bastardo,' he cursed himself aloud.

He'd been so set on letting her look after herself. If she thought she could, then she was welcome to it. But he had been hurting when he'd said it. Angry. Afraid of losing something—someone—he treasured. Scared she would leave. She'd left anyway.

Of course she thought she could protect herself. She

had done so for two years. In that time she hadn't thought she could come to him.

But what if he had been the kind of man she could have confided in? She didn't need him. Charlotte didn't need anyone. He was certain of that. She had more strength, more tenacity in her than anyone he knew. But he *wanted* her to need him.

'What have I done?'

He wanted to protect her. To cherish her. To be the man she allowed in her life. She allowed so few in.

Idiota, *she's just like you and you let her go!*

He wanted to be the man she ran to, not from. And she had run from him because she was right, in that moment: he had tried to control her. Hold on to her. Like he tried to control everything. Like he held on to the vineyards. But holding on that tightly tended to crush things, and that was exactly what he had done to her.

'You're mine.'

Enzo could kick himself. She'd told him how she was treated. Of course she would see his words as proof that he, too, wanted to own her. He needed to find her, to beg her forgiveness. He was possessive. His whole family was. They held on to things. That was how they amassed centuries' worth of wealth. That's what his father had done with the vineyards instead of sharing them with the woman he was meant to have loved. What Enzo had done too. What, he suddenly realised, Emilio had attempted to do. Emilio had only ever had his mother's love. Of course he would have wanted the vineyards she gave him.

'Maybe this could be a chance to get some of your family back.'

Charlotte had seen what he could not. Of course she had. She was always so perceptive. He'd always known that for someone of her intellect, being his PA was nowhere near challenging enough. But she'd always celebrated his wins as if they were her own. Just like him, she wanted to leave a mark, but her only option was to do so through him. How unfulfilled must she have been? Enzo felt his fists clench. He strode back to his desk, sitting so hastily his espresso cup rattled in its saucer. He had wasted a week. He wouldn't waste another second.

Charlotte wanted more. Why wouldn't she? A woman that smart and loving deserved the world. He leaned over his laptop, fingers flying over the keys. He was going to find her and tell her that she could have everything she wanted. She didn't need to settle for a job just to have a life. It wasn't one or the other. She didn't need to live like a hermit. She didn't need to choose safety over friends or love.

Love.

The word made Enzo's mouth go dry and his heart race. In a cowardly act, he'd shunned love, but now he wanted it.

'I don't want to change you when I...'

He was so sure she'd been going to say she loved him. He only recognised now how badly he'd wanted to hear her say it, even if he hadn't been ready. He'd wanted to hear it because he felt it too.

'I love her,' he said under his breath. 'I love her, and I let her go.'

He slammed his hand against the polished wood, cursing loudly. How could he have been such an idiot?

But he would make it right. He would find her, and he would bring her back.

She'd been gone a week already. She could be anywhere. But there was one way he might be able to find her—and protect her while he did so.

He was going to track down Gordon Kim and Grant Campbell.

After Milan, he'd known he would need some insurance and had called on one of his fixers to dig into Kim's and Campbell's pasts, everything they wanted to keep hidden. What he already possessed might be enough to threaten them into leaving Charlotte alone, but that didn't feel like enough for Enzo. He needed them to suffer a punishment from which they would never recover. When he was done, no one would ever do business with them again. Business would be the least of their worries.

He owed Charlotte that much. Even if she'd chosen to walk away from him, he would still protect her. He'd made a promise, and he kept his word.

They might even lead him back to her…

Hours ticked by like minutes. When he finally had enough and went to trace where the men were right now, his blood ran cold.

'*Cazzo!*' he cursed.

They *had* led him to Charlotte, but not because they had followed her to her new home. No, because Charlotte was in Perth.

And getting married to Campbell.

Enzo wouldn't let that happen.

How had she ended up back there? How quickly had her father found her? Enzo was certain Charlotte was smart enough to evade Kim. Something about this didn't sit right. And not just because the woman he loved was marrying another man. A man Enzo was now actively trying to ruin.

Time was up. Enzo had to act immediately or Charlotte would suffer. And there was no way in hell he was about to let that happen.

He grabbed his phone. 'Get the plane ready. We're going to Perth.'

CHAPTER FOURTEEN

SEATED AT THE very spot on the plane he had last sat with Charlotte, Enzo drummed his fingers on the polished wood table. This was where he'd let her get lost in the thoughts that had taken her away from him. For a man who made so few mistakes, he had certainly made a massive one that day. Anger at himself battled with the fury he felt towards her father.

He had never felt so impatient to land in his life.

Hurry up. He willed the plane to go faster. He needed to get to Charlotte before she was caught in a trap she would never escape. Even if she never wanted to marry Enzo—and that thought hurt—he still wouldn't let her marry this day.

Enzo could have tried to while away the time, perhaps with work, but he didn't. He needed to suffer for his idiocy.

He felt every minute as if it was an hour. The moment the doors were opened and the stairs attached to the plane, he was racing down them and snatching the keys from the driver he'd ordered without even a greeting. He knew the only person he could rely on to get him to the church in time was himself. He was certain he would be getting a few speeding fines, but he didn't care.

He started the low-slung sports car with a grunt and floored it in the direction of the church. He'd spent the five-hour flight compulsively studying the route. Every second counted. Darting between slower vehicles, he paid no attention to wagging fingers and shouted curses. He cared about nothing but getting to Charlotte. And when the grand church surrounded by beautiful gardens rose up in front of him, glorious in its Gothic architecture, he turned in sharply, bringing the car to a screeching halt right in front of the large doors.

Slamming the door shut, he sent up a silent prayer that he wasn't too late. If he was, he would find a way to free Charlotte regardless. He ran up the stairs, throwing open the heavy wooden church door with a crash that had every head in the room swing towards him.

Silence.

For moment, no one moved. Not a sound was made.

A bible lay open in the hand of the pastor. Gordon Kim was halfway out of his seat, a look of shock and anger on his face. Grant Campbell, an unappealing man in every regard, held Charlotte's hands tightly in his.

Charlotte.

Standing there, in a dress that reminded him of a cake topper, her black hair all pinned up under a long veil. It wasn't her at all. Just a showpiece. It ratcheted his anger up even more. And when he looked at her face, at the shock and desolation, he wanted to sink to his knees and rip off the heads of everyone in the church in equal measure.

But that moment lasted a second. A breath.

With purposeful strides, he made his way down the aisle, but Gordon marched towards him. Whispers rose in volume.

'Get out, De Luca,' Gordon ordered.

'No,' Enzo growled, standing at his full height, looking down on the man he had never met but loathed. He took one step forward, and Gordon stuck out his arms in a pathetic attempt to stop him.

'If you know what's good for you, leave.'

'Funny, I was about to say the same thing to you.' Enzo bared his teeth at the man. 'Get out of my way. You have more to worry about than your daughter's wedding.'

The momentary look of fear in the older man's eyes was all Enzo needed to see before he walked around Gordon and approached the altar.

'Same goes for you, Campbell.'

Hatred and rage warred on Grant's face, but Charlotte's voice had Enzo ignoring him in an instant.

'Enzo, what are you doing here?'

The brokenness in the way she said his name was the most painful wound Enzo had ever had to bear, but just hearing his name on her lips after a week of agony was the sweetest joy.

'I'm sorry,' he said.

'For what?'

'This.'

Despite the fact that Grant hadn't let go of Charlotte's hand, Enzo scooped her up in his arms. Loud gasps echoed around the church. Grant was forced to break his hold as Enzo carried her down the aisle and into the sunlight.

'What are you doing?' Charlotte's question was a half sob against his shoulder.

'Can you trust me again?' The answer seemed like the most important thing in the world. Enzo's heart ceased beating as he waited for the answer. But he didn't wait long.

'I have always trusted you,' she replied, instantly.

He nearly sagged with relief. Maybe he still stood a chance of undoing all the damage he'd inflicted. Enzo hurried to the car and placed her in the passenger seat, the ridiculous dress almost comical as he strapped her in.

'Enzo, you can't,' she said frantically. 'My father—'

'*Tesoro*, there's nothing he can do to you or me. I won't let him.'

'You don't know him.' Her eyes filled with tears that spiked his rage. How had Gordon threatened her? Enzo vowed to find out and make the man hurt even more than he'd already planned.

'I promise, and I always keep my promises.'

'I know, but—'

'But nothing, Charlotte. Let me protect you.'

Charlotte swallowed thickly and nodded.

Before anyone could rush out of the church, Enzo was racing away. He drove them a short distance to the coast and parked the car amongst the numerous others. When he turned to look at Charlotte, tears slid down her cheeks.

'The ocean,' she said. 'How did you know to bring me here?'

He wiped away her tears with his thumbs, remembering seeing her sit at the fountain after they'd nearly kissed. 'I know you, Charlotte. I know your heart. I can see over your walls.' He had noticed how much she loved the water when they were in Italy. At his home in Ravello. While they sailed. He wanted those days back. No, he wanted better.

'I owe you an apology.'

'For stealing me from my wedding?' She gave him a watery smile.

'No. I am quite proud of that, actually.'

She huffed a laugh, then shook her head. 'What are you really doing here, Enzo?'

'I'm here to tell you that I'm sorry. I'm sorry for what I said, *tesoro*. I'm sorry for holding back. For lying.'

'Enzo...'

'For someone who hates lies, I became very good at it. I lied to myself, and I lied to you. After Gia, I didn't want to be in danger of being used, of being hurt, so I convinced myself that I couldn't love again. It was a lie. Just like it was a lie to say that all we had was a physical connection. It's more than that. I love you, Charlotte. And you were right to walk away because you do deserve a love that should be shouted from rooftops. I want to give you that, but I want to love you in secret too.'

Charlotte had prayed that she would hear him say the words. For him to tell her he loved her. She'd imagined it would make her feel like flying, but instead it broke her heart even more. The words didn't change her situation.

'You can't say this to me, Enzo. It doesn't change anything. I trust you, but you won't ever trust anyone.'

She watched him look into her eyes. The thumb caressing her cheek stopped.

When he spoke, his voice was low. Scraped raw. She heard a vulnerability in it that she hadn't heard in him before. The master of the world, the most powerful man she would ever know, and he cast away all those layers of defence so she could see him. And before she knew it, she was reaching for him, taking his face in her hands.

'You were right when you said my heart is scarred. It was, but, Charlotte, you healed it. Not in Italy, but over these past two years. As Celeste, then as yourself. By being someone I could trust.'

'Do you trust me?' She tried to control the hope that flared in her gut.

'Completely.' He smiled then—small and gentle, but the purity of it was like gazing at the sun. Her sun. 'It took me a while to realise it, but I may have always trusted you. I leaned on you, Charlotte. I trusted your opinions even when you tried to make them seem like my own.'

She felt her cheeks redden. She'd always thought that she had done a good job at hiding her opinions in his, but he had seen through her. He saw over her walls. She wasn't lost in a maze any more. She didn't want to put up barriers between them. Except one still existed. The reason she was marrying Grant at all.

'And I will continue to do so for the rest of our lives,' Enzo went on. 'My only hope is that you learn to lean on me too.'

But she couldn't. Not when the marriage still had to happen.

'Enzo—'

'You were wrong about one thing.'

'What's that?'

He took her hands and placed them on his neck. 'You said I see you as a possession, but I need you to know that I don't. I just wanted to hold on to you, *tesoro*. I need you, but I went about it all wrong.'

Charlotte looked at her hands on his neck, remembering his words.

This space is reserved.

His vulnerability. What he'd told her. This was Enzo submitting to her. One of the most powerful men in the world submitting to *her*. A woman who ran. Who feared. And Enzo had been doing this all along. Offering her control. Telling her it was okay to take charge. Unlike her father and Grant, who tried to lead her by the neck. Showing her every chance they got that they owned her. And she had compared Enzo to them.

Guilt roiled in her belly. She'd been angry, and she should have never said it.

'I was jealous at the ball,' Enzo said. 'I hated the thought of anyone else getting to be with you. Seeing you the way I do. I just wanted you. Please, Charlotte. Please give me a chance to prove how much I love you.'

Her father's threat rang in her head. 'I love you too, Enzo! With my whole heart. But it doesn't change anything. I can't be with you. They will never let us be happy.' Everything she could ever want was right there before her, but she couldn't reach for it. The leash her father placed on her wouldn't allow it. She was breaking on the inside. So much worse than when she walked away, because now she knew how much Enzo loved her. Now she could see a future where they could grow old together. Dangling before her. A cruel taunt.

'*Tesoro*, how did they threaten you?' The passion and love in his voice were instantly turning into cold anger.

Unable to stem the flow, she let tear after tear fall into the layers of her wedding dress. Her voice cracked, her throat raw. 'Not me,' she managed.

Understanding lit Enzo's features. 'Your father threatened me.'

Charlotte nodded. 'And De Luca and Co.' She sniffed and tried desperately to take a breath so she could speak again. 'I couldn't let it happen, Enzo. I can't be the reason you and the company suffer.'

Before she even knew what was happening, Enzo was unbuckling her and pulling her onto his lap. She barely noticed the cramped confines of the seat, because right here was where she longed to be. With Enzo. In his arms.

'I don't deserve you,' he whispered as he kissed her. Hard and bruising. As if he couldn't keep what he felt

within himself any longer. Charlotte revelled in it, returning his passion, pulling him closer. Never wanting to let go.
Kissing the man she loved in the dress she wore to tie herself to another. She felt Enzo's nails scrape against the fabric, wanting to rip it off her as much as she wanted him to.

She didn't want this kiss to end. She wanted to be here
with him for ever, but he was pulling away. His hand
moved up to her veil as he looked into her eyes and pulled
it free, tossing it aside.

'You never have to go back,' he said, punctuating every
word by removing another pin holding her hair up. Her hair
tumbled around her shoulders, releasing the pressure on
her scalp. And she knew right then, from the confidence
in his voice, that Enzo had found a way to neutralise her
father. And whatever it was, Gordon wasn't going to like it.

'What's going to happen to my father?'

'Let's just say Gordon and Grant are going to have some
very extensive legal trouble for a long time after everything I uncovered. And even if they somehow find a way
around that, which I doubt, there isn't a single bank that
will touch them after this.'

That was the power Enzo had. Centuries of it at the
tips of his fingers.

'Have I overstepped?'

She saw the seriousness of the question in his green
eyes, understood then what it meant to be his. He protected viciously, but he would undo everything if she gave
the word. He held on to what was his, not by squeezing
the life out of it but giving it a safe space to thrive. The
question gave her a chance to run—but the choice to stay.

'No. You haven't.' She smiled. So did Enzo, and he
reached to wipe from her cheeks the tears that had gone
from grief and fear to joy.

'Tears aren't meant for your eyes, *tesoro*. They remind me of the night sky at sea. They hold the stars. I will protect you so fear never dims them again.'

Charlotte kissed him. There was no possible way for her to tell him what those words meant to her, so she showed him. 'Take me home, Enzo,' she said against his lips. 'Take me home to Sydney.'

The smile he gave her was blinding and the kiss breathless.

'First we need to get rid of that ridiculous dress.'

Charlotte laughed. It *was* ridiculous. 'I look like a cupcake.'

'You're definitely delicious.'

'I love you, Enzo.'

He kissed her again, and she heard him breathe against her lips. *'Tu ed io per sempre.'*

Charlotte might not speak Italian, but her heart understood the words. She agreed. Charlotte and Enzo would be for ever.

EPILOGUE

One year later

ENZO STOOD IN the kitchen doorway, watching Charlotte nibble on *cornetti*, a cup of espresso beside her computer. Her back was to the spectacular view of Sydney, her attention firmly focussed on Isabella's face on the screen.

'Don't you worry, everything will be ready before you arrive,' the housekeeper said.

Charlotte had been excited to spend the Italian summer in Perlano and spent a lot of her time making arrangements with Isabella, who had come to treat Charlotte as her own daughter.

It hadn't taken Enzo long to forgive Isabella for not telling him about his brother's visit. In fact, Enzo had forgiven Emilio entirely. It had been like a crushing weight lifting from him. It was Charlotte who had helped him find that peace, and while Enzo might never bring himself to trust people implicitly, he at least recognised that he could trust those in his life. Even his brother, who had been leading part of the company successfully for years.

The beloved sound of Charlotte's laughter filtered through the quiet penthouse. It warmed his heart to see how well she and Isabella got along. Charlotte had been nervous to tell her about her true identity, but it had been a short conversation, with Isabella insisting she could always tell who she was in her heart.

He was proud of Charlotte. Not just for taking back her life but for living it to the fullest. Black-and-white photographs of her now hung in an artful grid in the entrance to the penthouse. The focal piece of his home. She had reconnected with her friends and had a thriving media presence.

His Charlotte had joined him in the light.

Enzo waited as long as he could stand for her to finish her call but soon ran out of patience and stepped behind her, wrapped her in his arms and kissed her neck.

'*Ciao*, Isabella.' He smiled at the screen. The twinkle in the elderly lady's eye told him she knew what he was about to do. Without warning, he ended the call.

'Enzo!' Charlotte scolded.

'I couldn't wait any longer, *tesoro*.'

He spun her around on the bar stool and kissed her as if he was a soldier returning from war. Her moan ignited his blood. With each day it felt as if their attraction only grew. So did his love for her. He hated being away from her for even a second, his business trips becoming even more efficient than before so that he could return to his love.

A month after they had returned from Perth, Charlotte was asked to take over her father's company, but she'd refused. Not only that, but she had also cut ties with every single one of her family. But Enzo couldn't let her languish as his PA, so he'd offered her a chance to head up her own department because there was no one he trusted more than her. He wanted his family's legacy in her hands too.

'You can never wait,' she teased.

What she didn't know was that he *was* waiting—waiting for them to return to Perlano, because in his pocket, safely tucked away, was an engagement ring. His mother's ring. Emilio had handed it over to him when they had last seen each other. Every time Enzo felt it, his heart jolted at the future that he could see. Charlotte, beaming and happy. His children running around the estate just as he once had. It would be a good life.

First, they had to get back to Perlano, and then he would take her to the vineyards that they so loved, that his mother had loved, and he would ask her to marry him.

'You have no idea, *tesoro*,' he said and kissed her once more.

* * * * *

Did you fall head over heels for
Strictly Forbidden Boss?
Then you're sure to adore the next instalment in
The De Luca Legacy duet,
coming soon!

And don't miss these other stories
by Bella Mason!

Awakened by the Wild Billionaire
Secretly Pregnant by the Tycoon
Their Diamond Ring Ruse
His Chosen Queen

Available now!

ITALIAN'S
PREGNANT
MISTRESS

CAROL MARINELLI

MILLS & BOON

Dear Sister Anne

Love always

Sister Carol

PROLOGUE

A NEW YEAR.

Professionally, Dante Casadio had no resolutions.

He was at the top of his game.

And while the skies might be raining sleet, in the boardroom of a top Milan legal firm people were loosening ties and sipping water as things heated up.

Dante's silk tie remained beautifully knotted, his glass untouched.

It was the end of the second week after the Christmas break—and apart from a brief trip to Lucca he had been in his office most days.

The New Year had started as the last had ended—with his exceptionally famous client insisting, 'She can't do this!'

'Nobody is doing anything,' Dante responded in rich Italian. 'It's an extremely reasonable offer.'

'We'll let the judge decide.'

Vincenzo, his senior paralegal, cast Dante a worried glance.

'I mean it,' the client insisted. 'I'll see her in court!' he continued angrily, but Dante said nothing.

Emotional outbursts didn't faze him.

In any capacity.

Be it at work with an overwrought client, or at decadent play with a beautiful lover, his impenetrable barrier was maintained.

Always.

If anything, he found such displays mildly interesting. Possibly because he allowed for so few emotions of his own.

Certainly he never shared how he was feeling with another.

The client, though, was more than ready to share his!

And, rather loudly, he did.

Dante's haughty face remained impassive throughout the rant, and finally he was winding up.

'No, absolutely not!' the client concluded. 'She's not getting her hands on the chalet in Switzerland. Hell, she doesn't even ski.'

Still Dante said nothing.

'I can't believe you're charging me for this so-called advice...' He sneered and tossed the file towards Dante. 'I thought I was hiring the best in Italy.'

There were many people sitting in the boardroom.

The best of the best.

Attorneys, paralegals, a psychologist, his client's PR, as well as his assistant... This eleventh-hour meeting was well attended, by the best of the best, and yet a year on they were getting precisely nowhere.

Dante was rarely wrong—but his client was not concluding his rant. He was escalating.

'I made one mistake!' he shouted. 'One!'

As a colleague tried to defuse the situation with calming words, Dante resisted rolling his eyes.

One mistake?

Please...

As a very sought-after and rather infamous family law attorney, Dante was cynical to the extreme—and he didn't believe a word anyone said. Whether directly, or by omission, Dante knew full well that everyone lied.

Himself included.

But more to the point...

'It's irrelevant,' he said.

His measured, sparse words only further incensed the client, and a vein bulged on his forehead as he refused to accept the fact Dante had calmly delivered—even if his client had strayed, in Italy it was no-fault divorce.

'Legally, your extramarital affair is irrelevant.'

In the heightened emotional world of family law Dante's

stony logic was invaluable, and that was why, despite his enormous fees, he was incredibly sought after.

He was not, though, famed for hand-holding.

Dante left that to others.

'You've hired me to deal with financial, property and succession matters. That I can do. However, if you feel you need more time with the practice psychologist...'

'I don't need to see a damn psychologist. I need to speak with my wife.'

'That's the last thing you should do,' Dante warned him sharply. 'The very last thing. Do not contact your soon-to-be *ex*-wife.'

His client sucked in his breath at this reminder of the status of his marriage. 'You're a cold bastard, Casadio.'

Indeed, he was.

As his client thumped the gleaming table Dante Casadio did not flinch.

Vincenzo, his paralegal, was startled, though, and a couple of the other attorneys sat up straighter, perhaps wondering how they would deal with things if this exceptionally high-profile client completely lost his temper.

Rather than clearing the office of staff, or warning the client to calm down, Dante stood up to his well over six-foot height.

There were no signs of confrontation in his stance.

He didn't so much as look at his client.

Nor did he stalk out.

Instead, he picked up the paperwork that was so angrily being discussed and took a moment to ensure it was in the correct order.

Dante liked order.

His suits were handmade here in Milan. His shoes also. His shirts and ties were from a little further afield—Paris. He liked the cut of a Charvet shirt and remained loyal to them. His thick black hair was trimmed weekly, he shaved daily—even at weekends—and if he was attending a function, as he often did, he shaved twice.

After tapping the paperwork several times on the desk,

to ensure it was neatly aligned, he placed it in the rich navy folder.

A tense silence filled the boardroom. All awaited his response, perhaps wondering if he was going to excuse himself from the case...

Of course not.

Dante was more than used to this.

'We shall speak in my office,' he said, and with the file in hand walked to the exit. As he reached the door, he added, 'Immediately.'

He was over the drama—and, as well as that, he had an unexpected phone call to make.

Prior to this meeting Antonia, his PA, had informed him that Sev, his older brother, had called and asked that Dante call him as soon as was convenient.

He and his brother weren't speaking, and the fact that it wasn't Helene, Sev's own PA, who had called had been of instant concern.

'An emergency?' Dante had checked, concerned that something had happened to Gio, their grandfather.

'No.' Antonia had shaken her head. 'But he asked that you call him back today, if possible...'

And he would—just as soon as he had a moment.

Walking into his office, Dante truly wondered how people could be so attached to *things* that would surely cause nothing but pain.

Aside from a small envelope in his office safe there was nothing he would miss.

Actually, it would be a relief if even that was taken.

Dante had no photos on his desk or shelves, no mementoes. It was the same at his luxurious Milan penthouse, and at his stunning property in Lucca.

Once he had considered the gorgeous Tuscan town home. Now it was a place he avoided until it became...

Unavoidable.

Like at Christmas, or anniversaries.

Why would anyone want constant reminders of anything? Dante thought.

He certainly didn't.

Although he hadn't always been this dispassionate—quite the contrary... As a child he'd been the wild, cheeky one, his charm undeniable, his smile melting hearts...

More so as a teenager and young man.

That smile had won him better favours by then. He'd adored sex and had been passionate lover. A faithful one too—at least for the brief time any tryst had lasted. For he adored women and made it very clear it was just sex...

Good sex.

And lots of it.

With a side serving of charm.

But those days were long gone.

His parents were dead, and he and his brother's once close relationship was severed.

He didn't want to *think* about happier times, let alone feel. And so he didn't.

His relationships were now deliberately remote and brief. He trusted no one and his career was his sole focus.

Dante, despite his client's current anger, knew that come next Christmas there would be champagne delivered from him and he'd be recommending Dante to colleagues and friends.

Not now, though.

His client stormed in through the door and slammed it closed.

Dante remained seated.

Somehow, despite the status of his client, Dante remained the absolute authority.

Ice versus fire.

And when it came to Dante Casadio ice always won.

Nothing could melt him; his angry client was like a blow torch against a vast glacier...

His client attempted to start where he'd left off, perhaps not understanding that he was in Dante's office now. 'I mean it. She's not getting—'

'Enough!'

Dante called for him to be silent and as the incensed client—angry, offended—met Dante's gaze, no doubt about to remind his attorney of just who he was talking to, the tirade was abruptly halted. There was something in Dante's brown eyes that could, when they so chose, halt an army.

'Take a seat.' Dante gestured to the chair in front of his desk and waited until he had done so. 'If you thump my desk, I shall ask you to leave. If you thump me, I shall see you in criminal court.'

'I just—'

'I've heard enough,' Dante interrupted. He pushed the neat file towards him and stood. 'We can speak again once you have read the proposed settlement in its entirety.'

He walked to the window, staring at the impressive structure of Milan's cathedral.

The documents would take some time to go through, but Dante was used to that.

His intention had never been to specialise in family law, but then, Dante had never lived his life as others intended.

Sev had.

Or rather, he had tried to for a while.

What did his brother want?

God, he hoped Gio was okay.

His grandfather, Gio Casadio, was the only warm place left in Dante's heart—even if he didn't see him that often. He was the only reason he kept a property in Lucca, and his sole reason for returning home.

Even if it killed him to do so.

Dante hated going back...

Their parents had assumed that both the Casadio sons would want to continue on with the lucrative family business in Lucca—a vast winery in the Tuscan hillsides. Yet no one had glimpsed what lay ahead.

At eighteen, when he'd first moved to Milan to study law, Dante's intention had been to focus on corporate law. Sev, the older of the two, had focussed on the hotel industry. Their parents—their father especially—had assumed that their combined skills would progress the business.

Their father had been good at assuming.

No one could have predicted that the once close brothers would fall out on the eve of Sev's wedding.

That Dante, the best man, would be wearing a row of stitches and a black eye almost as dark as his bespoke suit.

Or that the groom's fingers would be too swollen from throwing punches to get his wedding band on.

Not even the sudden and tragic death of their parents and Sev's wife Rosa in a helicopter crash had reunited them.

If anything, the tragedy had driven the brothers further apart.

Oh, they communicated—generally through their personal assistants—on matters such as the winery, or their grandfather's vast property in Lucca, or his well-being.

The brothers themselves spoke rarely and on a needed basis only.

What did Sev want?

It was then that his client spoke. 'I miss her.'

Dante said nothing, but felt a rare surge of sympathy for his client.

'How we were…'

For a brief second Dante closed his eyes and saw himself and Sev, two little boys running through the vines at home, or playing on the gorgeous walls of Lucca that surrounded the medieval town. They had been so close and, yes, he silently acknowledged, he missed being a brother…

'Listen…' His voice was husky, and he cleared his throat as he snapped his sharp mind back to work. 'Listen to me,' he said in more measured tones as he turned from the window and retook his seat. 'Time is not on your side. Unless you can reach agreement, six weeks from now we go to court and the judge decides. Now.' He put up a hand to stop his client from speaking. 'I don't need to hear about regrets and mistakes or that you miss her. Not in this office. I sort out the finances, the divisions of property, the legalities. I have worked extensively with your wife's attorneys, and this is more than a fair deal. If it goes to litigation, while I shall of course do my best to represent your interests, I don't believe the judge will award you anything close to this.' He gestured to the folder. 'Combine that with my fees and you'll be looking at losing a lot more than a chalet in Switzerland.'

'I've already lost.' His client buried his face in his hands. 'What do I do if I still love her?'

Dante was the last person to offer relationship advice.

'Wrong office,' he said, albeit kindly. He would not kick a man when down.

'Please…' His client looked up. 'Tell me…'

'I've never had a successful relationship nor do I want one.'

'Dante…?'

While he would never offer relationship advice, on occasions such as this, when he was invited to…

'Some mistakes you cannot come back from.'

'It was just once…'

Dante was about to conclude the conversation, but his client was being honest now.

'It was more than once. And I regret my indiscretions more than you could know.'

'Believe me,' Dante corrected with a grim smile. 'I do know.'

'What can I do? Please, just…'

'Okay,' Dante said, and then sat for a moment in silence, considering not an ex-lover, but the loss of his brother. 'Even if hurts, you have to try to let the other go with dignity and grace.'

'What if I can't?'

'Then it ends in court.'

Before his client left his office, Dante offered his hand, as well as one last word of advice. 'Do *not* contact your wife.'

Alone, Dante made his call.

'Hello?' Sev said.

'You asked me to call?'

'Yes, hold on.'

Sev got rid of whoever was with him and switched to video call. Dante stared, unsmiling, into his phone at a slightly older version of himself.

There were differences. Sev's eyes were grey, whereas Dante's were a deep brown, and Dante had a scar through his left eyebrow. And, though their hair was the same thick glossy black, Sev wore his a little longer. Both were tall and broad, and had similar features—strong jaws and straight roman noses. They were clearly cut from the same cloth.

Once Sev had been the more solemn of the two, although now they almost shared that podium...

'How's Dubai?' Dante asked, hating the polite small talk, but attempting to take the dignified route he had suggested to his client.

'Hot,' Sev said, perhaps hating the forced conversation too. 'How are things in Milan?'

'Cold.'

'Just a couple of things to discuss,' Sev said. 'Helene mentioned that you haven't RSVP'd regarding the ball. I can't attend this year.'

'Well, I shan't be going,' Dante responded.

He attended many events representing their grandfather's winery, but the spring ball in Lucca was one he avoided.

'It's important to Gio. We're the main sponsors.'

'We?' Dante provoked. 'I'm not an owner, and neither are you.'

'Dante...' Sev said, in a wry use of his name. Technically their grandfather was the owner, but the brothers dealt with the management of it, and both knew it would eventually pass to them. Hopefully not too soon. 'Have you been able to visit the winery lately?'

Dante stared back at his brother. He loathed going back to Lucca—especially to the winery. He could still see the wreckage in the hills every time he visited.

'No,' he said finally, and, even though they were not talking, he knew it was in moments like this that he wanted conversation. To ask his brother if he shared the same visions, if the nightmare of that day was all he could see whenever he returned home. 'I find it—'

'Inconvenient?' Sev snapped. 'We all know you're busy, Dante. So, when *will* you be back?'

'I don't know,' Dante said, knowing that Sev was now getting to the real reason for this rare call. 'In a couple of weeks, maybe. Why?'

'I called Gio yesterday…unexpectedly.'

Neither brother called him Nonno—and not just because it didn't work well in business matters. Dante, back when he'd had a heart, had been the cheekier of the two and had started to call him by his name. He had been unable to understand why he got told off when he did.

'But he *is* Gio…' he'd said, and hugged his *nonno* so fiercely and called him by his name with such love that it had stuck.

'He seemed a bit vague,' said Sev.

'As do you,' Dante pointed out, for usually their conversations were more specific. 'He struggles with his new phone; though I tried to show him how it worked at Christmas.'

'How was he then?'

'Just Gio being Gio,' Dante said. 'A bit…' He turned his mind back a couple of weeks. 'A bit morose, maybe? He was talking about…' He hesitated, loath to mention the date the brothers hated most. The one time in the year when they were forced together. 'He wanted to start making plans for the ten-year memorial. I told him it was months away. He certainly wasn't vague then.'

Dante's frown deepened as his brother spoke again. 'He was alone. Apparently the domestic staff are off for a couple of extra weeks.'

'Mimi's there, though?' Dante checked, because even if most of the household staff were on leave Mimi, his grandfather's housekeeper, would be there.

'I'm not so sure,' Sev said. 'Dante, he was in his robe and still unshaven at midday.'

'Gio?' Dante shook his head. 'Perhaps he was—'

'I took a screenshot,' Sev said.

'Okay.'

Dante gave the one-word response as he looked at the photo.

And Sev, even if they weren't talking, knew his ways. He stayed silent and let Dante think...

His grandfather was a very formal man. Always up with the birds and immaculately dressed for his morning stroll along the walls. This shot of him unshaven and in a robe meant something was wrong.

Still silent, Dante glanced at Sev. For a brief second he felt his brother's eyes on the scar that ran through his eyebrow. The scar Sev had put there. He watched as Sev hastily pulled his eyes back to meet his brother's gaze.

They *never* discussed that time.

'Delete that photo,' Sev warned. 'I'll do the same.'

'I'll go and see him,' Dante told his brother. 'I'll just arrive unannounced.'

'When?'

He knew he had a packed schedule, and a date tonight, yet he had to think hard to remember her name and none of it really mattered, Dante realised.

'Now.'

'It's just a hunch,' said Sev. 'I'm not asking you to drop everything.'

'It's Gio,' Dante responded.

'Yes...'

'Hopefully it's nothing,' Dante said. 'I'll let you know when I've seen him.'

'Thanks.'

There were no goodbyes.

From either of them.

Sev rang off and Dante sat in silence, staring at the image of his grandfather, who seemed to have aged a decade in the past couple of weeks.

He cancelled his date.

Actually, he ended his association with her there and then.

Nothing mattered other than Gio.

He buzzed his PA.

'Change of schedule,' he told Antonia. 'I need to be in Lucca tonight.'

CHAPTER ONE

SUSIE BILTON'S SMILE was present and correct.

Her blonde hair was neatly pinned back. Her black dress was immaculate. And her black apron, with the elegant Pearla's logo spun in gold over one pocket, was neatly tied. She wore the requisite black tights and, because she would be on her feet for the next six hours, black rather sensible shoes.

The team were being briefed by Pedro, the head waiter. But her eyes drifted to the busy kitchen—to Cucou, the head chef, who was laughing as he twirled fresh pasta like a skipping rope.

'Susie?'

'Sorry,' she said, and tore her gaze from the kitchen and back to Pedro.

Having been in Lucca for four weeks, working over Christmas and New Year and taking language courses during the week, Susie understood most of what Pedro said.

'We have a birthday. The cake is a surprise, so don't offer birthday wishes until then. And an engagement.'

He smiled, and so did the staff. The restaurant was on the walls of Lucca, and very elegant, and was often a chosen venue to celebrate precious times.

Pedro took them through the choices on the menu tonight. 'Cucou has prepared a ricotta and spinach ravioli with a walnut sauce...'

Susie found her gaze again drifting to the kitchen, to the slight frenzy taking place as they prepared for a busy night. It was a noisy, busy kitchen, and there were often shouts and sometimes bursts of laughter. She would give anything to be a part of that team…

Maybe one day…

Though not at Pearla's.

When she'd applied to work here, Susie had told the manager that her goal was to work in the kitchen, that she would do anything…

Anything.

Honestly, she'd be happy washing the dishes or peeling onions. Anything to be given a chance in the kitchen of this beautiful five-star restaurant. She didn't understand how they would let her loose on the clients, but not in the kitchen.

Actually, she did understand…

It was the reason she was here.

The really good Italian restaurants, even in England, required you to be fluent in the language to work in the kitchen.

She'd tried learning Italian at home, but her ex had rolled his eyes at her attempts. He hadn't understood how cooking wasn't just work, it was her passion.

She couldn't blame him for that. Not her parents, nor her sisters, and none of her friends understood the frustration she'd felt working as a cook in an Italian restaurant that was part of a large chain. Yes, she'd got to cook—but to a set menu. And it had involved a lot of heating up pre-prepared food, or adding the chain's salad dressing to a standard version of salad. She'd wanted to create her own. But first of all she knew she had to learn…

That was why she was in Lucca, taking lessons each weekday morning at the language school, and to pay her way she was waitressing whenever she got a shift.

'There's also a reduced bar menu,' Pedro was saying, and Susie felt tension in her jaw as the waiting staff were told the kitchen was short-staffed tonight.

Again.

It was common even at the most exclusive venues.

As the staff dispersed the first customers were starting to enter, but Susie held back.

'Susie…?' Pedro frowned.

'I could help,' she responded in Italian, but she saw the flicker of impatience on Pedro's face. He really didn't have time to listen to her stumble through her words, but surely her Italian had improved since she'd arrived?

'You do help,' he responded in English. 'I know it is irregular, asking you to deliver meals…' He gave a small shudder—food delivery was not usually an option, yet for certain guests exceptions were made! 'Gio—I mean, Signor Casadio—hasn't called yet, but if he does…'

'I meant in the…' Susie started, but then realised that Pedro had perhaps deliberately misunderstood. He knew she wanted a chance in the kitchen—she'd asked often enough!

'Susie…' Pedro sighed. 'Please, there are guests waiting.'

'Of course.'

Burning with a blush, she turned and approached her first table for the night. The guests were English, so no practising her language skills there.

It was a busy Friday night—so busy that her blonde hair started spilling out of its pins, and Pedro sent her to the cloakroom to fix it. In the mirror she saw her flushed face and, very rarely for Susie, the glitter of tears in her vivid blue eyes.

'Susie…?' Her name was being called as she came out. 'Kitchen!'

She felt a lurch of hope—but no, Cucou was putting the finishing touches to the birthday cake. It looked stunning, and had been made by the maestro himself.

She watched as Cucou wiped the edge of the plate.

'Perfect,' he said, more to himself than to Susie.

'It looks far too good to eat.'

Susie smiled, trying to make conversation, to be noticed by Cucou, but he wasn't really listening.

'It's my sisters' birthday today,' she said in Italian, as Pedro lit the candles on the cake. 'I'm sure their cake isn't—'

'Sister!' Pedro abruptly corrected Susie's Italian. '*Her* cake…'

The correction was unnecessary—for once Susie hadn't

mixed up her plurals or tenses or whatever. 'No, I meant *sisters*,' she said. 'They're twins.'

For the first time Cucou seemed interested in what Susie had to say. He actually asked her a question. 'Are they identical twins?'

It was the same question everyone asked. *Everyone!*

'Si,' Susie said.

And then she stood there, her lips a little pursed, as Pedro and Cucou proceeded to chat about some identical twin brothers who lived nearby. How, even if they came to Pearla's separately, they ordered the same meal, inadvertently dressed the same at times.

Typical, Susie thought as Cucou proudly lifted the cake, that the one time he'd spoken to her it was about her sisters.

Out they all walked, Cucou carrying the cake, and Pedro, Susie and the wine waiter behind with champagne, descending on the couple as the lucky birthday lady let out a cry of surprise and delight.

'How beautiful!' She smiled at her partner. 'You never forget.'

Gosh, she really was teary tonight, Susie realised. Only it wasn't the little party here that was causing her slight upset tonight. It was the little party undoubtedly taking place tonight back in London that had her feeling a little...

It was a feeling she would rather not acknowledge.

Anyway, there wasn't time—the delightful Signor Casadio had again made good use of his new phone and she was to take over his meal.

It had been New Year's Eve when he'd first rung the restaurant.

They had been so busy that all calls were going to the machine, and yet Pedro had been startled when he'd heard his voice and had immediately taken the call.

'Of course, Signor Casadio, it would be our pleasure to bring your meal over.'

Susie had frowned as Pedro had hung up the phone.

'I thought the restaurant didn't deliver?'

'We do when it's Gio Casadio asking,' Pedro had snapped, and then dashed off to speak with Cucou.

Susie had assumed the reason she'd been chosen to deliver to him was because she was new and could most easily be spared. Or possibly they'd been forced to acknowledge that she did have some culinary skills. Susie had been told she must cook the fresh pasta once she was there, serve the meal, grate the truffle and cheese, and suggest a wine from his collection.

'I'll be there for ages,' she'd protested.

'As long as is needed,' Pedro had insisted, seemingly prepared to take the shortfall in staff despite it being New Year's Eve.

And today it was still the case, because now, two weeks on, at around 8:00 p.m., Susie pulled on her trench coat and hastily wrapped a pretty scarf around her neck as Pedro came over with the bags.

'There's also a fruit compote and a light yoghurt.' Pedro dropped his voice. 'For his breakfast tomorrow...'

Susie's smile was more natural now as she nodded—she was loving how they were very discreetly taking care of this elderly man who had found himself home alone.

For reasons the staff would never discuss...

'Do you want to take your break straight after?' Pedro checked.

'Yes,' Susie said. 'Thank you.'

Susie wasn't just delivering a meal. No, she would be preparing coffee for the morning, putting blankets on the couches... just a couple of little jobs in an attempt to help the delightful Signor Gio Casadio.

Stepping out into the cool night, she walked along the gorgeous walls that surrounded the medieval town.

All her life she'd been walking on walls, Susie thought, though none as glamorous as these, treelined and wide. There were dogs being walked, cyclists... She walked on the correct side and looked out to the very old town, saw the Friday night lights and heard the music.

She felt as if she'd been born outside an exclusion zone.

Always on the edge of the real action and gazing longingly in.

Born thirteen months after stunning identical twins, Susie was very used to not turning heads and going unnoticed. Only it wasn't the old ladies beaming at the twins and not at her that had hurt...

Well, it had hurt a bit...

It wasn't even that she'd always felt like an extra at their joint birthday parties...though it had made her feel a bit invisible at times.

As she'd told Cucou, it was their birthday today, and she felt far away from the little party taking place at home. Far from any friends as she stood at the bottom of the career ladder, in a town where she didn't belong, and acknowledged the ache inside her.

Lonely.

She'd always felt it.

'Stop it!' Susie told herself and picked up her pace, refusing to feel sorry for herself.

She had a lot to be happy about. Once her Italian had improved, she would be off to Florence to do a cooking course. And before that her parents were coming to Lucca to spend some time here. Best of all, their visit would coincide with her own birthday.

As for men... With one relationship to her name—one that hadn't worked out—she was alone by choice.

Single and loving it—wasn't that how she was supposed to be feeling?

She came to the huge iron gates of Signor Casadio's vast property—far too big for an elderly man to manage alone.

At the urging of his housekeeper, Susie had arranged for some of the furniture to be moved, fashioning a kind of bedsit arrangement in the dining room, and she adored their chats as she prepared his meals in the attached butler's kitchen and served his dinner—even if he was rather maudlin.

Last night he'd wept with shame because his grandson had called and seen him in his robe...

'I hate this phone,' he'd sobbed. 'I hate it that Sev saw me like that.'

'It's okay,' Susie had said. 'I'm sure he didn't even notice…'

Now she walked up the path, past the fountains and stone benches and bare winter trees, looking up at the dark building and hoping that Gio had heeded her gentle prompts to shave and get dressed.

Walking beneath the portico, she headed around the vast building to the beautiful French windows that led off the dining room. She knocked on the glass and then pushed down the handle, her smile widening in delight when she saw that Gio was indeed dressed and shaved. Not only that, but spread out on the table were necklaces, earrings…the family jewels—and she rather hoped she knew why.

Perhaps Mimi would be getting a ring after all!

Mimi, his housekeeper, had walked out on New Year's Eve, Gio had told her. She wanted more.

At first, Susie had assumed she wanted more money—but no. She'd gleaned from Gio the fact Mimi wanted more acknowledgement…more respect.

And during her daily talks with Mimi, who was keeping an eye on Gio from a distance, via Susie, she'd found out that Mimi wanted to be more than Gio's secret mistress.

Susie had blushed at that.

Gio had told her a little about it too…

'Signor Casadio…' she said now, and smiled.

'Ah, Susie…'

He half stood, and she waved him to sit back down. And then, before Gio had time to inform her, she knew there was another person in the room.

'I have a guest,' Gio said, with a wry edge to his tone. 'Usually, I am informed prior to his arrival.'

'I wasn't aware I needed an invitation.'

The unexpected guest stepped forward.

He was still in his coat, his black hair a little damp from the rain, and had clearly just arrived. It had to be one of the grandsons—Gio had shown her photos of them, though they were all from a long time ago. Before Gio's family had been torn apart by a dreadful tragedy.

She knew she should be relieved that one of the grandsons was finally here.

And in a moment perhaps she would be both pleased and relieved that someone was here for Gio.

First, though, she must attune herself to his beauty.

Her skin had to cool from the blush that had emerged, her mouth had to work out how to move, and she somehow had to step down from the high alert her senses had been placed on.

No photo could truly have prepared her, for it wasn't just his physical beauty, but the dark eyes and the way, though he stood by a wall, he somehow commandeered the room.

'My grandson,' Gio informed her. 'Dante.'

'Oh,' Susie croaked, and then made the foolish mistake of attempting small talk while blindsided by beauty. 'The cheeky one!'

Her little quip dropped like a stone between them.

He wiped the smile from her face with a sharp frown.

It was then that she realised the foolishness of her words. Of talking to this imposing man in the terms Gio had used as he'd reminisced.

Dante was the younger one.

The cheeky one.

The funny one.

The loving one.

She wanted to die. Of all the ridiculous things to say! The impish, cheeky little boy that Gio had spoken about was no-where to be seen. This man's lips were almost scathing, with no trace of a smile, and his eyes were suspicious—as if she were some kind of intruder.

Susie rather wished the marble floor beneath her feet would open up and swallow her.

'Sorry.' She gave her head a shake, wishing she could re-tract what she'd said. She was about to flee to the kitchen, but Gio was speaking again.

'No doubt he is here in Lucca to check up on me.'

'I live here,' Dante said, removing his suspicious gaze from Susie as he addressed his grandfather.

'No,' Gio said, rummaging through the jewels in front of him. 'You live in Milan; you have a property here that stands mostly empty. You forgot about home a long time ago.'

'That's not true, Gio,' Dante said.

There was a slight husk to his voice, and he closed his eyes. Both weariness and pain flickered across his features, and then he spoke on.

'I was here at Christmas, and I'm here now.' His eyes opened then, and he stared at his grandfather. 'Where's Mimi?'

Gio gave no answer.

'I'll sort out dinner,' Susie said into the tense air, and was more than happy to go into the small butler's kitchen. Trying to pretend he didn't affect her so, she attempted to be polite. 'Are you staying to eat?'

'No,' Gio answered for him. 'I'm sure Dante has a date to keep.'

'Yes,' Dante said, his eyes still on his grandfather. 'I shall be staying for dinner.'

'Sure.'

Susie worked quickly, putting on water for the pasta before she'd even removed her scarf, then preparing Gio's Moka pot for the morning, filling it with water and coffee and putting it on the little burner.

She was just unbuttoning her coat when Dante came into the kitchen.

'What's going on?' he asked.

'Sorry?' She gave a nervous half-laugh.

'Why is he here alone?' he demanded in a harsh whisper.

She could hear the accusing tone…as if it were her fault.

'Why didn't you call me?'

'Call you?'

Under his vivid scrutiny she was perplexed by his question, and trying not to notice that his eyes were as brown as chocolate. A very dark chocolate… Certainly they weren't sweet.

'How?'

'You pick up the phone.' He snapped his gaze away and commenced walking around the small kitchen, opening cupboards. 'He's clearly sleeping downstairs; he shouldn't be here alone.'

'I agree, but—'

He wasn't waiting for explanations. Instead he peered into the rather empty fridge. 'There's barely any food in the place.'

And suddenly Susie, who rarely spoke up for herself, decided an exception might well be called for. 'He's *your* grandfather, not mine.' Her voice came out a little more harshly than she'd intended. 'I'm doing what I can.'

She took off her coat, hung it on a hook and felt his eyes drift over her attire and down to her black apron.

'Who *are* you?'

'I work at Pearla's. I'm here delivering an order,' Susie told him.

He didn't respond—just stalked off.

Her heart was thumping as she put the pasta into the water and sliced fresh olive bread, still warm from the oven. Her lips were tense, her shoulders too, as she listened to Dante questioning Gio.

'Where's Mimi?'

'At her sister's.'

'Why?' Dante demanded. 'When did this happen?'

Susie screwed her eyes closed, trying to stay out of it as Gio made some excuse about Mimi wanting a pay rise.

Dante clearly wasn't buying it. 'Then give her more.'

'Don't tell me what to do.'

'Are you living down here?' Dante asked. 'Sleeping in the dining room?'

'It's better to keep only the one room warm,' Gio retorted. 'We have to think of the planet, Dante.'

'Gio! I'm asking seriously, now. What the hell is going on? Sev told me that you were—'

And Susie could stay back no more.

'Ouch!' she yelped, and grabbed a tea towel and wrapped it around her hand. 'Ow…ow…'

Dante came to the door. His coat had been removed and he wore a charcoal-grey suit. His tie was slightly loose, but apart from that he looked dressed for both a stylish office and a photo shoot. Still, as gorgeous as he looked, he was far from sympathetic, and he looked impatiently at her wrapped hand, and then over his shoulder, as if to call for someone.

Clearly he was very used to summoning staff, and she watched as it dawned on him there was no one to summon.

'What's wrong?' Gio called out.

'Nothing, Gio,' she responded. 'Just a little cut.'

'Susie…?' At least Gio was concerned.

'It's fine, Gio,' she called to him. 'Dante's taking care of it.' Then she met his eyes and mouthed, *Don't!*

'What?'

'Don't mention him being in his robe yesterday,' she whispered.

He frowned, clearly about to turn away and leave her to bleed to death, but then with a slight hiss of frustration he put the conversation with his grandfather on hold and started opening the cupboards, eventually producing a little first-aid box.

'He's embarrassed,' she said in a low tone as he rummaged in the box for a sticking plaster, though he was clearly listening. 'He was devastated that Sev saw him in his dressing gown. I promised Gio that Sev wouldn't have noticed.'

'Okay.' He closed his eyes and inhaled deeply. 'He's dressed and shaved now though?'

'Yes.' She nodded, not wanting to break a confidence and choosing not to tell Dante that she'd gently suggested to Gio that he tidy himself up a bit. 'Just don't tell him Sev noticed.'

'Very well.' He nodded curtly. 'Let's sort out your hand.'

He took her wrapped hand and she noticed the contrast of his olive-skinned fingers against her pale forearm. His hands were cold, his fingers long, and an expensive navy watch face peeked from beneath his cuffs. She watched the sweep of the seconds ticking away, far more slowly than the beat of her heart. His touch was deft and firm, and the effect was both unexpected and unknown…

She watched tiny goosebumps appearing on her own flesh, and her nose seemed to twitch as it was treated to a gorgeous citrussy, spicy scent, as if it were trying to decipher whether it was his skin or his hair that smelt so divine.

Mute at his touch, she stood stock-still as he unwrapped the tea towel and exposed her hand.

'Where?' he asked, turning her hand in his own. 'Where's the cut?' He peered at her blemish-free hand and the clean white tea towel, then let out a mirthless laugh as he realised her ruse. 'Were you faking it?'

'Yes,' Susie said, only her voice sounded strange…as if her throat was inflamed. Actually, it felt a little as if it was. 'Go gently on him.'

He frowned and then, still holding her hand, he lifted his head and met her eyes. She knew from both Gio and Mimi a little of this fractured family's history, and that Dante's arrogance tonight was because he was scared for his grandfather. Gio had been right when he'd said that that Sev would turn up, or Dante. She hadn't really believed him—had privately thought that one dressing gown day wouldn't have his grandsons come running—yet here Dante was.

'He's a bit fragile,' Susie said.

'Yes.' He gave a nod. 'I'll go gently.'

'Good.'

'I'd better put a plaster on you, or he'll notice.'

'Indeed,' she agreed, because Gio was as sharp as a tack.

And so she stood, her heart thumping loudly, as those long-fingered hands peeled the backing off a little plaster.

He looked at her pale hands, as if considering where to place it. Then he chose her palm and positioned it over her life line. And as he lightly pressed it into her flesh he unknowingly answered a question that had perplexed her for months…

Why had she ended a seemingly fine two-year relationship?

Something had been missing.

She simply hadn't known what.

It had been okay…

But never had she felt this level of attraction.

Pure, unadulterated, physical attraction.

Attraction so immediate and intense that were he to kiss her now it would seem almost appropriate.

She looked to his mouth, and then down to her hand, still held by his, and somehow, rather than kiss his face off, she reclaimed it.

'Thank you,' she said.

'No problem.'

He, of course, seemed entirely unaware of the seismic shift taking place inside her.

'The sauce!' she yelped, certain it must have burnt dry. And yet as she dashed over she saw it was barely close to a simmer. 'I'll put the pasta on and then...' She was trying to recall Cucou's orders. 'Wine...' she said. 'A Sauvignon will pair nicely with...'

'Thank you,' he said, with a slightly wry edge.

He left the kitchen then.

Thank goodness!

Soon she was bringing out plates. They were both seated at the very large dining table and that pleased her, because before Gio had been eating on the sofa. He looked brighter for the company, Susie thought.

Dante must have been to the main kitchen, and was now pouring wine.

'Thank you,' he said as she put down the plates. As she went to offer cheese, he took the grater. 'I've got it,' he said, and grated cheese over Gio's dinner.

She tidied up the kitchen and filled the sink with hot soapy water, as she did every time, then fetched her coat, pleased to hear the low hum of conversation and even the sound of Gio's laughter as she pulled it on.

'I'd better get back...' she told them. 'The restaurant's really busy.'

'Is your hand okay?' Gio checked.

'It's fine.' She held up her palm and showed him the plaster. 'Just a tiny cut.'

She wrapped her scarf around her neck and stepped out

into the night, grateful for the chilly air, certain her face was on fire.

It was a relief to close the large gates behind her and step onto the walls.

She'd have liked to sit for a moment, just to relive that moment when time had seemed to slow down...when everything had stopped. To sit for a moment and dwell on a pompous, arrogant man who clearly loved his grandfather deeply.

Oh, she hoped he'd tread gently.

Thanks to Susie's acting skills Dante was treading gently.

'You said you spoke to Sev...?' said Gio warily, resuming the conversation once Susie had left.

Dante was grateful that she'd interrupted him. The last thing he wanted to do was embarrass his grandfather.

'What did Sev say?'

'That he can't make the ball.'

'Can you?'

'No.' Dante shook his head.

'But a Casadio has to be there.'

'Could you go?' Dante asked, wondering if this might be his way into a rather awkward conversation.

'No, that was where I proposed to your *nonna*...'

'I know,' Dante said. 'But...'

He wanted to point out that that had been a very long time ago, but he knew it wouldn't go down well, so he gave up on that suggestion.

'I really can't,' he said. 'I've got a big case that looks as if it's heading for court.'

'You mean a divorce?' His grandfather's lips curled slightly. 'Marriage is sacred.'

'If I was a criminal defence lawyer, would you blame me for my clients' sins?'

'I guess not.' Gio gave a reluctant laugh. 'Who's the client?'

'I'd rather not discuss it.'

Dante did not bring his work life to the dinner table, and although Gio would only have to glance at the news in a few weeks' time to find out who his grandson was representing, Dante would not be the one to tell him.

Gio had more immediate concerns. 'What else did Sev say?'

'Not much.'

'It's good to know you two occasionally talk.'

'Of course we speak.'

'Dante!' Gio rebuked. 'I might be old, but I am no fool. You two haven't spoken since…'

He paused, but they'd had this discussion many times over the years, so Dante was certain Gio had been about to refer to the accident.

'Grief affects people differently,' Dante said. 'Sev lost his wife and—'

'And you two fell out long before the accident.'

There was a clatter as Gio threw down his cutlery and broke the unspoken rule of the Casadio men left behind, venturing into territories that by mutual silent consent they all avoided.

'The night before Sev and Rosa married the two of you fought…' He got up and took down a photo, holding it out in front of Dante. 'You didn't get that scar from falling while celebrating! And Sev's hand was so swollen from hitting you, Rosa couldn't get his wedding band on. I didn't believe you then and I don't believe you now. You said something to Sev about Rosa, didn't you?'

Dante almost lost his poker face, inwardly startled by his grandfather's question, but he had trained himself well and kept his features impassive as he responded. 'I just asked him if he was certain that marriage was what he wanted.'

'Why?' Gio demanded.

Dante twisted the last of his pasta on his fork, even as the knife in his heart twisted tighter. Gio had loved Rosa, he was certain. There was no way he could tell him that two years prior to the wedding he'd slept with Rosa—nor that she'd told him she might be pregnant in an attempt to trap him and that night he'd been concerned Rosa might be playing the same tricks on Sev.

Instead, he offered a very diluted version of his thoughts around that time. 'I thought I was looking out for him.'

Gio made a small hissing noise that said what he thought of Dante's actions. 'You should never come between a man and his choice of bride.'

'I know that now!' Dante said tartly. 'Thanks for the late advice.'

To his surprise there was a small burst of laughter from Gio, but then his face flicked back to serious. 'You should have come to me.'

Dante responded with a thin smile.

'Did Sev tell you I was looking unkempt?' asked Gio.

'What?' Dante feigned a frown.

'Dante...?'

Had it not been for Susie he would have answered honestly—after all, Gio had invited him to speak. But he looked at his proud grandfather and heeded her plea to tread gently.

'I have no idea what you are talking about. What do you mean "unkempt"?'

'I didn't know it was a video call. Sev caught me at the wrong time.'

'Okay.' Dante thought for a moment before he responded. 'You're looking very smart now. Are you feeling better?'

'Somewhat.' He nodded. 'Susie said if I shaved and put on my best clothes I might feel like going for a walk...'

'Did you?'

'No, but I did take out the jewellery...'

'So I see.'

He glanced to the coffee table, at the necklaces, bracelets and rings all strewn across it.

'What else have you been doing?'

'Not much.'

'Can you tell me what's wrong?'

'Like you, there are things I would prefer not to discuss.' Gio moved the topic on. 'How long are you home for?'

'I'm here all weekend. So I can do whatever needs doing.'

'The dishes tonight?'

'I can give it a go.' Dante's smile was wry. 'I'll sort out a temporary housekeeper tomorrow.'

'I don't need that.' He looked at Dante. 'If you want to help, then pay a visit to the winery. I haven't been able to get there...' He frowned. 'I know you don't want anything to do with the place, and I'm sure you and your brother will sell it the second I'm gone, but while I am alive—'

'Gio,' Dante cut in. 'I care about the place.'

'How?' Gio asked. 'How can you care for it from Milan?'

'Okay, I'll go,' Dante agreed, even though it was the last place he wanted to visit.

The helicopter had taken off from there, and it was there where everyone had gathered, waiting for news, or confirmation, watching the fire in the hills. Even the drive there was hell now, winding past churches where weddings and funerals had taken place.

'What else can I do?' he asked.

'I have to sort out the jewels. They haven't been cleaned and I—'

'I'll take them to someone in Milan,' Dante cut in.

But Gio instantly declined. 'No! I want them to be taken care of here, where I had them made.'

'Fine.' Dante nodded. 'Gio, can I ask if Mimi is coming back?'

'I don't know,' Gio said.

Dante watched as his grandfather fought with himself, perhaps wanting to talk, yet refusing to.

'You said you would do the dishes,' he said eventually.

'Sure.'

Dante collected the two plates and took them through to the butler's kitchen. Not completely useless, he went to put them in the dishwasher—but then he saw the sink filled with soapy water.

She'd filled the sink for Gio, he realised.

That was kind of her.

She *was* kind, he realised.

For the first time in ages...perhaps since university...he did the dishes, rinsed the glasses, then walked back to the dining room that had somehow turned into his grandfather's bedsit.

'Are you going?' Gio asked.

'I think so.'

'I was going to watch a film…'

God help me, Dante thought as he sat on the sofa with a large brandy watching Sophia Loren, ever beautiful, in black and white.

'Your *nonna* loved this.'

'I know.'

Because Gio had repeatedly told him.

His gaze drifted from the screen and he noticed the changes since Christmas: more photos had been moved here, as well as the television and his grandfather's old gramophone. Most confusing, though, they were seated on the heavy couches that belonged in the formal lounge, and there were blankets folded on one.

'How did the couches get in here?' Dante asked.

'Susie,' Gio said.

'How?' Dante asked. 'She's tiny.'

But Gio didn't answer. He was gazing at the voluptuous Sophia, obviously thinking of Nonna.

Dante's mind drifted to the rather slender waitress who had somehow rescued the night.

'You should have spoken to me first,' Gio said suddenly, pulling him from his thoughts.

Dante looked at the screen and saw the film was over. 'When?' He frowned.

'If you were worried about Rosa, you should have come to me rather than go to your brother.'

'Leave it, Gio…' Dante warned.

Oh, it really was time to go.

He stood and retrieved his coat. 'I'll come over tomorrow, before going to the winery.'

'Dante, please…you should have come to me.'

'Gio…' His eyes briefly closed in weariness, but before he could go on Gio spoke again.

'I had my reservations about the marriage, too.'

Dante was sure he'd misheard, and was almost scared to move in case he reacted too much only to find out he'd got things wrong. He was a master of the impassive, yet it took him a full second to wipe the flash of shock from his features before meeting Gio's eyes.

'But you loved Rosa!'

'I love Sev,' Gio said. 'And because of that I tried to care for Rosa. But I was sure her family were trying to get their hands on my winery.'

'Did you ever share those reservations with Sev?'

'Never.' Gio shook his head. 'Only now—only with you.'

'Good,' Dante said. 'Because as it turned out he loved her.' He pointed to his scar. 'It's better that you didn't say anything. When I questioned the marriage, it broke us.'

'You told him you thought her family had pushed for the marriage?'

'I suggested it as a possibility,' Dante agreed.

'What made you suspicious?'

That he would not be revealing to Gio. His grandfather had been a one-woman man, and had long disapproved of Dante's rather casual ways. He didn't need to know that he'd once slept with Rosa…nor the rest of the sordid tale.

And Sev must never know.

'Just a hunch,' Dante settled for saying. 'I was studying property mergers…succession laws.' He shrugged. 'Goodnight.' He kissed his grandfather's cheeks. 'I'll see you tomorrow. Let's hope for a better day.'

He walked along the walls, his collar up against the cold, and called Sev.

'He's okay,' Dante said to Sev's message bank. 'But Mimi seems to have left. Gio won't discuss it, of course, but there's a girl who's been helping…'

He paused, thinking how terse he'd been with Susie. How tonight could have gone so differently had she not faked a small injury. And on this dark night his face moved into a slight smile.

'I'm staying for the weekend; I'll hopefully know more tomorrow.'

Actually, he hoped to know more tonight.

Dante walked further along the treelined walls, loathing being back more with every step, for there were memories everywhere…

'Dante!'

He could almost hear Rosa calling to him, the sound of her heels as she ran to catch him, and he recalled his annoyance that two years on from their one-night stand she still tried to leap on him when he was home from university.

'Dante, please.'

He walked faster, but it was as if the past was chasing him tonight.

'We need to talk.'

Rosa had grabbed at his arm, but he'd shaken her off.

'There's nothing to talk about,' he'd told her. *'Seriously, Rosa. Stay the hell away.'*

'Dante, you have to listen to me…' she'd urged. *'There's to be an announcement tonight. Sevandro and I are getting engaged.'*

On a hot summer's day he'd felt the blood in his veins turn to ice. The music festival had been on, and he'd been able to hear the music from the valley beneath pounding, to see the revellers everywhere, and somehow he had known in that moment that his life would never be the same…

'No.' He'd shaken his head. *'Sev's never so much as mentioned you.'* She didn't even call him by the name family and friends used. *'No.'*

'It's sudden.' Rosa had nodded. *'Sevandro spoke to my father yesterday. Dante, please, he cannot know about us.'*

'There never was an "us",' Dante had reminded her—as he had many times before.

Usually she begged him to reconsider, but on that day she'd agreed.

'It was a one-off.' She'd taken a deep breath, blinking back fake tears. *'Sevandro can never know. You mustn't tell him.'*

'You don't get to dictate our conversations.'

Then he'd looked at the woman whom he knew had tried to get him to commit by using the oldest trick in the book.

'Are you telling Sev that you're pregnant?'

'Don't be so personal!'

'Personal?' Dante had checked. *'This* is *personal—Sev's my brother.'*

'And your brother is in love with me,' Rosa had said, her voice defiant rather than pleading, no sign of tears. *'Sevandro loves me. If you tell him what once took place, such a long time ago...'* She'd shrugged. *'Take it from me, Dante, you will lose your brother.'*

Perhaps he should have listened to Rosa, Dante thought now as he came to Pearla's and leant on the archway nearby.

While he hadn't told Sev what had taken place between himself and Rosa, he'd tried to broach the topic. He'd used the same excuse he'd given his grandfather tonight, only with a slight twist. He'd told Sev he was studying family law.

To no avail.

On the eve of the wedding he'd been a little more direct, implying that Rosa was trying to force his hand, and that if Rosa was telling him she was pregnant...

He hadn't even finished speaking before Sev had knocked him out cold. Dante would wear the scar of that attempt at conversation for ever.

And Rosa had been right.

He'd lost his brother...

'Ciao, Susie...'

The sound of the name hauled him from dark memories. Glancing over, he saw Susie walking out of Pearla's. Her coat was open. She tied her scarf, then stood opening and closing her umbrella, which seemed to want to invert...

'Susie?'

She put her umbrella up before looking at him. 'We meet again.'

'And not by chance,' he said. 'I would like to apologise...'

CHAPTER TWO

'*SUUU-ZEEE...*'

Somehow Dante made her name sound sexy.

She'd known it was him before she'd even looked over, and her broken umbrella had felt easier to control than the flurry of butterflies escaping in her chest.

She gave him her best version of brisk as her umbrella snapped up into an imperfect shape. 'We meet again,' she said.

'And not by chance.'

Oh, he was actually here to see her!

'I would like to apologise.'

'Apologise?' Susie checked, so stunned to see him waiting for her that she forgot to be shy. 'You mean for being rude earlier?'

'Yes,' he agreed, and she thought he almost smiled.

She'd heard of people taking your breath away, but he took more than that, and for a second she wasn't capable of words, or even of walking off. She was choosing to prolong the encounter, only she did not know what to say.

He solved that with a question. 'How's the "cut" on your hand?'

'Much better.' She held up her unblemished palm, the plaster gone. 'I heal quickly.'

'You do.' He nodded.

It was the oddest moment of her life. He was looking at her, and the conversation was pleasant, yet she actually recalled that moment where he'd touched her hand, and how his touch had made her heart seem to flutter in her throat.

It felt the same now.

He couldn't have noticed, of course, for she just stood there, a little stunned at her own thoughts, as Dante spoke on.

'I overreacted. Sev had called me and I was expecting…' He gave a helpless shrug. 'I don't even know what I was expecting.'

'I get it.' She nodded. 'It's nice that you came to check on him.'

'Always,' he said. 'I'll stay for the weekend and try and sort a few things out for him. It's kind of you to have helped. Also, we need to discuss money.'

'We don't.' Susie flushed.

'You're English,' he said. 'So I know discussing money is painful for you.'

She laughed, just a little bit, but it was enough that she relaxed a little and could look him in the eye. 'Seriously, there's no need.'

Her lips pressed closed. She did not want to reveal the arrangement she had with Mimi.

'You're clearly doing more than just dropping off meals.'

'I'm not.'

'So you get the morning coffee ready for all your clients. Fill the sink? Move furniture?'

'No,' she admitted. 'But I really don't do much.' She gave a small shake of her head. 'I don't think Gio would appreciate this conversation.'

'Perhaps not, but *I* would appreciate knowing what is going on.' He relented a little. 'I want to help him, too.'

'I know…' She hesitated, not wanting to break her new friend's confidence. 'Look, I just do a little here and there… not much at all. I think…' She looked at his pale face, his dark eyes, and for a second all thought stopped.

'You think…?' he persisted.

'That I should go,' Susie said. 'It's late…'

Somehow he made her want to be indiscreet. And not just with Gio's secrets. He took the cold air away; he made the night somehow shiny.

'It was a long shift,' she added.

'Of course.' He nodded. 'Where do you live?'

She pointed in the direction of her apartment.

'I'll say goodnight, then. Again, I am sorry for earlier.'

He gave her a nod and walked off, and Susie stood there, a little unsure what to do. Her apartment might be where she'd pointed, but her favourite ice-cream shop was in the direction Dante was headed!

And after a very long shift she wasn't missing her treat.

She gave him a small head start and then followed him along the pathway, hoping he wouldn't notice...

Dante didn't notice her at first.

It wasn't her clumpy shoes that had him turning around. More that he turned to catch another glimpse of the woman, Susie, who been the sole reason he'd smiled a few times today.

And then he saw her—a few steps behind him.

He frowned, and got back to walking, but he could hear her footsteps now, so he turned again.

'I'm not following you,' she told him. 'I like to get an ice cream at the end of my shift.' She'd caught up with him now. 'I think about it all night.'

'Do you?'

'Yes.'

'What flavour?'

'I don't know yet,' Susie told him as they took the steps down from the walls. 'I'm trying to work my way through the list, but I adore the red velvet.'

'Then get the red velvet, surely?'

'I want to try new things. My ice-cream-at-night habit only began when I started working at Pearla's.'

'When was that?'

'I've been there a month now. I started a week after I arrived.'

She told him she was here studying the language.

'And I'm off to Florence soon, to do a cookery course, but I have to be fluent to do that... I'm going for total immersion.' She looked over to him then. 'I ought to be speaking to you in Italian.'

'*Lieto di accontentarla,*' he said, but then he saw her slight frown and translated. 'Happy to oblige.'

'Thank you, but please, no…' She drooped. 'It's nearly midnight and my brain's a bit fried.' She peered over at him. 'I'm sorry, too.'

'For what?'

'I was mean.'

'When?'

'When I said about Gio being *your* grandfather…'

'He *is* my grandfather—and you were right to stick up for yourself. That's not being mean.'

'It felt mean.'

'Not in my world,' he said, but she wasn't listening.

He saw her eyes actually light up—clearly the ice cream had come into view. Her chosen venue was popular, because even this late there were people lining up in the street.

'Do you want one?' she offered.

Dante was about to decline, and tell her he wasn't a fan of ice cream, but he'd already been rude enough.

'Let me get these.'

'No, no…'

'It's an ice cream, Susie,' he pointed out. 'What flavour?'

'Oh, God!' She looked at the board, as anxious as if he'd demanded the answer to some impossible mathematical equation. 'Pistachio,' she said. 'Actually, no… Espresso…' She shook her head.

'Red velvet?' he checked, and she gave a resigned nod.

'I'm so predictable,' she sighed as he ordered. 'What are you getting?'

'*Amareno,*' Dante said. 'Sour cherry.'

Soon they stood with their chosen ice creams. He could see her eyes on his.

'Thank you,' she said.

'You're welcome.'

'Well, I'm that way…' She gestured with her head. 'Goodnight.'

'*Buona notte.*'

* * *

Oh, my...

Her brain certainly wasn't too fried to appreciate being wished goodnight in silky Italian by someone so delicious.

Susie walked off with her treat and a whole barrage of new sensations, and wished Gio had warned her how devastatingly handsome his youngest grandson was...

'Susie?'

She was barely two steps into her journey home when he halted her.

'Can I ask one question?'

She turned around and stood a short distance apart from him. He was beautiful in the rain. 'You can ask...although whether or not I'll answer...'

'How did you move the furniture?'

She let out a small laugh and then beneath her umbrella, ice-cream cone in hand, she flexed her arm. 'I'm deceptively strong.'

He nodded, but instead of leaving it was Susie who now prolonged things. 'I also have a question.'

'Go ahead.'

'You said I should have called you. How?'

'You pick up your phone.' He shrugged and stared back at her for what felt like a full moment.

A moment during which her toes curled in her clumpy shoes and she gripped her umbrella as if it were a pole that might secure her against walking towards him.

'But I didn't know who you were...where you worked, or...'

'It would have taken two minutes to find out.'

'Please...' she retorted, disbelieving him. 'Goodnight, Dante.'

This time she walked away, but he'd conjured up so many questions that he'd made her giddy.

Her ice cream was especially delicious, even if it wasn't sour cherry, and it was completely devoured by the time she pushed in the code for the vast door of her apartment block.

She collapsed her umbrella and left it in the stand, then

climbed the many steps and opened up her door, catching sight of her reflection in the large hall mirror as she did so.

Her face was flushed and her eyes were glittery and she looked as if she'd been very thoroughly kissed. In fact, she was breathing as if she had been, and she couldn't quite blame the stairs!

Her flatmates were either asleep or out, so Susie took herself to her bedroom and flopped down on her bed.

Bewildered.

More than that, fascinated.

She started scrolling through her phone.

Yes, it took less than two minutes for her to find him, but even so… As if this suave, accomplished attorney would have called some lowly waitress back. As if her message would even have been passed on.

Feeling curious, and oddly liberated, she dialled the number of his law firm.

'Hello…' She spoke into a machine. 'My name's Susie Bilton. I'd like to speak to Dante Casadio.' She swallowed as she said what she might have said had she considered calling him about Gio. 'It's a personal matter.'

She rang off and spent the next few moments looking at images on her phone. Staring at the many, many beauties who had accompanied this man on many, many glamorous nights out.

As if he'd even get her message!

Dante quickly relieved himself of his ice cream at the request of a beggar.

'Please,' Dante said, handing it to him. 'Enjoy.'

He was soon at his residence, at the top of Corso Garibaldi.

Usually he would have alerted his part-time housekeeper that he was coming home. Perhaps that was the reason for the unlived-in air as he stepped into his immaculate home. His case was still in the entrance hall, where he'd dropped it off before heading straight to Gio's. There were no lights on…no drinks or food left out…

Not home.

This had been an empty shell when he'd bought it. Rather like himself. Over the years it had been restored to its original glory, yet it brought him no joy, no peace. If anything, the more beautiful it got, the more it reminded him of how hollow he felt. And now it served just as a reminder of the silent commitment he had made to keep a residence here as long as Gio lived.

After that…

Dante was far from naïve, and he knew Gio was getting on. Of course he worried about him. But there'd always been Mimi…

He knew Mimi was not just the housekeeper, but had gone along with Gio. He always gave notice before he went over, and never commented on the many little things he noticed.

But now clearly his grandfather was unhappy, and Dante knew he had to address it.

How?

He went to the sink and washed his hands, sticky from the ice cream. His intention to garner more information had proved futile. While he admired Susie's discretion, it irked him that she'd told him nothing.

If he saw her tomorrow then he would speak to her again. Directly this time.

He'd ask what she knew about the situation, and not get waylaid with language schools, cooking courses in Florence or ice-cream flavours…

Dante rarely got waylaid.

Susie had called herself predictable.

Oh, no.

Susie was far from that.

CHAPTER THREE

Susie awoke to the bleep of her phone and ignored it.

Then her flatmate Juliet's violin practice commenced, so she buried her head under the covers. Especially when Juliet's bow, or whatever it was called, kept missing certain notes.

The same notes.

Over and over.

She shared the apartment with Juliet, who was English, and Louanna, who was a local.

It was Saturday, and she was determined to have a lie-in. There were no Italian classes at the weekends and nowhere she needed to be until she met Mimi later this morning.

Should she have told Dante that Mimi was giving her daily private Italian lessons so that she could keep an eye on Gio from a distance?

No, because Gio didn't want his grandsons knowing about his relationship with Mimi.

Dante...

He dropped into her consciousness as she tried to sink back into sleep.

What would he say if he knew that Mimi had walked out on Gio because she was tired of being passed off as his house-keeper?

Surely he already knew?

Those knowing brown eyes wouldn't miss much.

Susie lay on her side, her own eyes determinedly closed, and yet he refused to exit the stage of her mind. If anything, the spotlight shone brighter upon him, highlighting the scar above one of those knowing eyes.

Gio had shown her a photo of Sev and Rosa's wedding, so she knew the injury was from then. And Mimi had told her how fractured the brothers' relationship was now.

She recalled how he'd frowned as he'd pulled back the tea towel on her hand, and his slight smile as he'd realised there was no cut… How her skin had turned into goosebumps and she'd held her breath as he'd attended to her fake wound…

Louanna's rather loud voice cut into her lovely sleepy recall, as she informed anyone who wanted to know that coffee was ready, then thankfully the violin stopped.

Susie had given up on sleep now and reached for her phone, delighted to see she had a message in the little Sisters Group they shared—a short message with a link attached.

So excited!

Frowning, muzzy from sleep, she was about to click on the link—it looked like an estate agent's advert—when the message was deleted.

It took her a moment to realise that she'd been sent the message by mistake.

It happened now and then—and it hurt every time. This message perhaps more than most. She'd already guessed from a couple of things her mum had said that the twins were thinking about sharing a flat.

The rapidly deleted message only confirmed it.

She could hear Juliet and Louanna chatting and laughing in the kitchen, and even though they were lovely Susie felt a bit of an outsider.

It wasn't just the fact that she was a temporary housemate that kept her a little apart from them. Music was her flatmates' energy and their main topic of conversation.

It reminded her of when she was younger, listening to her sisters chatting in the next room.

Gosh, she'd felt left out.

Every night it had sounded as if there was a little party going on, with her listening as Celia and Cassie chatted and giggled or, in later years, cried about a broken heart or whatever…

She was going to go out for breakfast, Susie decided, and speak Italian all day.

No exceptions!

She pulled on some thick black tights and a black jumper, and then wriggled into a burnt orange corduroy pinafore that added a blaze of colour, determined to cheer up and stop being so mopey.

'*Buongiorno!*' Susie breezed into the kitchen.

'Good morning,' Louanna smiled. 'How was…?'

'Ah-ah!' Susie halted her with her hand. '*Italiano.*'

Louanna obliged, telling her that her dress was very colourful and she had a passion for orange. Or something along those lines. Then she asked if she was working tonight.

Susie affirmed that she was, and said that, yes, the restaurant had been busy last night.

'Do you know Mimi?' Louanna asked, as if surprised. 'I saw you with her in a café.'

'Yes.' Susie nodded. It wasn't just her lack of vocabulary that had her holding back from mentioning Gio. She didn't think Gio would like having his personal life discussed, so she'd never mentioned the home deliveries. 'She's helping with my Italian.'

Louanna turned to Juliet. 'Mimi was once a very famous opera singer.'

'Wow…' Juliet said. 'I love opera.'

And back to talking about music they went…

The rain had dried up, though Susie's trench coat and scarf were still required as the weather was crisp. Still, the sky was the palest blue, and the clearest it had been since her arrival, and it was wonderful to wander through the laneways.

Unexpectedly, she had fallen in love with Lucca.

She meandered through the ancient cobbled streets, just drinking in her surroundings.

She went past the gorgeous opera house, where Mimi had once performed… She would love to go to the opera. It was something she'd never considered before, but here in the birthplace of Puccini it was everywhere.

All roads seemed to lead to the Piazza dell'Anfiteatro, a public square in the heart of Lucca, and she entered it through one of the archways. It was more like a circle, surrounded by tall pastel buildings—an amphitheatre where gladiators had fought. Now, where once the audience had watched on, it was cafés and restaurants, umbrellas and tables.

Wandering around the perimeter, she was soaking it all in while trying to select where to stop for breakfast.

'Hey…'

Susie stilled, the deep voice causing her to startle, and she looked over to the stunning sight of Dante, seated at a café table, sipping coffee and looking rather too gorgeous for a lazy Saturday. He wore a black jumper that must be cashmere, and even dressed casually he looked groomed and elegant. And he was beckoning for her to go over.

Susie went.

'We meet again,' she said, and smiled.

'Everyone meets here,' he informed her.

'How was the sour cherry?' Susie asked.

'Like sour cherries,' he replied, and gestured to his table. 'Would you like to join me?'

'So long as you're not going to interrogate me about Gio,' she said. But even though he made no promises not to do so, she took a seat.

'I was just about to order.' He signalled to the waiter.

'Is there a menu?'

'No need. I was just getting pastries, bread…'

Susie frowned. 'For all you know I might be gluten intolerant.'

'Then you shouldn't have had that cone last night,' Dante said, then conceded, 'I'll ask for a menu.'

'It's fine.'

Gosh, he was confident. Or perhaps it was just the way things were done here, she mused as he ordered for both of them.

The waiter commented on the gorgeous morning and Dante nodded. Then he attempted to draw Dante into conversation and said how nice it was to see him back…

'Thank you.'

He was rather terse with the waiter, which Susie thought was a bit of a red flag, so she pursed her lips as he shut down the conversation, but when the waiter had gone she spoke up.

'He's just making conversation,' she said. 'Believe me, I know how hard that can be.'

'I went to school with him,' Dante said. 'He was nosey even then.'

'Oh!' She gave a half laugh. 'Sorry. I thought you were being rude. I didn't know there was history.'

'There is history on every corner. You wait—we shall soon be the talk of the town.'

'I'd love to be the talk of the town,' Susie said, and sighed. 'It's my ambition.'

He offered a polite smile at her little joke, but then frowned. 'You're not joking, are you?'

'I'm not,' she agreed. 'I'm sure I'd soon tire of it, but…' She smiled at the very gorgeous Dante. 'Just once.'

'It's actually quite easy to achieve here,' he said. Taking a bread roll, he tore it, then dipped it in honey. 'Aren't we supposed to be speaking in Italian?'

'Not on a Saturday,' Susie lied, forgetting her earlier vow. She wanted to concentrate on the conversation, not on the language. She didn't want to be stilted with Dante. 'It's nice to have a day off—at least from classes.'

'Well, I'm glad to have caught you. I did want to thank you.'

'You already have.' She shrugged.

'Susie, I know about Gio and Mimi. At least, I think I do.'

'What about them?' she asked.

* * *

Dante admired the fact that she remained discreet.

'I've long since guessed she is more than a housekeeper.'

Still Ms Discreet said nothing.

'Gio doesn't know I know.'

She met his eyes then, and he saw more than blue. He saw the curiosity that danced in them, and he saw the softness of her lips as they asked an unrelated question.

'Sev's the older brother?'

'The serious one,' he said, watching her blush as she perhaps recalled her comment last night. 'What about you?' he asked, those blue eyes steering him off track and forgetting his intention to be more direct.

'Me?' Susie checked.

'Do you have siblings?'

'Two sisters. They're—' She abruptly halted and Dante couldn't fathom why.

'Older or younger?' he probed.

'Older.'

'You're the baby?'

'Hardly.'

'I meant the favourite.'

'I wouldn't go that far...' She rolled her eyes. 'You're an attorney?'

He nodded. 'My speciality is family law. According to Gio, I do the devil's work.'

'Oh!' Her eyes widened in slight surprise. 'You must hear some tales.'

'I try not to.'

'How could you avoid it?'

'We have a large practice. I deal with the division of assets. Passing the tissues is not my forte.'

She laughed at that, and he found that he smiled as they chatted.

And not about Gio.

He saw now the honey tint to her pale blonde hair and noticed the pretty curl of her fair lashes. She wore the coat she'd had on last night and the same scarf. Because they were seated outside, he did not know how she was dressed beneath.

He recalled her slight figure as she'd removed her coat last night. And he remembered, because he'd held her hand when she'd pretended to cut it, the scent of her hair.

Dante found himself in an unexpected guessing game, wondering not just about the clothes beneath the coat, but also about what colours they might be. She'd been in her uniform last night, and today he found himself searching for clues.

It was something he did at work, of course, and in the courtroom at times—trying to fathom the person he was about to question or challenge.

Only this wasn't work.

And Susie was nothing like the women he dated—sophisticated women who knew that his black heart remained closed and that the only place Dante Casadio lasted was in the bedroom.

He caught her gaze and, to his own surprise, when she smiled so did he.

He didn't usually.

Smile.

And if his phone hadn't beeped he might have studied a little more deeply the shades of blue in her eyes.

'Damn…' He glanced at his phone. '*Scusi*, I have to…'

'Of course.'

He left the table to take the call and she sat there, looking out to the square. She felt the waiter looking over, so resisted checking her reflection in her phone.

Gosh, this morning felt thrilling.

She had to meet Mimi soon, and usually she loved their hour together, but this morning she was tempted to cancel… just for more moments with Dante…

'Sorry about that.'

His voice, though it was now familiar, still made her jump.

'It's fine.'

* * *

'No, it's not.'

He let out a low, wry laugh and took a sip of coffee, and then he looked up at her eyes, and then down to the full lips that had stayed closed when he'd pushed for information on his grandfather. Somehow he simply knew she was discreet.

'I have a client... My last words to him were, "Don't contact your wife." Hah!'

'I'm assuming he didn't take your advice?'

'He did not.'

He reached for his coffee, to take another sip, yet even as he lifted the small cup he replaced it.

Was it her patient silence that gave him pause, or was it that she didn't demand information?

Or was it something about sitting beneath the umbrellas in Piazza dell'Anfiteatro on this gorgeous Saturday with her gentle conversation and beauty that had his guard down a touch.

'He got drunk last night and wrote a six-page letter admitting his failings, offering to change.'

'Oh!' She gave a small giggle.

'And he mailed it.' He hissed in annoyance. 'If he'd sent an email I could at least have read it.'

'Do you read a lot of love letters?'

'Only if I'm being paid to,' he said, and now she really laughed.

The bigger surprise for Dante was that he wanted to tell her more.

Without names or identities, of course...

Perhaps that was it, he pondered.

Susie was from England.

After this weekend he would never see her again.

'I told him yesterday to stay back,' he went on. 'I knew it could only cause trouble. People say and do things they regret when they're upset.'

'I don't.'

Her response caused him to frown, his eyes narrowing, and he leant forward a little in an invitation for her to elaborate.

'I just go quiet.'

'In relationships. Or…?' Dante knew he was fishing.

'In everything, really. Work, family…'

Fishing did not suit Dante. He moved to being direct.

'Are you in a relationship?'

'No.' She gave a tight shrug. 'Not any more.'

God, but he wanted her to elaborate. Instead, she asked about him.

'You?'

'I don't do relationships.'

She lifted her eyes to his and he knew now was the time to make his position absolutely clear.

'I don't get involved with my dates.'

'How can you date and not get involved?'

'Because they are all very short-lived.'

'So, you've never been serious with anyone?'

'Never,' he told her. 'Nor will I ever be.'

'Wow… I'm sure you've broken a lot of hearts.'

'Oh, no.' He shook his head. 'A good time is had by all,' he said, in a low, silky voice. 'So long as both parties agree. Dinner…a nice night…'

'Hey,' the waiter said, bringing out another coffee, his smile aimed now at Susie. 'I didn't catch the name of your English friend…'

'Susie.'

Dante's smile was tight. He loathed the implication—but of course there was. Because he'd never sat in this square with a woman. He'd never brought his dates here. Even as a teenager he'd known to keep all that well away from home, where gossip flared and no forbidden deed went unnoticed.

And so he cut the gossip straight off. 'She has been helping out with Gio.'

'Ah…'

Susie felt the relegation from casual coffee date to Gio's housekeeper or nurse.

She'd thought they'd been flirting—just a bit—but it

dawned on her then. The real reason Dante had been hoping they'd catch up. He probably wanted to ask her if she'd be Gio's temporary housekeeper.

No, she did not want to be on Dante's payroll.

Her heart sank.

Of course someone as suave and utterly gorgeous as Dante wasn't going to be seeing her in any way other than as an employee.

'Susie, I was wondering—'

'Please don't,' she broke in. 'The answer's no.'

Frowning with curiosity he met her eyes, as if he hadn't expected Susie to address their situation so boldly.

'I'm very happy at the restaurant.'

'Sorry?'

'You were going to offer to pay me to check in on Gio, or...'

'No.' Dante shook his head. 'That wasn't my question.'

'Good.' She let out a small laugh. 'I adore him, but...'

'I get it.' He took a sip of coffee.

'No,' Susie said—because it wasn't that she didn't want to help Gio, and frankly she needed any work she could get. 'I think of Gio as a friend. I like our chats and helping out. I don't want to get paid for it.'

'Susie, that wasn't my question.'

'What was it, then?' she asked, certain it would be something about Gio.

'Would you like to go for dinner tonight?'

'Dinner?' Susie frowned. 'To talk about your grandfather?'

'Oh, no.'

She swallowed. The café's heaters must have suddenly been turned up, because she was boiling beneath them. Truly. She wanted to fling off her coat or tip a bucket of ice over her head.

Never had she been so boldly propositioned.

Never had she thought she might be.

And certainly not by this most sexy, gorgeous man, who somehow turned her on with nothing more than a touch.

It startled her how badly she wanted to lift her eyes to his and nod.

For him to take her there.

Wherever 'there' was.

She'd almost forgotten to breathe, Susie realised as she dragged in a long breath. And she wished…oh, she wished she was brave enough to say yes. To just get up from this table and be led to his bed.

Only she'd never been brave in that department.

And, in truth, she didn't really like sex.

At least, she hadn't to date.

'I'm actually working tonight,' she said.

'That's okay.'

'I'd love to, but I do have work, and if I don't give enough notice…'

'Susie.' He smiled, and she wished she could smile so easily when rejected. 'It's fine.'

No, it wasn't fine.

It was Susie who had said no, and yet she was the one fighting not to pout.

'It's not that. I…' What could she say? That she wanted to?

She looked at his eyes, which seemed to draw her to unknown places. She reached for her purse. 'I ought to get going.' She wasn't lying. 'I have to…' She paused and went a little bit pink. 'I'm meeting a friend. Juliet,' she added needlessly. 'And I'm running late.'

He waved away her offer to pay half and she felt his eyes on her as she left.

'Susie!' Mimi was in an absolute panic. 'Dante is here.'

Her violet eyeshadow was bright, but her signature eyeliner was absent, and though she still cut a fabulous dash, she was a little dishevelled.

'*Si?*' Susie said, and pointedly switched to Italian, telling Mimi she had met him last night. She didn't mention she'd just left his table. Oh, and that he'd offered her a night of passionate sex.

'*Avocatto!*'

She frowned, thinking of avocados, and then caught herself

and laughed at her own mistranslation—Mimi was bemoaning the fact that he was an attorney.

'He will think I am after Gio's money and the winery. He and Sev will do all they can to dissuade him...'

'Mimi!' Susie slowed down the rather frantic pace. 'Surely the brothers know you're not really his housekeeper?' She looked at probably the most glamorous octogenarian on earth. 'You were an opera singer...'

'A lot of artists fall on hard times.' Mimi sighed. 'Well, that's what we told the boys.'

'Boys?' Susie giggled at Mimi's description of Dante and his older brother, but then checked herself. Mimi really was distressed.

'We told them that when I first moved in,' she said, then halted, her face suddenly brightening.

Susie quickly found out why.

'Dante!' Mimi was suddenly all smiles. *'Buongiorno!'* She switched to English. 'Susie is here.'

'We meet again.' He looked directly at Susie, making her want to squirm.

'I am helping with her Italian,' Mimi told him.

It was Dante who switched to Italian now, asking Mimi if he could speak to her. But of course she was desperate to get away from him and declined, blaming Susie, telling Dante she had paid for an hour-long Italian lesson.

'Ciao!' Mimi said, and hurriedly walked off.

Before Susie could follow there was a brief second when she was alone with Dante.

'Juliet?' He called her out on her lie.

'I should have just said...'

'Did Mimi put you up to helping my grandfather?'

'I'd rather not say...' She could hear Mimi calling for her. 'I'd better go.'

Except she stood, almost as if she was waiting, certainly hoping he might offer dinner again.

He didn't.

'Susie!' Mimi called again.

And she knew she should be relieved that Mimi had dragged her away.

'I cannot believe my bad luck,' Mimi moaned. 'I just hope Gio doesn't tell him about us. I want that ring on my finger before the grandsons interfere.'

'Limited bar menu,' Pedro told the team. 'We are short in the kitchen again.'

Susie felt her jaw grit—and not just in frustration at waitressing.

She should perhaps have been proud of her own restraint, but instead, in the hours that had passed, her regret at declining Dante's offer had increased tenfold.

Perhaps it was for the best, Susie mused now as she waited on tables. She had absolutely nothing suitable to wear for dinner with someone as sophisticated as Dante, and certainly nothing daringly unsuitable in the underwear department...

The thought of one night, no strings, might have appalled her once upon a time—but that was before she met Dante...

Right now, she ached for that one night.

There were a lot of shouts and a lot of laughter in the kitchen. It would seem Cucou was in great spirits tonight. She felt like a cat out in the rain, peering in as she collected some orders.

'Hey, Susie,' called Nico, one of the pastry chefs. 'Cucou said you have a twin.'

'No!' Cucou laughed. 'Not Susie.'

Not Susie.

That should be stencilled on her forehead.

Chiselled on her grave.

Not boring, plain old Susie...

And then everything changed. Or rather, life got interesting.

'Signor Casadio.'

She looked up at Pedro's effusive greeting—he was clearly thrilled to have Gio back in the restaurant. 'We have missed you,' he said to the elderly gentleman, and then he nodded to his stunning companion. *'Signor.'*

'Pedro.' Dante nodded, and then his eyes skimmed past Pedro, and somehow, in a room full of people and noise and all things wonderful, he found her.

Thankfully she didn't have to wait on his table, or the gorgeous pale grey linen shirt he wore might have become the worse for wear.

Instead, she waited on her regular tables, chatting to the guests, trying out her Italian.

She never caught him looking at her, it was absolutely subtle, but she had never felt so aware. She was certain he noted her every move, heard her every word—and then, of course, Gio saw her.

'Susie!' He half stood to greet her. 'It is so good to see you here. So nice to be out.'

'It's lovely to see you too, Gio.' Susie smiled.

'He wanted to go elsewhere.' Gio gestured towards Dante. 'He said I must surely have eaten enough food from Pearla's.'

'Oh!' She smiled, and raised her eyes a fraction. 'That's disappointing to hear.' From the corner of her eye she saw Dante's wry smile at the riposte, aimed at him, then her words were all for Gio. 'Well, we're all thrilled you chose to visit us.'

Should she be disappointed that Dante hadn't wanted to come here tonight?

It didn't feel that way—not in the least.

Perhaps his arrogant pride *had* been a little dented?

She chose to think of it that way, and happily got on with her work.

She was clearing a table of plates, and busy wishing she was doing something else. Shaking a cocktail—or even carrying one. Instead she passed Dante with an armful of crockery.

'Break, Susie,' Pedro said, and she nodded.

'*Scusi...*'

Dante had put up a hand, and though the table was not her own, she of course had to go over.

'*Signor?*'

'We'll be getting our coats...'

'Of course.'

'Unless…' he looked to Gio '…you want dessert? Some ice cream, maybe?'

'Please,' Gio dismissed, 'since when did you want dessert?' He looked up to Susie. 'He doesn't even like ice cream.'

'People have been known to change their minds,' Susie said, and smiled at Gio, though again her words were for Dante.

Oh, she hoped he understood what she was trying to convey. But perhaps he didn't get it at all, because he stood glancing at his phone as Pedro helped Gio into his coat.

Then he glanced up and his eyes found hers again.

Oh, gosh.

There was a rush of excitement such as she'd never known. And the searing heat of the kitchen was nothing compared to the heat of his look. She ignited inside.

He was dangerous. He made her feel reckless. How, with one look, did he tell her that she knew so little about her own body?

She'd had just one boyfriend and things had been okay.

Sort of…

Okay… What a pale word. What a pale experience her sex life had been. And now she stood, feeling her body tighten, her breasts full beneath her dress. And low, low in her stomach she felt as if she wore some kind of internal corset that had tightened so much that even the tops of her thighs tensed.

Passion.

He promised passion and she had never known it, Susie realised.

At the end of her shift she stepped out, wondering if he'd understood.

And there he was, holding an ice cream.

'Here,' he said. 'Luckily it is a very cold night.'

'Sour cherry?'

'Of course.'

It was sharp and sweet and utterly her new favourite.

'Did you even try it last night?' she asked.

'No.'

'Try it now.'

But he declined, and they walked down from the walls into the street…where the music from the bars blended with the street performers…and she ought to feel shy, but she was too happy for that.

There were gorgeous sounds coming from the music school as they passed, and she listened to the plucking of a cello.

'My flatmates attend here.'

'Really?'

She nodded, popping the last of her cone into her mouth. 'Their practising drives me mad, but it's so lovely hearing it out here. It makes me want to dance.'

'Then let's dance,' he said, and took her hand.

She hadn't thought their one night might be romantic, and she'd never thought she could feel glamorous in clumpy black shoes, but as she danced under the dark sky the tiny side street was the most romantic, sensual place in the world.

'You make me feel light-footed,' she said, as his face came down to her cheek. 'I can't dance. But…'

'You can,' he told her. 'You can do anything.'

'I haven't done very much at all,' Susie said, and she rather thought they weren't discussing her dancing any more. 'I'm very, very boring…' she warned.

'I don't think so.'

He lowered his head and she stretched to meet his mouth.

This was no awkward first contact.

It came as a relief.

The weight of his mouth on hers felt perfect, and he was heavenly to kiss and to be kissed by. His lips were like velvet, his chin rough, and his body so warm. Closing her eyes at the bliss of his tongue, she tasted him back, and it was both passionate and so good.

His hand slid under her coat and hooked her waist. And then he either pulled her towards him or maybe she just shaped herself into him, as if a mould had been cast.

'I stand corrected,' Dante said. 'I do like sour cherry ice cream.'

He went back for another taste and she clung to his head,

kissing him back. The music was silent now. And truly she didn't care if the students were all leaning on the windows and looking out as he kissed her against a wall…

Actually, she did.

Her eyes sprang open. 'I was worried…' she gasped. 'That we were being watched…'

'We're just kissing.'

'Really…?'

She couldn't quite get her breath, and she could feel him hard against her stomach, and she felt swollen herself, just too hot to be out in the cold.

'Come on,' he said, and she nodded as he took her hand and they started to walk.

Still holding her hand, he led her to his house.

They reached Coro Garibaldi… 'How far?' Susie asked as they walked along the elegant avenue.

'Nearly there…'

Except they kept stopping for kisses. And even as they climbed the steps to his door she was impatient. It wasn't just a matter of him taking out his keys, she was almost inside his jacket, trying to find them.

Kissing and laughing, they almost fell inside.

'I'll get the lights,' Dante said.

And that might have been his intention, but first he took off her scarf and hung it over the banister, then he removed her coat and his.

'Let's go to bed,' he suggested.

But she sat on the stairs and removed her horrible shoes and groaned in relief.

'You ache?' he asked.

'I ache,' she agreed, wincing a little as he picked up one foot. 'Please don't.'

She was worried her feet might not be the freshest, but then she stopped caring as he massaged her calf, and then picked up the other foot. And as his fingers dug into her taut calf she found her toes creeping towards his erection.

His hands came to the hem of her dress and slid under it.

She lifted her bottom from the stairs and he dealt with her stockings and knickers in one go.

'Bed,' he told her, and stood her up, as if he was ready to carry her if he must.

But then they were kissing again, all traces of sour cherry gone.

'Dante...'

She wanted to explain how unlikely this was, how completely wonderful it was to be too desperate to get to his bed. She was at his belt, feeling him through fabric, and then pulling at his thin jumper. He pulled it over his head and she used her palms to feel his chest. She kissed his flat nipples as he undid her hair.

She liked the semi darkness, but she wanted light to see if his body was as completely magnificent as it felt beneath her hands, or when it was pressed against her. She was almost climbing up him, and he lifted the hem of her dress and gripped his hands onto her bare bottom.

'Please...' Susie said, nervous that this intense feeling might fade on the way to his bedroom, desperate not to lose the new freedom she'd found.

And when he lifted her up, she wrapped her legs around his waist.

Dante was not one for frantic sex in the entrance hall—or, really, frantic sex anywhere. He was always in control. But Susie was light and hot and coiled around him, and clearly they weren't going to make it to bed.

And yet it wasn't frantic...it was slow and delicious, but with a raw edge.

He held her thighs as she wrapped her arms around his neck, and then he lifted her and lowered her onto him. Her breathing was ragged, and she stared at him as he moved her a little, then moaned as he squeezed inside her.

Susie had never had sex standing, and yet she'd never felt further from falling, held in his arms as he moved inside her.

He was so strong, and he held her so securely, that she focussed on the sheer bliss of his thrusts.

Deep and slow.

He sucked her bottom lip and she looked at him with glinting eyes.

'Keep looking at me. Keep looking,' he told her.

And now their eyes were locked, and she felt hot and slick and on the edge of orgasm.

'Dante…'

She wanted to look but her eyes were closing, her neck arching. He was still thrusting, and she felt herself moving, pushing against him, chasing something that had eluded her for ever.

She closed her eyes and just sank into bliss, too selfish to move, pleased that Dante was taking care of that. He was thrusting in and she caught another glimpse of that elusive thing. She clung tighter, and then his sudden shout had it captured. There was a zip of energy, low in her spine, and she let out a cry of delight as he released himself into her.

She felt tender even as it faded.

Still turned on as it ebbed away.

She looked at Dante and smiled. 'I've never managed that before.'

He stared.

'I've always…' She stopped.

'Faked it?'

She nodded.

'Let's go upstairs.'

CHAPTER FOUR

SUSIE WOKE WITH her face buried in the side of Dante's chest, and it took her a moment to work out not so much where she was, but how they'd made it to his bed.

He'd carried her.

All limp and sated from her first orgasm.

He had carried her here, and then they'd done it again.

With Susie on top.

Gosh.

She rolled onto her back and saw stars. Literally. His ceiling was an artwork of stars and moons and angels and just so many beautiful things that she thought she could stare for ever as she remembered last night.

And then what had mattered little last night suddenly mattered a lot, and she screwed her eyes closed.

Oh, God. They hadn't used anything.

'I know.' His deep voice answered her frantic thoughts and she turned anxious eyes towards him. 'Common sense seems to have eluded us both last night.'

'I can't believe it,' she groaned. 'I mean...' She had known they were unprotected, and so had he! 'I'm usually so careful.'

'You said you were on the pill.'

That's right...

Somewhere before their second time they'd both rather feebly addressed the matter.

'I am.'

Susie nodded. She was more cross with herself than him.

Or simply stunned that she, Susie Bilton, could so completely lose her head.

'Then we have nothing to worry about. I've never had unprotected sex.' Perhaps he saw the doubt creep into her eyes, because he added, 'Susie, last night really was an anomaly.' He seemed to consider. 'Maybe it's because…' His voice trailed off as he attempted to rationalise what had occurred. 'The change in routine.' He turned and gave a slow, triumphant smile. 'That must be it.'

'That is the most ridiculous excuse ever,' she chided lightly. 'So, I'm a change in routine?'

'You are.'

'I'm not sure I want to know your usual routine.'

He gave a soft laugh. 'I meant I've never brought a lover here…'

'Never?'

'Absolutely not—you saw what that waiter was like this morning…way too interested…'

'It was lovely, though, wasn't it?' Susie said.

'Very,' Dante agreed, although he didn't tend to discuss such events afterwards.

He was about to climb from the bed. Do his usual and offer coffee, to be polite, in the hope that she'd say no. Especially as—bonus—he didn't have any milk.

It didn't feel like a bonus, though.

The bonus was her wide-eyed smile.

'Twice,' she said, and took a happy breath.

Yet still he lay there.

Usually Dante loathed morning conversation, and he had sometimes wondered if he was the only guy on earth who didn't particularly like morning sex.

Well, he liked the sex part… Just not feeling like a louse afterwards, for wanting her gone.

But this morning he wanted to prolong the conversation. He looked over at the woman in his bed and did not want her gone.

She was looking up at the art on his ceiling. 'It's gorgeous,' she said. 'So much detail.'

He joined her looking skywards. 'It was beneath plaster when I bought the house. The previous owner gave up on a full restoration and concealed it. The dining room has one too.'

'Gosh…'

'I found someone in Florence to restore it.'

He had admired it at the time, and on occasions since, but his times here were brief, and generally fraught with memories as he was often here attending memorials. Even celebrations like Christmas made Gio morose and, of course, at times, there was the strain of himself and Sev putting on a front, pretending they still had a relationship…

No, he'd never really taken the time to appreciate what was before his eyes, where planets and stars fought in a deep crimson sky.

But there was a little frown on her face. Perhaps she was still cross about their carelessness last night?

'So,' Dante said. 'What's your excuse?'

'Hmmm?'

'For last night.'

What *was* her excuse? Susie thought, and was quiet for a moment as she lay pondering his question.

'I don't have one,' she finally admitted, and saw him turn to the sound of her quiet bemusement. 'I don't know.'

She wasn't being evasive—she simply didn't know how to describe what had happened to her.

'I've never forgotten myself like that,' she admitted.

'Forgotten yourself?' he checked.

She didn't know how better to describe it, but there had been the light stroke of his fingers on her stomach and then…

She'd had one relationship and so little to compare…

'I just lost my head,' Susie said, and she even tried a little joke. 'Too much ice cream!'

'Do you want coffee?' he asked.

'I do.'

As he rolled from the bed and dressed, she looked at his stunning long legs and taut bottom, and watched as he pulled on some clothes. Gosh, she wanted him to climb back into bed.

'Are you leaving me here?'

'I'm getting us coffee. I didn't let anyone know I was coming.'

'Anyone?' she checked,

'I have a housekeeper. I would usually let her know when I'm staying.'

'Your home's stunning.' She looked at the bold red walls. 'It's incredible. Just…'

Susie didn't quite know what else to say. It was like something out of a lifestyle magazine. But for all that it was lavish, there was nothing here that spoke of *him*. She looked at the ornate wardrobes and for a brief second wondered if there were even any clothes in them.

She let the conversation die, happy to watch as he raked his fingers through his hair to comb it and ran a hand over his unshaven jaw.

'How do you have your coffee?' he asked.

'Lots of milk.'

'I shan't be long.'

It was a little awkward. She lay there silent, but managed a half-smile as he let himself out, then lay there some more and waited for the cringe of utter regret to spike now that she was alone.

Except…there was none.

Now the conversation had been had as to their recklessness, there was none.

She didn't regret last night at all.

It had been a complete revelation.

A small part of her had thought that deep longing and fevered want didn't exist for her.

Hauling herself from his delicious bed, she made her way to the bathroom. It was all marble and gold taps. No stars on the ceilings, though, but still decadent.

Bathed and smelling gorgeous, from all his lovely soaps and

such, she wrapped herself in a huge towel and stared into the full-length mirror that leant on the bathroom wall… She tried to think of practical things, like where she'd left her clothes.

And although she would have loved to climb back into the high, rumpled bed, she pinched his comb instead.

Back in the bedroom, her eyes were drawn to a thick golden card. She couldn't help but peek—and then was startled when she got caught…

Dante stood at the door and informed her about what she was reading. 'The Lucca Spring Ball.'

'Yes. It looks incredible. Mimi's told me about it.'

She turned and saw that he had brought up not just coffee but her clothes. It really was time to leave, Susie realised as she replaced the thick card.

'Sorry…' She took the coffee from him and truly didn't know how they should be together. 'I wasn't angling for you to invite me.'

'I would hope not,' he commented as he moved to lie sideways on the bed and watch her dress. 'Given it's six weeks away.'

'And we're just for one night.' She'd got the message and wanted him to know that she had. 'Anyway, it's my birthday that weekend.'

'How old will you be?'

'Twenty-five—and my parents are coming.'

'Is that nice?'

'Very.' She smiled as she clipped on her bra. 'I can't wait to have them here on my birthday.' She separated her knickers from her tights, wishing there was a more elegant way to do things. 'And have them all to myself.'

'All to yourself?'

'On my birthday.' She knew she sounded petty and jealous—possibly she was—so she shook her head and smiled. 'What are you doing today?'

'I'll check in on Gio…see if I can get him to talk. We're not brilliant at it.'

'How come?' she asked. 'I mean, you're very direct.'

'Do you talk easily with *your* family about difficult topics?'

'No,' Susie admitted. 'I just…' She slipped on her dress and sat on the bed to do up the zip at the back.

He watched her wrestle.

It was by far safer.

Dante was conflicted. He wanted her gone and yet he wanted her back in his bed—and the latter did not sit well for him.

Last night had perturbed him, and his continued desire for her this morning was doing the same.

'I'm not very good at this,' she admitted suddenly, and he felt a twist inside at the tense rise in her voice. 'I mean, I don't know how I should be…'

'It's okay,' he said, and gave in on not helping. Sitting up, he dealt with her zip, and then he held her hips for a moment, with her back to him. 'It was a great night.'

'Yes…'

'I leave for Milan this evening.'

'I know that.'

'I have to go and see Gio,' he said, as if reminding himself there was a reason he should not prolong this encounter. 'Sort out all the old jewellery. It's a job he has been putting off for a long time.'

'Yes.' She nodded. 'I'm sure it will be difficult.'

'He gets upset…'

'I meant…' She swallowed. 'It will be difficult for both of you.' She let out a breath. 'They're not just his wife's jewels…' she ventured. 'There's your mother's jewellery too.' She didn't turn her head. 'He showed me some.'

'Yes,' said Dante, rather pleased that her back was still to him, and a little stunned to hear his silent dread about today being acknowledged. 'He has most of it.'

'Most? Do you have some?'

Her enquiry, Dante thought, was gentle. And it was a natural question, an invitation to ask if he'd kept some sentimental pieces. But when he'd said 'most' that wasn't what he'd meant.

He briefly thought of the small stones in his safe in Milan, but it was by far too painful to go there.

Even in his own head.

And if ever one day he did, then he would be alone.

Ensuring the agony was wiped from his features, he turned her around within the circle of his hands, her hips beneath his palms, and looked up at her damp blonde hair and pale face.

Why were they ending things here? Dante asked himself.

'I'd better go,' Susie said. 'I have homework...'

Her voice was a little strained and high.

'What's your homework?' he asked.

'Greetings, thanks and farewells.' She smiled at him. 'How do I say *Thank you for last night*?'

'Try,' he told her.

'Grazie per la scorsa notte?'

Dante gave in.

'I could help you with your homework.'

'Really?'

'Stay?'

He saw Susie tense as he said the word, as if her body was warning her...

'I have to go and visit the winery,' he told her, and then he looked up at her blue eyes. She was uncertain whether to stay, and that helped—because he was uncertain if he should have asked. 'It's not exactly fun—I have to speak with the manager and such—but we could get lunch?'

'I'd like that.' Susie nodded.

He pulled her down onto his knee. 'You'll have to try and keep your hands off me, or Gio and Mimi will find out.'

'I'm sure I can manage.'

She felt shiny with pleasure—not just because this wasn't goodbye, it was the way he made her feel.

'I'm not so sure I'll be able to,' he told her, and they shared a slow kiss, his jaw rough and his tongue exquisite. And it was so much nicer to kiss than to say goodbye.

'You have to go to Gio's,' she reminded him as his hands moved her dress up.

He turned her around so she straddled his lap.

'I know I do,' he said, with both a smile and a dash of regret.

But even as he went to tip her from his lap she resisted. Not demanding more kisses…she had something to say.

'Talk to Gio about the jewellery…'

'Sorry?'

'You said it was difficult to get him to open up. I think talking about the jewellery with him might help…'

'We've already spoken about it. I told him I would take it to Milan.' He halted, recalling the conversation. Gio had been talking and he had shut it down.

The jewellery was a painful topic for Dante.

For all of them.

'Okay,' Dante said. 'I'll give it a try.'

Now Susie stood. 'I ought to pop back home…' She gestured to her dress. 'Get a change of clothes.'

Then she thought of another rather essential matter—her pills, sitting in her bedside drawer.

'Meet back here?' he checked.

She nodded.

'I'll order a driver.'

'Pick me up if it's easier.'

'I've got a lockbox,' he said. 'I'll give you the code. Just let yourself in whenever.'

'You're sure?' she checked.

And no, he wasn't sure—because Dante did not give out such information, or have people in his space without him. And yet all his rules seemed to be falling by the wayside.

This was more than he'd expected, or perhaps even wanted, but it was hard to let go of bliss, hard to shut the door on such a delicious reprieve.

'Meet back here,' he affirmed.

* * *

Juliet and Louanna were both practising. Susie could hear the violin and the cello as she climbed the stairs to her apartment.

She went in quietly and headed straight for her bedroom.

Staring into the large wooden wardrobe, she looked at the clothes she had hanging there. A pair of jeans, a spare uniform. Some rather boring jumpers and a couple of thick skirts that she wore with boots.

Certainly nothing that matched her mood.

And her mood was…

She examined her feelings for a moment, as if reaching in and feeling the touchstone of her soul, and knew she was happy. Exhilarated…

Grabbing her toiletries bag, she went and brushed her teeth and then reached for her pills.

Today was Sunday…

So why were Friday and Saturday still in their tiny igloos? *Today*, she said to herself, *is definitely Sunday.*

And it would seem her brain had ceased being sensible on Friday.

The moment Dante had stepped into her life.

'Breathe,' Susie told herself aloud. 'It will be fine.'

She changed into fresh clothes—jeans and a lilac jumper— and then Louanna called out.

'Are you up?'

'Yes,' Susie said, realising as she headed out to the lounge that they hadn't noticed she'd been gone all night.

'You look nice.' Juliet smiled. 'Are you on your way out?'

'Yes, I'm going to a winery.' Susie nodded. 'With a friend.'

'You should try De Santis,' Louanna suggested. 'For cheap wine, it's pretty good.'

'We were thinking of Casadio.'

'Hah!' Louanna said. She rolled her eyes and offered an Italian saying. *'Costare una fortuna…'* A warning that she would pay a very high price.

'I'll keep it in mind.'

'You're not going to the restaurant there, are you?' Louanna checked, running her eyes over Susie's jeans. 'It's very elegant.'

'She looks lovely,' Juliet jumped in.

'I'm just saying…' Louanna shrugged. 'I'd want someone to tell *me* if I wasn't suitably dressed.'

'Thanks, I think!' Susie said, smiling to Juliet, who rolled her gorgeous green eyes. 'I'd better go shopping…'

There was steady rain, so the shops were quiet. She looked in the beautifully dressed boutique windows, but it was all a bit intimidating.

Susie wasn't offended by what Louanna had said—well, a touch, maybe—and she did appreciate the heads-up. More than that, it had been for ever since she'd shopped for something nice to wear. She'd been saving for her trip, and before that…

She thought of her ex, who hadn't ever seemed to notice when she'd gone all out, so in the end she hadn't bothered.

Everyone had been surprised that she'd ended things between them—even Susie had struggled to justify it to herself. The relationship hadn't been awful, or terrible, or any of those things, but she had suddenly seen how she'd hidden her true self. She had wanted to be more adventurous—not just in bed, but in everything. But she'd stuffed down the little hurts rather than voice them.

Passing the ice-cream shop, she thought of Dante waiting outside the restaurant with a cone.

She didn't quite get how a simple thing like an ice cream could mean so much.

Was it that he'd thought of her when she wasn't there? Queued up to get the treat because he knew it was something she liked? That he'd known she secretly wanted that flavour… that he'd noticed.

He made her feel noticed. And even if this was very temporary, it was thrilling, and an adventure, and under his delicious attention she was discovering herself.

She ventured into one of the shops, but she had no real idea what she was looking for.

'For lunch where?'

The assistant who had offered to help nodded when she said she was going to a winery in the Tuscan hills.

'Perhaps these?'

She held up some gorgeous black jeans, but then pulled them back when Susie explained that it was Casadio.

'The cellar door, or the restaurant?'

'I think…' She had no idea. 'I don't know…possibly the restaurant?'

'Hmm…' The assistant clearly considered this a conundrum. 'Okay,' she said, heading over to a small rack that sadly wasn't a discount one. 'You can dress these up, or…'

She held up a grey woollen dress, but Susie's eyes had lit on another.

It was the palest blue and the softest wool, and if she was going to splurge for the first time, then… She took a breath. She might as well adore her purchase.

The wool was thin and soft, yet snug, and the neckline was a little scooped, but not too low. There was a thick belt in the same wool, but that dressed it down too much.

'Look.' The assistant showed her a gold belt and looped it round her hips. 'With stilettoes, you could even go to a party.'

'Yes.' She laughed. 'But I don't really go to many parties.' Sometimes she was a waitress at them…

But yes, absolutely this could work for a glamorous party.

And for lunch with Dante.

'I love it.' Susie nodded.

And she loved the pretty underwear she bought too.

Arriving back at his place, she found the key in his lockbox and stepped into his gorgeous home, hiding the bags because she didn't want him to know the effort she had gone to.

She looked around the kitchen at the gorgeous copper pots, the huge ovens that could cater for a small party, the wooden bench… There was even a little herb garden in the window, and yet from all he'd told her he was rarely here.

She walked through the hall and into a lounge. The walls were a silky navy and there were beams that ran across the high ceilings. Every room was a masterpiece. It was like viewing a stately home, Susie thought, as she peered into a beautiful dining room.

Yet there was nothing of *him*.

No photos, no mementoes.

She went back to the kitchen. He didn't even have one fridge magnet.

Susie collected them wherever she went. Possibly it was one of her many weaknesses.

It unnerved her a little that his house, while stunning, was so impersonal, and it reminded her that Dante got attached to no one. It would be wise to keep an emotional distance.

Yes, the sex was incredible, and he was too, but to get too close to Dante could seriously hurt.

CHAPTER FIVE

DANTE WASN'T CLOSE to anyone—though he did make an effort for Gio.

'Hey…' He gave him a kiss. 'Is there anything you want me to discuss with Christo at the winery?'

'No, just make sure he is happy…ask if there's anything he needs.'

'Of course. I spoke to him last week.'

'Face to face is better, Dante.'

'I know.' He took a breath. 'So, you want to get these cleaned?' He took a seat and picked up one of the bracelets. 'This was Nonna's, yes?'

'No.' Gio shook his head. 'That was my grandmother's.' He looked at the sapphires, then paused as Dante picked up a string of pearls. 'They were your mother's.'

'Yes.' Dante nodded, assailed by memories of her and his papa about to head out. He put them back down, instead lifted a heavy emerald choker. 'This was Nonna's?'

'There's a stone loose,' Gio said. 'I should have had it looked at ages ago. She liked them to be cleaned at least every year.'

'We'll sort it.'

'When?'

'I can call the jeweller…' He paused, thought of his hectic week, but decided, for Gio, he would take some time off. 'I could see if we can go in tomorrow.'

'Tomorrow?' Gio sounded a little panicked. 'We'll do this tomorrow?'

'If you want.' Dante nodded, and was reaching for some

rather awful earrings when his grandfather finally stated his truth.

'Mimi is not my housekeeper.'

'Okay...' Dante said, picking up the awful earrings.

'She never was my housekeeper.'

'Mimi makes you happy?'

'So happy,' Gio said. 'And I make her happy too. After her Eric died she cried for two years, and I understand that. When I lost your *nonna* I thought my life was over, and then the accident... I never thought I would be truly happy again. But when Mimi sings...' He wiped his eyes. 'Sometimes she looks at me and sings and my heart soars again.'

'If you make each other so happy, why isn't she here?'

'Mimi wants to make things official.'

'I see.'

'And I have to sort all these first,' Gio said. 'Take care of the past that I've been neglecting. I don't want to be sad and lonely. I want to hold Mimi's hand on my morning walk.'

'Then do it,' Dante said, and gave Gio a hug. 'Make it official.'

Gio mopped his eyes. 'It's time to be happy, Dante. To move on from the past.'

'Yes.'

'Not just me.'

'Gio, I have moved on. Don't worry about me.' Dante was practical. 'We'll get the jewels sorted. I'll come with you.'

'I was going to use this central stone for her ring.' Gio picked up a ruby bracelet. 'The stone is so beautiful...and rubies are very romantic.'

Dante didn't care for rubies. He had two in his safe that no one knew about... He pushed that thought aside. 'Perfect.'

'I thought so too.' He was suddenly defeated. 'However, Susie said no.'

Dante frowned. For a second he wondered if he'd given himself away by reacting to Susie's name.

'She said I should get a new stone for Mimi—something I chose myself, that is just for her.'

'Why?' Dante asked, and he wasn't just being his usual unromantic self. It was because he was happier to pursue the conversation when the topic was Susie. 'You have more jewels than you know what to do with. I am sure Mimi would love this.'

'I said the same. The ruby is spectacular. But Susie seems to think Mimi would want a new stone.'

'It wasn't Nonna's,' Dante pointed out, but he saw Gio flinch, and knew it was still a delicate matter for him. 'It's a beautiful ruby…it's been in your family for years.'

'Yes.' Gio nodded. 'That's what I thought. I was going use the gold from the chain I used to wear when I was younger, but Susie said even the gold should be new.'

'New?' Dante frowned. 'When it's melted down gold is gold.'

His grandfather gave a low laugh at his wry response. 'I said the same, but I'd invited her opinion and she suggested I choose something new and special, just for Mimi.'

'It's a ring, Gio. I don't know what Susie's going on about.'

'Susie has twin sisters,' Gio told him, and then added, 'Identical.'

'And…?'

'They're very close in age—just a little over a year older than Susie is.'

'And?' Dante said again, a little perplexed as to what that had to do with anything, but curious. 'Is one of them a master jeweller?'

'No.' Gio laughed, and Dante was pleased to see the sparkle in Gio's eyes had returned. 'Susie was always getting things handed down to her. Clothes, toys…'

'That's hardly the same as jewellery.'

'She seems to think so. Apparently, she always felt left out—their birthdays were always grouped together, and their presents were similar. I have to make this just about Mimi.'

'Mimi's not a twin, and she doesn't have any sisters who are twins…' Dante didn't get it.

'No, but she is unique.'

And then Dante got it a little bit more. Susie ached to be the talk of the town, for attention, for the spotlight to shine briefly on her, to stand out rather than fade into the background. And he felt a twisting ache in the black hole that existed where his heart had once been.

'Yes,' Dante agreed. 'She is.'

And he wasn't really talking about Mimi—he was thinking about Susie, and how he was now determined to make this day a little special.

Susie was ready on time, and when a dark car slid up outside she wondered if perhaps she was meeting Dante there.

She slipped on her coat and was just tying up her scarf when Dante came rushing through the door.

'Two minutes,' he said.

'How was Gio?'

'Come up,' he said, stripping off and dashing into the shower. 'Talking about the jewellery helped.'

'Good.'

She sat on the edge of the bath, enjoying watching him quickly wash, then frowning when he dashed out and lathered his chin to shave.

'I thought we were in a rush.'

'We are.'

'It can't be that much of a rush,' Susie said, 'if you've time to shave.'

'Call an ambulance if ever I don't,' he teased, wiping his jaw and then pulling on a black shirt.

Within a matter of moments he was back to looking like a *Vogue* model, elegant and polished, and soon they were headed out to the car.

'It's not fair,' she grumbled as they sat inside.

'What isn't?'

'How lovely you look in so little time.'

'You look lovely, too,' Dante said, looking at the mascara on her lashes, her glossy lips, her hair freshly brushed and worn down. 'You've really helped with Gio.'

'What happened?'

'I'll tell you when we're there.'

'I can't wait.'

But for now it was nice to simply relax as the car took them out of town and into the gorgeous countryside. Dante showed her fields that in summer were a blaze of yellow, filled with sunflowers. Then the car slowed down as it climbed the hills and they passed a church that was somehow familiar.

Then she knew why. She recognised it from one of the many photos Gio had shown her. It was the church where Sev had married.

She glanced at Dante, who was going through the messages on his phone.

'Is this it?' she asked, as a sign for a winery came up, rustic and pretty and very Tuscan. 'It's gorgeous.'

'That's not it,' he said, with an edge to his low voice. 'That's the De Santis winery.'

'Oh, I've heard it's good. Well, for cheap wine…'

'It's like vinegar,' he said. 'Always rushed through. It's Sev's wife's…or rather his late wife's family winery,' he explained, and there was still that edge to his voice.

'Rose?'

'Rosa,' he corrected, and it was as though he had to keep his mouth from curling with distaste just saying her name.

Susie knew there was a lot of tension around the wedding.

Looking out at the grey rolling clouds, she tried to remember who had told her what. Mimi had told her on their walks about Sev and Rosa's wedding in the beautiful little church, and the tragedy of the funeral just a few months later. Gio, too, had shown her photos of his gorgeous family outside the church.

Susie hadn't known Dante then—but she'd seen his cut and black eye.

'We're here,' Dante said.

Unlike the De Santis winery, Casadio's wasn't quaint or rustic. The dark signage was sophisticated, the driveway long, and clearly it was a slick operation.

Dante parked, and as she climbed out Susie saw there was a large shop. Then they walked around the side, and spread before them was a hillside full of vines and a gorgeous outdoor area with tables.

'Dante.' A gentleman came out, all smiles, and greeted him effusively.

'Susie, this is Christos.' Dante introduced him. 'Our manager.'

Christos led them up to a gorgeous restaurant that was every bit as luxurious as Pearla's, yet very relaxed and spread out. He spoke in rapid Italian, but thankfully Dante translated easily.

'He's asking if you would like a tour while we talk, or to relax on the couches?'

'Oh.' She looked at the huge roaring fire and as she took off her scarf she opted for the couches. 'The couches sound lovely.'

'We shouldn't be too…' Dante started, but as she slipped off her coat he found out what it meant to be lost for words.

He'd only seen her in her waitressing dress, or naked in his bed, or wrapped in a sheet, and he was momentarily stunned. Her dress was the colour of the sky in spring, and it was somehow demure and sexy as hell all at once.

Or was it sexy because he knew what lay beneath?

Everyone else seemed unperturbed. Christos's wife was taking her coat, Christos himself was guiding her to the couches. So Dante, refusing to react like some awkward teenager at a party, went over to the bar, turned his back on her and chatted to the bar manager.

He would really rather have joined Susie on the couches, but instead he walked through the cellars with Christos. Then he met with the vigneron and listened to all he had to say. Then Christos suggested they walk through the vines.

Being shown through a place where he had once played hide and seek, where he had run, where he'd once had a happy family, was hell.

He liked Christos—he just did not want to be playing owner today.

Especially when he had the intriguing Susie waiting.

Oh, she was so far from predictable…

She was sitting on a huge leather sofa, gazing out at the view that he saw only in nightmares, with a vague smile on her face.

'Susie?' He interrupted her wherever her daydreams had taken her. 'Do you want to eat?'

'Yes!' She didn't stand, though. 'I was talking to the chef, and he said we could do a tasting here. They'll bring all the foods and wine over.'

'A tasting?' he checked. 'They'll explain all the wines, all the food…'

'Yes.'

'Why don't we just get a table and eat? A tasting is very…'

'Sociable?' She laughed.

'Yes,' he said, sitting down beside her with a sigh. 'Okay we'll do a tasting.'

He signalled to a waiter and told him to go ahead, but when they were alone again he turned to her.

'Before they start, I'm going to tell you something.'

'Okay…'

'No one else knows this…' He cupped his hand and whispered in her ear. 'I don't actually like wine.'

'Seriously?'

He pulled his head back and nodded. 'Why do you think I went to study law?'

'Are you telling the truth?'

'I can drink it. And at family events and functions here, or events that we sponsor, I do. But…' He rolled his eyes. 'I might as well be drinking cheap De Santis wine; it all tastes the same to me.'

'Does it?'

'Almost.' He gave her a smile. 'De Santis is exceptionally bad. Still, I don't really get it. It is all Gio talks about—and Christos. Sev knows his stuff too. So do you…'

'I don't.'

"'A Sauvignon will pair nicely…'" he quoted her, teasing. 'I'm playing…' He gave her a smile and looked down at her dress. 'You look stunning.'

'Thank you.'

'You do,' he told her. 'I feel like they just opened my case at customs…'

'I don't understand what you're saying…'

'Unexpected goods inside.'

She started to laugh.

'Seriously, I am here on a sort of business lunch, and all I want is to make out with you on the sofa…'

'Better not,' Susie said. 'It'll get straight back to Gio.'

It was fun.

Even if Dante didn't much like wine.

Possibly *because* Dante didn't much like wine!

It made her smile as he listened intently and swirled his drink.

Susie just sipped it.

'Yum,' she said about the 'peppery red with a hint of black-currant', as described by their server. 'It is peppery.'

'Yes…' Dante joined in her little joke. 'With a hint of black-currant.'

And there was more 'yum' as she ate thick olives and gorgeous meats and cheeses from this very beautiful land.

'Wait…' Dante said, and then he trickled truffled honey over some cheese. 'Now try it.'

Susie closed her eyes as she tasted it. 'Oh, my goodness…' It was incredible. 'I have to get some to take home.'

It was a lovely, long lunch, and finally they were on the dessert wine, and Christos was explaining to them what they were tasting in great and long detail.

'I like this one,' Susie said. 'I might get some.'

Finally the tasting was over and the social side done, and they both sat back on the couch and smiled at each other.

'That was actually good,' Dante said.

'It was. I might bring my parents here when they visit.'

'Do,' Dante said. 'Speak to Christos when you book.'

'You can pay for my lunch today,' Susie said. 'But not my parents'.'

Susie intrigued him.

As Gio had said, she was delightful. He found her forthright, but at times shy, and very kind.

But there was so much more to her. Little bits of which he had found out today.

He wanted her to tell him more herself.

'Are you going to tell me about Gio?' Susie asked, surprised she'd waited so long to ask. They'd been enjoying each other so much…

'He told me that he was in love with Mimi.'

Susie smiled, utterly thrilled that Gio had finally told his grandson, as well as curious to know how Dante had taken it.

'How do you feel about it?'

'Feel?' He paused with his glass on its way to his lips. 'Relieved that he's told me and very pleased that he's been talking to you. How did you get him to talk?'

'He was quite…' She hesitated. 'I was worried the first night I took a meal over to him.'

'Was he upset?'

'No…' Susie thought back. 'I think *determined* better describes his mood then. He didn't tell me anything then—just said that he had all the numbers he needed in his phone.'

'My fault.' Dante rolled his eyes. 'I gave him a few lessons on how to use it and put a few numbers in…like Pearla's…'

'He wasn't so great the next night,' Susie told him. 'He started to talk about his late wife, and how marriage is sacred. He showed me a few photos.' Susie smiled. 'I came out and Mimi was waiting for me. I didn't know who she was, of course.'

It was nice to be able to tell Dante now.

'She was beside herself, but determined to stand her ground. She asked if I could do a few things for him—without Gio knowing, of course.'

'How did you sort out the furniture? He told me you moved it yourself.'

'No!' Susie laughed. 'I took him for a walk and while we were out Cucou and Pedro came, with a few of the pastry chefs. They've been really looking out for him—discreetly, of course. He's very loved.'

'Yes, and he and Cucou go way back. They have been friends for ever.'

'How do you feel about it?' Susie asked again, thinking of Mimi's doom and gloom predictions where Dante was concerned. Although he really didn't seem bothered. Or perhaps they weren't close enough to discuss such things as his grandfather's estate? 'Do you have any concerns?'

'I had concerns when I found out he was alone in that vast house,' Dante said. 'But I'm pleased for him. God knows, he's been through it...'

So had Dante, Susie thought, yet he spoke only about Gio's pain.

'He says it's time for him to be happy, to move on from the past, and I want that for him. He didn't deserve what happened.'

'Nobody deserves that,' Susie said, and frowned when Dante didn't answer. 'Nobody.'

'I know,' Dante responded.

He didn't sound entirely convinced.

Surely he didn't blame himself?

He'd never spoken about the accident, though, and she wasn't sure it was her place to ask, or even how she'd do it, and so, instead of delving, she asked about his brother.

'Does Sev know about Gio and Mimi?'

'He's going to call him today.'

'You haven't told him?'

'No,' he admitted.

'Did he have his suspicions too? About them being a couple?'

'Probably—he's very sharp.'

'But the two of you have never discussed it?'

'We don't really talk about things like that.'

'Like what?'

'We don't talk about much,' Dante said. 'Just how Gio is, and the business side of things.'

And perhaps she oughtn't delve—they were nibbling little chocolates and drinking dessert wine, and according to the rules they were together for a good time, not a long time—but Susie found she couldn't quite let things go.

'Were you ever close?' she asked.

'Yeah.' He nodded, but didn't elaborate. Instead he asked her a question. 'Are you close?' he asked. 'With your siblings?'

'I guess...' Susie started. But, given she wanted to know more about Dante, it felt wrong to hide part of herself, and so she shook her head. 'We're not as close as I'd like to be. My sisters are inseparable: they work together, have their own little chat group, and they'll be living together soon. I found out yesterday that they're getting a flat together. By accident,' she added. 'They haven't actually told me yet.'

'So how do you know?'

'They sent a text that wasn't meant for me...' She could feel her heart sink just as it had when she'd received it—just as it did whenever she felt pushed away or excluded. 'It was quickly deleted, but I'd already seen it.'

'Damn phones,' he said, and gave her a gentle smile. 'I hear it happens all the time—not that that helps.'

'It actually does help,' Susie corrected. 'It's not like discovering an affair, or anything, but I knew it wasn't meant for me and it hurt.' She took a breath. 'They're twins...'

'Gio mentioned that,' Dante told her. 'So, you feel left out?'

'Not just left out. I was never let in.'

She could feel tears stinging her eyes, but hoped she could blame the low afternoon sun streaming through the glass. She was certain she sounded pathetic—especially to someone who had lost so much. Yet he was the first person she'd ever really opened up to...the first person who had insisted she be herself.

'They'll tell me when they're ready.' She shrugged. 'I'm pleased for them, really.'

'Liar.' He smiled as he called her out. And then he gave her something to think about. 'Would you want to share a flat with them?'

'No!' She gave a half-laugh, but it soon faded. 'It would be nice to be asked, though.' She sighed. 'I must sound very jealous.'

'Are you?'

'Of course not.' She shook her head, possibly a little too quickly. 'My mother often accuses me of being so, but...' She decided she didn't want to be *that* honest! 'I do love them. They're great, honestly. And they're gorgeous.'

'So are you.'

'No, they're seriously beautiful—they turn heads wherever they go.'

Dante listened to her denial, and even as she lied to his face, still she made him smile. She was so jealous. He could feel it—could see it choking her as she spoke. And he adored her for it. Adored how she tried so hard to speak nicely of people... how she insisted everything was perfectly fine.

'Why are you smiling?' Susie asked, a little bemused by his expression.

'You turn heads.'

'Stop it,' she said, feeling his eyes on her mouth and aching to kiss him.

'I could very easily make you the talk of the town,' Dante told her, looking at her lips, still glossy with truffled honey. 'I could kiss you here.'

'Perhaps not,' Susie said, not feeling quite so brave at the prospect of people knowing about her fling with Dante.

And it wasn't because she'd be embarrassed—it was more that she could glimpse Monday, and Tuesday, and all the days afterwards, possibly having to laugh it off to Louanna, or whoever, after he'd gone. The pastry chefs, too, were always delighted to gossip…

She saw it again—that glimpse of having to shrug it off. Pretend it didn't really matter.

She looked into brown eyes that seemed to be just waiting for them to be alone, and she blushed pink in the face of such blatant desire, feeling warm in her dress, and in the heat of his gaze, and she simply didn't know how a Sunday could be more perfect…

'Do you want to go back?' Dante asked, with a purr of suggestion. 'Examine those unexpected goods?'

'I do.' Susie nodded. 'But…'

Yes, she did want to go back, and discover herself with him. To do some more of the things she'd missed out on. And yet she knew, or rather guessed, that this place must be agony for Dante. There was a darkness to him here, a pain that felt almost palpable at times. Or perhaps she recognised the loneliness she so often felt. Having no one to really talk to—even if in Dante's case it was by choice.

'It's so nice…sitting here talking. Or aren't your temporary lovers supposed to say that?'

'I told you,' Dante said, 'you can say whatever you want. You're not used to that?'

'Meaning?'

'You don't often speak up?'

'Perhaps…' Susie admitted. 'Okay, then.' She would speak up. 'I'd like to stay here a bit longer. What time do you fly?'

'Damn!' he said, and sat up quickly. And then he saw she was startled. 'It's okay, I'm not panicking at the prospect of more conversation. I have to let my pilot know.' He took out his phone. 'The helicopter is booked for this evening.'

'Helicopter?' She frowned as his call was swiftly dealt with. 'You surely don't…?' She halted. 'Sorry.'

'For what? You think I should be avoiding helicopters, given what happened?'

And, while she was all for speaking up, Susie knew this might have crossed the line. 'I shouldn't have said anything.'

'There's only one commercial flight a day from Milan to here,' he said. 'And I am not chartering a whole plane just for that. As Gio would say, we have to think of the planet!'

'Doesn't it scare you?'

'No.' He shook his head. 'I flew on a helicopter straight after I heard about the accident. I just wanted to get back to Gio.'

Her hands met his and touched the tip of his fingers. 'I'm so sorry.'

'It was a long time ago,' Dante said, and then he looked to the window, and the grey, heavy skies that must be so unlike that clear, bright day. 'I could see the smoke as we flew over...' He pointed to the hills. 'Right there—just where the snow caps the middle one. A little way up...'

'You saw it?'

'I can still see it,' he admitted.

'So you hate coming home?'

'I do,' he agreed. 'Though not so much this time.'

He gave her hand a squeeze, and it was Susie who wanted to pull back.

He'd said it so nicely, yet she couldn't help but feel like a diversion. A little respite from the pain of his past. But then who could blame him for that? And wasn't he a little respite for her? A boost to her confidence? Someone she felt brave enough to try new things with, to discover her body with and soothe her wants with his skilful hands?

Yet right now it wasn't just sex. Only the tips of their fingers were still touching...

Dante had never spoken about it—not really, but Gio had got to him. He'd seen the doubt in his grandfather's eyes when he'd insisted to him that he'd moved on.

He had.

Surely he had?

Yet aside from practical reasons he'd never told anyone about that day. Oh, he'd listened to Gio endlessly go on, accepted condolences, but he'd never talked about it.

Possibly to prove to himself that he could, he decided to tell Susie.

Susie—whom he'd never see again after this day.

'My parents were coming to Milan to visit me. They were taking me for lunch…they wanted to talk. To be honest, I wasn't looking forward to it. I'd just finished university and was starting an internship in Milan.'

'They wanted you back here in Lucca?'

'In part. But I think it was more to discuss why Sev and I were not talking. We'd had an argument a few months before that.'

Susie nodded. 'Gio showed me the wedding photo.'

'Yeah…' He gave a resigned half-laugh. 'I'm not getting into that, but…'

She saw Dante reach for the wine he didn't much like and take a sip, then put down his glass.

Then she felt his fingers come back to her own. And even if neither was really one for holding hands, possibly they were on ice-cream nights…as well as on days when they discussed their worst moments.

'Rosa had a specialist doctor appointment in Milan—that's why she was with them. She wasn't coming to lunch…'

There was an edge to his voice when he spoke about Rosa, but Susie said nothing, just listened when he gave his sad conclusion.

'They crashed just after take-off.'

'How did you find out?' she asked, imagining him waiting in a restaurant. 'Did you guess something was wrong when they didn't show?'

'No, I got a call from Christos. He said I had to get back here. They didn't know how bad it was, but I think he knew…'

His hand felt like ice—so much so that she wanted to hold it tighter, to warm it, but she dared not move, scared that he'd pull his hand back or stop talking.

'We all came here, waiting for news. Gio's reaction was dreadful. He collapsed, and seemed to know straight away there was no chance they'd survived. Sev was in the Middle East... The guy had to fly back not knowing if anyone had. I told him there was still hope...' He gave a wry smile. 'I'd seen the wreckage, the fire, but I really thought there might be a chance they'd got out. They hadn't, of course.'

'How do you...?' She swallowed. 'Sorry, stupid question.'

'How do you cope with something like that?' He asked the stupid question for her. 'Gio took to his bed—perhaps for a year. Sev went back to work a week after the funerals. I don't think he's stopped working since.'

'And you?'

'I was practical—calling people, sorting the funerals, seeing the lawyers, going through the wills...' He gave a dark smile. 'That said, I was up before dawn every day, scouring the accident site.'

'Looking for what?'

'Something.' He took a breath. 'Anything.'

'Did you find anything?'

'Not really. In the end I hired a specialist company—they had tools to comb the hillside. They salvaged a couple of small things.' He raised his eyebrows, as if surprised that he'd said that. 'I've never told Gio or Sev that anything was found.'

'Can I ask why not?'

He shook his head and it was left at that.

The gorgeous, lazy afternoon had turned sombre, at least for Susie. Dante, though, was talking normally to Christos as she put on her coat. Then she realised that this must be his normal—that he lived daily with all the sadness she'd felt hearing his story. No wonder he couldn't bear to come home...

'For you,' Christos said, handing her a beautiful basket of all the wines and cheeses she'd especially liked, and some truffled honey too.

'How gorgeous!'

'Susie's bringing her parents here in a few weeks,' Dante said as they left—only Susie wasn't so sure now, wondering how it might feel to be here without Dante.

It was a forty-minute drive back through the hillsides, and

Dante looked out of the window this time—at the De Santis winery as they passed, and the church where Sev and Rosa had married...where Rosa now lay.

She heard the whir of a window closing and saw the divider between them and the driver was now shut. Dante's hand came to her hair. She turned fully around and was met by desire.

She guessed this was Dante's preferred method of escape.

It was her preferred method now, too.

Because all the horrors that had been discussed seemed to fade, his tongue chasing them away, his kiss raw with passion, his hands tight around her waist.

There was no more talking, because it hurt too much, and it was so nice to be kissed in the back of a car, to feel his hands slip between her thighs.

'Those tights are an issue,' he told her, his hand creeping up her inner thigh.

'Dante...' She looked towards the closed partition.

'We're just kissing,' he told her.

But she knew he lied—because even if that was all their shadows appeared to be doing, she could feel his hand moving further up her thigh, then the firm massage of his palm through her tights...

She wished they were gone too. But they remained. And he cupped her warmth and stroked her, and then he left her mouth. His head was heavy against her as he kissed her neck and the stroking of his fingers did not stop.

'Come on...' he urged her—as if it was necessary...as if her pleasure was completely required.

His mouth was high on her shoulder—or was it the base of her neck? But it was wet, and thorough, and she felt a low spread of warmth. His mouth returned to her lips, as if he knew before she did what was happening, and then his lips were over hers, but not moving, swallowing her gasps as her bottom lifted a touch and her thighs closed tight around his hand.

'Nice...'

She wanted to close her eyes, to rest her head back, to catch her breath. So she did.

And it was Dante who pulled down the hem of her dress, so they were only holding hands as the car swept into his driveway, and Susie had never felt happier, or bolder, or more desperate to get inside.

'Grazie,' Dante said as the car door opened.

She forgot the basket of goodies, but he remembered and carried it up the steps, then opened up the door.

They stepped into his home and she shrugged off her coat. She caught the smoky scent of fire, and wondered if it was from her, but then she glanced into the lounge.

'Someone's been in.'

'The housekeeper.' Dante clearly did not want diversions.

'Is she in here?' Susie asked, walking into the room.

'Of course not,' he told her.

And Susie was about to turn, more than ready to be taken straight to bed, but then his hands came down to her waist and slid up to her breasts. She felt the press of him behind her and relished the roam of his hands and how he wasn't shamed by his desire.

He turned her, and she wanted to be stripped, wanted her clothes to disappear. She knew he felt the same because his jumper was off, so she kissed his chest, the flat nipples, and she wanted to sink lower, but fought the desire as she'd never done that before.

And yet her hands slipped down as they got back to kissing and she felt him through fabric, felt how he hardened beneath her palm, and her fingers ached for more contact.

She attempted to undo his belt as they kissed, but thankfully he dealt with that, and then she was holding him, stroking him, feeling the velvet skin on her palm. She looked down and was fascinated, and the desire to sink down and taste him refused to relent.

Her mouth moved as if of its own accord and she followed the trail her lips made, closing her eyes as they bypassed his chest. Her mouth strayed lower and kissed his stomach, tasted his salty skin.

He was too tall for comfort, and for a moment she kissed his thighs. And perhaps he saw her struggle, because he guided her so she sat on a couch. Susie had no idea of its colour. Apart from the gorgeous fire, she hadn't really taken in her surroundings. It was ridiculously comfortable, though, and the cushions soft on her bottom. She relished her unhurried exploration, holding him and dropping little kisses along his length, and then suddenly she became aware she was fully dressed.

'Should I take off my clothes?' she asked, and looked up to see his frown. 'I've never done this.'

'Do you want to?'

'Oh, yes.'

'Why do you think you have to get undressed?'

'To turn you on?'

'That's not an issue,' Dante said, and his hand closed over her own.

Together they stroked his thick length, and then back to her came the deep pull of desire, and there was no reason to resist it.

'I love that you've never done this,' he said in a gravelly voice.

But perhaps her tentative mouth knew what to do, because when she took him in, he made a breathless sound that she knew from when they were in bed.

She tasted him, and his hands guided her as she took her time, taking him in, then a little deeper...

Dante had more control than most.

Not to impress his lovers—more because he held back, even in bed.

Sex was usually necessary and frequent.

In contrast, this was ponderous and tender.

There was an internal fight building in him. At first he thought it was frustration, at her untutored mouth taking him too gently, or her hand gripping too lightly. But then he realised the fight was with himself. The temptation he was fighting wasn't to place his hand over hers and show her how to move more roughly, nor to move her head lower and tell her she would not hurt him.

No, it was none of that.

He was fighting not to stroke her hair, not to smooth it back so he could see her, not to touch her cheek.

And so he told her how good she felt, how good he felt.

But he held back on telling her of the light and the joy she had brought to him.

'Non ti fermare!' he told her. 'I want to see you,' he added, smoothing her hair back, seeing the reddened cheeks that had been so pale before.

She was lost. But she was no longer shy or unsure, just loving the taste of him, and the feel of his hands smoothing back her hair, over and over, then cupping her cheeks tenderly.

And his thrusts didn't daunt her. She was hot between her legs, her breasts heavy beneath her dress. She was aching below and deeply turned on.

There was a slight flurry of panic as she felt him swell, and rush, and then it was the sexiest moment… Because she heard him shout, as if his own climax had caught him unawares, and she tasted him, on the edge of her own orgasm as she lifted her head.

His eyes were closed, but he pulled her up to join him, both standing breathless, their only regret that there was no bed to sink into.

'Come on,' he said.

His bed was made and it was bliss to be stripped before she got into it. He even took her boots off.

'What's this?' he asked of her silver underwear.

'I bought it today.'

They lay together and she adored just lying there, talking, half asleep and yet awake.

'You were in a relationship for…?' he asked.

'Two years.'

'And yet…' He let out a reluctant laugh. 'I don't want to think about it, but…' he was clearly curious '…you've never…?'

'No.' She shook her head. 'I told you: we were very boring in that way.'

'That's not boring. That's…' He thought for a moment. 'Sad.'

'Yes,' she agreed. 'I tried to liven things up, but…' She sighed. 'I don't think he was that interested in me.'

'Yet you stayed?'

'No, I ended things…' She looked up. 'He's the only person I've slept with.'

'Okay…' He was obviously thinking. 'So, what drew you to a man with no passion?'

'It wasn't that bad,' she said, and laughed. But it soon changed. 'It wasn't that good. I just didn't know it. We're good, aren't we?' she said.

'Yes.'

His hand stroked her arm and her hair, and then moved back to her arm. 'I'm going to return the favour,' he told her.

'Please, no…' She cringed at the very thought. 'I could never…'

Then she paused, because until a short while ago she'd never thought she could want to take someone in her mouth. She thought for a moment, but then shook her head.

'No,' she said. 'I don't think I'd like that.'

What she really liked was this: lying half awake, half asleep…sharing confidences…as if some kind of truth serum had been slipped into them while they slept.

CHAPTER SIX

'HOW IS IT Monday already?' Dante asked.

'You've got to go to the jewellers.'

'Don't remind me.'

'It will be nice.'

He didn't answer that.

'You've got class this morning?' he asked.

'I do,' she said. 'Then a lunchtime shift.'

She stared into the thin morning light, loving being wrapped in his arms, and asked the question she was dreading the answer to.

'What time do you fly?'

'I haven't booked it yet.' He yawned, and was silent for a moment. Then, 'Perhaps I could fly back early tomorrow morning.'

Susie swallowed, her delight at the prospect of another night tempered with a lick of uncertainty. It was all very well for him, with his million and one exes—he was clearly used to goodbyes.

She thought back to her one attempt yesterday. That had been hard enough. Now, it felt near-impossible to say goodbye without crying. Oh, she wanted to be sophisticated, and to kiss him and walk away. But, while she'd accepted this was temporary, her emotions were joining their little sex party.

'I thought you only did one night?' She tried to speak as if it were to tease or joke. 'We're already on two.'

'I thought I only had one night when I said that,' Dante pointed out.

She thought back to him asking her to dinner—that was before Gio had decided to go to the jewellers. 'So, you do have longer relationships?'

'I wouldn't call them "relationships", but, yes of course. Short-lived, but not just one night.'

'Do you ever get involved? Too involved?'

'No,' Dante said. 'Now, I should shower and get ready, or Gio will be waiting for me in his hat and coat.'

Dante was lying. The truth was he didn't get involved, and always left at the first sign... And if he said that to Susie... Well, it would mean he'd been the same with her as with others.

Never.

This weekend had been a complete exception and he knew he should end things.

What the hell was he doing, suggesting another night?

Yet, he wanted another night.

He came out of the shower and Susie was lying there, gazing at the ceiling. And then she looked over to him.

'Can I ask something?'

'You can.'

'When you end things...'

'It's not just me that ends things. I always make it clear that I don't want to get too close, and...' He paused, took a shirt from the wardrobe, and then answered the question. 'If it *is* me ending things, I just say it's over.'

'And?'

'My assistant sends flowers...a gift.'

'A little bauble?'

'I don't gift jewellery,' Dante said. 'Antonia generally chooses.' He buttoned up his shirt.

'Does Antonia write the card?'

'I think the florist does,' he responded. 'I'll make coffee.'

'I like milk,' Susie said. 'I'll get my own coffee on the way.'

* * *

She didn't want a card from his assistant, or flowers, or a gift.

As she showered and dressed she tried to pull herself out of a slight panic. She was torn between wanting another night and the farewell that was surely to come.

They left together, but as Dante walked down the steps Susie stopped, in the middle of wrapping her scarf, and saw all she'd missed last night.

'Oh!' She was taken aback by the view...the sheer beauty of where they were. Behind the elegant houses she could see the Tuscan hills. 'You can see the hills!' She spun around, and whichever way she looked the views were to die for. 'And the walls.' Everywhere she looked it was like a postcard. 'It's so gorgeous... How did I miss this?'

'We were a bit distracted.'

'True.' Susie laughed and, refusing to be rushed, stood and gazed down the almost deserted avenue.

Dante, who'd seemed impatient to get on, followed her gaze. 'It is stunning,' he agreed. 'In spring, the magnolia trees flower.'

'They're all magnolia trees?' She stood, trying to picture it in bloom. 'They're my favourite flowers.'

'Come the spring, you're in for a treat.'

'No...' She shook her head, hit by a sudden wave of pensiveness. It was possibly not fitting, over flowers she would never see, yet it briefly knocked her off kilter, and she could feel her smile slipping away, her shoulders drooping. 'I'll be in Florence by then,' she said.

Her voice sounded hollow, when usually she spoke of Florence with excitement, but it dawned on her that possibly it wouldn't be a floral display she'd be pining for.

Oh, God!

She looked down the street and then back to Dante. The collar was up on his coat, and he looked brooding and completely irresistible, and for the first time she glimpsed the hell of getting over him.

Did it really have to end?

Were there never exceptions to his temporary lover rule?

Any chance for an extension?

She'd been so happy with one night. Deliriously happy with two. And now...?

'Susie? Everything okay?' he checked.

Why not tell him what she was thinking? Susie pondered. For it was as if last night had somehow freed her—as if the liberty he'd brought to her body had also converted her mind. She would tell him how she felt. And maybe...just possibly...

'I was just...' she began.

But it was as if some sleeping guardian angel had been startled awake and had grabbed her by the collar of her trench coat, squeezing her throat tight on the surely forbidden words.

Do not fall for him, Susie, the angel warned.

You might be a bit late, she replied silently, though thankfully the moment of madness was over.

She liked the honesty between them, how he'd told her to speak up and say how she felt, but in this instance she knew that honesty possibly wasn't the best policy when dealing with a playboy of Dante's calibre.

So she pushed back her shoulders, conjured a smile and dashed down the steps to his side.

'I just adore magnolias.'

Sure enough, Gio was dressed and ready.

'You're late,' he told Dante.

'No...' Dante glanced at the clock and saw he was actually on time.

He didn't point it out to Gio, though. He knew this was very emotional for him.

They were silent as they passed the church where Dante knew his grandparents had married, then they turned and walked along a small cobbled street. Naturally Gio knew practically everyone they passed, and stopped for a greeting, but as they approached the small group of shops he paused.

'I want to ensure all the jewels are taken care of,' he said. 'And then I might have a private conversation with Signor Adino.'

'Of course,' Dante said.

'It might take some time.'

'No problem.'

The jewellers had been there long before Dante was born, with its dark wooden façade and gorgeous windows that displayed both modern and antique jewels.

'You and Sev used to look at the watches here.'

'We did.'

He'd forgotten that. They had been there often. Not just with Gio. Mamma would sit trying on rings, and all the other things that had seemed boring, and he and Sev had stared at the clocks and watches.

He saw the flash of his own stainless-steel watch now, as he rang the bell for their private appointment. The store would be closed to others.

'Welcome, Signor Casadio,' said Signor Adino as he opened the heavy glass door. 'Ah, and Sev...'

The jeweller stopped and laughed at his mistake, and Dante felt the sweep of Signor Adino's eyes briefly register his scar.

'I knew it was you who made the appointment, Dante, but for a moment I thought you were Sev. It's been such a long time.'

Such a long time.

He'd excluded himself as much as possible from life here for more than a decade.

Signor Adino locked the door behind them as Gio walked over to the rear counter and placed down the black jewellery pouch that contained so much of his life. His shaking hands opened it up—he clearly wanted to do this himself.

'There is a stone loose on this choker,' Gio said, and his voice was trembling as the jeweller put on his magnifying glasses. 'I remember you making this for her...' Gio took out a handkerchief, then turned to Dante. 'He's a good salesman. I had to purchase a silver hand mirror—'

'So Signora Casadio could see it when she put it on!' Signor Adino carried on.

Only Dante wasn't listening. He was staring at the spread of jewels on the black velvet—some dulled, but still attempting to shine, some that had belonged to his mother. There was even the cross and chain his father had worn when they were small.

It was the pieces that were missing that punished him the most.

Lost in the accident on the hills.

He thought of the two stones sitting in his safe back in Milan. He would really prefer to leave Gio to it, and yet he stood beside him, watching as each piece was laid out and one by one the jeweller made notes in a handwritten ledger.

Who the hell still used carbon paper?

Finally, the list was complete and the copy handed to Gio, who watched as the jewels and so many of his memories were carefully taken out to the back of the shop to be lovingly tended to.

'Are you okay?' Gio checked with Dante, when surely it should be the other way around.

'Of course.'

And with the past taken care of, the jeweller returned and smiled to Gio. 'I have everything set up for you, Signor Casadio.'

'I might be a while,' Gio said.

Dante nodded, watching as Gio moved behind the counter, no doubt to choose the stone for Mimi's ring.

He wandered around the small store, looking at the watches. There was a beautiful old gold one...

He glanced down at his own luxury watch and told himself he did not need another one. Anyway, he didn't wear gold.

And then from nowhere a memory assailed him, of standing on this very spot, with Sev beside him, not with his mother looking at rings, but with his father at the counter. Collecting a ring.

Turning to Sev, he had asked a question. 'What's an eternity ring?'

Slamming closed that memory, he walked away from the watches and crossed the floor of the tiny jewellers in two strides. For a while he stood unseeing, staring at the lavish displays, wishing to God they weren't locked in.

Then a burst of laughter from the office hauled him back to the present, and he looked with mild interest at some of the more modern pieces.

His attention was held by one. A necklace of sunflowers—a beautiful swirl of gemstones and precious metals—and beneath it a sticker that proclaimed it sold. His eyes moved to rubies arranged like a field of wild poppies and set in white gold. They weren't slender chains…more like subtle jewelled garlands with leaves.

He pulled his head back when he realised the jeweller had come out of the office and was standing behind him.

'Signor Casadio wanted a few moments alone.'

'Grazie.' Dante nodded, grateful for the time taken and the kindness shown to his grandfather—and he knew it wasn't just because the Casadios had once been regular clients, it was how things were done here. 'Are these your work?' he asked.

'They are.' Signor Adino nodded.

'Exquisite.'

'Thank you. They are a labour of love.'

Perhaps he could break another rule? He wasn't one for gifts, or romantic gestures, and certainly gave nothing as personal as jewellery. But he and Susie had got personal, and even if it could never last this weekend had meant a lot.

He'd heard the edge in her voice as she'd asked about the gifts he gave, about how he would end things.

Nicely.

Nicer than he'd ever been, perhaps?

'Do you have magnolias?'

'I don't.'

'Anything similar?'

'No…' The jeweller shook his head. 'These two are bespoke pieces—they are being collected this week. They are certainly not impulse purchases,' he scolded lightly. 'They take weeks to make. First a design is decided on, then the mould is cast…'

'So, not for me then?' Dante got the message and gave a wry laugh. 'I was just…' He didn't know quite what he'd been thinking, but then he smiled and looked up as Gio came out. 'Okay?'

'Yes.' Gio nodded and came over to thank Signor Adino profusely.

'So,' Dante said as they walked back to Gio's. 'What did you choose?'

'That is for Mimi to reveal,' Gio retorted. 'I haven't even asked her to marry me yet. Haven't I taught you anything?'

Dante saw him back to his house, and then his grandfather said he was going for a sleep.

'You no doubt have a flight to catch,' Gio said as he fare-welled him. 'Thank you for taking the day off today.'

'Any time,' Dante said. 'Well, not any time,' he warned as he kissed Gio goodbye. 'No getting married too soon; I have a case coming up…'

'I know you do.'

Gio certainly looked happier than when he'd arrived, Dante thought as he walked along the walls in the direction of home.

At times he had felt happy too.

But he knew he couldn't stay in bed with Susie for ever.

He sat on a bench and thought of how their conversations had started to deepen.

He'd wanted to know more about her.

And yet…

It was still hell to be here.

He thought of all those jewels splayed out on the velvet, and his grandfather thinking him cold because he could barely bring himself to look at them.

Susie was right. Old memories tainted the future.

Perhaps he would suggest she come to Milan this weekend?

He thought of her busy schedule, and the scant direct flights.

Then he closed his eyes in despair as he realised Gio had been right to doubt he was over the accident.

Dante got on and off helicopters with little thought. He just accepted that he had to, and took the risk…

But he could not stand the thought of Susie up in one.

'Susie?' The language teacher smiled. 'You are distracted today.'

'Sorry…'

Susie apologised, and tried to focus on the class, but her mind was in a hundred different places, and when it was time for a break, rather than find coffee and a chat she slipped off in search of peace.

The school had a magnificent balcony and Susie stepped out—just for some air and a moment.

Gosh, she was going to start crying, she thought, trying to remind herself that a few days ago she hadn't known him. The last time she'd attended class Dante hadn't even factored into her life. Perhaps it was better that she fired off a message now and told him she couldn't make it tonight.

Or maybe she'd decide after her lunchtime shift?

Then she stilled, for there on a bench he sat, staring out to the hills. She pulled back from the edge of the balcony and tried to tell herself to just go back to class.

Then she watched as he tipped his head back, as she might at the hairdresser's. But that only described the motion he made—it didn't explain why that movement had tears spilling down her cheeks.

She was witnessing agony.

'How was class?' Dante asked, letting the exhausted Susie in.

'It was okay,' she said.

'Work?'

'Long,' she admitted, taking off her awful shoes.

He helped her with her scarf and coat.

He sounded normal, and he certainly looked beautiful—no sign of the man she'd seen sitting alone and despairing on that bench.

'How was the jeweller's?' she asked.

'It was okay,' he told her. 'I'm not allowed to know what he chose for Mimi, of course. I meant to call Maria...'

'Who's Maria?'

'My housekeeper. I forgot to tell her I would be here to-night. I was going to ask her to get some food in. But I'll call for something—or we can go out?'

'Or I could make something?' Susie said.

'You've been at work.'

'I work most days,' Susie said, and smiled. 'And I eat most days too.'

She liked how he laughed and kissed her, and it was heaven to be back here. Really, she'd been stupid to think she couldn't han-dle it. It was just one more night, and she wanted to be here, so...

'Anyway...' She wriggled from his arms. 'I've been dying to get into your kitchen.' She laughed at his expression. 'Don't worry, Dante, I just miss cooking. There are only two little gas rings at the apartment, and a microwave and a toaster.'

'I really don't have any food.'

She opened up his cupboards and then peered into his fridge. 'And you had the cheek to tell me off about your grand-father's meagre fridge contents!' She saw a lonely tub of ricotta and a couple of other cheeses. 'I'll be fine with these.'

'You're sure?'

She nodded. 'There's a recipe I've been dying to try,' she told him, taking down a bag of walnuts from a cupboard. 'You've got most things I need.'

'Do you want some wine?'

'No, thank you.' She pulled out some flour and looked at his glass. 'I thought you didn't like wine?'

'Hmm...' He put down his glass and rather elegantly hopped onto the large marble bench, watching her pulling out jars he clearly hadn't known he had. 'I'm seriously hungry,' he warned, obviously not believing that nuts, cheese and some flour could be turned into much.

'I know.'

'Hey, Susie? What if your cooking is terrible?' he asked, making her smile. 'Do I have to pretend I like it?' he teased.

'Since when did you ever do that?' She smirked. 'You can give me your usual honest opinion.'

She was loving this…making pasta, stretching it, running it through the machine and watching as the lovely soft white sheets came out.

Dante sat watching her. It was unusual to see anyone other than Maria in his kitchen—and certainly he didn't sit and watch his housekeeper cook.

'I've got to go to court,' he told her. 'The wife read the husband's letter yesterday.'

'But he only posted it on Friday.'

'Through her door. Where he shouldn't even have been.'

'Gosh…'

'And he's not supposed to contact her, so another rap on the knuckles for me. He's offered, in his own handwriting, far more than had been agreed. Now he wants to change his mind. What a mess…'

'Do you like the wine?' she asked.

'I do…' He took another sip of wine, unable to voice more, because he could hardly believe he was drinking wine and thinking about the winery.

Thinking about taking on a little more responsibility for it.

He was grateful for the loud buzz as she blended walnuts, yet the large kitchen still felt peaceful.

Gio had never legally passed the business on to Dante's father, even though it had caused a few arguments…

'You'll get it when I'm gone,' Gio would declare. *'For now, it stays with me.'*

And that had proved important when tragedy had struck…

'My father had very big ideas for the winery,' he told her. 'Though Gio wouldn't let him get his hands on it. Rosa's family did too. They wanted to blend the two of them…'

Susie looked up.

'But Gio was having none of it. He would say, "You can do what you want with it when I'm gone..."'

'Did you ever want to be a part of it?'

'No—nor did Sev. Maybe we would have got involved somewhere down the line, but we wanted our own careers first.'

He watched as she placed little balls of mixture on the sheet of pasta, and found that watching Susie made it all too easy to voice his thoughts out loud. To *want* to voice them.

'If my father had been a shareholder on his death that share would have passed to Sev and I. And any of our spouses would have had a stake.'

'Ah, but you're going to be single for ever,' Susie said.

There were little parcels of ravioli all over his bench now, and she was concentrating on her sauce.

'Sev wasn't single.'

'No,' Susie agreed, and turned to him and offered a sympathetic smile. 'Rosa died, though.'

'Where there's a will there's a family...' Dante said. 'Do they say that in England?'

'I don't know.'

Susie gave a small laugh and got on with tasting her sauce.

Dante knew she didn't get it that if Gio had not been so wise then Rosa's family might have had a claim. It was the sort of thing that had kept him in the library for hours, long before her death, reading all the details in the books that lined the walls.

While he'd never anticipated losing his family, Dante had always been sure the De Santises had been trying to get hold of Gio's rich, fertile land and become a part of the successful winery business.

He took a sip of his wine—blackcurrant with a hint of pepper...

If the De Santises had had their way they'd be drinking vinegar by now.

Yes, Gio had been wise.

And, yes, perhaps he should have spoken to him—at least about the legal side…

Not about the sex or the pregnancy that never was.

That would be too much for Gio.

Too much for anyone.

'Nearly there,' Susie said, walking past the bench as she went to get a large copper saucepan.

He trapped her with his legs as she passed. 'It looks great.'

'You haven't tasted it yet.'

'Can I help?' he asked, knowing it was almost done.

'You can lay the table.'

'Or…' He pulled her in, looked at the flour on her cheeks and on her black dress, and found he was more than happy not to think about the De Santis family any more. 'We could eat in bed…'

'I want it to be nice.' She looked at him. 'I haven't cooked in for ever.'

'I shall lay the table, then.'

He did indeed lay the table—the grand table in his dining room—and he even lit candles.

'Susie!' he called as she passed by with plates. 'In here.'

She stepped in and her jaw dropped—not so much at the stunning polished table and the jade walls, but at the silver candelabra.

'I meant the coffee table… And candles?' she commented as she put down their plates. 'That's very romantic of you, Signor Casadio.'

'I think the food calls for it,' he said, turning out the main lights.

'We'll see…'

'Take a seat,' Dante said, and held out her chair.

'Thank you.'

Susie felt nervous as he sat down and looked at what she'd made. She always did when she tried something new, but somehow tonight it mattered more than ever.

'Ricotta ravioli with a walnut sauce…'

* * *

Dante looked at the food before him. He had eaten in many, many fine restaurants and this wouldn't be out of place in any of them—and all made from the scant selection in his cupboards.

He looked at the little garnish of parsley. 'It looks very nice,' he said, then turned his plate and nodded.

He picked up a fork and sliced a piece of ravioli, then took a mouthful and tasted it as carefully as Gio would taste wine.

Susie almost wished he'd just dive in and declare it 'nice' or 'awful', as her ex had. But then she'd hated it when he did that.

Dante took his time.

'Okay…' he said at last, when he'd swallowed the first mouthful. And she knew he wasn't saying that about her food.

He thought for a moment, and took another taste of her walnut sauce, before delivering his conclusion.

'Tell Cucou that you want a trial.' He looked right at her. 'Demand it.'

'I can't demand it!' She laughed away the very thought. 'Is it nice, though?'

'Susie, I was always going to be polite, no matter if it was nice or not. I was always going to say it was delicious, because I am polite and you cooked it. But this belongs in any top restaurant I have eaten in. I want to eat it all immediately. Even if you offered sex, right now on the table, I would want to finish my food first.'

'Honestly?'

'Offer me sex on the table and I'll prove it.'

She laughed, and yet she felt close to crying. It was the first time someone had really, properly talked with her about her cooking.

'Tell them you want a trial,' he repeated.

'I already have. They're not interested. I don't have experience… I can't speak the language.'

'Tell them food *is* your language, and then suggest they give you a chance or you'll walk out.'

'I need the job.'

'Susie, they're testing you. You have to be tough to survive in a kitchen like that. They would not have you preparing food for my grandfather if they didn't think the world of you. He is a very well thought of man here.'

'Yes…'

'Stand up for yourself. You might find they are just waiting for you to do so.'

She'd never considered such a thing.

It was a gorgeous night.

'I don't know what was better,' Dante said a whole lot later, as they lay there breathless and sated. 'The food or the sex…'

Such a gorgeous night…

So much so she forgot to dread the morning.

Even as it arrived…

CHAPTER SEVEN

'I LIKE THIS…' Susie admitted.

'What?'

'Lying in bed talking…'

They hadn't really slept, and now morning was creeping in. No beams of light, but she could see their hands knotted together on his stomach as she lay with her head on his chest. And as brilliant, as dazzling and as whirlwind as the weekend had been, and as fabulous as the sex was, it was these quiet moments, just talking, that she'd cherish deeply. It was where they were closest to one another, and the truth serum seemed to reach its peak dose around dawn…

'I hear Juliet and Louanna chatting most mornings,' she told him.

'Are they partners?'

'No!' She thumped his chest lightly. 'They get up before me, that's all. I hear them discussing their music, and people I don't know. It just reminds me…'

'Of what?'

'Growing up, I had my own room,' Susie explained. 'While my sisters got to share.'

'*Got* to share?' he checked. 'Wouldn't you want your own room?'

She laughed. 'We don't all live in mansions. It was a three-bedroom home. Usually the eldest gets their own room, but the twins wanted to be together,' she explained. 'All my friends said I was lucky.'

'But you didn't feel so lucky?'

'It sounded as if they were having a party every night. And then came discussions about boys and make-up and...'

'What about birthdays?' Dante said.

'What about them?'

'I think Gio said you were close in age to the twins?'

'They're just over a year older.' She took a breath. 'So our parties were all lumped together. It was a case of two against one,' she said. 'I always wanted to have a fairy party or dress up...'

'What did your sisters want?'

'To go to the cinema, or the zoo, or...' She thought back. 'I remember this man with reptiles came to the garden.' She shuddered. 'I was very young.'

He laughed. 'What's your first memory?'

'I can't remember.'

'Come on...'

'I was in my pushchair...' Clearly, he wasn't up on the names of baby paraphernalia. 'A stroller? And I saw a lady smiling and saying nice things about me to my mother. Then the twins came out of the shop with my father and she just started admiring them...' She gave a muted laugh. 'I threw my dummy out.' He frowned. 'Pacifier?'

'Ah...' He smiled. 'For attention?'

'I threw it again and again. See? I'm not nice.'

'Are you jealous?' he asked.

She was about to defend herself—to answer as she had before and say of course she was not—but she felt hot tears splashing out, along with the truth.

'So very jealous.' She left his arms and sat up, almost leapt out of bed, as if startled by her own truth. 'So damn jealous... The twins, the twins, the twins...' she parroted.

And out burst almost twenty-five years' worth of stored bitter tears.

'Hey...'

Emotional outbursts did not move him, but feeling her crumple, seeing the wet tears, hearing the choking voice, he was both horrified and stunned that their light, playful conversation had turned so dark.

Dante had been provoking her for the truth, but the depth of her pain stunned him. And yet he was oddly pleased to hold the real Susie, to feel this hot ball of emotion in his arms.

'You can be jealous,' he told her. 'Why not?'

'It's wrong, though. I love them, but…' She was really crying now. 'There was a school play…'

She told him how stunning they'd been as angels…and how heads always turned whenever they passed. And about the shared bedroom again. Out it all came.

'They even got beautiful names—Cassandra and Celia, I got Susan.' She halted, as if stunned by her own vitriol. 'Oh, God, I sound so…'

'Jealous,' he said. 'And no wonder.' He was practical. 'Next time your mother accuses you, say, *Yes, I am jealous, so perhaps you could be more thoughtful.*'

'I doubt that would work.' She closed her eyes and took a breath and he pulled her back down. 'Do you get jealous?' she asked.

He thought for a moment. 'No.'

'What's *your* first memory?'

'I think getting a smack.' He laughed. 'I wandered off on the beach.' He thought of his mother. 'My mother was furious.'

'Scared?'

'Yes. That was the only time I saw her angry. When I was in the jewellers yesterday—' He stopped. He really hadn't meant to go there. But then he looked at her wet lashes and reasoned that she'd told him some painful stuff. 'I remembered being there when my mother chose some stones for a ring. She was laughing. Then a few weeks later we went with my father to pick the ring up. I asked Sev what an eternity ring was.'

'What did he say?'

'I can't recall,' Dante admitted. 'You remember I told you that I had people comb the accident site? They found two rubies from that ring.'

'And you haven't told anyone?'

'No, it would be too much for Gio. He cried over a loose stone on Nonna's choker...'

She frowned, clearly still not getting it.

'I don't know if my mother took her ring off, and that was how the stones didn't shatter in the fire,' he said. 'Or...'

She was still frowning, so he was more direct.

'There was nothing of them left intact.'

'Oh, God,' she said, which was entirely the wrong thing, but he found he didn't mind.

'It's fine. Gio doesn't need to know. They're in an envelope in a safe. I don't look at them or know what to do with them. I spend most of my life with people who are fighting over things and I don't get it. I can't imagine fighting over a house, or a yacht, or anything.'

'Why haven't you told Sev?'

Dante shook his head, and although it was clear he was telling her to leave it, Susie saw he was looking right into her eyes.

It was the first time in her life she'd truly felt close to another person—as if it was in this room, in this conversation, that she completely belonged.

Susie stared into his dark eyes and told herself that was ridiculous.

She had family, friends, work... And, yes, she was loved.

But in this moment, she was in the right place, and nothing and no one could invade it.

His hand brushed back the hair on her forehead, and they were still staring at the other.

'Suuu-zeee...' he said, changing the topic in the nicest of ways. 'I think it's a beautiful name.'

'Only when *you* say it.'

He gave a very gentle smile as they continued to stare right into each other's eyes.

'Maybe...' he said, and moved to kiss her.

She saw his eyes draw nearer, felt the warmth of his skin even before their lips had met, and she knew she was about to be kissed.

It was thrilling, even though she'd been kissed by Dante many times. This kiss was soft, as were his hands, and feeling his mouth on hers caused an involuntary sob...

She revelled in his citrussy cologne and the warm caress of his tongue, in how he stroked the side of her aching breast as her arms coiled around his neck. His head moved down and he took her breast in his mouth. She heard herself moan again, felt the slide of his hands on her hips, the tempo moving to a mutual urgency.

He pulled the pillows from the bed and she lay beneath him. And even though he moved to his elbows it was the lower weight of him that had her breathless. His hungry kiss made her feel as if she were being crushed by desire.

'Dante...'

His mouth was at her ear, kissing the shell, and there were myriad sensations. His thigh was between her legs, and she was already parting them, and his groan as he squeezed inside her spoke for them both.

She arched up and pressed her hands into him, her body begging for urgent relief, but his thrusts were slow and measured.

'Slow down,' he told her, denying her haste.

'I can't.'

She spoke not just for her body, but for every part of her. She did not know how to slow things down now he'd appeared in her life. She was aching with desire, tearful at the prospect of missing him, and reckless with her heart. All Susie knew was that she wanted more than she'd had. It was as if everything was in tune—as if loneliness had been banished and she could not hold back.

And suddenly she felt a rush of fury that he was holding back, taking her slowly. So she arched again, impatiently. 'Please...'

And at her urging Susie found out just how much he'd been holding back.

He took her with an intensity she hadn't realised until now that she craved.

'Suuu-zeee...' he said, as perfectly as he had that first night, calling her name as only he could. Filling her, consuming her, and making her temporarily his.

And she didn't want it to be over, didn't want their time to end. Her eyes flicked open, only to be met by his.

A single look that evoked a thousand questions.

'How?' she asked as he took her.

For a second she thought he might answer her nonsensical question, but instead Dante closed his eyes, and went back into his head.

'How...' she demanded and if she had nails, they would have dug in his back, but instead she clung on. She kissed his salty shoulder and wanted to bite. Again fury rushed through her—for how could he want her in this moment, then say goodbye the next.

And it was goodbye, for he was releasing into her.

How could they be over, she wanted to beg, but there were no words left. Feeling him come, hearing his passionate shout had her fury twisting into desire, delivering an orgasm so deep it took all thought away.

When her eyes opened she saw his were closed as she dragged breath back into her lungs.

'How?' Susie asked again, as intimate pulses faded.

Of course he didn't answer.

Dante rarely allowed emotion in the bedroom.

Pleasure, yes.

But his heart had been sealed so long ago he'd forgotten it existed.

Yet it had emerged in recent days and now it thumped in his chest.

He took in a deep breath, knowing there was no way ahead for them.

He'd heard her question.

How did they do this?

Certainly he didn't want her to be endlessly here waiting

for occasional visits, but nor did he want her whirring her way through the air to Milan.

For what?

They were too close for comfort. What had felt right a moment ago now felt unfamiliar and unwelcome, and he knew he was too dark for her light.

He could hear her talking, apologising for her feelings. Oh, she didn't allude to the question begged in the throes of love-making instead admitting to being embarrassed by her earlier tears and what she'd revealed about being jealous.

'So there you have it,' Susie said. 'The fatal flaw...my Achilles' heel.'

'It's really not that bad,' Dante said.

And then, as she often did, Susie practised her Italian.

'Qual è l'azione peggiore che hai impegnato?'

Dante frowned as he deciphered her dreadful pronunciation. 'What is the worst action I have ever committed?'

He started to smile—he knew she'd got the words wrong, and had been trying to get him to share—but then his smile faded.

He reached down to rescue one of the pillows that had been scattered by their lovemaking, but then he put his hand behind his head and lay flat.

He was tired of carrying his secret.

Possibly he knew his truth would deal with things and push her away for ever.

How?

Dante knew how to end them—'I slept with my brother's wife.'

Susie looked over at him. Watched as Dante stared at the ceiling...

'Is that why...?'

She didn't finish the question. Of course that would have caused the brothers to fall out.

But then Dante gave a small shake of his head. 'Sev doesn't know.'

For a second she wanted to sit up, to hug her knees, to re-sist looking at him—for surely there were few betrayals worse than that? But she was held by the agony in his eyes, and she knew that whatever her own feelings were on the subject he surely didn't need to hear them.

She didn't doubt Dante was already burning in his own guilty hell.

She had never been entrusted with something so big, and she touched his arm, not knowing what to say, but trying. 'Was it...?' She tried to keep the shaky note from her voice. 'Did it go on for long?'

'It was once.'

He closed his eyes and took a deep breath, and Susie thought he was trying to banish the memory rather than summon it.

'I was in Milan, a student. I'd just passed my first-year exams.'

She frowned, trying to get her head around things. Surely Dante had been at the end of his studies when Sev had got married? She stayed silent rather than speak.

'Even back then I never got involved with anyone who came from here. But she was in Milan for a visit and we met up.' His laugh was both dark and resigned. 'We were nineteen—you know what it's like...'

Susie had had no idea what *anything* was like at nineteen—at least not on the dating front. She'd been awkward in herself, working shifts in a kitchen bar and...

Hiding, Susie realised.

She'd been hiding even back then...

Only her rather pale and drab past wasn't the issue now, and she listened as Dante told her what had happened between him and Rosa.

'We both agreed it was to be a one-off.'

Never had Susie been more grateful for her reticence—for holding back and not automatically voicing her thoughts. It meant she hadn't jumped straight in and was able to speak in an unaccusatory tone.

'You were nineteen. So, they weren't married at the time?'

'God, no.'

He dismissed that as if he were brushing off a fly, and then he looked over at her. 'But it didn't end brilliantly. She suddenly seemed to think that our brief hook-up meant we were going out. That was never what we agreed.'

Susie fought not to react—not to show in her features that she didn't like that term...*brief hook-up*. Not because of any moral code or such—she just didn't want it applied to her.

To them.

She didn't want what they'd found to be labelled as a 'hook-up'.

'So, for you it was just casual...?' Her voice tripped over the words. 'Like us? Like this?' she checked, speaking through lips that were possibly a little pale and taut.

But then she checked herself, doing her best to put her own issues with Dante aside—whatever they might be—and do her best to focus on him.

Dante looked at her and wanted to say, *It was nothing like us. Nothing like this...*

'We didn't do a lot of talking,' he said, and even as he answered he knew he'd said it all wrong.

Her short nails dug into his skin then, and she pulled her hand back as Dante continued.

'I told her from the start that I didn't want a relationship,' he said. 'I made it clear we were never going to be serious.'

'But she fell for you?'

'I don't know...'

Dante sat up in bed, his elbows on his knees, and Susie lay silent.

Susie didn't really know what to say, for as she looked at him, gorgeous in the morning light, on the bed still rumpled and warm from their time together, her body still thrumming from the breathtaking attention he'd given her, she could see both sides.

But contemplating how Rosa might have felt wouldn't be helpful right now—because no matter how sure and brave she'd been at the start, no matter that she'd sworn to hold on to her heart, when they said goodbye it was going to hurt.

Dante had seen her features change, could feel Susie's eyes on his back, and knew she was struggling to find the words to say.

He sat waiting for relief to come at having finally told someone.

Wasn't confession supposed to be good for the soul?

It didn't feel that way, and there was certainly no sense of relief.

He felt ill as he examined what he'd said, and even though Susie didn't press him for information, he carried on out loud. 'Rosa wanted to tell people about us,' he said. 'She kept calling…asking when I'd be back in Lucca…angling for me to take her to the ball. That would have been practically announcing our engagement…'

'So, she wanted to get serious?'

'Oh, yes—and I don't doubt her parents were behind it.' He turned and looked at Susie, still lying there, her eyes huge as they met his. 'They had big plans for their old shack of a winery.'

'What?' Her eyes snapped closed and her lips tightened. 'I've heard you be blunt before, but never mean…'

'Because I save it for those who deserve it.'

Dante shook his head and got out of bed. How the hell was he supposed to tell her all of it if he had to censor every word?

'Just because you hold everything in, it doesn't mean I have to,' he told her.

'Meaning?' she bristled.

'Just that.'

'I think you can say difficult things and still remain nice.'

'Fine,' Dante responded. 'I'll tell you *nicely*, then.'

And so he did. He gave her the cleaner, condensed version.

'I cut things off, and the rare times I was home I kept well away from Rosa, or even any conversation about her. Two years later I was walking on the walls when Rosa came running. She told me she and Sev were about to announce their engagement.'

'He didn't know that you'd slept together?'

'Of course not.'

'And you told him just before the wedding?'

'No,' he refuted. 'I tried to broach the subject… I said some things I perhaps shouldn't have.' He pursed his lips the way Susie had. 'Let's not go there. I'm sure you wouldn't approve.'

'Dante…'

Her eyes filled with tears and he could not bear to see them. He hated it that all he ever caused was hurt.

'Sev let me know my opinions were not welcome,' he told her.

'Dante…' She reached out to touch his shoulder, but he tensed and stood up.

'So there you have it.'

'What?'

'The worst action I have ever committed.'

He walked towards the shower, but she halted him with a question as he reached for the door.

'You mean sleeping with Rosa, or not telling Sev that you had?'

It was a very good question.

One he didn't answer.

Couldn't answer.

Instead, he climbed into the shower, and as the water hit him there was finally relief that he'd told her.

They'd been getting too close; he knew that very well.

Given Susie's reaction now, that would no longer be an issue.

That was the relief.

Dante was self-aware enough to know that in revealing the truth he was effectively ending them. But better to cut things off now than be standing in a jewellers considering romantic gifts, or walking back into the bedroom and asking if she wanted to come to Milan.

No.

He didn't want anyone.

But even as the water cleansed him he felt contaminated—as if he brought nothing but despair into the lives of everyone who had ever mattered.

Susie knew she'd handled things badly.

As Dante showered she lay there for a while, knowing damn well that she'd been busy comparing their weekend of passion with what had happened between him and Rosa. And when he'd disparaged Rosa's family winery, she'd flinched. Not so much at what he'd said, more out of dread that one day she'd be similarly relegated to the past...a little footnote he referred to with derision because she'd been stupid enough to bare her heart.

She'd been shocked at first...worried that he'd been having an affair while Sev and Rosa were married. And when the relief of getting it wrong had hit her she'd been too involved in her own tumbled feelings to really listen to Dante, let alone say the right thing.

Now, as he came out of the shower, she just hoped it wasn't too late.

'Dante...'

'Let's leave it, hey?' His suggestion was kind. 'My car will be here soon. I don't want you leaving here upset.'

He said it nicely, but the implication was that it might be better for her to get dressed.

'I've thought about it,' Susie said. 'While you were in the shower.'

He shot her a slightly incredulous look. 'Oh? So do you have a solution?' He buttoned his shirt. 'I've been considering it for more than a decade.'

'Dante, please...' She felt like a plane that had been going round and around, attempting to land for a second time, only the conditions on the ground hadn't really improved. 'I think you should try telling Sev. It's been so many years. You've both lost so much. Could you write to him?' she suggested. 'Like your client did to his wife?'

'I am going to be dealing with the fallout of that letter today.' He looked at her then, and actually smiled. 'I've tried, believe me, but I can get never get past the first line… *"Dear Sev, sorry if this comes as a surprise…"'*

'He's your brother, though, and from everything I've heard you were once so close…' Her voice trailed off as he glanced out of the window.

'The car's here,' he told her. 'I can drop you off.'

Susie didn't want to get dressed, but she did.

She didn't want to leave, but she could hardly chain herself to the bed.

And she did not want to cry, but she felt very much as if she might.

'Hey…' Dante did not want it to end like this, and he took her in his arms. 'I shouldn't have told you.'

'I'm glad you did,' she told him.

'No, you're not,' he said gently.

He could see the doubt swirling in her eyes, feel the ache in her to fix something that was broken beyond repair.

And it was.

Of that he was certain.

But even if his car was waiting, and even if he might well miss his plane, Dante chose to take the time to let Susie see just how impossible things were for him and Sev.

'Will you answer me something honestly?' Dante asked.

Susie gave a nervous laugh, a little worried as to what he might ask. 'Am I on the witness stand?'

'You are,' he said, and took her face in his hands.

It was just nice to be teased a little as they faced the difficult topic.

'We've had a good time,' he said. 'Agreed?'

'Yes…'

'And we're both clear that it should end neatly?'

'Yes.'

'With no hard feelings?'

She didn't answer quite so quickly then, because while there might not be hard feelings in the way he meant them, there were going to be difficult feelings—and certainly they'd hurt.

'Susie?' He was awaiting her response.

'No hard feelings,' she agreed—because she didn't regret what had taken place between them, nor ever would.

'Okay,' Dante said, and his hand moved to her arm. 'Now, what if in two years' time…?'

His hand paused, the fingers hovering over her arm, and she felt her skin goosebump, as if stretching to retain contact.

'What are the names of your sisters?' he asked.

'Cassandra and Celia.'

'Okay, what if Celia comes to visit, tells everyone she's met a guy, and she's hoping he'll propose this weekend…'

Susie's heart sank as she envisaged it.

'His name is Dante…'

She swallowed.

'And he's really good-looking,' he said, coaxing out a smile.

'Arrogant?' she checked.

'Absolutely,' Dante said. 'As well as brilliant in bed. Oh, and he's an attorney in Milan.'

Her smile faded then; this game was so hard to play.

'I don't know…' Her mind darted at the dreadful conundrum. 'I think I'd tell her.'

'What if I'd already met the rest of your family and told them we were getting engaged?'

'I…' Her certainty was gone.

And the more he spoke on, the more she didn't know.

'What if I then caught you alone and told you how much it would hurt your sister if you ever told her?'

'I'd probably do what you did…'

'And then I tragically die.'

Susie started to cry as she truly saw the hellish position he was in.

'Would you tell her then?' he asked. *"Hey, Celia, I never told you at the time, but before you were married Dante and I..."*

'No.' She stopped him then. 'I would never tell her.'

'There you go.'

Susie stood still, wishing there was something better she could offer, and then she looked at Dante, a man who dealt in broken relationships for a living, and knew he would have examined every angle.

'I'm so sorry for what happened,' she told him.

'It's hardly your fault.'

'I *am* sorry, though; it must have been awful.'

He nodded.

'It still is?' Susie ventured.

He didn't answer; instead he gave her the nicest kiss.

But it was a slow and light kiss, a never-to-deepen kiss, and as they pulled apart Susie ran her tongue over her lips and they tasted of goodbye.

It was time to do this.

'I should go.'

She pulled on her boots and put her lip balm in her bag, and then she went to the bathroom and packed her toiletries in seconds. She came out as Dante was throwing a couple of last-minute things into his hand luggage.

'My driver just texted,' he said. His voice was a little husky, but then it wasn't even 6:00 a.m. 'I need a file...'

'I'll go,' she told him.

And there were no more kisses, no suggestions that they might meet again. She sort of waved at the door, but he was ramming a folder into his case, so she clipped down the stairs, pulled on her coat and collected her basket of goodies from the winery.

Dante closed his eyes as he heard the door close.

He'd seen the glittery tears in her eyes and he actually got it for once. Sometimes saying goodbye really was hard.

And he loathed how matter-of-fact he'd been, when he hadn't felt that way at all.

'Merda,' he said, cursing himself as he headed down the stairs.

To do what?

Call her back?

Take her back to bed and then say goodbye all over again?

He paused, saw her scarf on his banister and recalled removing it. He remembered their passion, their conversation, and everything in between.

He did not wrench open the door. Nor did he call her back to get her scarf and haul her into bed. Nor did he whisk her off to Milan.

Instead, he reminded himself of what he'd told his client.

Let her go with grace.

He put the scarf back over the banister and then went and collected his case. He headed out to the waiting vehicle and tried not to catch one final glimpse of Susie walking along the walls, carrying her basket...

CHAPTER EIGHT

ODDLY, WHEN IT felt as if the world was ending, she didn't cry. Instead, she greeted a couple of early-morning locals as if life was beautiful…as if the world was normal. There were even tiny buds on the trees that hadn't been there on Friday,

'Mi scusi,' someone said, and Susie smiled and stepped aside.

She was surprised at how calm she was, that she wasn't in floods of tears. But if anything, she was relieved.

Relieved that she hadn't burst out crying on him—or, worse, asked him when or if they might see each other again.

'Permesso…' a morning jogger scolded her.

But she barely noticed—was just relieved to make it to the apartment and climb the steps and be home.

'Hey…' Juliet smiled. 'Goodness, did you win a raffle?'

'I might have.' Susie smiled. 'Help yourself.'

'Seriously?' Louanna pounced on the offer, and was soon smearing truffled honey on crackers.

Oddly numb, Susie showered, tidied her room, caught up on a few calls, and then put on her uniform for work.

She was doing brilliantly, she decided. Over him already.

'Woo-hoo!' Louanna suddenly called from the lounge. 'Casadio!'

Frowning, Susie walked through—and there Dante was on her television screen.

'If I ever need to get divorced,' Louanna said, 'I am going to him.'

'What's it about?' Juliet asked.

'The divorce of the century,' Louanna said. 'Casadio is ruthless…he's trying to get a judge to agree to proceedings being delayed.'

Good grief!

Dante looked beautiful—as if he'd rolled over and gone to sleep after she'd left, and then been shaved and groomed by angels before stepping into a dark suit and his court robes.

'His robes…' Susie croaked—and then realised she'd said it out loud.

'Toga,' Louanna translated. 'They're in the Supreme Court.'

Dante even smirked as some journalist hurled a question at him.

Unlike his client, who walked alongside him, Dante was utterly calm, a little scathing, and completely immaculate.

He didn't even offer a 'no comment' as he walked from the court with his entourage, his *toga* billowing behind him.

Had she really been in bed with him just this morning?

She headed to work, bumping into a few more people along the way.

There was something fizzing inside her.

How could he be so completely fine?

Dante was far from fine.

There'd been an air of disorder when he'd arrived at work. As his client's letter had arrived while he was away, and an order had been broken, it meant he'd had no choice but to rock up to court.

And, no, the judge was not pleased at the stalling tactics—and no, there would be no more delays.

She'd glared at Dante. 'I don't like a circus outside my courtroom, Signor Casadio.'

And best of all, when he'd returned to his office, his head still spinning, Antonia had tried to bring him up to speed on lesser matters.

'This can surely wait?' Dante had said.

But Antonia liked a clear desk as much as he did, and had persisted. Relaying urgent messages, the names of other clients who were also about to stuff up, several requests from the press.

And now there was the personal stuff...

'Signor Adino, the jeweller...?'

'Dealt with.'

'Helene...' She glanced up, to confirm that he knew she meant his brother's PA. 'Helene would like to know if there is anything pressing regarding your trip home. She's more than happy to assist...'

Damn Sev. Too wrapped up in his own life to get on a plane himself, Dante thought. But now he wanted a full report.

He could wait.

'Oh, and a Susie Bilton left a message,' Antonia said. 'She said it was personal.'

'Grazie,' Dante said.

Merda, he thought.

Dante really didn't hear the rest, but he managed to nod in enough right places that finally he had the office to himself.

He'd tried to end it nicely this morning—had really thought she'd understood that there would be no repeats, no follow-up, no more...

He'd destroyed everyone he'd ever been close to, save for Gio, and he was not going to risk it with Susie.

Their weekend had been a rare one, and one to never repeat.

He'd been certain when he'd told Susie what had happened between him and Rosa that that would be it.

Now it was time to be his bastard self.

He dialled her number.

'Susie,' he said.

'Dante?'

'My assistant just informed me that you called.'

'Scusi...' she said, and he heard someone swear at her.

'Where are you?'

'Walking to work.'

'So why is someone swearing at you?'

He tried not to think of the last time he'd seen her walking on the walls. How he'd teased her about Mimi being Juliet...

Instead he got back to the point. 'And why did you call? Antonia said it was for personal reasons. I didn't think you were needy, Susie.'

'Needy?' She let out an incredulous laugh. 'I actually called you last Friday.'

'Why?'

'Because you told me I'd be able to find you in two minutes.'

He saw another image, this time of Susie standing under the umbrella.

'I didn't think you'd ever get the message or call me back.'

'Well, I have.'

'Just as well it wasn't a real emergency with your grandfather,' Susie said. 'It took you long enough.'

'What are you talking about?'

'I'm just pointing out that had there been a problem, you wouldn't have been around.'

'You're making no sense.'

Wasn't she? Susie asked herself as she was almost mowed down by a cyclist.

It finally registered that she was walking on the wrong side of the path. Possibly that was why everyone had been a little testy with her this morning.

'Susie…?' he said.

'I'm going to go,' Susie said, her voice a little high. 'I'm at work.'

Oh, she was fine.

Utterly fine.

If anything, she was angry. How dared Dante call her needy! She stood there as Pedro allocated the team and told her the tables she was working.

'No bruschetta,' he said, and then told them everything else that was off the menu. 'We are short in the kitchen.'

Then he clapped his hands and everyone set off to work. Except Susie.

'Problem, Susie?' Pedro said in English, as if she might not have understood his instructions. 'I said you're to work the bar tables and—'

'I understood what you said,' Susie said, in such a determined voice that, along with Pedro, she blinked in surprise. 'I'm so sorry, Pedro, I'll finish my shift, but after that I'm going to look for something else…'

He frowned.

'It's very disheartening to be told no without any consideration…to not be given even a chance…'

She was possibly saying what she wished she could say to Dante, Susie conceded, but Pedro would have to do. 'To be just written off.' She reached for her apron. 'Actually, I think I should just go home now.'

She marched to the little staff cloakroom, ready to go home, where she might take her scissors to that damn basket and tip the contents in the bin.

She halted and sat down on the small bench.

Oh, gosh, she wasn't okay.

Not at all.

She had been a public liability walking on the walls, and now she'd thrown in her job.

Oh—and now she understood what Dante had meant about walking around thinking you were being normal.

Then, at the thought of him out on the hills, searching, she started to panic, wondering how on earth she could get home without breaking down.

Never—not for a second—had she thought you could fall this hard for a person in a single weekend.

A single long weekend, she corrected.

A deliciously long and very wonderful weekend.

She'd never thought she was capable of this depth of feeling. It seriously hurt.

And it wasn't just her own pain she was dealing with. She seriously ached on his behalf too.

Gosh, she'd cried over her ex—but that had been more out of guilt for ending something that hadn't mattered enough.

Dante had made her feel like herself, feel important, feel wanted and adored and special. And he'd told her about Sev.

They'd shared so much…

'Susie?' There was a knock at the door and then Pedro put his head around it. 'You have a shift tonight in the kitchen,' he told her. 'Be here at four for prep.'

Thank goodness for work…

For exhilarating, exhausting shifts at the restaurant.

Now Susie wore the kitchen's huge black and white pants with a white top and apron. They were by far too big, but Susie loved them. And it was much easier to tackle mountains of to-matoes or onions than to address issues of the heart. And there was language classes and homework on top of that.

Susie was happy to collapse into bed each night and fall into an exhausted sleep.

It was in the silence of morning that she glimpsed despair and lay there so lonely, remembering how she and Dante would lie and talk…sometimes lying on their stomachs, facing each other, or on their backs looking over from their pillows…or the sheer pleasure of being held…

Then Juliet's violin would start!

Yes, she had every right to tell her to stop, but Juliet was apparently struggling at music school. As well as that, she was sweet and kind, and yesterday had even asked Susie if everything was okay.

Of course it was!

Work was increasingly brilliant. Soon she was no longer constantly chopping, and there were times when Cucou called her over and gave her a little demonstration, or asked her to taste something…

'My *sofrito*…' Cucou said now, speaking lovingly of the onion, celery and carrots he was frying in butter, and Susie's eyes were like a hawk's as she watched what he added.

Sofrito was the base for many Italian dishes, and every *nonna* and every chef guarded their own recipe. Parsley went in, she saw, and she noted the aromatics he added…

He gestured for her to try it and she took a little tasting stick. 'Oh, my…' she groaned at the sheer perfection. 'I need to add more butter to mine, and…' She looked at Cucou, who was smiling to himself, and was certain she hadn't seen all that he'd added. 'There's something else…'

He carried on stirring.

'Will I ever find out?'

'No.' Cucou shook his head. 'I shall take it to the grave.'

As well as work there were wonderful hours spent with Mimi—and not just walking on the walls. Sometimes they would go to the shops, or for coffee, and this gorgeous Saturday they were in Mimi's sister's home. Or was it Mimi's home? Susie still hadn't quite worked it out. But there they sat, going through old photos as Susie practised her Italian.

'This church is beautiful…'

'Very good,' Mimi approved, and turned a page in the album. 'Now say something about this photograph.'

'Goodness…'

It was a photo of a much younger Mimi, standing centre-stage in the amphitheatre. She was poured into velvet, her hair in ringlets, and clearly singing her heart out as the crowd watched spellbound.

'Look at you!'

'I was so beautiful that night…my voice soared.'

Mimi stretched her arms up like a ballerina and held the position as she recalled it, then gave a contented sigh as her hand came down. Susie wished she had a tenth of Mimi's fizz and confidence.

'I was singing for Eric,' she said, and smiled. 'He had asked me to the ball.'

'Are you hoping Gio will ask you?' Susie said, perhaps angling to know what was happening.

Apart from the little Dante had told her, it would seem he and Mimi were still living apart, although Mimi seemed a lot happier. In fact, she laughed now at Susie's question.

'Oh, no. The ball is very traditional. You only ever take one woman. It is different these days, but for some of us the tradition remains. Gio proposed to his beautiful wife there. It was where I met Eric...' She looked at Susie. 'You should go—Gio can get you invited!'

'I can't. My parents are visiting that weekend,' Susie said. 'As well as that, I don't have anyone to go with.'

She thought how dismissive Dante had been, even at the thought of inviting her. And although her thoughts darkened, she tried to lighten her tone.

'Anyway, I wouldn't have a clue what to wear. Let alone be able afford it.'

'I have a thousand gowns.' Mimi waved her excuses away. 'And I have been many sizes. Come.'

She took Susie upstairs to a gorgeous high-ceilinged room, with many full-length mirrors and an ornate dressing table with angled side mirrors.

'This is where I sing now, but it was once my dressing room,' Mimi said as she opened up what looked like an entire wall of wardrobes.

'Oh, Mimi...'

Susie stared at the array of beautiful gowns as Mimi pointed out some of the costumes she'd worn. Enchanted, Susie went through the dresses. Silks, velvets, frothy tulle of many shades and moods, vivid crimsons and sensual violets, as well as a dazzling russet. They were all labelled with the venues they'd been worn at, as well as the dates.

'Rosina,' Mimi sighed, taking out a black velvet dress. And perhaps she saw Susie's frown. 'I sang Rosina in *The Barber of Seville*.'

For a tiny second Susie had thought Mimi was talking about Rosa... Gosh, that last conversation...her last time with Dante. No matter how Susie filled her days, he was never more than a thought away.

Then came a brief diversion as her hand paused over a dusky gown. Susie wasn't sure if it was a pastel grey or pink, but the fabric was as soft as feathers to the touch.

'Oh!' Mimi gave a cry of delight, replacing her Rosina costume and coming over. 'What was I thinking? I actually hated that poor gown.'

'Why?'

'I usually prefer block colours. But this designer was famous for his achromatic designs and I wanted to own one. By the time it came to the final fitting I'd decided it was too subtle for me.' She put on her glasses and read her meticulous notes, then separated the layers of the skirt. 'The slip is Paris-pink, the chiffon a dove-grey.' She took it out and held it against Susie. 'I was very precious then—I believe I ended up wearing saffron.' She peered at the label again. 'It's never been worn. Try it.'

Susie couldn't resist, and slipped behind the curtains and undressed. Then she peered at the frothy gown wondering how to get it on. 'Do I...?'

'Step into it,' Mimi said from outside.

It felt like stepping into heaven. It was glorious, even allowing for the straps of her bra, and she stared at her image, a little pale and washed out, as Mimi chatted away.

'In Milan, I had four people helping me into it.'

Dante was in Milan...

That was all it took and he was back at the forefront of her mind. Gosh, no matter how Susie tried she could not keep thoughts of him at bay.

The curtain was swept back and Mimi stepped in. 'It's heavenly,' Susie said. 'Although even done up I think it'll be a bit too big...'

'It's corseted,' Mimi said. She instructed Susie to take off her bra, then took a little implement like a crochet hook to do up the back buttons. 'Arthritis,' she explained, and then, with not a jot of awkwardness, she stared at Susie in the mirror and jostled her breasts.

'Ow!' Susie said. 'That hurt!'

'I barely touched them!' Mimi laughed as she arranged the skirt and then looked at Susie's reflection. 'Oh, Susie...' She gave her verdict. 'It's perfect.'

'No, I think you were right about the colour,' she said. 'I do look pale in it.'

'Because you are pale,' Mimi said. 'This plays it up.'

Mimi lifted Susie's hair, as if trying to decide if it should be worn up or down.

'Please think about going…you'd be the belle of the ball.'

There was the sudden threat of tears. But Susie hadn't cried since she'd first torn off her apron and demanded a trial in the kitchen. And she was not going to cry now.

'It's gorgeous,' Susie said, 'but…' She shook her head. 'I really can't.'

'Surely your parents would love to see you all dressed up and enjoying yourself?'

'Not if they've flown over to see me!' Susie laughed, though it wasn't just the fact that her parents were coming that held her back. It was the thought of attending the ball alone when she'd have given anything to attend with Dante.

He hadn't messaged, and certainly there hadn't been any flowers.

Susie wondered if he even thought of her at all…

CHAPTER NINE

DANTE WAS DOING his level best not to think of Susie.

His vague plan to send her a gift and some flowers once the court case was over kept changing.

Perhaps a handwritten card, rather than one written by the florist...

But even that seemed too impersonal.

She had her parents visiting that weekend in the middle of his court trial, but perhaps he'd send something after that?

Then he would snap himself out of it, tell himself that the hollowed-out feeling he seemed to have acquired since he'd returned to Milan would be gone by then.

Certainly there was enough work to bury himself in. Both the client and his soon-to-be ex-wife seemed determined to have their day in court, and there were plenty of other clients...

And there was always family.

'Dante!'

Gio was sounding chirpy this morning, and had been for several mornings prior. Dante was starting to rue the day he'd showed him how to use that smart phone.

'Hey, Gio,' Dante said. 'How are you?'

'Good,' Gio said. 'I know we spoke yesterday, but I have good news—Mimi and I are getting married.'

'Congratulations.' Dante found that he was smiling. 'Did she like her ring?'

'She's not wearing it until the wedding. We want to keep it very small; most people can find out about it once we're married. Just you and Sev... Mimi's sister...'

'When are you looking at?' Dante asked, pulling up his calendar.

'Valentine's Day.'

'Gio…' Dante frowned. 'That's two days away. You mean next Valentine's Day?'

'I'm eighty-four, Dante,' Gio snapped. 'Of course I don't mean next year.'

Dante screwed his eyes closed in exasperation. He had honestly thought any wedding would be a couple of months away, when Susie had gone.

'Gio, I have that big case commencing next week.'

'That is why we are doing it before. It is just a lunch. Are things so bad between you and Sev that you cannot stand to be in the same room for my wedding?'

'Don't be ridiculous.' He pushed out a lighter tone, while squeezing the bridge of his nose between thumb and forefinger. 'Of course I shall be there…' He asked the question he wasn't sure he wanted the answer to. 'Where is the lunch to be?'

'At home. Mimi insists on cooking for us.'

Dante found there wasn't the expected wave of relief that there would be no encounter with Susie at Pearla's…

'I have eaten rather a lot of restaurant food lately.' Gio laughed.

'Are you still getting home deliveries from Pearla's?' Dante had tried not to ask before, but today he couldn't help but delve.

'Sometimes.' Gio laughed. 'Mimi refuses to move back in till after the wedding, so I order now and then—but not as much. Things changed.'

'What changed?'

'Susie stopped bringing my meals. And I miss her a lot.'

God, so did he.

The hollowed-out feeling he'd had since he returned to Milan had morphed into a black hole of regret that felt as if it might consume him.

'She's working in the kitchen now,' said Gio.

'Oh?' Dante said, as if it meant little to him. But he stood from his seat and started to pace as realisation dawned.

Susie would be in Lucca.

And not just for Gio's wedding.

She didn't need to go on that course in Florence. She was working in the kitchen of one of the best restaurants in Italy. Which meant every time he returned, Susie would be there.

'Dante? About the wedding…'

Gio brought him back to the reason for his call.

'We are not going to let anyone know—not until the wedding papers are signed.'

'I understand.' The whole town would be there otherwise. 'I'm so happy for you both.'

'Two brides to your zero!' Gio laughed. 'My love life is better than yours.'

'It is.'

'But if you want to bring a guest,' Gio said. 'Someone special…'

Of course he would like to bring a guest. How much easier the day would be with Susie by his side. It would make facing Sev a whole lot easier. But he was not about to use Susie as a shield.

And, of course he wanted to call Susie tell her he was returning for one night…perhaps arrange to see her after the wedding.

But that would set a dangerous precedent.

'No,' he told his grandfather. 'It will just be me.'

Susie had never really been one for Valentine's Day. And Lucca was such a romantic city that it seemed to ram home her loss as the big day approached.

Museums were holding special events and there were beautiful floral displays everywhere. Pearla's was booked out for both lunch and dinner, with Cucou planning a special menu…

Was it the same in Milan? Susie pondered as she awoke on the dreaded day. Were there red roses by the fountains? Was there so much romance in the air that Dante would pause and finally think of her? Would flowers finally arrive from him today?

She lay listening to Juliet playing. It was a different piece than usual, and actually rather beautiful. It made her think of Dante, although that wasn't unusual. Everything did these say.

She checked her phone, chiding herself for vague hope, while knowing damn well he wouldn't call now…

It had been weeks of nothing and she knew his big case started on Monday—no doubt he was busy working, or out with some gorgeous beauty who understood that when Dante said he didn't get involved he meant it.

As she did most Saturdays, she called home.

'How are you, darling?' Mum was sounding cheerful.

'Busy,' Susie said. 'One more week till you come. You need to tell me your flights…' She scrambled for a pen. 'I'm really looking forward to seeing you.'

'And we're excited to see you too—but I'm afraid it's not going to be until April.'

'Sorry?'

'The twins' move has been brought forward. They're moving that weekend.'

Susie felt her heart plummet as she was told how they needed Dad to shift some heavy stuff…how there was simply no other day…

'But, Mum…' Susie tried to quash her wail of despair. 'I've booked the days off.'

'I know you have, darling,' Mum said. 'But their landlord wanted tenants in immediately, and they'd have lost the flat otherwise. You know that we'd do the same for you…'

Actually, Susie didn't!

'But it's my birthday…'

'Susie!'

Mum gave a little laugh—the one that she always used to warn her that she was being petty. And possibly she was. It wasn't a milestone birthday…it didn't actually matter…

Except it did.

She wanted one birthday where it was all about her.

One cake that was her own, and not just another candle

stuck in beside the twins' double ones, which always seemed to shine so much more brightly.

'Susie, we *are* coming—it just won't be next week.'

'Mum, please—'

'Now, stop being silly!' Mum gave her little warning laugh again. 'You sound as if you're jealous.'

'I am.'

'Pardon?'

'I am jealous,' Susie confirmed. 'I'll call you next week. Bye.'

Ending the call, she took a breath and waited for guilt or panic to arrive. But bizarrely she felt a bit better for having said it.

She went into the kitchen and smiled at Louanna, who was dressed in black. *'Buongiorno...'*

'There's coffee in the pot,' Louanna said.

'Are you working?' Susie asked.

'It's Valentine's Day in Lucca—there's a lot of love and music to be made.'

She looked up as Juliet came in. She was also dressed in black, her red hair up in a chignon and pearls in her ears, clearly in for a busy day also.

'But no love for us today...' Louanna sighed. 'We just get to watch other people be romantic. I'll get packed up.'

'I didn't wake you, did I?' Juliet asked as Louanna went to sort out her cello.

'I was up anyway,' Susie said, and smiled, deciding not to take her grumpy mood out on everyone else. 'You sounded incredible.'

'"Una Ve Poco Fa",' Juliet said. '"A Voice I Once Heard". It's a gorgeous piece.' Then perhaps she saw the strain on Susie's face. 'Are you okay?'

'Of course.' Susie nodded, then shrugged. 'I just found out my parents aren't coming next week.'

'I'm sorry... I know you were so looking forward to it. You've been quiet for a while, though, and you are very pale.'

Susie saw a flicker of concern in Juliet's eyes and did not want it to be there. Juliet didn't know about Dante, no one did.

'I'm honestly fine. It's just the new job, all my course work...'

'If you ever want to talk?' Juliet offered, before she and Louanna headed out.

Susie didn't know how she felt, let alone what she might say.

It wasn't Juliet's early practice sessions, nor was it even that her parents were no longer coming.

She kept waiting to feel okay—to wake up and know she was over Dante.

It was the first time she'd been alone in the flat in for ever. Mimi was busy today, so there would be no walking on the walls. And, yes, she had homework for class, but for now it could wait.

Two minutes into her peaceful moment her phone rang.

It wasn't Dante.

And it wasn't her mum, saying she'd thought about it and they were coming next week after all.

Nor was it a florist staggering under the weight of red roses, calling to be buzzed in...though she briefly flared with hope.

'Susie!' It was a frantic Pedro. 'Can you come in early and help with prep? We have a function—a last-minute booking.'

'Sure.'

'And I know you won't be happy, but after prep we need you to do some waitressing...'

'Pedro...' She did not want this, but of course it was a feeble protest. Her apron-flinging moment had been a brief one. 'When do you want me to come in?'

'Now.'

Even though Pearla's wasn't yet open, the restaurant was hectic on this special day. The pastry chefs were all frantic, and Cucou barely looked up—just pointed her to a mountain of parsley.

'Prep that, then help Phillipe with the *arancini*.'

But, as busy as it was, Cucou still found time to teach.

'Susie…?' He called her over and she gazed upon his *sofrito*—buttery, silky, salty perfection. 'Do you see the gloss?'

'Yes…'

She put in her tiny little spatula and took a taste, and then she looked at Cucou, about to tell him she knew his secret, for she could taste anchovies.

'Good, yes?' he asked.

'Perfect.' Susie nodded.

Certainly she wasn't about to disagree with Cucou, and she was grateful when Phillipe came over and tasted it too.

'To die for!' he declared.

'Are you waitressing at the wedding?' Cucou asked her.

'Is it a wedding?'

He nodded. 'If so, the cake needs to come out of the chiller exactly twenty minutes before serving—no earlier…' Cucou gave her some more somewhat unusual instructions, and perhaps saw her frown. 'It's a tiny wedding…just a party of five…'

Cucou opened up the massive chiller, and if this Valentine's Day had proved challenging for Susie so far, it suddenly became impossible.

Gio and Mimi

The names were piped on the cake elaborately, and there were little hearts and bells… And if there was a God, then he was playing tricks on her, surely?

'Gio and Mimi are getting married?' she croaked, hurt that Mimi hadn't told her. 'When?'

Cucou glanced at the huge clock. 'About now…'

He closed the box on the precious cake.

'Susie…?' Pedro called. 'You need to get changed.'

As she headed for the cloakroom she braced herself for a second hurt.

Dante.

Dante won't even be there, Susie told herself as she slipped on her stockings and wriggled into her black dress, remembering his hands on the zip even as she reached for it. Remembering his hands on her hips and how in that moment their promised one night had turned into three…

Of course he'll be there, she argued silently in her mind as she put on her ugly sensible shoes and then tied her black apron on.

And if he was going to be in Lucca then he'd want to see her, surely?

Call her?

Warn her so she could at least warn her heart!

But then what did one weekend with a waitress mean to a man like Dante?

He'd made her feel special and adored, but she didn't doubt he'd done the same to many women.

He wouldn't be here, she reassured herself as she tied her hair into a low bun and put a slick of lipstick on.

It felt odd to step into Gio's through the staff entrance and not the main kitchen.

Pedro was his usual self—behind the scenes he was frantic, but she knew he would be all polished smiles when the wedding party arrived.

'Susie and Camilla, you are here in the butler's kitchen, serving…'

'Can't I work in the main kitchen?' Susie asked.

'You're a waitress today,' Pedro reminded her sharply.

Oh, God.

She would like to run…go and hide in the lovely garden and drag in some air. Instead she walked through to the private dining room, where the table was being hastily dressed for a very elegant wedding breakfast—more candles, of course, as well as silver-framed photos on occasional tables. To her surprise Juliet and Louanna were there, as well as a tall gentleman—obviously their conductor—and a harried-looking older lady.

'Susie…' Juliet called.

She gave a quick wave. Now and then they'd worked the same venue, but there was no time to stop now. They were busy tuning up, and Susie was busy accepting platters from the main kitchen.

Then she was directed by Pedro to hold a champagne tray at the door.

'Wait…' the conductor was saying, and Susie couldn't work it all out—because surely there was no such thing as a surprise wedding?

Yet there was Mimi, looking stunning in an emerald gown, giving a shocked gasp as she stepped into the dining room.

'Gio!' She laughed, and kissed the groom as the music started.

Susie stood still as hands reached for the champagne flutes on the tray she held. No matter how she tried not to notice, she knew which hand was Dante's.

'*Grazie*, Susie,' he said.

'You're welcome.'

Mimi was still happily protesting. 'This is beautiful…but I wanted to cook for my wonderful husband, my new family.'

'You think I would have you cooking on your wedding day?' Gio was delighted as he held a chair for his bride. 'Sit, my love.'

'I am not going to sit,' Mimi said. 'I have to *sing*.'

'Great…' the other man in the party said under his breath as he took a drink from Susie's tray. 'That's all we need…'

Susie looked up to get her first glimpse of Sev. His comment had clearly been to himself rather than to Susie. In fact, he didn't even deign to spare her a glance—just took a glass and raised it.

The music paused as Mimi smiled to her small audience and then looked at her husband.

'My love gets stronger every day…my voice not so much. Forgive me…'

'You have the voice of an angel,' Gio said.

Mimi looked towards the string quartet. '*"Una Voce Poco Fa"*? "A Voice I Once Heard…"'

It was the piece Juliet had been practising this morning,

Susie realised. Perhaps Gio had told them it was Mimi's favourite?

There was silence, then a short musical introduction, and then Mimi reached out her hand towards her new husband, and for the first time Susie heard her glorious voice.

Susie knew nothing about opera, and hadn't really understood before how a song might know exactly how she felt—how a song might mirror the aching desire and the loneliness that had suffocated her since her parting from Dante.

God, she missed him so much…

As the song neared its conclusion Susie dared to look over, but of course Dante was looking at Mimi.

At first, she couldn't read his features. His chin was up, his lips slightly taut, and for the first time she saw that the very smooth Dante appeared slightly awkward.

'Bravo,' he said as Mimi finished.

Possibly it was to do with his brother being there, because there was no hint of awkwardness when he came into the little butler's kitchen a while later.

'I didn't know Gio was getting lunch catered here,' Dante explained. 'When he told me about the wedding he said it was just a family lunch and Mimi was cooking. The string quartet and the private lunch was a last-minute thing, apparently.'

'Good for Gio.' Susie pushed out a smile, not wanting to make a fuss. After all it was a very special day.

And it wasn't the wedding that hurt.

She understood why Mimi hadn't said anything; it was clearly a very intimate affair. What hurt was the fact that Dante had known he'd be in Lucca and hadn't even thought to call.

Clearly she was *nothing*.

'Susie?' He caught her wrist. 'I had no idea you'd be here.'

The first time he'd held her arm her skin had prickled with goosebumps, perhaps unsure how to react to a delicious stranger. Now, though, her body knew the pleasures his touch was capable of, and it flared in reaction. She looked up to those dark eyes, and down to the full, sensual mouth that she'd missed so much, and almost stepped forward to kiss him.

No!

She wasn't going to be caught kissing Dante in the butler's kitchen. He couldn't just pick up where he'd left off.

'I'm at work, Dante.' She wrenched her arm away and stepped back.

'I was just attempting to explain…'

He stopped when Mimi burst into the kitchen.

'Susie!' Mimi pulled her into a hug. 'I was *desperate* to tell you.' She held out her hand. 'But I knew if we told a soul…'

Dante left them, and Susie examined Mimi's stunning ring—reds, violets, greens, encircled with diamonds.

'It's a rare black opal,' Mimi said. 'Gio says it is for the colour I bring to his life.'

It was a very long, very gorgeous lunch, and thankfully the happy couple were so besotted they didn't seem to notice the strain between the two brothers—or perhaps they were used to it by now.

The speeches were short and informal.

'Mimi, you have brought so much happiness to Gio…' Sev smiled at his new step-grandmother, then looked at his grandfather. 'Gio, you deserve every happiness.'

'You do too,' Gio said, dabbing his eyes.

It was far from effusive, yet Susie could feel the love in the room, and she found she was holding her breath as Dante stood to make his toast.

'Mimi…' he said. 'It is wonderful to share in this day, to know you are now part of our family.' He looked to his grandfather. 'And Gio…'

He paused.

He really paused, and Susie felt her throat squeeze tight.

'We love you…'

Gio nodded. 'I love you boys too.'

The music recommenced, and Susie headed back to the main kitchen to take out the cake. She nodded when Pedro suggested she take a break.

'There's some lunch for you in the kitchen.'

Susie didn't fancy it, though, and just took a couple of *arancini* balls in a napkin.

'I might just go out to the garden,' she told him.

'Go through the side entrance,' he said, and nodded.

She slipped out and walked under the portico. It was a lovely chilly day, and it was nice to be cold for a moment, and to let a tear slip out. But she hastily wiped it away when she saw Dante had come out too.

'There you are…' He stood over her. 'Gio said you were working in the kitchen now. Congratulations.'

'Thanks, although I'm waitressing today—oh, and tonight.' She looked up, took in his lovely suit. She had sort of known he'd come out—or rather she'd hoped he might. 'How's your client? The one with the letter?'

'Driving me crazy. Court on Monday.' He rolled his eyes. 'I don't think either party is ready. The judge is right, I fear—it's going to be a circus.'

Dante wasn't outside by chance. He knew how awkward this wedding must be for Susie, but he'd been resisting calling her for weeks.

Resisting…

He glanced back at the restaurant. 'Mimi's going to sing again.'

'I think that's beautiful.'

'Maybe…but I get embarrassed when people sing to each other.'

'You!'

'I don't know why… I always have.' He couldn't help but smile as he took a seat on the bench beside her. 'Just my luck to now be related to someone who does it all the time.'

Susie couldn't help but laugh, and then she thought about Sev's comment. 'You should tell Sev—I don't think he's too keen on the singing either.'

She glanced over at his grim expression. 'Please…listen… I

thought about what you said. If it was you and Celia… You're right, I wouldn't tell her.'

'No?'

'I think I'd lose her if I did…' She was being honest, and it hurt, but it was true.

'So why do you think I should tell Sev?'

'If it was Cassie who'd slept with you, though…'

'They're identical twins.' He frowned in confusion.

'I mean if you took me out of the scenario—if it was just between them—well, I think she'd forgive her, or they'd somehow get past it, because they love each other and they'd work it through.'

'It's not as straightforward as that.'

'You could try?'

Susie honestly expected him to stand up and stalk off, but he didn't.

'Rosa told me she thought she might be pregnant.'

He snapped it out, as if it was something he'd never wanted to share.

'Do you think Sev would want to hear that?'

'I don't know…' Her voice shivered. 'Was she?'

'Of course not.' He looked around and made certain there was no one else about. 'She kept calling, asking me when I'd be home—that sort of thing. I reminded her we weren't a couple. Then she called and said she was late…that maybe the condom had broken. I knew it had not.'

'Accidents happen…'

'Not to me. I knew I'd been careful; I knew she was lying. I flew straight back—she wasn't expecting me to. I called her and asked to meet immediately. I said that she should see a doctor and that I'd come with her. She didn't want that, of course.'

'What did she want?'

'Marriage,' he said flatly. 'She suggested I go and speak with her parents and make things "respectable" before anyone caught on…' His laugh was black. 'I told her there wasn't a chance in hell I'd marry her, and that I'd want a DNA test before we spoke any further. Look, I'm not proud of how I reacted, but I was certain she was lying.'

'Why would she lie?'

'Why?' Dante repeated. 'Because she was trying to set me up—no doubt at the urging of her parents. There have been fights over this land for generations...the De Santis family have always wanted the wineries merged.'

'You really think she was doing that?'

'Susie, I spend half my working life sorting this kind of issue out. Family lines, succession, mergers of land... I didn't get interested in that side of the law by chance.'

Susie exhaled shakily.

'I told her she should take a test right there and then. I went and bought one.' He gave a mirthless laugh. 'By the time I got back from the pharmacy, lo and behold, she told me it had been a false alarm.'

'Her period had arrived?'

'Of course.'

'You never told anyone?'

'I wish to God I'd told my brother, but I didn't.' The regret in his voice turned to bitterness. 'A couple of years later I was visiting home, walking on the walls, and she came running after me crying, telling me that she and Sev were in love, that he must never find out about us. I thought she must have pulled the same stunt that she tried with me and told him she was pregnant. Sev's a lot more dutiful than me—or he was... I tried to talk to him a couple of times, but he just blocked me... On the eve of the wedding I was more direct. I said that if she was saying she was pregnant, it was no reason for him to marry her. Sev hit me—told me never to speak of Rosa like that. He said he loved her...'

'Do you think he did?'

'Who knows with Sev? I stayed back... I figured if he wanted to talk...' He shook his head. 'Then the accident happened. I tried to talk to him again, but he didn't want to hear it.'

'He might now.'

'No.' He looked over to where she sat. 'I've thought about your question…if I regret sleeping with Rosa, or not telling Sev.'

'And?'

'I wish I'd never laid eyes on her.' He stood. 'Sev and I are finished.'

He headed back to the party and Susie just sat there for a moment. Then glanced at the time and knew she had to head back.

Dante watched Susie leave the private dining room and saw her pass the west side windows. He tried to focus on something Mimi was saying, and to tell her he wanted to leave discreetly.

But no…

That would not be fair.

And when Susie returned—when the cake had been cut and the catering staff were packing up—he wanted to go into the kitchen and kiss her neck…turn her in his arms and lose himself in her for a moment.

But that would not be fair either.

'Dante?'

Sev was trying to be polite, for the sake of the wedding, and held up a bottle of whisky. Dante nodded, but he could see the hell in his brother's eyes even as he attempted to be civil and knew he'd caused so much of it.

Then Mimi took the microphone again. Briefly he met Sev's eyes and gave a small smile, one only the brother who knew him very well might understand.

Only Sev didn't return the smile, and Dante looked away.

God, but he wanted Susie…

Dante gave in then—pushed back his chair and walked into the kitchen. But it was empty, and everything was neat and tidy.

The staff were gone.

It was just family now.

Two feuding brothers, whisky and wine.

Oh, and music that was set to play late into the night.

What could possibly go wrong?

* * *

It was after Mimi's sister had left that Gio turned his attention to his grandsons.

The musicians still played softly; his grandfather's conversation was getting louder the later the hour.

'Dante, why don't you ever bring someone?' Gio demanded, seeming determined to sort out his grandson's love life.

Dante strummed his fingers on the table and gave a noncommittal smile.

Right now, he wished he had.

He kept thinking of Susie, and how he'd stalked off in the garden that day, after he'd told her everything.

'And you…?' Gio turned his inappropriate questions to Sev. 'Why are you staying in a hotel when you have a home here?'

'It is your honeymoon,' Sev quipped.

'Then why not stay at your brother's?' Gio persisted. 'Always you stay in a hotel…'

'I might want to find company.'

'Then bring her along.'

Sev gave a wry laugh and rolled his eyes, and then Mimi decided it was time to treat them all to another performance.

'Ah, I know!' Mimi said, and delivered her choice to the ensemble.

The violinists and viola player took up their bows, but the cellist abruptly glanced towards Sev. She was local, and knew this was perhaps not the best choice.

A beautiful soprano aria by Puccini. They were in Lucca, after all—his birthplace. So possibly it was a natural choice, and Mimi would have performed it often…

Except it had been sung at Sev and Rosa's wedding.

As well as at Rosa's funeral.

Gio didn't seem to remember—he was gazing at his bride.

Dante closed his eyes for a moment, then opened them to look at Sev, who was as white as marble, though there was clearly still some blood supply, given the muscle leaping in his cheek.

Mimi's voice seemed to be wrapping around them both, taking them back to those dreadful days.

'Mimi…' Dante went to halt her, but Sev told him to leave it, and so they sat through the hellish performance and briefly met each other's eyes. Sev's look was less than friendly as his gaze lifted to Dante's scar.

'Bravo,' Sev said at last, and stood and gave Mimi a burst of applause. 'Now, I really do have to go.'

'Not yet!' Mimi pouted, but thankfully Gio suddenly seemed exhausted and ready for guests to leave.

'And me.' Dante stood.

Sev was out in a matter of moments, so it was Dante who bore the brunt of the farewell hugs and kisses, but soon he was up on the walls, chasing his brother down.

'Sev!' he called out.

Sev told him to back off, only Dante ignored him.

When he'd caught up, Sev told him to back off again—only rather less politely.

'No!' Dante grabbed him. 'Listen to me. I should never have said what I did. I get it, okay? And I am sorry. But it's been almost ten years.'

'I said leave it,' Sev warned, and now he had Dante by the lapels of his jacket. 'Or I'll take care of the other eye. See how good you look in court on Monday then. Go to hell, Dante.'

'We're brothers.'

'Correction,' Sev said, and shoved him. 'We used to be!'

Dante walked off.

Possibly because he knew he had court on Monday…

More likely it was guilt.

For whatever reason he walked away, arriving home to an empty house, and the coral scarf Susie had left behind still draped over the banister.

He'd be having words with his housekeeper, Dante decided, picking up the long strip of coral silk and pressing it to his face, inhaling her scent, unable to resist any more.

The worst Valentine's Day ever!

Susie's knew that her long shift might be worth it come payday, but seeing Dante had been hell, and then serving happy couples late into the night...

She was utterly spent—more exhausted than she could ever recall being.

One more week of language school and hopefully then things would get easier.

There was no Dante waiting with ice cream when she stepped out of Pearla's—not that she wanted one. If anything, the thought made her feel a little bit ill.

Susie stopped mid-stride, a few throwaway thoughts starting to merge in her mind. There was a flutter of panic in her chest.

She walked more briskly, telling herself she was being ridiculous.

She'd missed one pill.

Or two.

Her breasts hurt...

Because she was getting her period.

She'd told herself that when she'd been trying on Mimi's gowns.

'Hey...'

The one time she hadn't been hoping, Dante was here!

He'd been leaning against the wall of the ancient apartment block, but stood up straight when he saw her.

'Shouldn't you be at the wedding?' she asked.

'It was time to go.' He gave a grim flash of a smile. 'Can we talk inside?'

'I'm not sure if my flatmates are in.'

'What? Aren't you allowed to bring men back to the nunnery?'

He must have seen from her expression that his little joke wasn't well received, and perhaps he thought he knew the reason, because he said, 'Susie, I had no idea you'd be there today. I was...'

'So you were just going to fly in and fly out? Not even...?'

Dante looked as if he hadn't had the best night either. 'I

have a home here in Lucca—am I to you inform you every time I'll be home?'

'Of course not.'

'Did you want that?' he asked. 'Did you want me to call you and say, *I'll be here for one night. I can't tell you why, but can I come over?*'

'No.'

She shook her head; she hadn't thought of it like that. No, she didn't want to be his on-call mistress.

'So what? Now that I know you're here, you thought you'd drop in?'

'If you'd let me finish… I was trying to say I had no idea you'd be there today, but I was pleased you were.'

Her head was still spinning—not just from seeing him, but at the possibility that she might be pregnant, and also…

She looked at Dante and realised that there was another problem.

It would be hell to be pregnant by the playboy attorney…

But to love him…?

As if to deny her own want, she snapped, 'What do you want, Dante?'

'This.'

He kissed her then—a fervent and deep whisky-laced kiss that tasted delicious—and she was in his arms, kissing him back with passion. Hurling herself at the exit that was Dante, desperate for escape from her thoughts.

His hands were everywhere, and Susie truly wished they were at his house. There they could fall through the door and be completely alone…

But then she hauled herself back.

It was only a temporary escape.

She pulled her head back, peeled her body from his. 'You'd better go.'

'Susie…' He took a breath and then released her. They stood apart for a moment, and Dante seemed to gather his thoughts.

'Can we talk?' he asked.

'Talk?' she scoffed.

'Yes,' he said. 'Please.'

She was still reeling, though. She knew they would end up in bed, and that she'd be in love with him just a little bit more.

In love and possibly pregnant by a man who couldn't commit to anything.

And so she'd give him a chance to talk.

One chance.

'I spoke to my mother this morning...' she told him.

He frowned. Clearly he had no idea what she was getting at.

'The twins are moving house next weekend, so they're not visiting me now till April.'

He frowned again.

'It means I'll be free on my birthday weekend. The weekend of the ball. You could come.'

'I'll be in the middle of a court case.'

It wasn't the answer she wanted. She wanted him to understand how much it hurt that her parents had cancelled visiting her on her birthday, for him to fix it, to tell her not to worry.

To tell her they were about more than sex.

But, as charming as he could be, he didn't step in—and he didn't wave a wand and say, *Susie, you shall go to the ball.*

'What are you saying here, Susie? If I ask you to the ball then I get to come upstairs?'

Susie flushed. 'I didn't mean it like that.'

'No...' He shook his head. 'You want to use me in whatever strange competition you have going on with your sisters.'

'I might be in competition with them,' Susie retorted, 'but I'd rather that than throw in the towel as you have with Sev.'

Dante abruptly turned and walked off.

And, as he did so he raised his arm as if he was doing just that—throwing in the towel on them.

Damn...

Susie ran up the stairs and wanted to immediately run down again. Instead she sat on the couch and buried her head in her hands.

Oh, she knew she'd handled that terribly. But the shock

of seeing him two seconds after she'd realised she might be pregnant...

'Susie?'

It was Juliet, carrying two boxes of pizza, with Louanna behind her.

'You missed all the fun,' Louanna said.

'It wasn't fun—it was awful,' Juliet groaned.

'The Casadio brothers...' Louanna said with glee.

Susie's heart sank. 'What happened?' she asked.

'Mimi sang *"O Mio Babbino Caro",*' Juliet said, sinking down on a chair. 'You should have seen the look that passed between the two brothers.'

'And...?'

'Apparently it was played at the older brother's wedding,' Louanna explained. 'And I think it might have been played at the wife's funeral too. I thought Sev was about to explode... Then apparently there was a fight on the walls.'

'No...' Juliet shook her head, and told her the gossip she'd heard while getting pizza.

Only Susie wasn't listening.

She closed her eyes in wretched regret for her handling of things.

Dante really had wanted to talk.

And kiss...

It was the worst Valentine's Day ever.

CHAPTER TEN

'HOW WAS CLASS?' Juliet asked Susie when she came in on Monday.

'Great,' she said, but her voice was rather flat as she joined her flatmate in the lounge.

Juliet didn't look so great either. She was sitting staring at the muted television and looked as if she'd been crying.

'Don't you have rehearsals?' asked Susie.

'No, I wasn't selected to play for the ball.'

Susie knew how that felt. 'I'm sorry.'

'I'm worried about my scholarship,' Juliet admitted. 'I'm not keeping up. I'm working at the store and the bar to pay my rent, and there just aren't enough hours to practise. I'm getting up at the crack of dawn…trying to cram things in…'

Susie moved over to Juliet's couch and gave her a hug. She was pleased that in this instance she hadn't said anything to Juliet about the noise.

'Can your family help?' she asked.

'God, no.' Juliet shook her head. 'I'm not giving up my music, but I do have to face things.' Then she paused and looked at the television screen. 'There he is…'

Susie tried not to turn her head too quickly, and attempted to feign nonchalance as she saw Dante, looking utterly together, walking towards the court.

'That's from this morning,' Juliet said. 'Clearly he wasn't in a fight—Louanna's such a gossip.'

Dante wore a dark grey suit and a dark gunmetal tie, and

his white shirt almost gleamed in the mid-morning light. He looked a whole lot better than Susie.

The footage ended and the scene flicked back to the court, where all the cameras were waiting for news outside.

Juliet spoke again. 'It was a difficult wedding.'

Susie tore her eyes away from the screen. 'I thought it was gorgeous.'

'Of course—but it was so sad. All those pictures every-where…and so many pieces we were told not to perform. And then Mimi…'

Susie closed her eyes and felt so selfish. She'd been thinking only of how hard it was for her. And that was what she regretted.

Dante had needed her, and instead of being there for him, or properly listening, she'd been angling for an invitation to the ball.

Then there was the sound of footsteps on the stairs and then the door opened and an excited Louanna rushed in. 'Turn the sound on!'

'What?'

'There's about to be a press conference.' She was unmuting the television. 'They're back together,' Louanna said. 'Again!'

The happy couple were smiling and holding hands, with their lawyers standing beside them, a little grim-faced, as a short statement was read.

'The past year has been difficult for both parties, who deeply regret getting third parties involved. They look forward to renewing their vows and moving forward.'

'See?' Louanna said. 'Only the lawyers win.'

Dante gave a short response and said he was pleased for his client and wished the couple well. He offered a tight smile, then shook his client's hand and walked back to his office, the rebuke from the judge still ringing in his ears.

'This case should never have made it to court, Signor Casadio.'

Once again, he was the bastard…

For two days he dealt with the press, with his staff, with the paperwork that had piled up, and then he went to his safe and took out a small envelope.

'I'm taking the rest of the week off,' he informed his PA.

Dante returned to his stunning apartment, and thought Susie was right—he could rent it out tomorrow, as a luxurious furnished penthouse, and apart from clothes and toiletries there was little he would have to take out...

He opened up the envelope and stared at the two small rubies in his palm. Again he recalled his mother with the jeweller, insisting on the stones she liked.

'Rubies...'

'Not diamonds?'

'I have so many diamonds...rubies are more beguiling...'

Then he remembered going back with his father.

'Just rubies?' he had checked.

'Si,' Signor Adino had said. *'She wants rubies only for her eternity ring.'*

Dante had turned to Sev. *'What's an eternity ring?'*

Now he remembered his response.

'Something infinite,' Sev had said. *'For ever.'*

But Dante had frowned.

'Even after you die?'

Dante had had a heart back then. He'd loved everyone so much. And at the thought of his *mamma* dying, Papa too, he'd started to cry.

'What have you said to him?' Papa had come over to them. *'Dante,'* he'd scolded. *'Stop.'*

Now Dante found he couldn't stop.

He hadn't cried at their death, nor at their funeral. Certainly he hadn't cried when Sev had hit him, nor at the needle going in and out as he'd been stitched up. Nor when he'd walked away from his life.

The day when Rosa had run up to him on the walls, pitched him against his brother, he'd muted all feelings.

Only since Susie had appeared had they started to return.

He thought of her in Lucca, happy in her new job. There

was too much damage there, too much left undone, and the foundations were too shaky for him to even think of returning.

Instead, he looked again at the rubies and took out his phone.

'Signor Adino...'

A gift, Dante decided. And then he'd let her go.

'Are you still sulking, Susie?'

Her mum had called her midweek.

'No,' Susie said—and she was being honest. 'I've got a lot on my mind. I've been offered an apprenticeship.'

'Susie! That's fabulous. You won't have to do that expensive course in Florence.'

'I know.'

She looked at her new white uniform, hanging on the door; Pearla's had had her name embroidered on the jacket and Cucou had handed it to her yesterday.

No, Susie wasn't sulking—but she did have a lot on her mind.

When the call ended, she put down the phone and went to her bedside table to look at the result of her first ever pregnancy test.

Like Juliet, she'd decided it was time to face up to things.

INCINTA

She couldn't be pregnant.

But the pink word insisted she was.

'No...'

Susie shook her head and then checked the instructions again, told herself the test was surely wrong.

Because she was *not* going to be pregnant by some family law attorney who was too cynical for words and couldn't even commit to a week ahead, let alone a relationship.

She started to cry, and it was like a dam breaking.

She'd been on the edge of tears so many times, but now, as her entire world shifted, she broke down.

She lay on her bed and hugged her beautiful white jacket. She knew she'd have to say no to the apprenticeship.

And of course she'd have to tell Dante.

But how?

She would head back to England and deal with things there, she decided. Because, despite what she'd said to Dante that morning, she did not want to be the talk of this town.

Oh, and she would be. The two brothers couldn't even have a small scuffle on the walls without word getting out. Imagine the gossip about an apprentice chef at Pearla's being pregnant by Dante Casadio...

She didn't want it for herself, nor for Dante, nor Gio...

No, she didn't want her baby to be a piece of scandalous gossip.

Nor an accident.

She was certain that was what *she'd* been. And it told her what she didn't want for her own child.

She wanted to be a confident, loving mother.

Not one who resented giving up her fledgling career...

The tears stopped then, and there was a very wobbly sense of calm...

She'd be okay, Susie told herself.

Not for a second would she think of this as an accident.

Susie limped through the week on autopilot.

She even made a cake for her own birthday...

Susie

Happy 25th

'When's the party?' Louanna asked.

Juliet sat with a little frown between her green eyes, watching Susie piping hearts and flowers...

'Tomorrow,' Susie replied.

'Good, because we're both working tonight—it's the ball...'

Susie looked over to Juliet. 'Are you playing?'

'Yes!' She beamed, though her features were as white as marble. 'But only because the understudy broke her wrist.'

'You'll be perfect,' Susie assured her. 'Oh, I wish I was going.'

'Maybe next year,' Louanna said.

And the shaky sense of calm Susie was perched upon cracked a little as she glimpsed this time next year, and the whole live person she'd be responsible for.

There would be no ball next year, or the year after that, Susie decided, and messed up one of her pretty flowers.

And anyway, the only person she wanted to take her to the ball was Dante.

'Are you okay?' Juliet checked. 'Your icing…'

Yikes.

And then it dawned on her that there was no Prince Charming required when she had a fairy godmother.

She didn't need Dante to make her wishes come true.

And while she still had the chance, she was going to embrace everything!

Everything.

'Susie!' Mimi embraced her.

'Is it too late to say yes?' she asked.

'To what?'

'The ball.'

'The ball?' Gio called out. 'But it's tonight.'

'Don't listen to him,' Mimi said, and then she gave her a bright smile. 'Of course it's not too late.'

She invited her in while she collected her coat. Then, 'Gio, my love, Susie and I are going to my sister's for a few hours…'

Dante peered at his unshaven reflection in the mirror.

God, he looked like Gio in decline.

Or Gio in love.

It was late on Saturday afternoon and he picked up the phone to make the call he had to.

He knew he couldn't look to the future without clearing the past.

'Dante.' Sev was curt when he answered.

'Can we talk?'

'No. I don't have time. I'm trying to get to Lucca *again*, to attend the ball, because you couldn't be bothered to—'

'Sev,' Dante cut in, and he thought of Susie and those words that had stung. He refused to throw in the towel. 'I've met someone.'

'I have to board.' Sev was not giving an inch.

'Her name's Susie.'

'I know,' Sev said. 'The waitress.'

'How do you know?'

'I'm your brother, Dante.'

'For the first time since the accident there aren't awful memories on every corner in Lucca,' Dante said, thinking how when he thought of home now he could see Susie on the walls, or standing under an umbrella. And when he looked at the hills, instead of seeing twisted metal and a graveyard, he thought of her sitting on the couch at the winery. 'Can you get that?'

'I wish I could get that,' Sev said.

'Can we meet? Can we speak?'

'Tomorrow,' Sev said, 'but I don't want to drag up the past.'

'I don't see how we can move on if we don't.'

'I have to go; I really am boarding now…' Sev told him— and then he swore.

'What?'

'It's delayed. I'm going to try and sort out another flight.'

'Where are you?'

'Edinburgh.'

Dante looked at his new, or rather old, gold watch. 'You're not going to make it.'

'You'll have to go to the ball.'

He was going to hell, Dante knew as he packed his tux, because if Susie found out he was in Lucca and at the ball she would never forgive him.

He called her from the car on the way and got her voicemail.

'Look, I know it's too late to ask you to the ball, but I have to attend. So I'm going to be in Lucca tonight. I wondered if…' He grimaced. It sounded as if he wanted to drop by for a hook-up. 'Okay, scrap that. I'll call you as soon as I can.'

Right now, he had a lot to arrange…

'Oh, Susie…'

Mimi had performed utter magic.

The dress was still gorgeous, the softest grey with a blush of pink, and now she was squeezed into a pair of very beautiful shoes…

She could have looked by far too pale—especially as she was feeling a little peaky—but the make-up had transformed her.

Mimi had always done her own stage make-up, and now Susie stared in the mirror with eyes that were vivid and blue as she blinked her long lashes. Her lips were a very pale pink.

Her heavy curls had been smoothed, and loose curls fell down over one shoulder.

She wished things could be different, but accepted this was how they were.

She'd felt alone all her life.

Maybe it was time to embrace it. To accept it and simply enjoy it.

'You are going to be very popular,' Gio told her.

He'd arranged for a car to take her, and had taken a walk over to Mimi's sister's to wave Susie off and then take a nice early-evening stroll on the walls with his new wife.

'You can tell me how Dante's speech is received,' he said.

'Dante?' She frowned, certain that Gio had got it wrong. 'He's not going.'

'No, he's there. Sev won't be arriving until later. So there will be a Casadio there tonight after all.'

Her heart seemed to stop for a second, even two, and then it skipped into overdrive, her pulse racing in her temples.

Damn him…

She felt her newly painted nails digging into her palms, frustration and anger building at the fact that he'd do this again.

Surely he'd have called?

Then she checked her phone. And as it turned out he had...

He was in town and he was going to the ball. It would seem he was hoping to drop by.

God, he had a nerve!

'Thank you, Mimi,' she said as she climbed into the car, battling her feelings and trying not to let the happy couple see.

'Now, remember,' Mimi said, 'it's all about the entrance.'

'Yes.'

'You pause, and then you smile.' She looked right at Susie. 'You *smile*,' she said. 'Even if it kills you. Even if it is a hostile audience.'

'Got it.' Susie nodded.

It was a pink sky evening, just coming into spring, and the narrow cobbled streets were lined with impressive cars, filled with beautiful people.

Dante was going to be there...

The anger and hurt she'd been holding in was suddenly met with a surge of relief—like headwinds colliding on a clifftop. She felt battered. Surges of frustration met with the sheer relief that Dante would be there tonight.

And this, Susie decided, was how she wanted to face him. This would be his memory of her when she called him from England or they met to deal with legal papers.

Not pale and washed out outside her apartment after a double shift at the restaurant. Cross and pleading with him to take her to the ball.

She could do this by herself.

All of it.

She wanted him to know that.

The car arrived at the magnificent building, beautifully lit, and she saw beautiful women and elegant men milling on the stairs in the portico.

And now it was her turn to arrive.

The door was opened and a gloved hand was offered, and she stepped out of the vehicle onto a rich navy carpet.

She stood alone.

And it was then that she saw him.

He was standing by a pillar—not leaning on it as such, just with the edge of his shoulder touching it. He was looking impossibly gorgeous in a tux, and he didn't even glance in her direction at first—just cast a bored eye over the stunning surroundings and skimmed past her.

Then he frowned and turned around.

And she smiled. Not because Mimi had told her to, and not to kill him or show him how brilliant her life was without him...

Simply, she was pleased to see him.

It was as if her lips hadn't caught up with her playing it cool, so it was an utterly natural smile, and it only wavered when he didn't smile back.

He just stared, and so did she, because...actually...he didn't look quite his usual self.

'Signorina...'

She was being called to smile for the cameras, and then she was ushered through a sea of people and colour and so much noise.

Glasses clinking...the hum of chatter...all spilling forward as she followed the music into the ballroom, where huge chandeliers spun beams of light.

She looked over to the orchestra. There was Juliet, her red hair glowing, her concentration fully on the music. But then she glanced over and gave her a gorgeous smile and a nod.

'You look stunning.'

She heard Dante's voice and turned slightly.

'Thank you.' She looked at him a little more closely. 'So do you.'

However, she looked at his unshaven jaw and was reminded of his comment about calling an ambulance if he ever went out unshaven.

But it was not her place to comment like that now.

She took a glass of champagne from a passing tray—then remembered she couldn't drink it. This pregnancy thing was all so new.

She stood awkwardly, holding her glass, and found that the thought of her baby was the one thing that didn't scare her tonight.

It was the thought of all the days when there would be no chance of seeing him.

Of lawyers and odd visits that Dante didn't even know about yet.

And she wouldn't be telling him here!

She kept her smile pasted on. 'Gio said you're making a speech?'

'A short one—unless Sev gets here in time...'

'He's coming too?'

'Yes.' He looked at her. 'I called him—tried to talk to him.'

'Oh?'

'He told me I lacked responsibility.'

'Did he?' Susie gave a little laugh. 'You don't.' Then her laugh changed. 'I got your message...'

'I apologise for that. It sounded tacky.'

'Just a bit.' Susie nodded.

'Would you like to dance?'

She wanted to say no—to be petty, to be bitter, and flounce off and dance with every other man in the room.

Only there wasn't a single man in the world she wanted to dance with more.

'That would be lovely.'

She had never danced to an orchestra, and she had never done any formal dancing—just watched it on the television. But either some of it had caught her attention or she had the perfect partner, because Dante made it smooth and easy, even when she faltered.

'Left...' he said, and then, 'Just one little step back...'

It was enough for her to dance without thought.

'I'm a fraud!' She smiled. 'I know only one dance step.'

'I don't think I'm thinking about your feet.'

'Please don't flirt.' She looked up at him.

'That's an impossible ask,' he told her.

But the compliments stopped, and they danced in silence, and she wished the music would never end.

For a while it didn't—but Dante was not here just for fun.

'I have to dance with a few guests,' he told her.

'Of course.'

'I don't want to.'

'Go.'

And it was fine being there alone. There were plenty of offers to dance, and gorgeous people to talk to, and even had Dante not been there it was something she wouldn't have missed for the world.

The tables were filled with scented blooms and gorgeous treats and she was *not* going home with Dante, Susie told herself.

Promised herself.

No matter how tempted, no matter how smooth his delivery, she would decline.

She would be leaving tonight in utter control.

'Scusi...' someone said, and she realised she was standing at one of the exits.

She moved a little closer to a table as the music was silenced and the speeches began.

There were a lot of thank-yous, and then an elderly, very distinguished-looking man took the microphone and spoke so fast that even with all her classes and language lessons she could barely understand what was being said.

'Sevandro Casadio...' the MC said, and then corrected himself. *'Scusi...* Dante Casadio...'

'Grazie...'

Dante thanked all the people who had already been thanked many times, and then he thanked Christos and his wife, saying that without their skill the wine would not be as rich. He thanked the orchestra, and then he spoke of how this night meant spring was here...all colour and beauty.

'My grandfather and his beautiful wife Mimi are delighted to support this night, loved by so many...' He slipped it in smoothly, and even if word had already spread like wildfire there were a couple of gasps of surprise and then applause. 'I haven't attended this ball for a very long time,' Dante said. 'And I know I have been absent too long.'

She'd been proud of how she'd mostly kept up with his speech, but then he said something she thought she didn't understand...or perhaps she was fighting not to cry.

'It is good to be here and to be home.'

He stepped down from the stage just as someone else knocked into her, and Susie realised she'd drifted towards the exit again.

She wasn't okay, Susie knew.

And she felt a tear splash down her cheek.

She didn't want to leave.

Ever.

She loved this man who was now talking to an elderly couple, who were congratulating him on his speech.

And then she saw him talking to Sev, and they didn't seem quite so hostile.

She felt another tear splash out, and quickly wiped it away with her thumb.

It was time to go, Susie decided.

But Dante caught her hand.

'Dance?'

One more...

His hand was close to the small of her back, the other was holding her hand, but they were too far apart. His cologne was light, heavenly...

'I just spoke to Cucou,' Dante said. 'He tells me I am dancing with his new apprentice.'

She gulped. 'I haven't accepted yet,' she said.

'Why wouldn't you accept? It's everything you wanted?'

'I'm not so sure,' she attempted, but her voiced faded. It was all too new and too raw to attempt to sound dismissive as she farewelled long held dreams and so she hurriedly changed the topic. 'I know this piece...' she said, referring to the music. 'Juliet stuffs it up every time.'

He smiled, and she looked up at his unshaven jaw. Dante was tense—perhaps because his brother had arrived.

He pulled her in a little closer and she rested her head on his chest, so she could peek at the orchestra. It would seem Juliet had nailed it.

'Perfect…' Susie smiled as the music soared.

'Yes,' Dante said. 'Perfect.'

And they were flirting with their bodies now.

His hand was a little firmer on her back, the other rested on her waist, and her hand, left to its own devices, was now on his chest.

'Susie,' he said, as the clock inched forward and the crowd on the dance floor thinned. 'When I called—'

'Please don't, Dante.'

'I didn't think to ask you to the ball tonight because—'

'Dante!' He'd said enough already. 'Please don't.' She pulled back. 'I'm going to go to the ladies' room.'

She did so, and she topped up her lipstick and looked at her glittering eyes, and his words stung.

I didn't think to ask you…'

Have some pride, Susie!

So instead of heading back to the gorgeous ballroom, because she knew where that would lead—straight to bed—she went down to the foyer and out through the arches to the grand steps.

'Running away?'

His voice was like a deft arrow and it halted her, but she didn't let it fell her. She just turned around and shrugged.

'No.' She shook her head. 'I'm just leaving the same way I arrived. Alone.' She looked at him then. 'I can't believe you didn't ask me.' He said nothing. 'You've ruined my night.'

'How?'

'I wanted one perfect night. A photo of us arriving together. One time. So I could look back and say, *Oh, that's the guy. And that was me.'*

'Susie, it is not ruined—'

'But it is.'

She stared at him and then the floodgates opened, after a lifetime of being not quite enough, not fitting in, not getting to shine...

'I wanted something just for me. For...'

Us.

She didn't say it; she clamped her mouth closed before uttering the forbidden word.

It was silly. There was nothing of *them*. It was just that if she was having a baby, and if they were going to be bound only by lawyers or whatever, she'd wanted one memory...

And it wasn't just about showing her family and sisters; it was so much more.

More than that...

To show their baby...

That's your father and me.

One photo before it all turned to bitter dust.

One magical night and he had ruined it.

'You didn't even *think* to ask me?'

She threw his words back at him and stood trembling with hurt as he came down the steps, all lithe and nonchalant.

'Susie, the ball was the last thing on my mind until you arrived. You turned my head,' he told her. 'When you got out of that car, I couldn't take my eyes from you.'

'Too late.' Her eyes were brimming.

'It's never too late.' He smiled at her anger. 'Come back to mine.'

'You've got a nerve...'

'I do,' he said.

And he kissed her right there under the lights, his jaw rougher than she'd ever known it and his mouth hungry and skilled and utterly perfect, persuasive...

It was by far safer to kiss him than to speak. She might tell him she loved him...that they were having a baby. So much easier to sink into reckless kisses that made her forget all her problems, her every care swept away by the dark, passionate tide he created.

'Susie...' His mouth left hers and now he lifted her hair

and kissed her neck, then her bare shoulder. 'Come home with me...'

Her stance was wavering. One more night...she reasoned.

And his kisses slowed a little, like turning down the gas, and he took her to a simmer.

She hated how they'd ended. It was her only regret in their turbulent time.

'You left your scarf...'

She laughed at this most illogical reason for returning to his house, but it was good enough for now. 'I did,' she agreed, and her eyes closed as he kissed her to confirm, and the bells chimed in agreement, sweeping in a new day.

Her birthday.

It was not as if a louse like him would remember, but for now it didn't matter—it was still the best birthday of her life.

'*Fai strada tu*, Dante!'

Susie told him to lead the way and, picking up her skirts with one hand, holding his with the other, they walked together through the cobbled streets.

'Your Italian is getting better every day,' he told her.

'Yes,' Susie said, tongue in cheek. 'We did terms of endearment this week.' She laughed to herself. 'Not that you'd know anything about them,' she added with a teasing twist. '*Ciccina.*'

'*Ciccino,*' he corrected. '*I* am the sweetheart.'

Oh, he was so far from sweet as he stopped their walk home to kiss her against a very cold wall.

'What else?' he asked as he kissed her shoulder.

'*Cucciolo,*' she said.

She'd called him a puppy—a very affectionate term, but certainly not one that described Dante.

And then they made it to the gorgeous avenue and inside his door.

'Come,' he said, leading her towards the dining room. 'We can dance here as we wanted to.'

'I don't want to dance any more,' Susie said.

Her voice sounded unfamiliar, as if there was a new tone,

one that had her shivering, and clearly it caused a reaction in him, for his hand halted as he pushed down the ornate handle. The dining door remaining closed as he stood utterly still.

'Dance?' he suggested again, and his voice was low too, husky.

He cleared his throat and turned around.

'I really don't want to,' she said.

Then he met her eyes, and perhaps saw the fire that was blazing there. There was no time for dancing.

'Oh, you know how to ruin plans,' Dante told her as he scooped her up in his arms.

'So do you,' Susie said, putting her hands around his neck.

She only let go when he dropped her on the bed.

She lay in a cloud of pink and grey and closed her eyes as he lifted the hem of the gown to reveal the pale pink flesh of her thighs, and then impatiently he moved the material higher, up to her stomach.

'Careful,' she warned. 'It's not my gown.'

'Shh,' he told her.

And although it was clear he'd wanted them downstairs, in the firelit dining room, instead here they were—upstairs, the bed turned back, the mattress plump and waiting...

He pulled down her lacy knickers and she lost a shoe as he pushed them past her ankles...

'Oh, Susie...' he said, in that low, seductive voice, and he lowered his lips to the soft flesh of her stomach.

And when he spoke her name like that she had no choice but to close her eyes...to feel adored and wanted, even if it could not last.

'What else did you learn to say?' he asked with desire in his eyes, as if goading her to tell him how she really felt.

'I can't remember,' Susie said, terrified that she might say something she'd later regret.

'What else?' he persisted, and his hot mouth moved down her stomach.

He stroked her, his eyes moving down, and as he found her tenderest spot she felt tight inside, tight with desire as his fingers slipped inside her. She bit down on her bottom lip as he explored her—and then he looked up and met her eyes.

'*Settemila baci per te,*' Dante said. 'Did you learn that?'

'No…' Although she sort of understood what he'd said. But she didn't really have the capacity to play the game right now, so she shook her head.

'It means,' Dante told her, 'seven thousand kisses to you.'

He lowered his head and delivered several of them.

How did he make this so easy?

He simply did. Because she parted so easily, and as his soft mouth caressed her, as he explored her so exquisitely, her homework continued. But it was in breathless attempts at words rather than practice phrases.

'*Mi piace…*it's nice,' she told him. '*Mi piace…*' she said again. Only her voice was more urgent now, and it told him it was specifically there that he pleased her. Then she told him what he had once said to her, and it came from a very natural place. '*Non ti fermare!*'

Don't stop!

He was so intense, so specific with his mouth, and he did not stop. Even as her hips lifted his mouth chased them. And then she gave up on their game, because she did not trust the words that might slip out as he took her to bliss.

How many kisses it took, she lost count. She felt as if she were floating, almost aching for him to take her, to make love to her, to fill her. And yet she never wanted it to end. Her hands were knotted in his thick black hair, and his delivery so honed she fought not to push him away, because she wanted it so.

It didn't take seven thousand kisses.

She climaxed under his skilful mouth and sobbed out words in a language she didn't know as she simply gave in…

She was trying to breathe, hoping she hadn't told him she loved him, but Dante wasn't listening anyway.

Unbelted and unzipped, he took her.

'There,' he told her, and she was on fire, clinging to the sheets.

He was holding her hips. And she was spent, yes, but still

being ravished, watching him through her half-closed eyes and adoring him.

Because she did adore him.

He climaxed with a hollow shout, and it felt as if the air he breathed out stroked her inside, and she found there was a little left to give as she orgasmed again to the last thrusts of him.

'I can't breathe…' she told him.

'You are,' he said.

And he turned her around on the bed and undid her gown. And she lay there, watching him undress. Then he dealt with the rest of her clothes, and with a few deft movements from Dante…

She was back in his bed.

CHAPTER ELEVEN

SHE HAD ALWAYS loved their mornings.

'Morning,' he said, stroking her spine, and she turned and smiled right into his eyes.

And even if she was unsure of what lay ahead, waking to Dante would always be perfect.

'You look like a panda,' he told her.

'I'm sure that I do.'

They just lay together and stared, and she didn't quite know what to say.

It was Dante who spoke. 'I didn't think to ask you to the ball, because for me the ball is a duty. Yesterday it was the furthest thing from my mind.' He sat up in the bed. 'I'll get coffee.'

'Tea for me.'

'Tea?' He frowned. 'Do you want some breakfast?'

'No, thanks.' Susie grimaced at the very thought, then saw him frown again. 'Too much champagne,' she said.

Dante nodded and picked up a towel. She lay back in his sumptuous bed, wondering how she could bear to leave, and how she could possibly stay.

Susie knew she was running away—but she didn't want to see the disappointment in his eyes. She wanted him to find out from a distance...

Tea? Dante raided his cupboards, but there was no tea to be had.

Then he went into the dining room to collect a certain box,

and saw the champagne that had been cooling there floating in a bucket of water.

Susie hadn't even had a sip of champagne last night.

And she hadn't yet said yes to an apprenticeship at Pearla's, when it was everything she wanted.

Dante wasn't a top attorney for nothing.

She was pregnant.

He waited for the punch in his guts, only it never came. But he did sit down at the dining room table for some time.

He rather guessed she didn't want to have the baby here. If he was her attorney, he'd advise her to be on a flight back to England straight away.

Susie was possibly leaving. With his baby. But instead of being angry he didn't blame her.

Had she known when he'd told her about what had happened with Rosa?

Dante put his head in his hands, thinking of their row after the wedding and all he'd said…

A baby.

Why was he just sitting there when he should be pacing?

Why wasn't he panicking that it was too soon or pounding up the stairs?

A baby…

He kept going back to that…picturing something he'd never imagined for himself. A daughter or a son…

After so much pain and grief, the thought of Susie having his baby felt like a rusty knife being pulled from his chest.

But before all that he had to know Susie's thoughts.

Dante knew his.

But they both had to speak the truth.

The tea took quite a long time coming—in fact she was half dozing when the bedroom door was pushed open.

'Happy Birthday to You…'

She started as a gorgeous Dante, who could actually sing, pushed aside his embarrassment, and she simply bathed in the glow as he came in carrying a tray. She sat up, stunned to see there was even a little cake, with a candle lit.

'You remembered.'

'Well, it's not like you let me forget,' he pointed out. 'A seven-year-old would be less excited.'

She let out a gurgle of laughter, then sighed in delight when she saw the beautiful cake, her name piped in pink with little silver hearts, and knew it was Cucou's work.

'It's wonderful…'

'Blow,' Dante said. 'I want some cake. It's your favourite,' he added.

'How do you know?'

'I asked the pastry chef. Raspberry, with liqueur and cream and white chocolate…'

He was slicing away and it was her first proper cake of her own.

Her favourite cake had his bed feeling like a little boat in an ocean storm.

'I might save it for later. Have a huge slice then…'

'Too much champagne?' He put the knife down. 'You won, by the way.'

'Won what?'

'Whatever this competition is with your sisters. They will be very jealous,' he said as he handed her his phone. 'You look stunning.'

'Gosh!' She looked at the picture of herself arriving at the ball and instead of feeling sad, felt proud to have gone alone. 'Go, me!'

'There are a few.' He scrolled through them. 'A back shot… Look at that poor guy on the stairs. Homeless from the neck up, as Gio would say.'

She laughed when she saw he was referring to himself.

And she had her photo. Dante was gazing at her, and she at him.

That's your father and me.

Yes, she had her photo.

She looked up. Did she dare tell him now? Shatter this perfect morning?

No, she decided, because that was for later. This morning was simply about her and Dante. The morning he'd brought her a cake and made it the best birthday ever.

'Here,' he said, and handed her a parcel.

It was wrapped in gold paper and there was even a wax seal, and a slender golden rope.

'It's beautiful…'

'I think you have to open it to say that.' Then he looked at her as a tear slid down her cheek. 'Why are you crying?'

'Is this from your PA? The bauble that ends it all?'

'No.' His voice was suddenly serious. 'This is from me. And I admit I'm nervous.'

'Why?'

'I have never bought a birthday gift before.'

'Never?'

'Not for a long time. Maybe a bottle of whisky for Gio. We don't really…' He fell into a silence that said more than words—for him, birthdays and family celebrations had stopped a long time ago. 'Hopefully you'll like it.'

He might not have wrapped it personally, but Dante had definitely written the little card attached.

Tutti bella.
Dante

Everything beautiful.

No kiss by his name, and yet her heart was thumping even before she'd peeled off the paper. She already loved it!

The box was walnut and gleaming, and when she opened it up Susie gasped. It was a circle of jewelled flowers, nestled in velvet. Then she saw that it was actually a necklace—and not just any necklace, nor just any flowers.

'Magnolias…' she breathed.

There were so many stones and different precious metals,

swirls of enamel. Everywhere she looked she saw more. Pale sapphires, pink rubies and little emeralds, seed pearls and delicate flowers.

'Magnolias…' she said again. 'It's perfect. Where on earth did you find this?'

'Locally,' Dante told her, and took it out of the box. 'Let me put it on you.'

'I want to see it…'

He wasn't listening, so she lifted her hair, and he fiddled with the clasp, and then he took a hand mirror from beside the bed.

'I have never seen anything so heavenly…'

'I should have given it to you last night.'

'No.' She shook her head. 'It's perfect for my birthday.'

She started to cry, her panda eyes spreading, and kept peeling tissues from the box he handed to her.

'Thank you.'

'You're very welcome.' Then he looked at her. 'And a good choice, given you won't be here for the magnolias.'

She went still.

'You're going back to England.'

'I never said that…'

'Aren't you?' Dante asked. 'Can't we both speak the truth?'

She swallowed.

'Susie, I wouldn't want to tell me either.'

Her eyes darted up.

'But can I tell you one thing? I know I seem ruthless, but I'm not to the people I care about.'

'Dante…' She was shaking a little, still unsure what he knew.

'*Incinta?*' he asked—pregnant.

'I'm late…'

'The truth, Susie.'

'I *am* late.'

'You don't have to break it to me gently,' he said. 'I think I already know. And I don't think you'd be talking about throwing in your dream job if you hadn't taken a test, and you didn't drink any champagne last night. You don't want cake now.'

'Yes,' she finally said. 'I am.'

'When did you find out?'

'I think I was starting to work it out at the wedding.'

'Poor thing!'

He actually laughed, just a little, and it was so unexpected— more so the hand that came to her cheek.

'I did a test on Wednesday,' she said.

'So, when were you going to tell me?'

'Once I got home.'

He removed his hand.

'I didn't want an argument, or for you to…' She shrugged. 'Do your attorney thing and make the DNA speech.'

'I was nineteen when that happened,' Dante said.

'I get that.'

'Do you want to go it alone?' he asked. 'Seriously, Susie? I *am* an attorney, but I am not going to plead for marriage or for you to stay here. I am going to do my best, whatever you want…' Then he added, 'I'll be around, though. For the baby. A lot.'

She looked down.

'Well, depending on work,' he amended, and she smiled just a little.

She looked up and met his eyes for the first time since she'd nodded and confirmed that, yes, she was pregnant.

'So, what do you want?' he asked.

'There'll be a lot of gossip if I'm here.'

'There's gossip now.' Dante shrugged. 'Susie, please tell me what you want, or what you think you want, or *something*?'

She was scared to, though.

'Okay,' he said into the silence. 'Shall I tell you what I would prefer?'

'Yes.'

'Marriage,' he said.

'Don't say that.'

'I am saying that,' Dante told her. 'That's what I want. Okay, I'll tell you my ideal and then you can tell me what you want.'

'We don't know each other,' she argued. 'We only met a few weeks ago, and you've been in Milan most of the time.'

'And miserable without you.'

'My God…' She looked at him then, her eyes angry. 'You couldn't even commit to a ball, you didn't even invite me last night, and now you tell me you want marriage?'

'I love you.'

'Okay,' she amended. 'Now you tell me that you love me and want to marry me.'

'I do.' He nodded. 'I've told you what I want—it's your turn now.'

'A pause,' Susie said. 'To let the news sink in and so you can get used to the idea.'

There was more silence, and then he arrogantly broke it. 'That's your pause—I'm used to it now.'

'You can't be…'

'Are you?'

'No!' she shouted, and then she heard her own voice and heard her lie. 'Yes…' She was bewildered. 'I'm not Zen with it, or anything, but…'

'Let's talk about us,' he suggested. 'The baby's fine—we'll work it out. What about us?'

It wasn't the baby that was the issue now. He would take care of their child, however she wanted to play it, and she loved him for that.

She loved him.

Susie looked at the man she loved, at his chocolate-brown eyes and his unshaven jaw, and she didn't want him *trying* to build a future with her just because he felt it was the right thing to do.

'I think it's too soon for it to be love,' she told him.

'So you want to wait? See what happens? How you feel in a few months? How I feel is not going to change.'

'I don't believe you love me, Dante. I think you're trying to do the right thing…make up for what happened with Rosa.'

'Do not bring her into our bed.'

'Or you're trying to make Gio happy.'

'Do you know what I do for work? I sit with men and women who have married for the wrong reasons, or stayed together for the wrong reasons, or who are breaking up for the wrong reasons. I am not going to lie about love.'

'So when did you decide you loved me?'

'You're annoying me now,' Dante told her. 'I'm the one looking like a fool here. I just told you I love you. Now, if you don't love me, say so. I can take it.'

'I do love you.'

'Good!' he said. 'When did you know that?'

Susie thought back, and it was a hard thing to pinpoint... Given their short time frame, she could hardly say it had crept up on her.

'Always,' she admitted. 'I didn't realise it, but...' She nodded. 'Always.' Then she thought that might be a bit much. 'Maybe a couple of days in.'

'Well, I don't know quite when it happened for me, but...'

'Please don't say it if you don't mean it.'

'I promise you I would not. I called our jeweller and asked for the necklace to be made on my first day back at work.'

Susie frowned.

'I think I got cold feet,' he went on. 'And then he sent the designs.'

'You had this made?'

'I did.' He nodded. 'It was to be a farewell gift; I was never going to tell you it had been designed with you in mind. That felt like a bit much. So yes, maybe I did get cold feet.'

She reached up and struggled to take it off, just to take another, better look. Dante knelt up in the bed and helped her.

'I heard you wanted something chosen specifically for you... your little jealousy issue.'

And then he made her smile and he made her cry as he talked her through the stones.

'Pale sapphire—that dress you wore. I was like a fifteen-year-old... I told myself it was just sex.' He pointed to the darker sapphires. 'Your eyes.' Then to the little collection of tiny diamonds. 'The bubbles in the sink at Gio's...'

Her breath grew shallow as he took her through their time together.

'The pink and lilac I left to the jeweller, and the grass is enamel, I think, maybe with little gems?'

'Is it a tiny ladybird...?'

'No,' he said. 'That was a late addition this Wednesday. I had the ruby flown to Signor Adino.'

The air went still.

'I know you wanted fresh stones, and new metals, but I have never known what to do with the rubies. One for Sev...one for me. I wanted something nice for it.' He thought for a moment. 'Yes, I guess I officially knew I loved you on Wednesday.'

Susie turned and kissed him. It was a kiss that wasn't anything other than a loving kiss, a blissful one, and the bed was still and steady now, all nerves gone.

'Marry me,' he said. 'Up in the hills. Because when I think of them now, I think of you.'

'Marry me,' Susie said. 'I get to ask,' she told him, 'because I loved you first.' She smiled.

'Well, I'm not so sure about that...'

It was a delicious debate to have.

EPILOGUE

SUSIE WAS FINALLY the talk of the town—and was very happy to be.

She'd arrived in December, was marrying in May... And, yes, there had been a lot of nudges as the restaurant's patrons peered into the kitchen at the new apprentice chef who was dating Dante...and possibly showing her pregnancy a little.

Now, on her wedding day, her little bump was irrefutable.

Her dress was a simple one—white, but with the tiniest hint of pink, and only if the light was right. It tied under her bust and flowed down to her pretty jewelled sandals. It was floaty and summery and perfect for a wedding at a winery in the lush Tuscan hills.

She held sunflowers, because they made everyone happy, and that was the only requisite on this gorgeous sunny day.

Oh, and she wore her necklace.

Susie hadn't wanted an engagement ring, and neither would she require an eternity ring. Even if not another soul ever knew that the so-called ladybird she wore on the necklace around her neck meant everything.

She could hear gorgeous music and, looking out, saw their guests. There was Juliet, her red hair stunning in the morning sun. And Louanna. She could make out Cucou and Pedro too.

Gio was seated with Mimi, but Mimi rose now, ready to perform and sing Susie up to the arch of flowers.

And then she saw Dante and Sev, walking together, and her heart swelled at the sight of the two brothers. Things were still very difficult between them—and, no, that particular conversation was yet to be had.

If ever.

For today, though, it was all pushed aside and they were brothers again.

'Okay,' her dad said as his phone bleeped. 'It's time.'

And so it was.

They walked down through the winery's restaurant and then out towards the vines, and it was stunning. Lavender and sunflowers waved in the distance, and the hills that had taken so much from this family seemed to be trying to make up for it today, for they were vivid with colour.

She could hear the wonderful string quartet, and she looked at the two brothers.

Mimi gestured to the bride to proceed, and then smiled at the groom and sang directly to him, telling Dante, in song, that his bride was approaching.

And as Mimi's glorious voice rose skywards something beautiful happened.

Both brothers looked down to their shoes, and then they turned to each other and shared a very tiny smile.

Then Dante turned and looked at his bride.

Susie was crying before she was halfway down the aisle, and although Dante didn't quite kiss the bride on her arrival, he embraced her.

'It's all good,' he told her.

And he looked down at her dress, took her flowers and handed them to one of the twins—he really didn't notice which one. The best man handed him a handkerchief and he dried Susie's eyes, but when Dante touched the little ladybird on her necklace they filled again.

'For eternity,' he told her.

'Yes.'

Both knew how precious this love was.

* * * * *

MILLS & BOON®

Coming next month

ACCIDENTAL ONE-NIGHT BABY
Julia James

Siena took a breath, short, sharp, and summoning up her courage, stepped into the lift that would take her to the one man in the world she did not want to see again.

Vincenzo Giansante.

'He'll think you're chasing him – and he's made it clear he's done with you.'

Siena's mouth tightened. Vincenzo Giansante had, indeed, made it crystal clear he was done with her – had walked out in the briefest way possible in the bleak light of the morning after the night before.

Well, now she was walking back into his life – to tell him what she still could scarcely believe herself, ever since seeing that thin blue line form on the test stick.

He has a right to know – any man does – whether I want him to or not.

The lift jerked to a stop, the metal doors sliding open. For a moment she just wanted to be a coward, and jab the down button again. Then, steeling herself, she walked forward.

Continue reading

ACCIDENTAL ONE-NIGHT BABY
Julia James

Available next month
millsandboon.co.uk

COMING SOON!

We really hope you enjoyed reading this book.
If you're looking for more romance
be sure to head to the shops when
new books are available on

Thursday 27th February

To see which titles are coming soon, please visit
millsandboon.co.uk/nextmonth

MILLS & BOON

LET'S TALK
Romance

For exclusive extracts, competitions and special offers, find us online:

f MillsandBoon

X @MillsandBoon

O @MillsandBoonUK

d @MillsandBoonUK

Get in touch on 01413 063 232

afterglow **BOOKS**

Afterglow Books is a trend-led, trope-filled list of books with diverse, authentic and relatable characters, a wide array of voices and representations, plus real world trials and tribulations. Featuring all the tropes you could possibly want (think small-town settings, fake relationships, grumpy vs sunshine, enemies to lovers) and all with a generous dose of spice in every story.

♪ @millsandboonuk
📷 @millsandboonuk
afterglowbooks.co.uk

#AfterglowBooks

For all the latest book news, exclusive content and giveaways scan the QR code below to sign up to the Afterglow newsletter:

SCAN ME

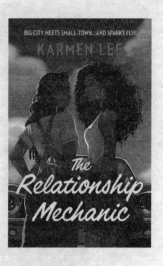

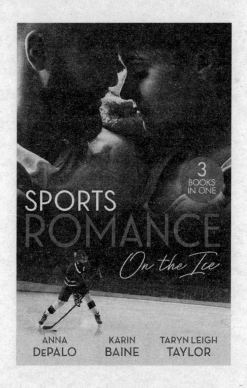

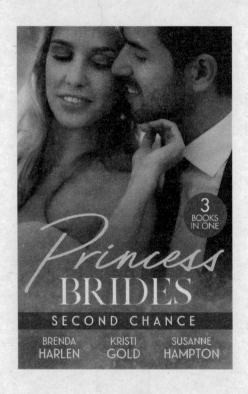